THE DARKENING SKY

'This was quite a read. Greene brings a lot t‚
psychiatry, forensics, medicine, society, car‚
they are delivered with ease and purpose. As for the strengths? For me, the
dialogue wins it. It's natural. It has wit without heavy punchlines. Greene handles
the reveal superbly and leaves you hanging until the end.'

'I have read many a crime book, but this book was different. I never for one
moment guessed how the story would unfold.'

THE FIRE OF LOVE

'There are lots of twists and turns and complex characters to keep the ending
from you and difficult to guess.'

'A good read that I would recommend to anyone who enjoys crime novels and
psychological thrillers. The writing is constantly good and interesting.'

THE GOOD SHEPHERD

'The story builds well with excellent attention to detail paid to the places that
the main characters visit.'

'I enjoyed this book. The characters were interesting and I felt the book was
well researched.'

'An excellent read, loved it.'

DR POWER'S CASEBOOK

'This is a little different to the novels but it is entertaining and well worth
reading. I enjoyed all the stories but 'The Dark' has to be one of the best short
stories I have ever read.'

'These short stories are written in Greene's own inimitable way and as always
the dialogue flows seemingly effortlessly as the stories unfold.'

SCHRÖDINGER'S GOD

'The best of the series so far. Hugh Greene never fails to deliver thrills and new
insights.'

'Greene is one of those artists who manages to make everything seem simple and
effortless, but the more you look at it the more detail you see, and the more you
can't help but admire those delicate touches.'

SON OF DARKNESS

'Suspenseful and cleverly plotted. It is thought provoking, as Hugh Greene's novels
usually are.'

'It's all here – Greene's meticulous plotting, convincing professional details
combined with archetypal horror from the distant past.'

'I feel that the author has created one of the most intriguing and dark worlds
within our own.'

Also by Hugh Greene

The Darkening Sky
The Fire of Love
The Good Shepherd
Schrödinger's God
Son of Darkness

Omnibus of Three Novels in a Single Volume
The Dr Power Mysteries

Short Story Collection
Dr Power's Casebook

Non-fiction
Hugh Greene & Judith Eddles
Dr Power's Meditation & Colouring Book
Dr Power's Book of Puzzles

Murder and Malice
A Dr Power Murder Mystery

Hugh Greene

Illustrated by Paul Gent

ISBN: 9798367455380

First Edition Published Worldwide in 2023

A catalogue reference for this book is available from the British Library

Typeset in Cambria and Calibri
by Judith Eddles

www.hughgreene.com

twitter: @hughgreenauthor

Murder and Malice

Structure of Allminster University

Vice Chancellor: Canon Ambrose Armitage

Executive Pro Vice Chancellor: Professor David Shacklin

Dean of Faculty of Healthcare:
Professor Bridget McFarlane (Nursing, Midwifery, Health Management, Physiotherapy, Social Work)

Dean of Faculty of Psychology and Media Studies:
Professor Ann Teesdale (Psychology, Drama, Media Production)

Dean of Faculty of Mathematics and Natural Philosophy:
Professor Nigel Kneale (Mathematics, Logic, Philosophy, Computing and IT)

Dean of Faculty of Social Sciences and Criminology:
Professor Johann Felfe (Sociology, Politics, Criminology, Probation Studies)

Dean of Faculty of Humanities:
Sir Robert Willett (English, History, European Languages, Archaeology)

Dean of Faculty of Physical Sciences:
Professor Simone Jauffret (Biology, Chemistry, Physics, Geography, Geology)

Dean of Faculty of Engineering and Technology:
Professor Immo Torvalds (Engineering, Chemical Engineering, Process Management)

Dean of Business and Enterprise:
Professor Erin Marsh, (Business, Finance, Accounting)

Registrar: Dr Nicholas Timmons

Bursar: Hamish Grieg, Solicitor

Executive Director of Human Resources: Karen Harvey

Prologue

She awoke with her cheek resting on the flattened, dry grass stems and the dusty earth beneath. A cool breeze was blowing across the warm land. The night sky turned above her slumped body. For a moment she watched the stars embedded in the velvet blue firmament. Without any light pollution from a nearby town's streetlights the stars stood out as clear pinpoints of light. Somewhat groggily, she fancied she could see the Milky Way, a golden white tear across the fabric of the night.

Her head felt heavy. When she tried to lift it, the effort proved too much and she laid it back down upon the earth. She felt as if she had woken into a new world and a new time. She lay there and pondered who she was, and what might have led to her silent vigil stretched out beneath the stars.

Her name was Savina Daidalos, of that she was sure. She was thirty-six, and after the recent death of her mother from a neglected diagnosis, she considered herself to be an orphan.

Savina sought her last waking memory before her deep slumber. There were a few images, which she tried to stitch and weave together into a narrative that approached coherence. There was sunlight on blue water – a blue so deep it looked like glistening blue jelly, the ocean below rushing past the hull of the ferry as she looked over the rail. There had been the crossing from the small island of Gozo to the greater island of Malta, the previous day. She remembered embarking upon the ferry at Mgarr, climbing up the gangway; the bridge between shore and ship resonating under her feet. She had a memory of sailing the channel and passing the tiny isle of Comino. There was no memory of arriving at Cirkewwa though. Her memory seemed fragmented; a shattered mirror of her consciousness. Had she been knocked out by a blow to the head, she wondered? There seemed no tenderness to her skull, just a leaden heaviness.

Savina fished in the depths of her mind for more memories, and it felt she had to go fathoms deep. There was a picture from months ago; her father getting into the plane and waving to her. It was like a film clip of just a few seconds long, but infinitely precious to her. He was waving out of the window from the passenger seat of the Cessna 182. The recollection seemed so vivid she could practically smell and taste it. She had no corresponding impression of her brother climbing into the pilot's seat by her father's side. Had her brother waved? She trawled for a memory of him on that last day, but could not catch one. Standing there at the airfield she had not thought anything out of the ordinary about their journey. Her brother was an experienced pilot. Her father had been happy, his manner oozing confidence. He had always enjoyed his business, the trip seemed to have inspired him and he had high hopes for his final investment. There had been no call for worry. They had enjoyed a last meal together at the Tmun restaurant on Gozo, before she drove them to the airstrip. The 'last times' haunted her, she thought. The last time she ate Bouillabaisse with her father, heady with trace aromas of Pernod and thyme from Comino. The last time he smiled at her. The last time he waved. A day later she was bereft, and filled with a disbelief and an anger she could not explain. The anger was so intense that it tasted acrid in her mouth and nostrils.

She had felt excitement as she travelled to the Research Station, watching the blue water speeding past as she made the ferry journey. It had not been an excitement so much as an agitated expectation generated by a hope that she would finally discover what had led to her father's last trip to England. What had drawn him northwards to that cold island? After the shock of the news of the plane crash in that distant land Savina had been as much use to her mother as a broken doll. Savina had sunk into a deep, clinical depression. There had followed weeks of pills and sessions with a kindly therapist. It had taken all her mother's love to re-build her, and then she too, all too quickly, was gone. And then the unanswered questions about the death of her brother and father had nagged her to pull the broken pieces of her life into order. She had forced herself to enter the tomb of her father's office, open the diaries on his desk and unroll the dry plans that lay piled on the table nearby. She had sparked his desktop computer into grudging life, cracked his passwords after hours of guesswork, and read those final emails about that last, huge investment of family money.

The encrypted email program on her father's computer yielded up all the emails her father had received and sent in the month before his death.

Of greatest interest to her in her quest to find reasons behind her father's final journey was a set of emails from a person simply called The Banker. He, or she, had agreed to meet him in England to discuss the terms of his last ever business investment. In return for a final payment of two million Maltese lira her father would receive a thirty-three per cent stake in the financial rewards from an innovation and research project based in Malta. The payment was to be converted into pounds sterling and paid, *in cash*, in England. Her father had bestowed such care on a titanium case he loaded into the Cessna at the airstrip. Even then Savina had intuited that the suitcase had not contained any clothes. Now she knew it had contained cash to fund research.

Attachments to the emails from The Banker to her father revealed themselves to be engineering drawings for something called a *saser*. This was what the millions of Maltese lira were for.

She discerned that a *saser* was a type of weapon. This had troubled her for days, and from this news flowed various unpleasant questions that she had kept to herself. At one time she had thought of asking her mother questions about what she had discovered, but some questions you never trouble your mother with, and her mother's health was failing – the consequence of ignoring physical signs for too long. With her mother gone, the questions assailed her again, and became louder. Where had her father's money come from? Had The Banker received the investment and where was any receipt? What assets might still belong to the family? She had seen no mention of these assets in her father's will or the estate as described by the shrivelled and wizened family solicitor in Valletta, Mr Esterhase.

The most troubling notion was that her father might invest in weapon research. This idea conflicted with her lifelong faith in her doting father. After his death however, she had begun to learn more and more of his life and the origins of the family fortune. He had trusted her brother with details of his business, but seemingly her father had protected his daughter from everything. Her education about the true nature of the family's business was an uncomfortable process. With regard to this particular final deal, Savina's researches on the Internet revealed that a *saser* was a device that focused sound waves, analogous in a sense to the focusing of light by a laser. She mulled over the acronym, *saser*, (expanded once in the emails to the full term Sound Amplification by Stimulated Emission of Radiation). This was the experimental device that was ostensibly kept within the walls behind her at Dingli. The device could emit highly coherent phonons of sound. Inaudible to those outside the focused beam the saser would deliver a 'kick' of sound that could inflict damage to liver or brain. Animal experiments were described citing brain damage and encephalopathy. Savina felt her stomach sink thinking about the animals mentioned in email attachments sent by The Banker. Her father had seen all of this, and yet still decided to back the project.

Savina debated with herself about the benefits and risks of contacting The Banker. She asked herself, again and again, had The Banker ever met her father in England? Had The Banker received and invested the money? Did The Banker know where the money had come from? Could The Banker explain to her why her own dear father would ever invest in such a cruel weapon?

One morning after her father's death she had awoken early and drifted down through the silent house she had shared with her mother in her last days, to her father's shrine-like study. She had re-read all The Banker's emails and her father's replies. She had mulled over her plans whilst drinking an Americano and, her hands shaking, composed a new email to The Banker. It was carefully phrased, asking just a few salient questions. She was particularly careful to give no detail about herself.

She had to wait two days before the reply came. Yes, the

investment had been made. Yes, the investment was all above board and perfectly legal. The research was genuine and even overseen by a University ethical committee. The research was conducted by a high-flying professor of Military Physics and Innovation, and any research results would be published openly in a peer reviewed journal. It was a very risky business – such research, but there had been promising preliminary results from the centre in Malta and, of course, thirty per cent of any profits from the research would be held in a Trust for the beneficiaries of Mr Daidalos's estate. The Banker tactfully included a whole paragraph of praise for her father's impeccable integrity and far-sighted vision in underwriting such research.

The last line of The Banker's email had hooked Savina and drawn her from the family estate on Gozo, over the bright blue channel on the ferry. It read, "I would like to reassure you that the late Mr Daidalos's investment was a prudent one, and that all is safe; I will be in Malta myself next week and will be so pleased to reassure you personally, show you round the research faculty myself and answer any questions you may have."

After a few more emails she had obtained her appointment with The Banker and booked her crossing.

She remembered the taxi had dropped her off at a road outside the village of Dingli. The road wended through a rough landscape, goats and sheep wandered, grazing and nibbling the spiky plants scattered across the unfenced brown scrub. There was a scatter of white- and ochre-coloured rocks between sparse clumps of grass. There was some white henbane and Sicilian snapdragon. She could smell their cream and yellow flowers. A few goats had raised their heads to look at the elegant young woman, clothed in a white pencil-thin dress, and red high heeled shoes. Their eyes stared at her with a mixture of indifference and evil intent, scanning her lithe body to see if she carried or wore anything worth eating. There had been the sound of squeals from a nearby pig farm, and the sickly whiff of the hogs and their ordure-strewn sties had made her wrinkle her nose in disgust. The smell was like decomposing meat and sour swill. The stink offended her before the breeze changed and sweeter air swept the odour of death away. She felt relieved to see, beyond the goats' scrubland, the broad sweep of the ocean, blue and sparkling in the afternoon sun. The scrubland fell away, yards from the road where she stood, and plunged down as part of a set of sheer cliffs, called the Dingli Cliffs; near vertical curtains of rock formed from strata of Coralline limestone.

She'd walked in the sun towards the research station, a squat, circular stone tower, topped by a huge, white, golfball-shaped radar dome, set behind a massive wall. Ostensibly this station had been to provide navigation to aircraft, but the complex had also housed an array of underground command structures during the War. And now, so The Banker promised, it housed a weapons research station, but to her it looked ramshackle, almost abandoned, and not the sleek efficient research facility she had imagined, all steel and glass with scientists in lab coats and a sleek reception area. She began to walk the hundred metres to the old wartime buildings. The sun was hot on her back. The effort of walking those yards brought out a sheen of perspiration upon her brow. Closer to the white walls round the station Savina saw three radio mast towers clustered around the dome, pointing straight up at the bright blue, cloudless sky. The tops of the walls bristled with rolls of spiky razor wire. Signs on the walls threatened potential visitors with prosecution for any trespassing, and announced 'Restricted Area. Strictly No Entry'. Other signs announced: 'MATS – Navigation Transmitting Site' and 'A.U. Jericho Institute Research Station'.

The large, wire-meshed gate seemed the only way into the walled compound. One portion of the gate was large enough to admit heavy lorries and the other was intended for pedestrians. Both portions of the gate were stout, heavily reinforced, and locked from the inside.

Savina felt intimidated and unwelcome. Part of her wanted to leave immediately without further delay, without causing any disturbance, but she also felt more compelled to find out about her father's final business transaction.

There was no intercom or bell at the gate. Casual visitors, or indeed visitors of any kind, were clearly not part of the installation's plan. Presumably, she thought, any deliveries at the installation were purely by prior arrangement. She resorted to calling out for attention; shouting through the wire mesh into the dusty compound beyond. There were a few vehicles parked inside, but no other sign of human occupation was visible. She shouted out again. Her voice echoed, bouncing off the walls inside.

Eventually a man peered out of a window in the tower, just below the start of the polygons that formed the huge white fibreglass radome, which had looked like a golf ball to Savina earlier. He frowned down at her through the glass and, with evident reluctance, turned away to climb down the stairs to deal with her. A door opened at the base of the tower and he made his way over to her across the baking asphalt of the courtyard, until he stood before her in his bright white shirt and crisply-ironed black trousers. He wore glasses and a goatee beard. His eyebrows formed themselves into a questioning look, but he said nothing.

"My name is Savina Daidalos," she said. "I have an appointment."

"Really?" he asked. His words dripped with scepticism. "Is that why you're making all this terrible noise? Disturbing the peace? Exactly who is your appointment with?"

"He asked me not to mention his name," she answered. "He promised to show me the research. My family funds the research here."

There was no sign that he understood her, had knowledge of any appointment, or even believed her. His face had become an impassive mask. Savina supposed he might often hear excuses from nosy sightseers who wanted to look inside the station. She began to doubt herself. Maybe it was all an elaborate hoax. Maybe there was no Banker and she now suspected, that like her father, she had been fooled. She hated the silence of the man standing before her. She feared the arrogance of his brown eyes.

"Please," she said. "I've come a long way. Taken the ferry from Gozo. Can you check, please?" He didn't move. He crossed his arms and regarded her, as though she was an exotic specimen. "The appointment was with a man who calls himself The Banker."

"There is no one here like that," he said, after a pause. "You would do better to leave. We are busy."

"It's hot. I've been travelling all day," she pleaded. "Can't you at least check with your supervisor? Please?"

"There is no one here with that name. This is a radar listening station. It's all automated. No staff here."

"He emailed me with the place and the time," she insisted, but in response he just shook his head.

"I will make an enquiry," he said suddenly. "Wait there." She was given no alternative but to wait, as he turned and walked without haste, back towards the radar tower.

Left alone, almost blinded in the searing overhead sun, Savina pondered summoning a taxi to get back to the ferry at Cirkewwa.

Ten minutes later the man reappeared at the doorway at the base of the tower. He had put on a dark jacket and tie, despite the temperature. She couldn't understand why he had decided to adopt a more formal look. He shaded his eyes from the bright sunlight and stared at her, taking in her tall, slim form, dressed in white, and by now, wilting like a bloom without water in the heat of the Maltese afternoon. He made his way over and again spoke to her through the grille of the gate, asking her this time for photo identification. She held her passport up against the grille. He glanced at the face in the photo and compared it to the perspiring face alongside it. He nodded and began to unlock the chains on the gate.

"Did you speak to The Banker?" she asked.

There was no reply. He swung the gate open just enough to admit her slim body.

"Are *you* The Banker?" she asked suspiciously. He paused and thought about the question, and slowly shook his head. He beckoned her through the gap in the gate before closing it gently behind her and re-locking it. He winced at the sound of the key scraping in the lock.

Without further remark he walked back to the base of the tower, and Savina walked behind him on the assumption that she was expected to follow.

He led her into the tower and sat her down on a wooden chair in a small room such as a security guard or cleaner might use for shelter or to keep equipment. A tiny room, all white walls and stone floor. As he said nothing and made no eye contact Savina was disinclined to make conversation, but felt obliged to attempt a further enquiry, "Is The Banker here?"

There was no reply and Savina found the silence frightening. She wondered whether the man was quite sane. His back was turned on her now and he was fiddling with something on a table. Savina felt slightly reassured when she heard the sound of a kettle being switched on and the chatter and chortle of it coming to the boil. There was the rattle of crockery and spoons, and the glug of water being poured. When the man turned round he held two mugs of strong tea, one of which he placed on a rickety table by her side. He nodded to her, encouraging her to drink. He sat down on a chair near the door to watch her as she sipped the hot tea, occasionally he nodded in tacit approval as the drink disappeared.

And that was the last she remembered before she awoke in the night, on the ground, outside the walls. What had happened to her in the hours after she had drunk tea in the little guardroom? She didn't want to think about what could have been done. Unconsciousness had ruled and only amnesia spanned the hours since she drank the drugged tea.

Savina shivered in the night air. A thin mist of dew made her clothes feel clammy against her skin. The presence of dew surely meant that the dawn was coming. Savina felt less groggy and she managed to get to her feet.

Something felt different now, she looked down at her feet and realised her red shoes were gone, removed whilst she was unconscious. Her bare toes were covered in dust as she walked uncertainly across the darkened scrubland away from the tower. She thought it best to make for the road wherever that was. Her knees felt unsteady and she felt unbalanced.

The sea was over to her left; she could hear the waves crashing on the rocks of the cliffs.

Suddenly, an altogether different and unnatural noise hit her physically. The noise was unbearable, like a sudden sharp shaft of bright clear sound, horribly loud, shaking the bones inside her head. She ran forwards in confusion and her shin collided with a rock in the dirt. She staggered and collapsed to the ground. The instant she fell and sprawled upon the scrub, the noise stopped.

Savina got up and once her head was upright the noise hit her again. She began to run, this time over to her left. As she broke away from a straight path the noise stopped. Then, seemingly, the noise sought her and the beam of sound found her once more. She again broke away to her left to escape the spike of intense noise that shook her head, like a pair of hands vigorously twisting and vibrating her skull. When she moved leftwards she discovered the noise could be escaped, and then within a few seconds, it found her once again and shook her, as if it was being aimed at her. When the beam of noise found her, she could not think, the imperative was only to try and escape its scream, its deafening, howling vibration. When it hit her, she felt a sensation of heat deep inside the bones of her head, she felt dizzy, sickness welled up inside her. All she could do was veer out of its beam, over to the left, and hope to outrun it. She ran blindly, panicked as she had never been before, her only thought to avoid the searing sound.

Savina felt the dusty ground slapping against the bottom of her feet as she ran. And suddenly she didn't feel the ground beneath her feet any more. There was just air, and falling, flailing her limbs as she hurtled downwards, down the vertical side of the cliff.

Chapter One
Michaelmas Term
4th November, 2004

Don't look for the meanings in the words.
Listen to the silences.

Samuel Beckett

Canon Armitage's sprucely-dressed secretary welcomed Professor Power for his 2 p.m. meeting with the Vice Chancellor.

She noted that Power was a tall man, a handsome man, a man who dressed for comfort rather than to impress, quietly spoken and only speaking when he could speak truly, politely, keenly and to good effect. She knew him to be a doctor of the mind who had published research worldwide; she had read his curriculum vitae before his appointment. She apologised on behalf of the Vice Chancellor and explained Armitage had just stepped out to get some lunch. She invited Professor Power to wait inside his office.

Power's professional curiosity was aroused by the opportunity to see the Vice Chancellor's office. The Vice Chancellor was something of a mystery and a source of speculation to his employees. The professor of theology maintained that there was a cloud of unknowing between mere mortals such as professors and the all-powerful Vice Chancellor. He wielded absolute power over the lives of thousands of students and hundreds of lecturers and professors. The statutes of the University had been forged in Victorian times. Committees at Senate level, and even the Board of Governors, had only an advisory role to the Vice Chancellor. The governors could appoint a Vice Chancellor, but not terminate their employment. The University was, to all intents and purposes the Vice Chancellor's personal fiefdom and he was more akin to a medieval princeling than an academic. The University bowed to his commands alone and, by ancient right, the University paid virtually no taxes.

Following his appointment, Professor Power still preferred to be known to others as Dr Power. Carl Power considered himself to be, first and foremost, a medical doctor, specifically a psychiatrist. He had been appointed a professor at the University several months before, and was still finding his feet in the byzantine world of academia. The new title, Professor Power, lent his name altogether too much plosive force. When he was purely a medical doctor the Vice Chancellor had been very keen to meet him and had fêted him at the Indulgence Cafe, a restaurant in Manchester, to win him over to the University. Power had been flattered to accept a part-time post, which allowed him to continue his independent medical practice alongside a University role. But after his arrival at the University the Vice Chancellor had virtually ignored him. Today's meeting would be the first since the Senate confirmed Power's appointment. The delay had whetted Power's appetite for information about the Vice Chancellor; he had asked his colleagues about the man and become aware that the gossip about him was mostly incorrect and mutually contradictory.

An unaccompanied visit inside the Vice Chancellor's office felt too good to miss and Power gladly followed the secretary into the oak-panelled room, and sat down in a deep, velvet-upholstered, armchair. He waited until she had closed the heavy door and then looked around the office.

He struggled to resist the temptation to look into every nook and cranny to read the Vice Chancellor's character. Eventually, as the wait dragged on, Power stood up uneasily and yielded to the impulse to walk about the room and investigate clues as to the nature of the man.

The Vice-Chancellor's office gave the impression of being modelled on a Victorian gentleman's club, with four deep, leather, armchairs set around the central medallion of a large, traditional Kashan rug. By the side of each armchair was a walnut pedestal table with three cabriole legs. Dr Power could imagine sinking into such an armchair and relaxing with a glass of tawny port poured out by some club servant.

On the wall nearest the door, atop a limestone fireplace, was a rectangular Louis Phillippe overmantel mirror with rounded corners, resplendent in gold leaf. In the grate was a log fire, steadily burning and lending a golden-amber warmth to the office. Power could see himself whiling away the hours before this fire, reading a good book, and sipping his drink as he turned the pages.

Nearby there was an ox-blood Captain's chair and an oak pedestal desk with a tooled burgundy leather top that appeared to have dimensions similar to a small aircraft carrier.

Power thought that the office could also be the Master's cabin of a nineteenth century merchant ship, given the captain's chair and the presence of a balustrade around the stairs leading down to some unseen deck below.

Practically every inch of the walls was filled by bookshelves, crammed with shining leather-bound tomes of theology, philosophy and law, arranged according to the leather bindings, they seemed unread and unloved. In a separate set of shelves built into a rotating cube near the desk there were some disparate volumes, which the Vice Chancellor might conceivably have read. There was *The Book of Art* by Gombrich, *Ways of Seeing* by Berger, *Mythologies* by Roland Barthes,

The Theory of Games and Economic Behaviour and Mullineux' and Murinde's *Handbook of European Community Finance.* Open on the Vice Chancellor's desk was a copy of *The Opening Game in Chess* by Pachman.

In the limited empty space between the wooden bookcases were a few portraits. One was of Armitage's predecessor, a flat and functional portrait of a narrow man in a stone-grey suit, looking out of the east window over the nineteen-eighties concrete quadrangle, built to expand the original college buildings. The first Vice-Chancellor's face was devoid of character, more that of a monolithic administrator than a fervent academic. Power was much taken by the other portrait in the room, an apparently original sixteenth century portrait of Margaret Beaufort. He stood in front of the portrait and admired the serene determination in her brown eyes. Her hands held an open prayer book, but her attention seemed elsewhere, off to the left of the painting, as if she was planning her future, or someone else's.

The Vice Chancellor's Office had two large floor-length windows, facing south and east respectively. The south window let the sun flood in during the winter and the east window harvested the morning light in summer. And in the wintry afternoon of that day what light there was threaded its way through the heavy mullions and muntins of the eastern window and fell upon an alabaster bust of a clean shaven, young man with a hand-tied bow at his collar. A small plaque noted that the bust was of Charles Dodgson, the academic and author. The mathematician's likeness was balanced on a fluted marble column, on a square base. The marble head gazed downwards onto a low table with a chess board set upon it.

Two upright chairs sat either side of the chess table. Power looked at the red and white chess pieces standing on the board. The Vice Chancellor clearly had a game in progress. Power suspected the white pieces were antiques made from natural ivory and that the red pieces were likely ivory too, but stained red. He assumed from the fact that this ivory was on display that any public nod that the Vice Chancellor might make to political correctness was merely superficial. Power observed that the pieces were carved with elaborate decoration; kings with domed tops and 'pineapple' finials, queens similar but of smaller size, knights as horses' heads, a rook as a raised turret with brickwork, and a single pawn with a baluster knop to the central section and again a 'pineapple' finial.

Balancing the bust of Dodgson on the other side of the window was a polished silver sculpture. Smooth and streamlined, it looked like a wingless bird soaring upwards in flight. Power wondered if it was by Brancusi.

What did these possessions tell him about Vice Chancellor Armitage? What could objects tell you about their collector? He mused on the books and sculptures. How much did they tell him of the University and how much of the man?

Power noticed that on the desk there was a copy of his very own book on psychopathology. He had written it some years ago and it had enhanced his reputation sufficiently to make him academically appointable. Power reasoned that the Vice Chancellor troubled himself to get to know the background of his staff. The book was halfway open, and next to it the Vice Chancellor even appeared to have made some handwritten notes from it on a sharp white piece of paper. Beside the notes was a white envelope addressed to the Vice Chancellor at home: the top was slit open with a letter protruding. Power saw that the frank mark on the envelope was from a doctor's village surgery and was naturally curious as to the contents, and wondered what was the matter with his health, but the thought of pulling the letter out and reading it, thereby infringing the Vice Chancellor's confidentiality, would have appalled Power. He was too tempted to ignore the notes the Vice Chancellor had made about his book however.

In moving around the desk to peek at the notes Power glanced out of the south window and saw a rotund figure bowling across the quadrangle. A steady grey drizzle was falling from the leaden November skies, and yet the figure wore no coat, just a crisp blue suit, which was becoming ever more softened by the relentless rain. The figure was carrying some bulging, brown-paper bags and a cup of coffee. He seemed oblivious to the students behind him who were pointing at him as he made a flustered rush across the quadrangle towards Power. It was Canon Ambrose Armitage, the Vice Chancellor.

Power moved away from the window, lest the Vice Chancellor look up and glimpse him moving round his office and he hurriedly walked back to the armchairs that sat round the Kashan rug and sat down, trying to look as if he hadn't been satisfying his curiosity by exploring Armitage's domain. He heard, in the distance, the sounds of a door opening and closing; the Vice Chancellor's private way into the building. He could hear the panting respiration of the man as he checked himself before the mirror downstairs. Then Power heard the heavy footsteps climbing the treads up to the office as Armitage ascended the stairs, and saw the broad, round, back of the Vice Chancellor as he neared the top. Raindrops had darkened the grey cloth of his once-immaculate suit. The latest drops to fall from the sky onto his back were still standing up on the cloth, sparkling as they reflected the light. The figure turned as it rounded the newel post. Professor Power stood up to greet him. Canon Armitage's face evinced a degree of surprise.

"Where did you come from?" he asked.

This was the kind of starter question that usually threw Dr Power. He tried not to gape like an open-mouthed fish, while he thought of a response.

"Good morning, Vice Chancellor," said Power. "Your secretary asked me to wait in here, I'm Carl Power."

"Yes, I know you are," said Canon Armitage, sounding slightly irascible. He gestured to Power to resume his seat and came to sit in an armchair opposite him, placing his paper bags of purchases upon the nearby table.

"I'm sorry," said Power. "I always get thrown by that question – 'where do you come from?' Ever since my first week at medical school." The Vice Chancellor raised an eyebrow and started unpacking the paper bags. He brought out a range of pastries in greaseproof paper, and a large cup of coffee in a paper cup. He took the top off the latte and sipped thoughtfully. Power thought perhaps he should finish his anecdote. "There was this viva we had in anatomy. I had to answer questions from the professor of embryology . . . embryology is the study of human development from fertilised egg cell to infant."

"I know," said the Vice Chancellor, munching on a pain au raisin.

"Well, he asked me the same question that you did," said Power. "Where do you come from? And I thought to myself, what a really difficult question to ask! I started talking about fertilised eggs, and zygotes and morulas, and differentiated layers and . . . well, as you might have guessed he only wanted to know where my home town was. He was trying to put me at ease. I kept trying to give him embryological facts and he kept saying 'No, where do you come from?' and I got more flustered as the question seemed to be getting quite philosophical in nature about . . . I don't know what . . . the spirit of life or something."

"I see," said the Vice Chancellor, most of whose attention was now taken by a plum pastry.

Dr Power, who had been feeling guilty earlier at inspecting the Vice Chancellor's room, now felt somewhat snubbed by Canon Armitage's primary focus on his appetite. Armitage snaffled cakes and guzzled his coffee and Dr Power could only feel that politeness dictated that he be offered something more than a ringside seat at the Vice Chancellor's unhealthy meal. Power looked at his complexion. His cheeks were ruddy and nose reddened, as if to testify to his overly high blood pressure. On balance, though, his complexion looked almost tanned as if he had spent a week abroad. It certainly lacked the usual pallor that might be expected in November.

The Vice Chancellor appeared to be approaching a state of satiety and slowed in his consumption of a third pastry, an apricot jam tart. Speaking through crumbs, he asked, "Why did you come here today? What did you hope for?"

"I wanted to talk to you about a project. When we first met, we talked about developing a medical school at Allminster."

"Quite," said the Vice Chancellor, finally laying down a crust of the jam tart that he no longer had appetite for. "I'm so glad you made the first move. We have the School of Nursing, of course, of course, but nursing is nursing. All a bit drab at the end of the day. Wound healing, qualitative research and grounded theory, hundreds . . . maybe a few thousands in research grants from well-meaning charities. Medicine is where it's at. Pharmaceutical research. Drug development, genomics, gene therapy; millions in research grants from the MRC, the Wellcome Foundation and the pharmaceutical industry. Absolute millions!"

"Still . . ." said Dr Power, thinking about the members of the clinical team and how many times he'd depended on nurses to help him in clinical practice, how they'd stopped him from making mistakes, even saved his life. "Nursing is . . ."

"Nursing is worthy," said Cannon Armitage. "And no one can say otherwise. But it's not medicine and a University is not a University without a medical school. It's nothing without that licence to mint new doctors . . . yes, that's what I want you to bring us Dr Power – a new medical school to complete the University's final stage of development."

As if by magic, the door opened, and a servant arrived from the Refectory bearing a tray with Darjeeling tea in a china tea pot, and a cup and saucer for Dr Power. The servant cleared the table of the debris from the Vice Chancellor's snack. Armitage, restored to the role of a host after the food he had eaten, poured Dr Power a cup of tea as a reward for the prospect of a new medical school.

"Developing a new medical school. Quite a task," said the Vice Chancellor. "Quite a hill to climb."

"I thought I'd like to find my way to the top of that hill," said Dr Power.

"I could show you some hills," mused Canon Armitage. "This hill is well defended. Plenty of people will stand in your way. You will be surprised. Anyway, how are you settling in? Where are you?"

"I have an office near the library," said Power.

"You may need to enlist the help of the School of Nursing. They will help you get to know the people who commission student places in health care subjects. You will need to win the lady dean of the School of Nursing over to your side. In fact I will send you on a tour of the deans. Sir Robert Willett is a knight who is the Dean of English and the Humanities. You will need the support of most, if not all, of the Senior Management Team. He is key to that. You don't know how jealous they all will be of a Faculty of Medicine. They view the University finances as one giant plum cake. Something finite. If you take a piece of the cake for medicine then they'll get less."

"But medicine will earn its way," said Dr Power. "More than earn its keep in time. The fees are higher, greater Government subsidies for instance."

"In time, yes," said Armitage. "But the initial investment in land, estate and staff will be huge. To misquote Blake, the deans would sooner strangle the infant medicine in its cradle than nurse your desire for a medical school." For all his gluttony, the Vice Chancellor was an astute man used to weighing people up and holding his own against the swollen egos of the assembled Senate, its deans and professors. He looked at Power carefully, measuring the worth of the man. He thought that Power seemed kindly, agreeable and reasonable; but that he could also prove a steely adversary to any dean who chose to oppose him. Power was in his mid-forties, with a distinguished bearing. "Where do you live?" he asked the doctor.

"In Alderley Edge," said Power, sipping the golden Darjeeling. He lived in a large Edwardian house on the Macclesfield Road.

"Alderley Edge – with all the footballers? I hear they've driven up the house prices."

Power knew that even though he was a leading consultant with a good practice, he probably couldn't afford his house on his earnings. The house had been inherited from his aunt.

"Any family?" asked the Vice Chancellor.

"I have my partner and a son, Jo."

"And you work for us part-time. The University can't match your normal full time earnings." Power nodded. "So you're effectively donating your time to academia. Being altruistic? Very public spirited."

A professor's pay was a fifth of what he might earn as a consultant. It was hardly cost effective. He had talked to his partner Laura of his ambition to develop a medical school, his hope to inspire new doctors with a philosophy of caring; instilling a sense of psychology and community into their hearts.

"What else do you do, for the rest of the week?" asked the Vice Chancellor. "Patients?"

"Yes," said Power, who couldn't have borne the loss of seeing patients. "I have outpatients, some medicolegal work, and I do some forensic consulting work."

"I once met someone who said that she had been treated by you. I know you wouldn't discuss her case so I won't say who. But she said that you were a good doctor, because you listened. Listening sounds a remarkably easy thing, or is it more complicated than that?" asked Armitage.

"I'm pleased she gave me a good report, whoever she is," said Power. "And listening is a more difficult art than most people imagine. A good listener has to concentrate on what is said, free himself of his own concerns and worries, empathise with the person in front of him, reach out, and prepare to be changed by what he hears, and in doing so overcome the fear of losing himself, of being . . . diluted . . . by what he hears."

"Ah," said the Vice Chancellor, nodding, but not remotely liking the idea of being changed by others words. "And you also said you did forensic work. Consulting work. For the police?" he asked, knowing very well what Power did, but wished him to expand upon it.

"I have done police work," said Power. "Like profiling work, advising SIOs, that is detectives in charge of cases. Now I mainly work with a friend, Andrew Lynch. He was a Superintendent, but he started . . . well, we both started . . . a Foundation. It's funded by charitable 'arm's length' grants from a multinational company."

"Ah," said the Vice Chancellor. "'Charity shall cover a multitude of sins'. What is the Foundation called?"

"The International Foundation for Justice. Andrew Lynch runs it. I advise when relevant."

"It sounds impressive. What does it do?"

"It looks at cases that police forces can't or won't look at. Cases that have puzzled people, been unsolved, or can't be progressed because the evidence available won't convince a jury of guilt 'beyond reasonable doubt'. Miscarriages of justice. Or cases the police don't want to look into too thoroughly. There are more of those than you realise."

"Hmm," said the Vice Chancellor. "The University is classed as a charity too. It gives us huge advantages as an organisation over, say, a company. We don't pay certain taxes – that's just one advantage. Suddenly that's a twenty per cent growth advantage over competitors. It makes Universities powerful entities. Like the nobles of old, the Vice Chancellors of Cambridge and Oxford, my colleagues, are so wealthy and have so much land, they are like dukes. They say, 'if only we had the power to raise an army we could take over!'" Armitage fell to musing on this idea for a second.

"Well," said Dr Power, steering the conversation back to the ambitious project that formed his own personal agenda. "I know that I'm only part-time. Part-timers sometimes aren't seen as equals by full-timers, but I'm willing to give the medical school my best efforts."

"You don't have the time to scheme for one thing," said the Vice Chancellor softly. "No, Professor Power, although your colleagues have more academic time, you have some advantages in any fight to build a medical school. You have my full blessing and the deans will know that. Go and meet them all. I will tell them to help you. And you are no ordinary pawn in this game. You are a doctor. You know medicine from the inside. And they do not."

"Yes, but I would hope to be more than a pawn," said Dr Power.

"That's easily managed. You can be the dean of the medical school once you cross over all the difficulties. That's a promise. Complete the journey for us and you can be the dean." Seeing Power had finished his cup of tea, the Vice Chancellor poured him another and asked, "What do you think of my study? It was a banal grey affair when I took over. The woodwork is all my addition. We rescued the panelling from a finance headquarters near the river."

"I like the portrait," said Power, inclining his head towards the painting.

"Not the portrait of my predecessor then," Armitage chuckled. "A man altogether without ambition, I'm afraid. No, the portrait you clearly admire is an original of Margaret Beaufort, the mother of Henry VII. The painting was one of a few painted by Holbein himself, some years after her death. The University bought it a couple of years ago. I remember bidding for it myself. It cost two hundred and seventy thousand pounds."

"I admire her courage," said Power. "Wasn't she thirteen when she gave birth? Her husband was twenty-four, and he died leaving her a widow when she was seven months pregnant . . . and he was her second husband. I admire her because, despite all that adversity, she became one of the most powerful women in history."

"Yes, of course, of course," said the Vice Chancellor. "and the portrait was valued last week at half a million. An excellent investment. Just like you, Dr Power."

Chapter Two

For the love of money is the root of all evil.
KJV, 1 Timothy 6:10.

Dr Power sank onto a damask couch in Lynch's office and offered up a tray of coffees he'd bought from the nearby cafè. "Coffee, Andrew?"

"Well, I could do with a break," said Lynch. "And what have you been doing today?" He closed the file he was working on and smoothed the cover down. From a cupboard painted in St Giles Blue built into the wood panelling in the corner of his office he removed a translucent box. "Pamela baked some soul cakes for All Saints' Day," Lynch opened the plastic box of cakes that his wife had baked and held it in front of Power for him to choose one. There were eight golden-yellow cakes inside, somewhat softer and larger than biscuits, with crosses made of sultanas across their upper surface. There was an appetising smell of cinnamon and nutmeg. "I remember the days when it was a custom to eat these," Lynch said. "Folks from the church would take them to people round the village, singing at various houses for the souls of the people inside. Well, that way of living has gone, I'm afraid, but we still have some cakes. Take two," he said. "We should eat them whilst they're fresh."

Lynch was a tall, well-built man with broad, powerful shoulders, and immaculately attired in suit and iridescent purple silk tie. His powder-blue eyes gleamed with an inquisitive enthusiasm for life. He had resigned early from his role as Superintendent at Chester's police headquarters and the change had benefited his wellbeing. Lynch was, more or less, self-employed now in that he and Power had founded an organisation to take on cases that the police had traditionally overlooked or exhausted without any conviction in sight. The Foundation, as they called it, was only a few years old, but it was well-financed by a philanthropic millionaire and the Fair Law Project and growing both in size and reputation. Where once it had just filled two small offices, it had now grown to occupy the whole of the Georgian stone barracks that sat next to the sandstone remnants of a castle built in Chester by William the Conqueror.

"How did your meeting with the Vice Chancellor go?" said Lynch. "You were worried about it."

"He likes my plan for a medical school," said Power.

"And? Tell me more?" Lynch performed the hazardous feat of extricating a piping hot black coffee from the cardboard tray without burning his hands on spilled coffee and sat in an armchair opposite Power. He knew his friend had been anxious about meeting the Vice Chancellor and surmised correctly that Power had driven from Allminster into Chester expressly to tell him how the encounter had gone. Lynch imagined all the paraphernalia that Power would need to develop for a new medical school – dissection rooms, lecture theatres, physiology and pathology labs – and the staff he would have to recruit – professors of biochemistry, anatomy, medical ethics and the like.

"I think Armitage backs the idea." Power's mind burgeoned with his dreams for the new school. A new medical school with a philosophy that put the community first, that enshrined the importance of the mind as well as the body, that upheld a new Hippocratic Oath for the twenty-first century. If Lynch could but see them behind Power's eyes there were images of new seminar rooms with serried rows of seats, new primary care teaching centres, and eager student doctors learning from enthusiastic and experienced teachers. Unlike Lynch his vision of a medical school did not include a dissection room. He had found he could not abide the dissection room during his own time at University. The smell of formaldehyde and pale, wizened bodies, muscles sliced open and grey like half-carved Sunday joints of lamb had repulsed him. Such a place would not feature in his school. No bodies would be picked at with scalpels and probes and dismembered by students heaving to disarticulate a greasy shoulder or a hip. Anatomy would be taught through the use of models, holograms and 3D imaging. "The project will take a heap of money though," said Power, sounding a cautious and realistic note. "Millions and millions. And Armitage warned me that the deans of other faculties might be against it – might even fight to stop the school."

"And what reasons would anybody have to oppose a new medical school? What could be more ethical and good than a medical school in the sight of God's eyes?"

"They will imagine, no doubt, that a new medical school might drain their resources," said Power. "And other faculties might realise they are not the jewel in the crown any more. Medicine costs, but also earns like no other faculty."

"Often the smallest evils in men's hearts have the most effect," said Lynch. "That people could stand in the way of something that would do so much good. What kind of people do they employ there? Spiteful children? In the end the Lord judges both the quick and the dead, but a medical school is an honest endeavour that trains doctors to keep the quick from the dead just a little longer."

"Well, I haven't met half of them yet, I'll let you know how I get on. You wouldn't expect to have to fight to start a new medical school, but if I need to fight my corner I will . . ."

Lynch nodded. He knew how tenacious and determined Power could be. "And how's Jo? And Laura?" Laura was Dr Power's partner and Jo was his son.

"Fine," said Power. "I'm meeting them in town later. Pizza and a film. Harry Potter," he paused. "And how are you, Andrew?"

"Terribly busy," said Lynch. Although there wasn't even a hint of reproach in his voice, Power felt a twinge of guilt.

"I'm sorry I haven't been in to the Foundation office this week yet."

"And no reason why you should. I would call you in if your particular expertise were needed. Actually, I think we may be getting some more help from a rather unexpected source."

"What do you mean?" asked Power.

"I had a visit from Inspector Beresford the other day. He asked to be remembered to you, and he still thanks you for your help on the Heaney case."

"Your old protégé is a first rate officer," said Power as decently as he could through a mouthful of soul cake.

"Well, whether he could ever have been truly called my protégé when I was in the Force, he wants out now, I'm afraid."

Power frowned, "Why? What has happened?"

"He says that he has been told he has reached his ceiling. He's stuck where he is, and will forever remain an Inspector. As isolated as a man in a wooden box. He perceives that the Force likes to have him on the books to prove they are 'diverse', but he's never allowed to show any real efficacy. He feels his job has become little more than a sinecure."

"But the case we all solved together, the Heaney case, that was one of the biggest cases in decades," said Power, only mentioning the case with a twinge of nascent anxiety that threatened to grow into the sharpest pang of remembered fear.

"He feels that if the senior officer of the Force had had any inkling of how significant the Heaney case would become they would never have assigned him to it. That's what he believes."

"And is what he believes actually so, in your opinion?" asked Power. Lynch nodded. "But he made a success of it, didn't he? Doesn't that count?"

"What he feels is true, I am afraid. He feels he's been shunted off onto a branch line, asked to front a team to 'model community engagement'. And you know Beresford, he's a bit more hands on than that. That's his perception. He feels they are inescapably prejudiced. And when the police want to sideline you, they do. He says, and I don't disagree, that the officers are like a gang and work together, clustered in a generation, around a few years of intake into the Force. Each member advances in his one career and takes pains to advance the colleagues who are most sympathetic to him. They ascend in a cadre, up the hierarchy, together. Like climbers ascending a peak, all tied together, co-operating. And it's great if you are part of the cadre, included on the rope line as the old boys inch upwards to the peak. At some point though one cadre of officers must supplant another. The old guard cannot stand forever, one by one they retire, nothing is forever. I know." Lynch looked at Power expectantly. "When the cadre that promoted you is gone, or if your face doesn't fit . . . you are suddenly all alone on the mountain." Lynch paused. "As I found out myself, when my values and beliefs became risible to the new guard.

And so I wanted to ask you something, Carl. What would you think if Beresford joined us?"

"I never expected we'd ever be discussing this," said Power. "In my mind I thought Beresford's career – his promotion – was inevitable, guaranteed by the Heaney case."

Lynch shook his head. "Sadly merit doesn't always count. He's been worn down over the years. You know what it's like when you're in an organisation and your face doesn't quite fit. When you get indirect messages from seniors in the up and coming cadre that you have nowhere to go? Little snubs, the way they keep a certain distance from you when you are with them. The way they won't meet your eye. It wears you down gradually, a little more every day, until you just can't take any of it any more . . . so what do you think? About his joining us?"

"We could do with his help," said Power. "Goodness knows we could."

"It could be an answer to a prayer," mused Lynch. He paused and looked more closely at his friend and wondered if he might tell him something else. "As a coincidence Beresford had been looking into a plane crash. You recall that plane that crashed into the farm?" Power said nothing, and Lynch began to suspect that maybe he had misjudged the moment. "He suspects that the crash wasn't as straightforward as it seemed. I suppose that nothing like that can be described as straightforward . . ." Power had stopped looking at him, and Lynch felt slightly nervous. "The couple in the plane may have been involved in organised crime. And to find out I need someone like Beresford who is dogged and keen, to chase the money that shadows all this. Follow that money and **that**, that's where the root will be found."

Power was looking away, through the window at the sky outside, and altogether disengaged. He did not want to have any reminder of the Heaney case, it had come too close to his home and family. Lynch realised that mentioning it had opened a gulf between them, fathoms deep. He could speak, but Power would not hear him. He had reminded Power of it too soon and now he was troubled by memories as persistent and bleak as bleached bones on a distant pebble shore. The tide would cover them and take them out to sea, but always return them on a new wave, washed afresh, to the brine bubbled shingle.

To move the conversation on, and away from a topic he found unsettling, Power said, "I'd better go. There's a pizza to be had and I don't want to leave them alone in town." He stood up, a thin and diluted smile upon his face; an attempt to portray normality. He coughed. "Thank you for the soul cake, Andrew. And, of course Beresford is welcome. Let him follow the money."

"Aye," said Lynch, thoughtful. "We'll wait for the money to speak."

* * *

"Good evening, Vice Chancellor."

Professor Shacklin poked his head around the sturdy oak door of Canon Armitage's office and saw the Vice Chancellor engrossed in the paper work on his desk. Armitage raised his head and peered at Shacklin over the rims of gold-rimmed reading glasses. From the angle he was looking, Shacklin's head looked disembodied, as if it were floating in midair, midway up the door. He allowed himself the luxury of a lukewarm smile at Shacklin's expense, and decided to exude an air of vague detachment as if he simply had no idea why Shacklin was there.

Professor Shacklin, doyen of all administrative enterprises at Allminster and Executive Pro Vice Chancellor, was an elegant, tall man whose dark hair was now thinning on top. His father, an industrial chemist, had hailed from an Anglo-Indian family and had emigrated from Hyderabad to Northern England in 1953.

Shacklin was obliged to prompt his superior. "You asked to see me at the end of the day, Vice Chancellor." His voice was oiled with obsequiousness.

The Vice Chancellor feigned a degree of absent-mindedness and looked out at the night sky beyond his office windows. In the glass of the sash windows he saw the reflection of the desk lamps and the flickering fire in the grate. "Oh dear, I hadn't realised it was so late. I've been so busy." He patted the pile of leather folders that he insisted his secretary always used for paperwork prepared ready for his signature. "Come in and sit down."

Shacklin entered with a smirk of pleasure. He liked being in the Vice Chancellor's office because he nurtured the hope that he, as Executive Pro Vice Chancellor (and, in his own mind, effectively the Deputy Vice Chancellor), would have this office on the Armitage's retirement. He liked to daydream how he would personalise it when the Vice Chancellor was gone. Shacklin snuggled his bony posterior into one of the plump armchairs in the middle of the room, and scanned Armitage's face. He liked to observe the redness of his complexion and the blueness of his lips, looking for signs of deteriorating cardiac health, or better still, imminent death. In his turn, Armitage looked at the gaudy ruby ring that Shacklin wore on his left hand and disdained its heaviness, detested its gaucheness, and simultaneously respected the ring as a symbol of Shacklin's ultimate inferiority.

Armitage had waited until his subordinate had quite settled himself down, and only then beckoned Shacklin to approach his desk a little more nearly. Shacklin hauled himself out of the armchair and stood in front of the desk, like a pupil before the Head. He began to feel uneasy.

"I saw Professor Power today," said Armitage crisply, his previously vague demeanour having evaporated. "Have you met him?"

"In passing, I think," said Shacklin. "Isn't he a psychiatrist? Best given a wide berth I'd say."

"Really?" said the Vice Chancellor, biding his time until Shacklin had fully committed himself to an opinion. He smiled blandly at Shacklin, who underneath his thinning hair still had a youthful face. "Do you know if the new Professor is settling in?"

"I don't think the dean of the Faculty of Health is too impressed. She feels he doesn't have the profile to have been offered a Chair and says there are more worthy candidates in her faculty and he has jumped over them."

"Some pieces have that ability in chess too," said Armitage. Shacklin frowned ever so slightly, wondering where the Vice Chancellor was headed with this analogy. "We can't be forever promoting that dean's league of nursey friends. There is a greater strategy that I am playing out here. I have to think of the whole University and where I want it to be in ten years' time. We can't rely on the old stock-in-trade subjects like nursing and English. We have to diversify and any University worth its salt has medicine and a decent reputation for research and the sciences. All that wretched dean of health can bleat on about is 'pedagogy' and the wonders of 'qualitative' research. What *is* that? What I am wondering, David," he paused here, deliberately using Shacklin's first name to imply that he cared for him. "What I am wondering, is whether you have an appetite for my strategy to expand the University and will champion it?"

"Well, naturally, Vice Chancellor, I would support whatever was necessary to . . ."

The Vice Chancellor smiled happily, as Shacklin had fallen so neatly into the position he had engineered for him. "Thank you, David. I want you to convene a meeting of the deans in the next week or so and introduce Professor Power to them. I'm counting on you to be very clear with the deans. You must support Professor Power. He is a good man and a significant asset to the University. We must move forward and we *must* have a medical school. You and I must brook no resistance by the deans on this one. The strategy is imperative. I expect you to be the Pro Vice Chancellor who is going to get this thing up and running for me. It's make or break for the University. I do hope you understand me on this. Have I been sufficiently clear? It's very important for the future of the University that you are the lead administrative player on Professor Power's team. I do not wish to be let down on this. I can't emphasise strongly enough how vital this is for *your* future here. I want the medical school up and taking its first students in less than four years' time. I want you to chair a weekly committee to implement the medical school project, and you will report directly to me on progress every week."

"But has Senate approved this plan, Vice Chancellor? Or the Degree Innovation Committee – they'd have to assess the merits, risks and the costs of a new award. I suppose it would be an MB, would it? I really would advise that we need the Senate's permission . . ."

"To all intents and purposes I am the Senate, David. They will back me on this. There is no need, and I have no time to wait around for their woolly-minded deliberations or backsliding."

"No, Vice Chancellor, no. I quite see that. You would like a meeting with the deans as soon as is convenient for them?"

"No. I want you to chair the meeting within the week. That would be most convenient to *me*, David."

"Of course, Vice Chancellor."

"And after chairing that inaugural meeting you can have a little reward, David." Armitage watched a mixed expression of puzzlement and hope form on the features of Shacklin's face. "You can have a trip to Malta for a few days as a thank you for gaining the deans' approval of the new medical school concept. You can spend three days there, but you do have an objective to complete. I'd go myself, but I am overworked as it is. I'll get my secretary to book flights and accommodation . . . for one."

"Yes, Vice Chancellor. May I enquire what the objective is?"

"I want you to discuss and agree a Memorandum of Understanding with the University of Malta on student exchanges under the Erasmus scheme. I will sign the Memorandum if our legal department approves the agreement on your return. I might also ask you to visit a research centre we co-fund out there. They are not sending progress update reports regularly. It's a concern to me." He paused and looked carefully at Shacklin, scrutinising his facial expressions to discern the thoughts rippling underneath. "Can I ask you what impressions you have of Professor Power?"

"I don't think I can say much about him yet."

"I understand that. He seems very agreeable, at least on the surface, and at times his manner may even seem vague. But I suspect that is because he doesn't want people to know what he is thinking. That might lure people into thinking he is naïve, but I should warn you to be careful how you behave around him. He is a highly professional, well-connected doctor, with a first rate forensic mind. He has solved numerous cases for the police, and is an expert in his field. We have all that expertise working for us at a University rate – a pittance for a man of his calibre – essentially he's volunteering his time here . . . so don't alienate him, we can't replace him; and don't underestimate him, however blithely inoffensive he might appear." Shacklin nodded. "I do hope that you understand everything I've said tonight, for your own sake."

Chapter Three

*Each player must accept the cards life deals him or her:
but once they are in hand, he or she alone must decide
how to play the cards in order to win the game.*

Attributed to Voltaire

The Vice Chancellor's office was carefully positioned so that it had the most favourable light during the day. The Executive Pro Vice Chancellor, Professor Shacklin, had an office in the diametrically opposite corner of the Senate House building. As per the nature of University hierarchies Shacklin's office was smaller and darker. It was carpeted and furnished to a lesser, shabbier standard.

It was also better than the cubbyhole that Professor Power had been led to, in a dilapidated part of the nursing school, on his first day. Power had taken fright at the loathsome cupboard of a room that had been offered to him as a temporary base to develop the new medical school, and negotiated an alternative that he might reasonably see a visitor in, but it still fell far short of what he might reasonably have expected.

Shacklin's office boasted a long meeting table, where he held interminable conferences from early morning until late at night.

His long-suffering secretary, Margaret, sometimes felt that her endless task of taking minutes in the room was like serving a life sentence in a low secure jail. She had a calendar on her desk made of numbered blocks. Visitors to her office space always commented that the calendar was incorrect. She did not comment. The figures on the blocks were actually counting down the days, months and years until she could claim her University pension.

Margaret had ushered Dr Power in to see Shacklin and retreated to her office space to finish her granola and yoghurt at her desk. There was fifteen minutes left of her lunch hour, before she had to take minutes for the deans' meeting in the Senate Room. Margaret could hear Shacklin's oily voice buttering Dr Power up through the thin wall that separated the secretarial space from Shacklin's office.

She took out her headphones and opened a file on her computer. To those observing it might look as if she was listening to Shacklin's dictation tapes. She was however listening, in her own time, to an audiobook, *The Blind Assassin*. The protagonist of the narrative had had a long and unhappy marriage.

Margaret's marriage by contrast had been fulfilling, but tragically brief. She had been widowed in a road traffic accident and left with little money and a two-year-old son. She had moved back in with her mother and to her old bedroom in the red brick villa near Grosvenor Park.

At first her son had been taken to the park every day in a pushchair by his grandmother while Margaret caught the bus out to the village of Allminster, where the University was growing. From the age of five her mother had put her grandson on the bus to King's school while Margaret scrimped to accumulate his school fees. With any money left from her meagre secretarial salary Margaret treated herself to carefully chosen second-hand clothes from Aquascutum and judiciously chosen perfumes like Aqua di Roma. She particularly liked its hints of mimosa and honeysuckle. Now she lived in the villa alone. Her mother had left her the house in her will, and her son, a computer engineer, now had his own family in California. Margaret dreamed of selling her house in the city centre and moving to Catalonia, where she holidayed most summers. Her attention to the audiobook wandered and she was suddenly thinking how kindly spoken and handsome Dr Power had been. She wondered what Power might have thought of her had she been her younger self.

Shacklin was hoping to glean some juicy details from Power about his recent cases. "The Vice Chancellor told me that you were the psychiatrist in the Lindow Farm case, and I've heard that the police consulted you about the murder of Sir Ian McWilliam. I gather you work with a detective, Andrew Lynch. Fascinating! Please can you tell me about the work you both get up to?"

Power frowned, not just because he found Shacklin's levity and prurient curiosity trampled on his personal notions of confidentiality. Unlike some psychologists and pathologists, who courted the media with their spectacular name-dropping, tell-all cases, Power felt even the dead deserved professional confidentiality. He also found the Lindow case personally upsetting. Power demurred, saying that professional obligation to the Crown Prosecution Service prevented him from discussing the details of past cases.

Shacklin adroitly covered any annoyance at the rebuff by a diversionary comment. "We used to run a national Masters in Criminology course for the police," said Shacklin. "It was a big earner for us, for years we took hundreds of students from all the Metropolitan forces, then the Academy of Law launched a competing course, which included bursaries for some officers. Half the price and free places, how could we compete? And the police are always interested in the bottom line. I once had an Assistant Chief Constable who described what motivated his officers. He said his officers had many agendas, but not one was about helping the public stay safe. He described them as the four Ps; pay, pension, promotion and perks. Is your colleague Lynch the same? I expect that he left the police to double his earnings?"

"Actually, no. Not at all," said Power. "He took a pay cut and jeopardised his pension. His motivation is simple. He just wants to see justice done."

Shacklin couldn't believe that anyone was not motivated by money, but decided not to challenge Dr Power.

"Well, to business. I saw the Vice Chancellor and he requested I convene a meeting of the deans of the faculties so that I can introduce the concept of a new medical school at Allminster. And also introduce you. You will be my guest at the meeting. It can be a bit daunting getting to know several new people at once, so I have asked Margaret to provide a list of the deans – to help you remember all the names."

He gave Power a sheet of A 4 paper. Power looked down at the list of deans and their faculties.

Structure of Allminster University

Vice Chancellor: Canon Ambrose Armitage

Executive Pro Vice Chancellor: Professor David Shacklin

Dean of Faculty of Healthcare:
Professor Bridget McFarlane (Nursing, Midwifery, Health Management, Physiotherapy, Social Work)

Dean of Faculty of Psychology and Media Studies:
Professor Ann Teesdale (Psychology, Drama, Media Production)

Dean of Faculty of Mathematics and Natural Philosophy:
Professor Nigel Kneale (Mathematics, Logic, Philosophy, Computing and IT)

Dean of Faculty of Social Sciences and Criminology:
Professor Johann Felfe (Sociology, Politics, Criminology, Probation Studies)

Dean of Faculty of Humanities:
Sir Robert Willett (English, History, European Languages, Archaeology)

Dean of Faculty of Physical Sciences:
Professor Simone Jauffret (Biology, Chemistry, Physics, Geography, Geology)

Dean of Faculty of Engineering and Technology:
Professor Immo Torvalds (Engineering, Chemical Engineering, Process Management)

Dean of Business and Enterprise:
Professor Erin Marsh, (Business, Finance, Accounting)

Registrar: Dr Nicholas Timmons

Bursar: Hamish Grieg, Solicitor

Executive Director of Human Resources: Karen Harvey

Shacklin continued, "If the medical school happens, its development will change Allminster irrevocably. And you, better than anybody, know that fundamentally, people hate change. The political and financial ramifications of a medical school will be profound. Will this mean a new Faculty of Medicine? Or will it mean that the existing Faculty of Health grows into a super faculty, larger than all the others? What happens if the Vice Chancellor channels funds into the new medical school and lets other courses and faculties wither on the vine? Allminster already has rather more faculties than other Universities, a by-product of rather rapid and haphazard growth in the nineties. So everyone is aware that the faculties and the number of deans need to be rationalised. They're nervous for their own future. The development of yet another faculty – Medicine – would be the catalyst for that rationalisation process. But, if I had to predict what would happen? The news of the medical school project will be generally welcome. We shouldn't see any overt hostility."

"I am surprised to think there would be any objections," said Dr Power. He looked at Shacklin's hands, which were moving nervously, dancing on his desk. His fingers were tanned, the knuckles dark. On the little finger of his left hand he wore a large gold ring which provided the mount for a broad ovoid ruby stone. Shacklin's grandfather had bought the ring, at great cost from Premraj Jain, Jewellers of Hyderabad, as a present for his only son on his emigration. Power's immediate thought was that the ring was grotesque, but he felt guilty about this summary judgment. He looked up at Shacklin's vanishingly pale, blue eyes.

"What the general public would rightly consider trivial minutiae are the stuff of all-consuming passion in academic circles," said Shacklin. "The rarified atmosphere of a University leads to the evolution of clever people with more than a few kinks and twists. And you'll find these people, for the most part, are brilliant at hiding them."

"Hmm," said Power, non-committally. "So, who will be at the meeting?"

"Well, the Dean of Engineering will not be there. Professor Torvalds rarely leaves his labs, which are in Crewe. He's working on developing an electric car to save the world. It'll never catch on. Professor McFarlane, on the other hand, would not miss the meeting for all the tea in China. She is the Dean of Healthcare. Delightful, lilting,

Dublin accent. Handsome, slim. Immune to male charms. I have tried, believe me. Bitterly envious, and would sell her granny to get my job. There's Professor Felfe, the criminologist, so quiet and so private – I don't even know his first name. And then there's Ann Teesdale from psychology. Strident – convinced that right is always on her side. She'd even have an argument with that statue of Dodgson in the Vice Chancellor's office. There's Professor Kneale, the mathematician. He's that person on the committee who always makes a negative point, but usually he's worth listening to as he is ruthlessly logical and often proved right, even if he annoys you initially. Professor Jauffret, Dean of Physical Sciences has just joined us from the University of Guadeloupe – she studied sea grasses and green turtles. She's convinced that sea grasses will help reverse global warming. I must introduce her to Professor Torvalds ... and last, but certainly not least, is our knight of the realm. Sir Robert Willett is our Professor of English and Dean of Humanities. He's a professor but I always forget whether he should be Professor Sir Robert or Sir Professor Robert. I just call him Sir," Shacklin chortled at his own encapsulated summary of the Board of Deans.

"Thank you for the run down," said Power, who realised he had already forgotten most of the names and details. "I'm not very good with names," he confessed.

"No doubt it will all become clear," said Shacklin. "I should let you know that I'm being sent to the University of Malta by the Vice Chancellor. I'm booked on a flight tonight actually. Perhaps you could make appointments to meet all the deans individually while I'm away? It would be a salutary idea to get to know them and to press the case for the medical school?"

"I met a professor of physics from the University of Malta," said Power, remembering when he walked the St James's Way in Northern Spain with Lynch. "He was called Ramon, I think."

Shacklin nodded, but he wasn't listening. "Tell me, Professor Power, what do you know about 'TopQuiz'?"

"The TV programme?"

"Yes, are you familiar with it? Do you watch?"

"Occasionally," said Power. "It began when University Challenge was taken off air. A similar format, but TopQuiz has three students on a team not four. Then they brought University Challenge back in the nineteen-nineties to compete with it, with Paxman as quiz master. When I was at medical school I appeared on 'TopQuiz'. We lasted for a couple of episodes."

"Yes," said Shacklin. "Somebody said you were on it."

Power was intrigued that people had been talking about him. He couldn't resist asking Shacklin, "Why do you mention it?"

"Oh, nothing. Just somebody may contact you about it. Don't worry, it's not bad. We'd better go to the meeting, I think. In my position it never does to be late. The Vice Chancellor loves to make people wait, but when everybody sees your job as a stepping stone to his it never does to let them gather together and plot without you there!" He sighed. "I forget you are a psychiatrist. You must think I am very insecure. I hate to reveal too much to people. They use it against you. The truth is I have worked very hard to get where I am. I'm here against the odds really. My father was an industrial chemist, what today we would call a chemical engineer, at Wilton in the nineteen-sixties. He died when I was ten. Overnight I became the man of the house. I actually think we lived on my newspaper round money for a while."

"How did he die?" asked Power.

"The doctor put mesothelioma on his death certificate. He worked for an asbestos firm in ... in the fifties ... well ... never mind." Shacklin did not want to say too much to Power and stood up. "The meeting won't chair itself, come on Professor Power."

* * *

The original building of Senate House was a gilded remnant of a large merchant's mansion overlooking the River Dee. In the nineteen-sixties a local architect, apparently enamoured with Ken Adam's design for the War Room in *Dr Strangelove* had grafted a brutalist concrete extension onto the Georgian merchant's house. The resulting extension housed the Senior Common Room and a large Senate Meeting Room with one wall composed entirely of a slanted plate glass window. The sloping ceiling of the meeting room had a large, deeply recessed, oval rooflight above a similarly oval, oak table with plump leather-upholstered swivel-chairs arrayed around it. The chairs were tall, and reminiscent of Neo-Futuristic thrones set on cone-like chrome bases. The meeting room's colour scheme of white stucco and shining steel floated on an ocean of thick, seagreen carpet.

Professor Shacklin and Professor Power walked into the Senate Meeting Room to find the deans already present and gossiping over cups of coffee and individual packets of biscuits; Viennese Whirls, chocolate cookies and custard creams. An alarming silence cut across their chatter as Shacklin and Power entered. Power felt all eyes were upon him. Shacklin steered him to a chair near the head of the oval table. One of the University catering staff in the room leant in close to Dr Power's ear and asked, "Would you like a cup of coffee, sir?"

"Thank you. Black, decaffeinated if you have that please, no sugar." A china cup of thin coffee was placed before him with a couple of custard cream biscuits on the saucer rim beside it. Power tasted the coffee. It was thin and watery, but piping hot.

"Hello everybody," said Shacklin. He looked at his watch. "Time we made a start on this Extraordinary Deans' Meeting, I believe." His secretary, Margaret, silently took her place alongside him, opposite Power. She unfolded her notebook and prepared to take minutes of the meeting in shorthand.

Power looked around. There were five deans in attendance. Their faces were unsmiling, and yet attentive. Power reminded himself that surely he was doing a 'good thing' in trying to found a new medical school.

Shacklin resumed his introduction, "We're here to welcome Professor Power at the Vice Chancellor's express request. I realise that this may be the first time Professor Power has met any of you and so perhaps if we could go round the table and introduce ourselves. I know we've had practice at introducing ourselves." He looked at Power. "Would you mind going first Professor? Just tell the meeting who you are and a bit about your background. We will come to your proposal later."

"Of course Professor Shacklin, thank you. Good morning everyone," Power looked around the table and made a brave stab at giving a smile to everyone. "I am Professor Carl Power. I've joined the University fairly recently. My background is as a researcher, an author, a doctor, specifically a consultant psychiatrist." Power noticed this caused one of the women far to his left to frown and start tapping the top of her pen against the papers in front of her in an agitated manner.

The dean on Power's immediate left turned to him and grudgingly acknowledged him. "Hello, Professor Power. I'm Bridget McFarlane, Dean of Healthcare, depending on what we discuss today, I think we should arrange a meeting with my sub deans so you can explain yourself to the Faculty."

It was the turn of an intense-looking , rather bushy-eyebrowed individual next. He avoided all eye contact with Power. He said simply, "Professor Nigel Kneale. Maths."

Next was a pale, grey shadow of a man, neatly dressed and with precise gelled hair. "Professor Johann Felfe, my sphere is criminology. I would, of course, be pleased to meet you outside this arena. Maybe sherry, or lunch, some time." Power nodded at the invitation, which he appreciated. Felfe was quiet but at least he seemed human. He thought that Felfe would be uncomfortable in any gathering of people.

Next came Professor Simone Jauffret, Dean of Physical Sciences; and the dean on the other side of the table was the woman who had frowned so markedly when Power introduced himself. She was a small, compact, raven-haired woman with a nose rather like a beak. She looked up and made eye contact solely with Shacklin. She did not deign to acknowledge Power in the slightest degree.

"Professor Ann Teesdale, Consultant Psychologist and Dean of Psychology. One of our largest faculties."

"Professor Teesdale's faculty also includes drama," said the dean on her immediate left. He was the last dean to introduce himself. He smiled engagingly at Power and his eyes twinkled with a humour that seemed wholly absent from any of the other individuals at the meeting. He reached over and shook Power's hand determinedly. "I'm Rob, Faculty of Humanities."

"This is Sir Robert Willett," said Shacklin to Power, *sotto voce* and with deference, "and now we are all acquainted perhaps I can talk about why I invited you to this Extraordinary Meeting. The Vice Chancellor asked me to hold this meeting to announce his intention to establish and develop a new project at Allminster. I must tell you that this is a project very dear to his heart. I emphasise that point."

"That's a warning," hissed Professor Teesdale to her neighbouring dean. As she noticed Shacklin's admonishing stare, she apologised, "Sorry for the interruption. But you're signalling that he will brook no opposition."

"And what is this new project?" Bridget MacFarlane purred in her lilting Irish accent.

"I was about to describe the project," said Shacklin. "The Vice Chancellor wants to introduce Medicine into our list of courses. He wants to build a new medical school offering the degrees of MBChB within in the next five years. He realises that this is a very ambitious target, but he is determined that it shall be done. And that is why Professor Power is with us. He will outline the scope of the project and the reasoning behind it."

"I think we all know what a medical school is," said Professor Teesdale, now frankly glaring at Power.

"Nevertheless," said Shacklin, "I think we should all extend the courtesy of listening to what Professor Power has to say. This would be a significant step in Allminster's evolution." He bestowed a thin smile upon Power. "Professor Power?"

"Well," said Power, wondering if he had just been thrown to the lions. "There is no medical school for around fifty miles in any direction from Allminster, and so there is a significant catchment area of potential student doctors in Cheshire, Shropshire and North Wales who might prefer to study here. We have a population around us of about five hundred thousand which is sufficient to offer a good range of clinical cases to teach upon. A new medical school would drive postgraduate teaching and medical research. Better doctors would improve the quality of services in the local hospitals and primary care. A medical school here would also boost recruitment – it's difficult to attract good doctors to a city without a medical school. Local hospitals and general practices sometimes have to advertise Consultant and GP posts three or four times before they attract a suitable candidate. And nationally, we have fallen behind other European countries – the UK has one of the lowest ratios of doctors per head of population. We have about two doctors for every thousand people, Germany has four and Sweden has five.

"My hope is to deliver a new medical school and a new medical course – a four year course – not a traditional five year course, because we would take in mature students – ones with existing degrees in sciences or nursing and evolve them into doctors. Our focus would be on training doctors into hard-to-fill specialities – general practice, emergency medicine. And we would focus on ethical practice and good communication; treating the mind as well as the body. Our new curriculum would be exciting and relevant to the twenty-first century, and also bedded on a new Hippocratic Oath. We would invite the whole multidisciplinary team to teach our doctors and we would use experienced or retired local consultants as mentors to our students to give them the benefit of the wisdom of older professionals and their experience surviving Medicine." Power was intending to say more, but paused for the briefest moments to look around in order to check whether his ideas were being understood and how well they had been received.

Bridget McFarlane seized on the opportunity the pause offered her. "This endeavour sounds immense, and highly costly. Has this even been discussed at Senate level or is it another of the Vice Chancellor's pipe dreams? Is there funding for such an ambitious idea, because I have to say right now that there is simply no money to be had from the other faculties to support this?"

"This is the kind of project that only the Vice Chancellor could initiate," said Shacklin. "The Senate will be asked to ratify the decision, but I think that the Vice Chancellor firmly believes this is his call. I for one wouldn't challenge him on that."

"I know that," said McFarlane. "You'd never challenge the old man. You wouldn't tell him to stop eating even if he was just about to explode through gobbling one too many doughnuts." Power noticed that the other deans seemed to be enjoying the ill-tempered exchange between the two senior figures. Only Professor Felfe seemed uninterested. He was making a private study of his fingernails. His facial expression was unreadable.

Power tried to pour oil on the troubled waters. "There's no medical school in the land that doesn't earn two or three times its costs. There are Government grants, years of tuition fees for every student and all the research income from places like the Medical Research Council."

"And what about the capital costs to set it up?" asked Professor Kneale. "I think Professor McFarlane may be more worried about that."

McFarlane retorted. "If I am, I am quite capable of saying so, thank you, Nigel. But since *you* raise it, perhaps Professor Power can enlighten us?"

"I think it's early days to expect Professor Power to present a business plan, Bridget," said Shacklin soothingly.

"He's a doctor," chipped in the spiky-haired Psychology Professor, Teesdale. "Doctors always expect to delegate their work to someone else."

Perhaps inadvisably Power replied to this. He had given much thought to the matter and gave voice to his ideas (and thereby lost ground). "I have considered the capital costs. To match other medical schools we would need around thirty million." There was a collective gasp from most of those around the table. Only Professor Felfe's face seemed to betray no reaction whatsoever.

"Maybe that's a bit high," suggested Shacklin. "I was thinking more of start up costs of a million maybe and then five million more spread over ten years?'

"Well," said Power, "We will start by teaching one year initially – the first year of around two hundred students – so not all facilities will need to be there on day one. However, a lot of the teaching at the start of any medical course is in subjects such as biochemistry, anatomy and physiology. Anatomy can be taught by dissection of bodies or, preferably these days, through prepared specimens and virtual computer demonstrations. You either need to invest in a mortuary and dissection rooms, or invest in superb anatomy prosections, like those by the *Body Worlds* creator? You know the man?"

"That creepy German doctor?" asked Professor Teesdale, with a tone that suggested both her disbelief and mortal offence.

"I am referring to Professor Gunther von Hagens, of Heidelburg," said Dr Power. "He has various labs across the world that make plastinated anatomy prosections – sections of bodies that are expertly dissected and preserved. He supplies anatomy departments of medical schools as well as putting on those exhibitions."

"I do hope we will not entertain such morbid atrocities here, that guy runs a freak show. Dead people set up to play cards. Appalling taste." declared Professor Teesdale.

"I don't particular like the exhibitions either," said Power. "But Dr Von Hagens also runs a serious business supplying anatomy labs. However it's taught, a doctor does need to know anatomy. It is essential," said Power. He spoke with quiet certainty and authority, but inside a small icy blue nugget of despair was freezing within his heart. Worse was to come.

"I understand that the Vice Chancellor is very keen we have a traditional medical school, Professor Power. I spoke with him, actually, about this very thing," said Shacklin, pleased to show that he had Canon Armitage's complete confidence. "He would like a dissection room and mortuary. He has looked into it and even talked about the special drainage required." It was Power's turn to be surprised. The Vice Chancellor had not mentioned this idea to him. Power disliked the notion of teaching anatomy to students by asking them to dissect cold, grey, and greasy corpses.

"Well," said Power, trying to underline the size of a medical school to Shacklin. "Medical schools are usually quite large – with many seminar rooms, at least three lecture halls, each with a capacity for two to three hundred students for lectures or plenaries, running all day, every working day, throughout the year. I think maybe when complete the Medical Faculty might need forty- to seventy-thousand square feet."

"That's the first we've heard of a new faculty too," said McFarlane, "The very first time anybody has ever said that. I think the Vice Chancellor needs to explain himself."

"Maybe Professor Power merely meant a new medical school, rather than a whole new faculty," said Shacklin soothingly. "And perhaps it is too early to determine the budget. We are talking in principle here, aren't we? The Vice Chancellor, I am sure, is, through this very meeting, making the deans aware of his intentions, in principle, at the earliest opportunity," he sought to neutralise the envy behind Bridget McFarlane's tirade. "I am sure that the Vice Chancellor would be very grateful if the Faculty of Healthcare could assist Professor Power in schooling him as to the planning of what is practical and achievable in the University environment. I am sure he has much to learn about curriculum development, and resources planning. The Faculty of Healthcare has much valuable experience after all, doesn't it?"

"I might consider a prominent role for our faculty," said McFarlane, scenting an opportunity. Power did not like the sound of the horsetrading going on at some level unfathomable to him. He didn't think he did need any schooling and had more than a grasp of what was involved in a medical school's curriculum and design. He had worked in several medical schools and helped instigate changes in their curricula. None of them had been small, and none of them ran on a shoestring.

Then the Dean of Psychology scenting that McFarlane might be willing to trade the Healthcare Faculty's acquiescence for a piece of the pie, broke in. She stood up, her spiky hair implacably rigid. Power wondered what gothic well of bitterness she had washed it in and if her state of perpetual offence had been ever-present since her days as a punk teenager. "I simply can't sit here and let all this roll over me," she said. "I'm not prepared to be a hypocrite," she gave a sidelong glance at Bridget McFarlane who simply smiled at her with feigned benevolence. "I will oppose medicine at Allminster. The Medical Model has been a disaster for human wellbeing throughout history, particularly mental wellbeing. I won't bow down to any palace set up for male medicine. We don't need the biomedical model any more. Doctors are just parasites on the weak."

Power wondered if the psychologist was deliberately adopting a standing position to dominate him and how best he should respond to the hissing bundle of spite looking down at him. He could stand up to challenge the domination, and perhaps appear aggressive himself, or seek to defuse the anger in her behaviour by exploring where her anger came from and what old relationship she was replaying in this new situation with him. Either strategy could lead to unpredictable results. He chose to try and counter the broadside by remaining calm and factual. Nevertheless, his inner anxiety at her challenge manifested in the slightest of stammers, which he hoped his wider audience might overlook.

"Medicine may have its detractors, but overall it has saved lives, increased life expectancy and raised the quality of those lives. What about the lives saved by eradicating the small pox virus, or preventing learning disability and blindness by vaccinating against rubella, or prescribing antibiotics for sepsis, public health initiatives for safe water – preventing cholera, or treating appendicitis with surgery before peritonitis kills a person. Aren't these all positives in medicine's favour?"

"I notice that you don't mention mental health in all that. You see psychological distress as a disease, and illness to be treated with pills. You use meaningless terms like schizophrenia – pretend that it's a disease that needs heavy medication – psychiatrists are nothing but power hungry abusers who peddle drugs. You want to start a medical school to perpetuate the myth of the virtuous doctor, but it's really all about control and money." She was shaking and red-faced. Her heart was pounding so much that her head was atremble atop her neck.

Power paused briefly. Once more he determined that the best response was not to challenge and inflame the situation. The possibility that Teesdale might even be ill herself briefly crossed his mind. He swallowed his anger and said calmly. "Psychology and psychiatry both rely on scientific method. There are plenty of studies that have been replicated to demonstrate the organic basis of schizophrenia in the brain. I'm thinking of the 1976 CT Scan study of Johnstone and colleagues and the MRI scan studies of Nancy Andreasen in the nineteen-nineties. Of course schizophrenia is just shorthand for what is probably a set of differently caused disorders. As time goes by we'll find those causes. In the early twentieth century we found that neurosyphilis caused about ten per cent of the cases in asylums and we are finding other causes all the time – like autoimmune disease, and prenatal links to flu epidemics." He paused. Teesdale was shaking her head vehemently, but most of the academics round the table were listening attentively to Power's words. "These are replicated findings. Surely psychology is signed up to the basis of scientific method?"

But Teesdale was loathe to concede any point. She was a fizzing ball of spite. "Well, aren't you a typical psychiatrist? Shroud waving and spouting irrelevances. Clinging on to white male privilege. I've taken the trouble to read your papers – and it was a chore I can tell you – unoriginal rubbish rehashing the medical orthodoxy, every one.

I certainly won't be supporting the introduction of your medical fascism here."

"Whatever judgment you might have made, please can we meet and talk things through?" asked Power. "Please do not stand in the way of a medical school that will serve the local community, raise standards in local healthcare, train a new generation of doctors. Those doctors – their education, culture and philosophy could be formed by the best of what Allminster already has to offer." (Although Power doubted now whether he wanted this particular dean anywhere near his students). "There are recruitment issues locally – a dearth of GPs, and the need for flexible working means that training numbers set when the workforce was predominantly male are just too low now as females often need to work part-time. "

"Pure sexism," hissed the psychologist.

"Whatever you say," said Power. "But the country needs MORE doctors – we have less per capita than any other European nation and our population is expanding every year . . ."

"Maybe we could train more nurses to take over doctor's jobs," said the Dean of Nursing unhelpfully.

"Doctors have some key skills that are vital," said Power. "Like diagnosis and expertise in prescribing."

"Nurses can do that," said the Dean of Healthcare, emphatically.

Professor Felfe was looking out of the vast plate glass window, watching the Vice Chancellor decant his portly self into his ostentatious car parked by Senate House and smoothly drive himself away.

"It takes five years at University and nearly ten years training on the job to be a consultant," said Power patiently. "That length of training guarantees safety for patients. Patients can't afford to see people who are not properly qualified. They shouldn't have to . . . it could cost them their lives after all."

"Shroud waving again," said the Dean of Psychology.

"Well," said Professor Shacklin. "I feel it has been useful to air all our points of view. The meeting today has had one aim – to introduce the concept of a new medical school at Allminster, and I think that our discussion has been very useful. I think it would be an idea, as Professor Power offered earlier to Professor Teesdale, for him to make an appointment to see each one of the deans and discuss the way forward. The Vice Chancellor has been very clear with me about his intentions regarding a new school and I must be equally clear with the deans here that he will brook no active resistance."

"I am terribly busy this month on staff appraisals," said Professor Teesdale. "I simply have no time to spare."

"Well," said Sir Robert, standing up, assuming that the meeting was at a close. "I am only too happy to meet with you, Professor Power. I think medicine at Allminster is a fantastic idea, and I will support it with all my energy. Count me in on your team. Medicine will diversify our Prospectus and it will earn the University much needed revenue. I would counsel you to arrange an appointment with the bursar as well as the deans. He can guide you as to the University's finances . . . or warn you in case the cupboard is bare . . ."

"That's a very good idea," said Shacklin. "Please add the bursar to the appointments you need to arrange whilst I'm away, Professor Power."

The Dean of Mathematics and Natural Philosophy, Professor Kneale, smiled at Power in a lukewarm way. "The bursar will tell you that the Vice Chancellor stretches the envelope of our resources pretty thin." He turned to Shacklin, "I wonder, Professor Shacklin, if the Dean's Meeting could minute that I am away for a week's annual leave from today?"

Shacklin nodded as Margaret took the minute down, and then closed the meeting. "The Vice Chancellor wishes there to be a regular steering committee set up, meeting on the medical school's progress, and I wonder if the deans could consider if they or a deputy from their faculty might wish to join."

This further offended Professor Teesdale. "It goes to show that there was no point in asking our opinions on the project if a planning committee is to be formed in any case. This meeting has been a complete waste of our time."

Shacklin's smile was unwavering as he brushed her comment aside. "Thank you all for attending today, it has been useful, I will report to the Vice Chancellor on your reception of the idea. As Professor Kneale noted his leave, I must also minute that I have been asked, by the Vice Chancellor, to go on a mission to the University of Malta."

"Some people have all the luck," said Bridget McFarlane. "A bit of sun in the Med while we weather grim November."

"I shall be working hard, naturally," said Shacklin.

"Are you taking your wife?" asked McFarlane, pointedly.

"I don't think so," said Shacklin defensively.

"Well, if she is not joining you, are you going alone then?"

Shacklin glared at her. "Thank you for coming everybody." Everyone stood up.

Professor Kneale started pocketing unopened mini packets of biscuits into his jacket.

Professor Teesdale glared at Power and left before anybody could talk to her. Professor Jauffret came over to shake Power's hand and seemed to apologise for her fellow deans when she said, "You managed very well in trying circumstances Professor Power. My faculty will probably support you. It is logical to do so, but we are wary of losing any of our budget to a new project." She gave him a warm smile, patted his arm and left. Power looked around; apart from Shacklin who was whispering to McFarlane just as she left the Senate Room there was only Kneale left. Felfe had disappeared unseen. Kneale sidled up to Power. Kneale smelt – an acrid waft of body odour assaulted Power's nose. He tried not to wrinkle his nose in disgust at Kneale's smell.

"An interesting proposition, Professor Power. It will be interesting to see how the Vice Chancellor explains the funding of such a project to the Senate. It will be a mathematical feat worthy of a Nobel Prize. And you have much opposition from your health colleagues, and Shacklin is an ambitious, altogether incompetent *Lothario*." Power didn't know what to say. "I don't expect you to say anything, Professor Power. You don't need to agree. What I say is not opinion, it's a matter of fact. Now, you're a medical man, tell me confidentially what do you think of our bloated Vice Chancellor? He should have died years ago of hypertension, diabetes and obesity. What is your honest medical opinion? How long has he got? A year? Six months?"

"I'm sorry," said Power, moving away from Kneale and feeling a sense of physical and moral distaste. Power wondered whether the acrid aroma of sweat was the smell of long-standing fear. "I couldn't possibly speculate like that."

"That's OK," said Kneale. "It's early days to assess him, I know. I'll ask you again when you've seen a bit more of him. Good day."

Power watched Kneale wander off. He couldn't quite believe what he had just encountered. The whole meeting had been very far from the kind of academic meeting he had been expecting and the behaviour of his supposed superiors at the University had confronted him with the uncomfortable feeling that they were driven by a range of different agendas, none of which aligned with the best interests of the University nor of Power's pet project.

"How did you think that went?" asked Shacklin, as he poured himself a final cup of coffee from the cooling vacuum flasks that the catering staff were even now packing away.

"To be honest, it was bruising and unpleasant," said Power. "This is a group of people who would prefer to see a crisis in an opportunity, rather than the other way round."

"Oh, don't be disheartened," said Shacklin. "You stood up to it well enough. It wasn't personal. They meet every new idea with similar displays of horror."

"Professor Teesdale – wasn't she personal? She called my research derivative and orthodox, I think. I find it difficult to recall. Her anger was mesmerising."

"You just have to press ahead," said Shacklin. "You'll need determination to survive here. I'm constantly running hard to stay still."

"I don't know," said Power. "I've worked in some very hostile environments with the most disturbed people; secure units, psychiatric intensive care units. But you know, I think there's none as mad as the sane."

"I'm sorry, I don't quite understand."

"I just mean that I find sometimes find that the symptoms of mental illness are easier to understand than the behaviour of the sane," said Power.

"Well, reflect on what worked and what didn't. Fine tune your figures with the bursar. When you mentioned that figure of thirty million I almost spilt my coffee everywhere."

"It's a reasonable estimate. Medical schools are big places."

"I was thinking of a few million as an initial capital budget," said Shacklin. "Seriously."

"We'd need more than that every year for salaries alone," said Power, beginning again to wonder what kind of looking-glass world he had entered.

"I'll see you when I get back from Malta, you can report to me on your meetings." He shook Power's hand and left the doctor standing alone in the Senate Room. Power left Senate House and began a gradual and thoughtful walk across the campus, through throngs of students heading home to their flats and rooms, across the gardens, to the red-brick building where they had given him an office. He used his identity card to open the electronic access and climbed the spiral stone staircase up to the floor where his office was. He crossed the marble-chipped floor to the heavy wooden door of his office and unlocked it. He just wanted to pick up his coat and briefcase and drive straight home to nurse his dented pride.

As he put his coat on he noticed something new about the office. There was a small, but heavy, business card left on the keyboard of his computer.

Power picked the card up. It was from Professor Felfe. Written on the back of the card was an invitation. "Can I invite you to meet me tomorrow at 12 noon, please? I will text you with the location tomorrow."

Chapter Four

*Il est encore plus facile de juger de l'esprit d'un homme
par ses questions que par ses réponses.*
Gaston de Lévis, Duke of Lévis

Power's outpatient clinic began at 8 a.m. precisely. He would see two new patients with student doctors in tow. The students were routinely sent out to learn psychiatry from the medical schools of the two big cities fifty miles' away. Power liked to finish at 11 a.m. This gave him an hour with each patient and a good while with each student discussing the diagnosis and management. By the end of his teaching clinic Power had taught on two cases – one of a twenty-six-year-old man whose heavily-tattooed body was causing him extreme distress. The static images of multicoloured snakes and dragons that he had lived serenely with for many years had recently taken on a life of their own, and in his eyes, had 'quickened' and were writhing and rolling beneath his skin. He had tried to gouge out the eyes of a slithersome red dragon with a red-hot penknife and now had two scarred, burnt out pits where the blade had seared into his flesh. "The dragon tried to wriggle out of the way as I stabbed the blade into him," he explained, before saying that the creatures were becoming even more bothersome by singing out at all times of day and night, keeping him from his rest. And truly the patient looked greatly wearied by his experiences.

Seeing how his mental disorder was devastating the life of this patient, Power was reminded of the psychologist, Teesdale, railing against the inutility of the term 'schizophrenia'. Power saw the savage cruelty of the illness before him, and how it dwarfed the sterile argument about what the illness was called. It was the suffering caused by the illness that mattered; to realise the enormity of the illness and consider what effective measures could alleviate its toll on the patient – nothing else. The academic discussion about what terms should describe the condition was futile in the reality of the moment.

Professor Power had wanted to admit this person with schizophrenia. To observe him, investigate his case and make sure he was safe. This would have been good practice, but this was no longer possible in a health service with diminished beds. Managers would tell Dr Power that the reduction in beds was 'progress', was safe, and they no longer wanted to listen to nurses or doctors in case they heard something they could not ignore. And so, despite Professor Power's better judgment, this patient was sent upon his way with tablets and a fervent hope that he would not harm himself again, and Power's requests for a community nurse 'would be considered' by the managers. After the consultation Professor Power discussed schizophrenia with the student doctors, all the while having unpleasant flashbacks to the meeting at the University, and Professor Teesdale's scathing attack.

The second patient, Mrs Alexander, a fifty-five-year-old widow related a tale of endless worry. Anxiety had driven her from her workplace in the busy shop where she once worked. Her whole working life: customers pressing questions, fellow staff demanding she work faster, the burdens of deadlines and travel had overwhelmed her, and relentless waves of panic had washed over her. The only way she found she could cope was lying on her bed in the stillness and the dark while the rest of the world carried on its business, laughing and chattering in the sunny streets below her window. The GP suggested cognitive therapy from psychology. For ten months she had lingered anxiously on the waiting list of the psychologists until they deigned to see her. Made medically redundant from her work she had dutifully attended all eight of the ration of sessions she was allowed. Her GP had asked Professor Power to review her, for she was, as she had told the medical student, "Not a bit better."

She sat trembling in the chair next to Dr Power. He asked what treatment she had received. She described questionnaires by the dozen, and sessions where she was challenged to reframe her overwhelming thoughts. "But the anxiety is there, just always under the surface," she said, "And it came on when things were going so well for me. They were talking about promotion. My first grandson had been born . . ."

"There was nothing that precipitated it?" asked Power? "No accident, or bad news or . . ."

"Nothing." She shook her head and her shock of curly brown hair moved in tandem. "It came on as a pounding in my head. My heart sometimes feels like a pile driver in my chest, I can hear it when I put my head on the pillow. And I don't sleep. I lie there in the shade; I sweat and just listen to my heart thumping away."

"And did psychology help any of this?"

"No, I think the psychologist got frustrated with me, angry even. He said I wasn't engaging in therapy and that it would be my responsibility if I didn't get better and back to work."

Power saw that even though the patient held her hands in her lap they trembled throughout the consultation. He asked her to put her arms straight out in front of her. The tremor of both her hands was clear to him, and the medical student by his side. Power noticed that her hair was thinning, and a sheen of perspiration coated the skin of her forehead.

"Do you often feel hot?" asked Power. "Do you go around the house opening windows?"

"I do," she said. "My son says the house is always cold. We argue and I tell him to keep the windows open when he tries to close them."

"I see," said Power. "Have you lost weight, maybe?" He could see her clothes were hanging off her slight frame.

"I've lost two stone," she said. "But I'm always hungry, always eating. I worry it might be cancer."

"Well, let's check one or two things out before we jump to any conclusions," said Power. "Has anybody taken your pulse?"

"No," she said looking puzzled.

"May I?" asked Power gently, and reached out to take her wrist. He felt for and counted her radial pulse for a minute then he put a thermometer in her mouth. After taking her temperature he measured her blood pressure. Finally he sought her consent to palpate her neck for a goitre. The he sat down. "I would like to run one or two blood tests. Has anybody done any blood tests since you've had anxiety?"

"No," she said looking alarmed. "The psychologist gave me a questionnaire and diagnosed generalised anxiety."

"On the basis of a questionnaire?" asked Power, frowning. She nodded. "Well, your pulse is fast – over a hundred and ten beats per minute. It's a bit irregular too. Your blood pressure is raised and so is your temperature." He turned to the medical student for an instant. "What blood test would you suggest?" The medical student was young, embarrassed at being the focus of attention, and said nothing, shaking his head. "Well," said Power. "I will run an urgent thyroid function test, and some others. I think it will probably show that your thyroid gland is running a little fast, and that is why you have been feeling anxious. I will ask my colleague, an endocrinologist, to see you for treatment, and if I am correct, you will be feeling much, *much* better in a week or so." Power rang his consultant colleague in the clinic down the hall and walked his patient through to see her. The endocrinologist emailed him the next week to confirm Power's diagnosis of hyperthyroidism.

His clinic finished for the day, Professor Power bade his students farewell and dictated his letters. As he was dictating the final paragraph his phone bleeped. It was a text from Felfe. "Professor Power – I suggest lunch at one at the Arkle restaurant at the Grosvenor Hotel. See you there."

There was both a certainty and brevity to Felfe's text. It was as if Felfe assumed, or rather knew for sure, that Power both wanted to talk to him and, furthermore, could attend the appointment.

* * *

Professor Felfe was already seated at the table when Power arrived. The restaurant had been approached through a maze of corridors, lined with pillars and lit by a skylight. The corridors' plush carpet felt expensively soft underfoot. Power had been glad that he had worn a suit for his clinic earlier that day and not something more casual, because the staff and guests at the Grosvenor Hotel were immaculately attired. Despite his Jaeger suit and tie, Power felt under-dressed.

Felfe was a small, bird-like man, with thinning grey hair and piercingly blue eyes. Today he was dressed warmly and smartly in a tailored grey tweed suit with an azure silk tie. A large white linen napkin was already spread across his lap. He gave Power a thin smile as he arrived. It was not the warmest of greetings, but despite the brevity of the smile it was genuine. He gestured with a hand to indicate that Power should take the seat opposite him.

Power seated himself and gazed around the Arkle restaurant. The nearby tables were empty. The lunch sitting was not busy and there were two couples on a table near the entrance. Power had rarely been in a Michelin starred restaurant. It was hardly the place for a working lunch, and Power wondered what impression Felfe was trying to convey.

"I am pleased to offer you lunch here," said Felfe. He spoke with a hint of a German accent. "The chef is Simon Radley. He makes sure that the vegetarian options are very good."

Power could not recall ever discussing his vegetarianism with Felfe, but Felfe certainly appeared to know about it. "Thank you for coming, you might have noticed my silence yesterday, I did not wish to speak at the meeting. I prefer to listen, that is when they are not talking drivel. Every one of them wants to add his mustard to the conversation."

"Mustard?" asked Power, not sure if he had heard right.

"It is an idiom, I spent time in Berlin in the nineteen-eighties, 'seinen Senf dazeugeben' it means to add their mustard. Everyone wants to speak at a committee. I prefer to remain silent. Nothing is achieved. The committee is an inefficient way of working, but they like them at the University as they give the illusion that someone is working. You will note that the Vice Chancellor avoids them. He does things. The deans just talk about things."

He and Power paused to consult the menu. When the waiter arrived Felfe ordered sparkling mineral water for them both, and for himself Felfe ordered a main course of grilled sea bass with sweet-and-sour beetroot and seared foie gras. Power chose the only vegetarian option, a celeriac lasagne with puy lentils, tomato and asparagus. "I would have ordered a Gewürztraminer, but we can't drink alcohol at mittagessen. Some colleagues will merely make trouble and spread rumours we are Alkoholiker. Such are those we work with. It is best you know now, so you can prevent their klatsch." Felfe gave his thin smile an airing.

"I appreciated your presence at the meeting, though," said Power. "Silence was preferable to the clamour of Teesdale, and thank you for offering me lunch." said Dr Power. "But what is your position on a new medical school? It seemed to be a very controversial idea for some deans."

Felfe allowed himself a dry chuckle. "I saw you trying so hard, and you were so earnest. You reminded me of myself thirty years ago. I saw an idealist being bullied for the purity of his vision. And so I thought I'd offer you some advice."

"Which is?" asked Power.

"All in good time," said Felfe. "It is best you first know something of the calibre and nature of the people you are dealing with. I thought you played it admirably yesterday, you played it with a straight bat – I think that's how the English idiom goes. And, of course, any normal sane person would support your ambition to create a new medical school. What kind of person would not? I will support it, for instance, although I am small cog in this machine. I was appointed by the Vice Chancellor's predecessor. I know, I accept, and I even welcome the fact that I am yesterday's man. I welcome it, because I am no longer seen as a threat to anybody. I can dissolve into the background, where I can get on and do my real work. The work that actually makes a difference."

Effortlessly, with a smooth balletic rhythm, the waiters arrived with searingly hot plates of steaming food. Power looked at the delicately arranged artwork of the food on the gleaming white porcelain and smiled. The scent of the perfection that was his meal wafted up from the dish to his nostrils and he sighed with pleasure. Power loved his food, always.

"I can only thank you for your support. It felt very lonely yesterday," said Power.

"Let me help you first by defining your opposition," said Felfe. "The primary opposition will be the Dean of Healthcare, Bridget McFarlane. Her faculty brings in most of the money in this University, so the Vice Chancellor can only afford to challenge her a little. You must enlist her support, even if you must compromise. She will put you down, and she is envious of you, but she is also attracted to you, despite her sexual attachment to her assistant dean. Forgive me for telling you these things, I see you raise your eyebrows as if you are surprised. But your patients reveal far more to you, I know. These are all facts I give you; you will need them all to understand the deep currents that flow beneath the surface at Allminster. Her assistant dean, Caroline, is a lesbian, and they have been together for ten or so years. Not that the relationship is altogether common knowledge. The Vice Chancellor likes to present himself as something of a puritan in those terms. He likes to protect his persona as a Canon of the church, and he worships all things respectable. So, they play the subtle game and whilst they do not deny the reality of their relationship, they conceal it from the Vice Chancellor. Armitage would frown on any relationship at work, and of such a nature particularity. Nevertheless, Dean McFarlane is not a pure lesbian, she is bisexual, and I can see she likes you. That may be useful to you. You need to understand that in the University everybody is sleeping with someone, (even if they are not meant to), and this explains much of what happens in the politics. I, myself, am too old for bed hopping." Felfe looked about to judge whether anyone could overhear his conversation, as the tables around were still empty, he felt sufficiently reassured to carry on.

"The antics of the Vice Chancellor's deputy, Professor Shacklin, are a distinct risk to your project, especially if he is tasked to nurture the medical school. His behaviour has the power to corrupt and infect anything he touches. He could contaminate and shrivel the most perfect rose." Power felt uneasy at Felfe's revelations. "This is not gossip," said Felfe. "These are facts you will need to know in order to survive. You cannot go into this battle naïve."

"I should be grateful to you then, I suppose," said Power a little uneasily.

"I have my reasons to help you," said Felfe. "Apart from the fact that my younger self would identify with you, they are good reasons, I think. Shacklin is a liability. At any time he might be removed from office in disgrace. He says he is married with young children, but no-one has seen his wife. If she exists, Shacklin keeps her well away from the University. The Vice Chancellor likes to meet his senior staff's spouses and views it as necessary that there is 'full support at home'. It is a wonder to me that Shacklin has stayed in the position given his wandering eye. He has bedded every secretary he has ever had, except his current one who's well able to keep his ilk at bay. But Shacklin has slept with numerous female lecturers and professors, and he has brazenly sent some flowers the morning after and charged them to the University credit card. He opposed the idea of a Code of Conduct in Senate, that is a Code for staff about staff-student relationships. And he opposed it precisely because he indulges in sexual relationships with students himself. Have I shocked you?" Felfe had noticed a hiatus in Power's eating. He sat with his knife and fork poised in mid air.

"I half expected something like that myself," said Power. "I had heard rumours of his womanising, but . . . still . . . the extent."

"I have definite proof," said Felfe, with certainty in his voice. "I don't say anything to you that cannot be verified. I have signed statements, which I might use when I can achieve most good for most people. Do I shock you?"

"No, no." Power stumbled over his words. "I'm just amazed that something hasn't been done by Human Resources to stop him."

"Complaints have been made," said Felfe. "Disappointed women, who found Shacklin was not sincere in any affection he simulated, innocent women who were used by him. But organisations have a way of shrugging off complaints they do not wish to entertain. And so it carries on – until that final overwhelming complaint of something so unforgivable that it demands change. I will wait my time. Did you know the porters and cleaners are worth cultivating in an organisation like this? They always know more than people think. They see the dirty laundry, sometimes literally, of their so-called betters.

"I have a signed witness statement from a cleaner who went into Shacklin's office at six a.m. He had been out the night before and was still ... er ... entertaining, lying naked on his back on a red velvet rug on the floor of his office. She described, accurately, a cafe-au-lait birthmark on his belly. The room was warm and smelt of the sex that had been going on all night. He was, to put it as delicately as I can, erect and inside a girl who was straddling him. I think you get the picture. Well, I have the cleaner's statement, but she has asked me not to use it, yet. She knows that her sworn statement alone is not enough to bring such a man down. He would deny the act and call her liar. And the student would not corroborate the cleaner's account if her degree was called into question. Now, I ask you, now you know all this, can you realistically expect any such man to be the noble champion of your project?"

Power shook his head glumly.

"*Da kannst du Gift drauf nehmen,*" Felfe whispered partly to himself. "Sorry, I mean to say you can bet your life on that. Perhaps you think I am too harsh. You think, well, we all have feet of clay?" said Felfe.

"No, no," said Power. "It's just ... just that ... I had imagined better of these people. Please don't think that I am some naive optimist. I'm no Professor Pangloss, but I always thought that a University would have the very highest level of ..."

"No University boasts perfection in these matters, I am afraid. We are constrained by the *ethos* of the people around us and trapped in the moment we are in, like a fly in amber. There is only so much I can do. I have plenty of evidence on Shacklin, but the time to act against him is not now. And Professor Teesdale, who berated you so angrily yesterday, and who shot arrows at your credibility. Well, her qualifications are not quite as she would have us believe. Her CV is largely correct, but in some parts it is just fantasy. She slept with an external member of Senate to get her post. I am collecting evidence on her CV, and then perhaps, who knows?"

Power had finished his celeriac lasagne. It had been exceptionally good, and as he regarded the empty whiteness of his plate he had been reflecting on what Felfe was telling him about his colleagues. Prior to meeting the deans Power had held great hopes that these senior academics would prove to be consummate professionals and pleased to work with him to develop a medical school for their University. However, he had found the deans little more than argumentative. Felfe had poured the fuel of unwelcome allegations upon the bonfire of Power's doubts. Learning of the deans' lack of integrity had made Power feel destabilised and uneasy.

He was also wondering just who Felfe was and speculating about what kind of person would keep dossiers and statements about his colleagues? Power was asking himself precisely how dangerous Felfe might prove to be?

Felfe continued, "I hope you don't think me too cynical, Professor Power. I am trying to make sure you are forewarned and thus forearmed. Your project has no chance of success if you do not know what forces you are up against."

"No, I can see that, and I am grateful for . . . for your good intentions."

"You will find Sir Robert will support you," said Felfe. Power was glad to hear that not all of Felfe's revelations were negative. "If Rob Willett says he will vote for you, then you can rely upon that. It's just that he is an empty vessel. He makes the most noise of them all, but he always . . . *sich zum Affen machen* . . . he makes a fool of himself."

An instant after their empty plates were cleared away, the waiter asked if they wanted dessert and coffee. "The baked chocolate and almond génoise is exquisite and comes with liquid cherries," he said. "And the banana tarte tatin is supreme." But Power was already starting to make his apologies.

Felfe suspected that Power was making excuses to leave. Power looked like a man who enjoyed dining, and he had hoped that the Arkel restaurant would captivate him. "I suppose I have disclosed too much to you," said Felfe. "I have been too honest, too forthright, and maybe that continental candour has made things unpleasant for you. I am sorry, but you already know that it is a friend who tells you the truth. The University is a distorted mirror image of reality that has a supreme monarch and a whole slew of pretenders to his crown. For example, I overheard Professor Kneale asking you about the Vice Chancellor's health. It is a constant topic of Kneale's conversation – what the average blood pressure of an obese man might be? Like an actuary, he worries about what the average age might be for a man of the Vice Chancellor's build to have a stroke? Charming."

"I am so sorry," said Professor Power. "I would love to stay for dessert, I really would. But I do have an appointment to attend to. It's been an excellent lunch. Thank you."

Felfe looked up from his seated position. He thought he might have a dessert and coffee on his own. "By all means, Professor Power. I haven't told you even half I meant to. I wish you well. Go carefully, and remember that I am happy to assist you whenever your project comes up against a brick wall. Which it will. Don't invest too much of your life energies fighting a battle that can't be won on your own. Come and see me, and maybe I can help take that wall down for you." He reached out to shake Power's hand. His handshake was firm, dry and warm.

As Power walked purposefully along Eastgate on the way up to the Cathedral he was filled with a mixture of disquiet. He had felt alarmed to be so quickly and effectively disabused of any faith he might have had in his colleagues. And yet, was it not ultimately a kindness for Felfe to prevent him being taken in by the superficial nature of his fellow academics? Was Felfe a beacon of truth in a hypocritical world or was he just a spiteful old gossip? Perhaps his conduct was just typical of Felfe's Berliner personality? Power wondered why he had been so quick to leave Felfe in the dining room? He reflected that he had practically fled. Power wondered if he had been unduly unsettled by Felfe's unremitting catalogue of negativity. Perhaps his old school loyalty to his professorial colleagues was misplaced, and maybe he should have stayed to hear the old man out. Felfe had said that he hadn't even started to tell Power all he knew.

* * *

Power walked through the streets of Chester, the air was crisp and the pavements were bustling with shoppers from Cheshire and North Wales beginning to prepare for Christmas, even though it was well over a month away. There was the smell of coffee and freshly baked bread from Chatwin's. Ahead, in the town square, a brass band was playing carols. The sound floated to Power on the afternoon air. The shops on either side of Northgate were piled high with red and gold decorations and overhead there were illuminations, bluey-white snowflake shaped stars, shining brightly against the grim clouds above. Power weaved his way between the clusters of shoppers and climbed the hill on Northgate Street, and then on his right, up steps, and along the ancient sandstone passageway to St Werburgh's Street. There looming above him was the massive stone bulk of the Cathedral. Power ducked into the porchway, hurried through the gift shop and into the nave. He saw groups of Chinese tourists and robed guides ushering people along the aisles.

He was looking for Lynch, as they had arranged to meet after his lunch, although Power had not expected to be at the Cathedral early. He knew that Lynch often spent time praying in the pews here, and wondered if he would be there ahead of their planned appointment, but today there was no sign of him.

Power searched in the cloisters to his left, when there was a sudden cough at his side. Power jumped and turned round. "I'm sorry," said Lynch. "Did I startle you?"

"A bit, but I was looking for you. I'm early, and just wondering if you were too," said Power.

"When it gets busy, like today, I go and hide in St Anselm's Chapel – it's over there in the corner." He pointed behind himself. "Up some stairs. It's quiet enough to get some peace to pray."

"I met Professor Felfe for lunch," said Power. "But I left before dessert and coffee. Should we find somewhere for coffee? It **is** a bit noisy in here today."

They left the Cathedral and crossed back onto Northgate to find a table in a bustling, steamy coffee shop. Lynch sat while Power arranged a tray of scones, a pot of tea for Lynch and a latte for himself. Lynch waited for the tea to brew before he poured it.

"You mentioned you'd dined with Professor Felfe. I think I know him from church. A quiet man. He worships at the Cathedral occasionally. He is a Lutheran, but there is no Lutheran church in Chester so he prays here."

"I don't know what to make of him," said Power. "He was so direct and earnest. The things he said made him seem a dreadful old gossip. He told me all about the secret lives of my colleagues at Allminster, I thought initially that he was tittle tattling, but I'm beginning to think he was genuinely trying to warn me about something."

"Why do you think to ask me about this old gossip?" Lynch grinned. "Are you implying **I'm** an old gossip too? That maybe all old gossips know each other?"

"Not at all," said Power. "You're not remotely like an old gossip. And I didn't know you knew him."

"I only know him a bit. We are on nodding terms across the pews of a Cathedral. It's not a close relationship by any means."

"Well, I wonder if you could look into him? Only I think there's more to him than meets the eye."

"Intuition, eh? I will see what information I can find, after the weekend," said Lynch, and poured himself a cup of strong tea.

Power raised his cup in a mock salute. "Here's to Friday and the end of the week!"

Chapter Five

*I believe that what we become depends on what our fathers
teach us at odd moments, when they aren't trying to teach us.
We are formed by little scraps of wisdom.*
Umberto Eco, Faulcault's Pendulum

Power had imagined that his son, Jo, might enjoy a themed day out. So, on Saturday, Power and Jo had set off from their home in Alderley Edge in good spirits. Towards the end of Saturday morning he wondered, like many parents do, whether his plan for the day had wholly misjudged the interests of his child, and whether in making his plans he had only been pleasing himself.

He had read the Alice books to Jo and thought that he might like to see where the author, Lewis Carroll, was born – Lewis Carroll being the pseudonym of Charles Dodgson, one of Cheshire's most famous sons. Dodgson had grown up in Daresbury village, and the drive to Daresbury was only twenty miles or so from Alderley. Power had kept to the old A roads, avoiding the anonymity of the motorway, and had enjoyed gazing over Autumn denuded hawthorn hedges, across the Cheshire potato fields.

Power enjoyed reading to his son, and over several evenings together they read through a copy of *Alice through the Looking Glass*, (which Power preferred to *Alice in Wonderland*). Jo had appeared to enjoy it, but traipsing around the field where Dodgson's childhood home had once stood and walking around the Gothic, All Saints church where Dodgson's father had been vicar had clearly not entertained the boy. Power enjoyed examining the depictions of the Cheshire Cat and the White Rabbit in the church's stained glass windows. However, Jo was pale and unmoved and plonked himself down in a pinewood pew, while his father took pleasure in Tenniel's engraved illustrations rendered in lead and coloured glass.

Jo only brightened when they left the church and crossed over the road to the Ring O' Bells for lunch. He brightened still further when his father ordered him scampi and chips and a tall, frosted glass of lemonade.

"Are you hungry, then? Is that what the matter is?" asked Power. Jo nodded and, belatedly, Power realised that Jo's lack of enthusiasm was more a case of hunger, rather than disinterest. "Why didn't you say?" asked Power.

"Grownups *never* listen," said Jo.

"I'm sorry. That sounds like a very *Alice* point of view." Power looked at the sepia photos of the locality in Victorian times on the cream-coloured walls of the pub. Between the photo frames were hand-painted quotes from the Mad Hatter inscribed on the walls. One of the phrases caught his eye.

"Have you guessed the riddle yet?" the Hatter said.

Power read the quote to himself a few times. The choice of quote didn't seem to fit in with the atmosphere of the bustling pub, the clinking and clanking of cutlery and crockery, the smell of beery yeast, beef, wine, chips and vinegar. The question 'Have you guessed the riddle yet?' might have been written by the moving hand of God Himself, asking his creations if they had fathomed the riddle of their all too brief existence on earth. Power looked at Jo, hopefully waiting for his food, and reminded himself not to overthink things.

"I suppose the meal won't be long," said Power.

"Jam tomorrow, and jam yesterday but never jam today," quoted Jo.

"Oh, very good," said Power. "Very apt." He smiled at his son and remembered how his father had paraded him around churches. His father, an architect, was often commissioned to look after the fabric of various churches. Power turned his thoughts into a narrative for Jo. "My dad used to take me round the churches he looked after. My dad, that's your grandfather, was an architect." Power observed that the wood-panelled room where they were sitting was divided into two by a low wooden screen that separated the lower half of the room from a raised dais. "This was a session room, once," Power said.

"What's a session room?" asked Jo.

"Like a small court room," said his father. "A justice of the peace would sit there on the raised platform, the dais, and dispense justice every month or so when someone had been caught being drunk or disorderly, or poaching on the Lord of the Manor's land, or was a vagrant . . . a homeless person."

"Did they chop anybody's heads off?"

"No, I don't think it was that kind of court. Just fines. Maybe a few weeks in jail. That sort of punishment."

Power reached in his jacket pocket and produced a small box with a travel chess set inside. He'd brought it along to amuse his son. "Would you like me to teach you how to play chess, while we wait for the food?"

"I already know," said Jo. "My other granddad taught me."

"Oh," said Power. "Well, that's good. We could have a proper game if you like?"

"Great," said Jo, sounding genuinely interested, and looking at the travel set Power held, "It looks like a Victorian Gameboy." Jo took the proffered chess set from his father. Some of the miniature pieces in the box rattled about as he set it down by his placemat. He lifted the mottled red lid and looked inside at the black and white pegboard and the scattered red and white pieces.

"I hope they're all there," said Power. "My dad gave me that set."

"They seem to be," said Jo, astutely sizing up the number of pawns and major pieces. "But there's a game already set up on the board."

"Oh yes," said Power. "That's the game in *Alice through the Looking Glass*. I set it up a few weeks ago, when we were reading the book. I set it up according to the illustration in the book so I could try and work it out. It's meant to be white to play, and to win in eleven moves. The moves in the game are supposed to mirror what happens in the book, or *vice versa*. You know Alice meeting the Red Queen and being told she can join the game as a pawn, and that she will be promoted herself if she makes it to the other side of the board. There's Alice," said Power, pointing to the white pawn on the board that symbolized her.

The waiter arrived with two plates of food; scampi for Jo and for his father a mushroom and ale pudding glazed in gravy, served with roasted vegetables. The arrival of the food precluded conversation for a while. Jo fell upon the food like a ravening wolf. Nevertheless, as he consumed the meal, Jo kept glancing over at the chessboard and the puzzle of its part-played game.

When Jo had eaten every chip and every breadcrumbed piece of scampi (leaving peas, lemon slice and tartare sauce untouched and shunned), he looked up at his father and pronounced his verdict on the chess problem.

"White doesn't need eleven moves to finish this game." Jo pointed to the White Knight. "You move him first to G3. The Red King moves to E5. The White Queen chases him to C5. The Red King retreats to E6. The White Queen chases him to D6 and White wins. White can win in three moves, not eleven."

Power peered over at the board and, in his mind's eye, ran through what the boy just said, moving the pieces about the board in his own imagination. "Yes, you're absolutely right. I hadn't seen that."

Jo grinned. "Are you ready for a proper game then?" He started setting up the red and white pieces in their places.

"Ah," said Power warily. It was clear that he would be facing a distinct challenge. "Yes, of course, but shall we order some desserts first?"

"If you like," said Jo. "But as soon as we've ordered we play; don't think you can distract me with that dessert dodge."

* * *

Power and Jo returned to Alderley late in the afternoon. Although it was only five o'clock when the ancient Saab crunched its way onto the gravel drive at Alderley House, the sun had just about set, and darkness was falling on their home. The house lights shone through the windows like a beacon, the amber glow of home spilling out onto the driveway. Power shivered as he got out of the car, in the sudden chill of the November night.

Power and his son tumbled into the hallway, chattering and clattering as they took off their hats and coats. Power locked the door firmly against the shadows of the night and, as Jo bounded upstairs to his bedroom to play, his father made his way through the hallway to the large, warm kitchen at the back of their house. He could hear music and smelt the scents of baking.

He found his partner Laura sitting ready with a large pot of tea and two cups. She was smiling and Power sensed that she had been eager for his return.

"Something smells good," said Power, sniffing warm syrupy smells, cinnamon and mixed spice.

"I had a go at making a fruit loaf."

"I 'knead' some of that," joked Power. He kissed her warm lips and sat beside her.

"The loaf is just cooling," she said. "But I baked some cherry scones before that. They are ready, would you like some?" She gave him a plate of golden cherry scones.

"Yes, please," said Power. He took a scone and sliced it in two. It was still warm in his hand, and he buttered it then spooned rhubarb and ginger jam on to each half.

"Did Jo enjoy his Lewis Carroll day?" asked Laura.

"I guess so," said Power. "There wasn't much to see. The land where the vicarage was. A little museum and some stained glass in the church . . . He enjoyed his lunch more than anything."

"He is remarkably like his father, isn't he?" Laura smiled.

"Perhaps he is," said Power. "But Jo's better at chess than his father. He solved a chess problem in seconds. And beat me at a proper game in minutes." He frowned. "On the drive back I was thinking about Lewis Carroll – Charles Dodgson – you know he practically founded the entire University using just some of his earnings from Alice? He was wealthier then than J. K. Rowling is now."

"I didn't know that, no."

"The Victorians were a philanthropic lot, weren't they?" said Power.

"Yes, they could be, when they weren't making little boys like Jo climb up chimneys or work cotton looms in factories . . ."

"That's right, I suppose," said Power. "How do we reconcile these contradictions about a society? These Victorians would happily bundle a twelve year old boy like Charles Dickens off to work in a blacking factory, but also design a great railway network or build a vast sanitation system and supply clean water to the public. And Dodgson . . . he wrote so beautifully, but he was . . . odd. Photographing his 'child friends'. Queasy stuff. His behaviour seems so . . . dubious. So how can we enjoy his books now, knowing what we do? Should we remember his contributions – should we celebrate his founding of Allminster?"

"Hmm, that's a puzzle," said Laura, anticipating her partner's wishes, but placing another warm scone on his side plate. "Nothing is perfect, I suppose. They say that the devil tries to put a flaw in everything and everyone, and if you focus on the flaws, that suits him fine. If all you see is flaws then he has won. Like that Leonard Cohen song:

> *Ring the bells that still can ring*
> *Forget your perfect offering.*
> *There is a crack in everything*
> *That's how the light gets in.*

"That is very philosophical. Thank you." said Power. "After the week I've just had I'm feeling negative about the University. I imagined that other medical schools might be selfish and try and stop us, but not the deans of my own University. I never anticipated that there would be opposition *within* the University."

Laura could see the sudden stress in his eyes and in the way he held his shoulders stiffly. "You don't need to work there," she said softly. "If they don't support you wholeheartedly, then it doesn't matter. You can walk away. Shake their dust from your feet. I know how it works. I was your private secretary for years. They are paying a pittance, and your time could be better rewarded elsewhere. You have a choice, so why stress?"

"I'll carry on for now. See how it goes," said Power. "I never like giving up. Sometimes you must persist. And in life, if you're not acting on your beliefs then they probably aren't real."

She smiled. "Speaking of persistence, would you like some good news then?"

He looked up from his plate, puzzling over an alteration to the tone of her voice. And as he looked more closely at her face, he could see a warm shine to her expression.

"Well," she said. "While you were out, I took a pregnancy test. And Jo is going to have a brother, (or a sister). Is that good news?"

"The best," said Power. "The very best."

Chapter Six

If you don't know where you are going,
any road will take you there.
George Harrison, Any Road, 2001

D r Power woke in the middle of the night and decided that the best and only way to resolve his anxiety about the new medical school was to seek the advice of the bursar. Power reasoned that if anybody was to know the state of the University's finances it would be the bursar, he would certainly know if the University could fund a medical school or not.

His anxiety about the project had become so acute over the weekend that Power drove into the University especially early on Monday morning. It was just after 8.00 a.m. when Power arrived, yet the bursar was already at his desk in his Senate House office, just down the corridor from the Vice Chancellor's office.

Hamish Grieg had been the bursar at Allminster since the nineteen-eighties, and his appointment predated all other members of the senior management team, including the Vice Chancellor. He still drove a leaky Mini Metro from his old student days. This was testament in itself to his extreme parsimony. He lived alone in a flat in the Cathedral Close, ate a single meal a day sparingly, and was thin to the point of cachexia. His skin was waxy and yellowed and his complexion looked to Power's eyes like that of an embalmed corpse.

His hair was white and thin, unwashed strands of it were draped across his balding scalp. He had blue eyes, which gazed out from within deeply set orbits. His office was cold, but when Power knocked on his door Grieg was only in white shirt sleeves.

"Good morning, Mr Grieg?"

"Yes? Good morning," replied Grieg. "May I help you?" He rose to his feet with a slow and determined grace, and stood politely as his visitor entered.

"I am Professor Power. I wondered if I could talk to you. I'm sorry for calling on you so early."

"I rise at five every morning and walk to the office rain or shine. That way I am sure that I am never late."

"You must arrive very early," Power said.

"I walk from the Cathedral to Allminster village and I am always here by six to go over the previous day's departmental returns. How can I help you?"

Power took a seat in a Spanish leather tub chair across the desk from the bursar. He expected that Grieg would sit down too, but he did not.

Grieg remained standing and explained, "When I have a guest I never sit. It is disrespectful to my guest."

"Nevertheless," said Power. "Please sit down, I will be uneasy if you remain standing."

"Oh, I couldn't," said the bursar. "I am not worthy to." Power thought that maybe the bursar was making a witticism, but the more he looked at Grieg's pinched and earnest face, the more Power realised Grieg was deadly serious. "How may I help you?" asked the bursar, as he resolutely stood to attention.

"Well," said Power, who was finding the bursar a perplexing character. "The Vice Chancellor has made me director of the medical school initiative."

"Ah yes," frowned Grieg, remembering back to the most recent Senior Management Team Meeting where the Vice Chancellor had outlined his new pet project. "The new medical school."

"Well, I was wondering if you could give me some guidance, really? The new medical school will need a new building with labs for anatomy, biochemistry, physiology, and pharmacology – all new subjects for Allminster – this will need to contain large lecture theatres and offices for the new academics who can teach these new subjects for the University – anatomy and pathology professors and lecturers . . ."

"I understand, but for new projects like this the Vice Chancellor usually seeks out the funding himself. He's quite adept at that."

"Oh, I see, well despite what you might have heard from anybody like Professor Shacklin, who mentioned an outlay of just a few million – the capital outlay for the new estate is likely to be around thirty million and the recurrent costs for salaries may be several million a year, and so I just wondered if the University is in a position to call upon the resources to cover that kind of capital and recurrent expense?"

"Professor Shacklin knows the value of nothing and yet he appears able to claim the cost of everything . . . still, I mustn't wash the University's dirty laundry in public. It's quite wrong of me and I should only talk about my business. I take care to balance the University's books, day upon day and week upon week," said the bursar. "It is my proud boast we have never made anyone redundant. And I cannot lie upon any matter lest I need to fast for a week. I control myself. I can not sin or I must mortify myself." He opened some buttons on his white shirt and showed Power the grey material underneath, worn close to his skin. "I was late to a meeting last week, and so this week I must wear the *cilice*."

Power felt baffled by so much that he had just heard. He had been expecting a conversation focused on facts and figures, spreadsheets and financial projections, instead he found he was being confronted with a most perplexing and seemingly challenged individual. "You must wear a *cilice*? What is that, please?"

The bursar came around the desk to where Power was sitting. He unbuttoned his starched white shirt. Underneath, Power could see Grieg was wearing a grey garment akin to a vest. Alarmingly Grieg offered his belly to be touched. "Feel it and you will see."

Very reluctantly Power reached out and touched the grey material that Grieg wore under his shirt. It was rough to his fingers like sackcloth, and mixed with fine black bristles from some unknown animal.

"I was twenty minutes late for that meeting last week and an apology was not enough. Not enough penance. So I will wear this all through this week to keep me to task and remind me to always be on time."

"Who makes you do this?" Power did not yet sufficiently comprehend Grieg.

"I must always be honest and efficient in my work, if I fail in my duty, if I transgress my code, I must always do penance. It's quite a simple philosophy."

"You're wearing a hair shirt, man," said Power. "Nobody needs to punish themselves like this; it's medieval. You will wear this . . . cilice . . . all week?"

"I will wear it during the day. When I leave work at eight o'clock I take it off before I go to bed. I rub ointment into any raw skin."

Power stared at him, unable to quite fathom Grieg's martyr-like approach to life. "There's simply no need for this behaviour. Do other people know you do this?"

Grieg's blue eyes swam with watery tears. "I make no secret of what I do, why should I hide my sins?"

Power did not know what to say. He felt he had glimpsed part of a whole life afflicted, restricted and constricted by a man's inner iron discipline and morbid guilt. Other doctors referred patients to Dr Power. He didn't simply encounter his patients anew in his everyday life. "Have you always done this or is this something new?"

"Always, always, since school," said Grieg.

"Boarding school?" asked Power.

"Fettes College."

Power struggled with a temptation to ask for more details, but to do so risked turning the bursar into his patient rather than a colleague, and Power hadn't come to see Grieg to do this. And yet, Power was fascinated by the morbid pathology that must underlie such behaviour; such abnegation and self-punishment. "All I wanted to do," said Power. "Was reassure myself that the University could afford a medical school," Power felt he needed to explain his mission once again. "What do you think?"

"I can tell you that I keep the University on an even keel. I ensure there is always a sufficient surplus to weather an unexpected storm. Please don't make me say anything more, for I would not wish to tell an untruth." Power suspected that he might trigger a new cycle of self-punishment in this man, if he pressed the matter. Dr Power considered that whatever lurked behind Grieg's self-punishing behaviour would need very careful defusing, but he did not feel he was the right man, at this time, to dismantle these particular psychological defences. Grieg went on, "All I will say is that the Vice Chancellor has a way of making things happen if he wants them too. He finds a way. He applies to the right places, so for Dean McFarlane's new healthcare buildings he seemed to know exactly which pocket of money to apply to at the Department of Health and exactly which CEO would sponsor the new sports department. If you have doubts you had best take them to the Vice Chancellor himself."

"Thank you," said Power. "Thank you for your time." He stood up and nodded to Grieg, before retreating quietly from the room, leaving the poor self-tortured man alone.

* * *

There was a bleeping from his phone as Power walked towards the University car park. He was heading towards a meeting with the dean of healthcare and she had insisted this be at the nursing school, so Power needed to drive to the hospital where it was situated. He answered quickly because he thought it might be a call about one of his patients.

Power heard an older female voice on the line. "Hello, Professor Power?"

"Yes. Hello?"

"It's Karen Harvey here, I'm the Director of Human Resources at the University. We spoke after the interview – when you joined us . . . do you remember?

There had been a sea of faces at his interview and Power could not recall anyone besides the Vice Chancellor. "Hello," said Power, wondering what was wrong as Human Resources rarely called anyone, other than for an emergency.

"I have been tasked with overseeing the University's commitments to various extramural activities," she said. Power felt no wiser for the explanation she had provided. "Professor Power, I am seeking your help as a mentor to a team of undergraduates."

"Oh, I'm not a sporting type," said Power hurriedly. "I wouldn't be much of a coach to any football or rugby team."

"It's a cerebral sport, Professor Power. I believe you were once on a TV quiz team for Liverpool University and got to the semi-finals. Well naturally, Allminster aspires to join *University Challenge,* but these days it really only seems the preserve of Oxbridge colleges. Difficult for a Northern University to break into. We have though, for the first time ever, got a team onto *TopQuiz* – you know – with the host Giles Masefield, and we were wondering . . . the Vice Chancellor was wondering . . . if you'd be kind enough to give our team the benefit of your experience?"

"Oh, I see." Power felt much more disposed toward the task now he knew no physical competition was involved. "What would that mentorship involve, please?"

"If you could meet the Allminster team and coach them on some techniques you found helpful; how to work together as a team, how to cope with the pressure in the studio, maybe go and support them at the filming of the episodes?"

"Oh, yes, well, thank you," said Power. "I'd enjoy that. If I can fit it in, I will."

"Very good, Dr Power, the Vice Chancellor said he could rely on you. Goodbye."

Power smiled as he got into the Saab. He enjoyed watching *TopQuiz* with Jo and he happily anticipated Jo's reaction when he learned his father was going to be involved in the programme.

* * *

Lynch closed the door to his office carefully. He unlocked his office safe and extricated a small, grey, cube-like device which he connected as an intermediary between his landline phone and its wall socket. He switched the device on, picked up the receiver and pressed it to his ear. He heard the burring noise of the dial tone, and entered a phone number, which he preceded by a PIN code generated by a second palm-held device. He listened to the ringing tone as it was routed hither and thither around the telecommunications system before it wended its way to the GCHQ's secure servers.

A voice answered. "Good afternoon. Please can you identify yourself?" Lynch always wondered if the voice was human or some artificial intelligence.

"Dovedale," said Lynch, which was his personal handle.

"Please input your personal identifier code now," the voice said, and an insistent red light on the keyboard flashed at him until he inputted the four digits required, then snuffed itself out. Lynch imagined the abstract nature of the encryption of the digitized audio wave, of remote handshakes and the salts used for transmission of keywords, all happening in the realm of some virtual cyberspace.

"Transferring you for your pre-arranged conference call now," said the voice.

Another voice came on the line, male and young. Lynch estimated the speaker to be about thirty years of age. "Good afternoon, Dovedale. Are you well?"

"Perfectly well, thank you. And yourself?"

"No complaints, I'm pleased to say." There was a slight pause. Lynch disliked these remote conversations. How could he ever engage with someone whose name he didn't know and whom he had never met? The voice of his handler was all he could recognise, and all else was kept deliberately anonymous. It felt a wholly sterile relationship, and so it was meant to be. "How can I help you? Or is the Foundation seeking to help us today?"

"I'm requesting information, as ever," said Lynch. He was rueful about repeatedly seeking something from his handler, but the Foundation paid handsomely for the privilege. On the other hand the Foundation was an approved independent agency trusted by Government and Lynch and Power had always delivered help when requested in the past. "Dr Power has encountered someone we need information about. Someone he has met in the course of some work at the University of Allminster, where he is a professor. He had an intuition about this individual, that there was more to them than anyone there knows. We wonder if we could request information about him."

"Dovedale, forgive me, but basing an inquiry on intuition – that's a long shot. Remind me – I seem to remember – is Dr Power a psychiatrist?"

"Yes," said Lynch. "His intuition has proven reliable time and again," said Lynch. "Dr Power is concerned about an academic with a background in Berlin, who appears to collect intelligence about his colleagues at the University. Dr Power thought there was a deal of 'craft' about him, if you see what I mean. I wondered if we could ask for a 'Pattern of Life' analysis."

"I see, you want a PoL, can you be more specific and give me a name for this individual, his occupation and a date of birth please?"

"Professor Johann Felfe. He is Dean of Faculty of Social Sciences and Criminology at Allminster University. Power has found out his date of birth, which is 10th November, 1930. He's still teaching at seventy-four. I suppose academics can go on longer than most of us."

The response of the handler at GCHQ was so instant that Lynch surmised there had been no need to feed the details into the database to find out about Felfe. "What can I say? Dr Power's intuition is proved correct yet again, but alas I cannot reveal any of Professor Felfe's details. What Dr Felfe chooses to reveal to you or Dr Power in the process of his work, is his concern. Only I would caution you to let Dr Power know that he should make contact with Felfe again. And furthermore, tell Dr Power to be extremely careful. He has stumbled, or rather is stumbling, into a really dangerous zone. If he doesn't want to make a mess of everything he should heed everything Felfe says. There you are, I can't say any more, and perhaps I have said too much. Is there anything else you would like to discuss? Bearing in mind I have said all I am going to say on the Felfe matter."

"Well, no," said Lynch who was at a loss for words. "Can I thank you for talking to me?"

"Of course, it's always a pleasure, Dovedale."

* * *

The Faculty of Healthcare was a brand new building; a modern pavilion of brick, glass and steel, without soul or embellishment. Power struggled to find a parking place by the faculty entrance and eventually had to park almost quarter of a mile away.

On the first floor, a signpost gave promise of the dean's suite, Power paused by an open door labelled 'Caroline Diarmid, Assistant Dean', and leaned in to ask if he was anywhere near the Dean's Office. The spiky, purple-haired occupant glared at him from under bushy black eyebrows and silently, and unwelcomingly, pointed in the vague direction of Bridget McFarlane's office. Power was just on time when he presented himself to the dean's secretary, but even so he was made to wait fifteen minutes before McFarlane phoned her secretary to invite Power into her office.

Power had imagined that he was being kept waiting while Dean McFarlane was finishing off her last meeting, but when he entered he could see she was alone. Her office was large and spacious, with a hint of a fragrance that Power could not quite place. The large windows flooded the office with afternoon light.

"Good afternoon, Professor Power," she said, motioning him towards a polished, beech-wood table with eight red-upholstered meeting chairs set around it. She waited until Power sat down and then chose a chair directly opposite him. He looked at her earnest appearance; blue eyes, cream-complexioned girl-next-door face, close-cropped hair and a half-smile of cultured innocence. "Would you care for some tea? And maybe a piece of shortbread made by one of my nurses?" She gestured to a large plate of golden shortbread, next to a bowl of fresh fruit on the table.

"Oh, thank you," said Power, "I've just had a cup of tea, but thanks all the same"

"Well, perhaps you'd care to nibble on some shortbread then?"

"No, no, "said Power. "Thank you, but I'm watching my waistline."

"Well, to business then since you can't be tempted," said McFarlane. "I'm so pleased that the faculty will be taking a hand in the new medical school." Power noted that although her cupid lips curved into a smile, her eyes did not. He wondered at the unwarranted speed with which McFarlane had moved from frank opposition to apparent co-operation over the medical school. "Where are you up to?"

"Well, let me say how pleased I am that your faculty has evolved towards a supportive position regarding the medical school," and Power deployed his smile too. He knew that the limited amount of genuine pleasure he felt probably equated to the minimal amount that McFarlane felt. Still, he supposed that he must remain diplomatic and civil in manner. "I met with the Bursar, Hamish Grieg today. To try and get some idea of the extent to which the University can support a new faculty."

"Oh, I'm not sure there will be a new faculty. Nobody has mentioned that; and that would be incredibly expensive. No, we need to look at another solution for hosting the medical school."

Power frowned. He sensed now, there would be some opposition to everything he mentioned in the meeting, and that Bridget McFarlane had a mirror agenda that reflected his, similar, but set completely about face. "Well, as I say, I met the bursar and . . ."

"And what did you think of our Mr Grieg?" asked McFarlane. "He's been bursar for ever and a day. A dessicated husk of a man. He lives alone in a flat in the Cathedral Close. He is solely devoted to building up a collection of reptiles, and they have each other for company. Pet slow-worms and the like. I ask you!"

"I thought he was . . . frightened – of himself mainly."

"How fascinating, I was forgetting you are a psychiatrist. Now we have a tame psychiatrist on the staff, I can ask you about people." She smiled gleefully. "Isn't he mad?"

Power felt repulsed. He determined immediately not to offer her the slightest opinion on anyone. He judged, correctly, that any unguarded comment he made about someone would be trotted out by McFarlane as a psychiatric opinion at any time that was inopportune for him and the medical school. Any comments he might make in all innocence could be used by her as a weapon to cause havoc for him.

McFarlane continued, hoping to provoke Power into an indiscretion. "He's so quiet in the management team meetings. Like Professor Felfe was in the dean's meeting we let you attend." Power noticed the subtle put down – the condescension behind her words 'let you attend' did not fail to hit home. "Felfe says nothing – just like Grieg says nothing."

"Have you read Borges?"

"I stick to scientific literature. There is no time for anything else."

"Borges said 'Don't talk unless you can improve the silence.'"

MacFarlane looked blankly at him. "Felfe is a loathsome man. He sits there like a sponge, absorbing everything and silently judging us. Feeling all superior in his little brain . . . he's a silent snake in the grass." She spoke venomously. "But I suppose Shacklin chairs meetings badly, or he'd get Felfe to say exactly what he's silently thinking of us all." McFarlane regarded Power for a moment. He seemed to be maintaining a very discreet silence of his own.

She decided to try once more to catalyse some reaction. "Shacklin is not ethically suited to head up your medical school project, have you thought about that?"

Power felt mildly bewildered. McFarlane was privy to different information than him and had known Shacklin for years. Power wondered what information he was not party to. Perhaps the Vice Chancellor had said something to McFarlane that day – maybe Armitage did want Shacklin to oversee the planning of the medical school. If so, that was his decision and how did McFarlane imagine

Power had any control over this? Was she proposing herself as an alternative leader?

McFarlane pressed her point. "He's sexually rampant." Her voice had become higher in tone. There was a red flush around her neck. Power saw a tremor of her hand and noted her stress. "Last month he even made advances to one of my nursing students – at an awards evening. The Student Union was presenting awards for the best lecturers of the last academic year. This student is the Union Social Secretary and she had him on her table during the dinner. Revolting man – leering at her throughout the food – and then during the speeches he started inviting himself back to her bedroom."

Power frowned. "That is troubling. Deeply troubling."

"More than troubling. Can't you chemically castrate him? Slip bromides in his tea?"

Although he had been guarding against being provoked into saying something he would later regret, Power found himself expressing a definite opinion before he could suppress the reflex. "I would have thought that was more of a role for Human Resources."

"Ah," said McFarlane, delighted she had got Power to commit himself and say something she could quote elsewhere. "You think so? Yes. But there is no code of conduct, or rule, at this University that prevents a member of staff from dating a student. Any reasonable person might think there should be, but that is **not** the case for most Universities. The Vice Chancellor sees the students as adults, and they are, of course, but some of us see the issue in terms of a power imbalance. The Vice Chancellor believes that it is all a matter of free will amongst adults. But I believe that he'll sack Shacklin if he can, if he strays just one more inch over the lines . . . and of course Dean Nigel loathes Shacklin even more that the Vice Chancellor . . . he'd like to be in Shacklin's shoes – in his Executive Pro Vice Chancellor role and the higher salary that goes with it . . . Nigel would positively kill for it. He's such a mean old man that he scrabbles to get all the on-calls going." She noticed that Power looked puzzled by the mention of 'on-call'. "Not like a doctor's on-call . . . well sort of. The University has an after hours' rota for the senior team – so there is someone on hand if the cobras escape from the biology lab, or if the books in the Library spontaneously combust, or if a student decides exams are all too much and slices their wrists. Well, Nigel Kneale would take every on-call he could get. The University pays two hundred and fifty pounds a night. It's so appropriate that he's a maths professor – he needs those skills to calculate his pay." She sighed and came to her point. "So, what's the plan, Carl?" She used his first name. "How are you going to build the Vice Chancellor his medical school? How do you get us from here, to there? What's your road map?"

Power smiled. His smile disconcerted her as she had not imagined he would welcome the question. She thought he had no idea. "Do you know the phrase 'If you don't know where you are going, any road will take you there.'" asked Power.

"Ah," she said. "You're quoting Lewis Carroll at me, surely."

"It's from a song by George Harrison."

"I think you'll find you're wrong," said Dean McFarlane. "I'm a bit of an expert on Lewis Carroll."

Power chose not to argue and instead returned to the point of their meeting and suppressed his inner irritation. He suddenly looked confident. "Well, I **do** know where I am going. I have very clear road map. We need to meet certain key people first . . ."

"I know everybody at the local level, all the people at Region who commission nurse places, all the representatives at the Nursing and Midwifery Council. I know every dean on HEFCE. My faculty can speak to all the appropriate people on the school's behalf."

Power now suspected she wished to ease him out of the project altogether, and that if she was given the chance she would do just that. "I need to speak to the General Medical Council to alert them as to our intentions. They will control our ability to award the degrees of MBChB. They have a statutory role to monitor and control our curriculum."

"Right, so my PA can set up a meeting."

"I have already set the meeting up in London."

McFarlane had not foreseen this. The annoyance that manifested on her erstwhile benign features was very clear. "If you give my PA the details I will join you at that meeting."

"Ah," said Dr Power nodding, but not quite saying anything. "And then I need to meet the medical deans at the nearest medical schools to assess what the feeling is about potential competition on their doorstep."

"I know all the deans, I can do that."

Power saw that McFarlane was writing some headings in capitals on an A4 paper pad. "The approach to the local deans must be very careful," said Power. "We do not wish to alienate them and then compete with them for hospital placements. And they could be helpful, by offering to sell us their curriculum or to be a contingent medical school for ours."

McFarlane's eyes narrowed. She was beginning to realise that behind his occasionally vague demeanor, Power knew exactly what he was talking about. She had mistakenly thought he was an empty vessel. Power watched her write down the phrase 'contingent medical school'. "And what is that precisely?" she asked. "A 'contingent medical school'?"

"A separate, long-established medical school to ours that is there to step in in case of contingencies. For instance, if the GMC need to pull the plug on the new medical school in its third year, say, then a back-up medical school would have to offer the students a place where they can study in their final two years. It's sometimes called a 'grandparenting' relationship."

"I see," said McFarlane, making a note. She spoke very softly now, without looking at Power, and saying, almost in a whisper, "You know he'll never make you dean."

Power felt uneasy, and wondered if she had really just said that. Had he heard her correctly? He watched her still writing on her pad, seemingly oblivious to his stare. Had she actually spoken?

Power now felt uneasy about explaining all the other necessary steps that he had already foreseen and arranged on the route to an Alminster medical school. He thought of the meetings he had sought and booked with the medical directors of local hospitals and lead GPs of the large primary care centres where Alminster students could practice their clinical skills, the meetings with potential professors of subjects like anatomy to discuss how best to teach anatomy, physiology and biochemistry in the most modern way. He wondered about telling her of the meeting he had booked with the Chief Medical Officer, Sir Liam Donaldson, to try and garner his approval in principle. He thought about all the problems he had envisaged and already solved and couldn't bear the thought of telling her, for her to slavishly note all his ideas and later trot out as her own.

Instead Power said, "It's so good that you are offering your help. If you can think of anything I've forgotten, maybe you would be kind enough to let me know, and we can discuss a way forward?"

"Weren't you going to say a bit more about your road map?" she wheedled.

"My mind's gone a complete blank," said Dr Power. He felt a little guilty for withholding his ideas and did consider whether he was being childish. However, he thought that revealing all his plans right now would be naïve. He sensed hostility behind her smile. He felt there was no one he could trust but the Vice Chancellor himself, and questioned why Canon Armitage had surrounded himself with such a team as the deans. "Thank you so much for your time, Professor McFarlane," he said. "Maybe we can meet again soon?" Power stood up, signalling that he was leaving.

"Of course," said Bridget McFarlane, smiling her best smile and holding out her hand to shake. Power noticed her handshake was moist. Underlying anxieties, he thought. What about? "Don't forget to let my PA know about the dates of these meetings."

But Power was already out of the door, hurrying down the corridor outside, past the surly assistant dean's office and bolting for the stairs.

* * *

Power hurried down the stairs, feet clattering on the concrete treads. He was shaking with suppressed anger. Deliberately, he slowed his pace and forced himself to breathe more calmly. He sought out the café. There seemed to be one in every building, if you knew where to look. The healthcare building had one by the front entrance, styled as a coffee shop and self-service bistro. Power took refuge in a black Americano and a slice of lemon drizzle cake.

When Senior Lecturer, Mason came into the café she saw a tall, handsome man with dark hair sitting at one of the tables. There was a touch of grey in his hair, just at the temples. He was resting the side of his head against his left hand, elbow on the table. With his right hand he was demolishing a slab of yellow cake with a fork.

She bought a pot of tea from the counter and carried her tray over to where he sat.

"Excuse me," she said. The distinguished man looked up and she could see his eyes were a warm, deep-chestnut brown. "You're Professor Power, I think?"

"That's right," his eyes crinkled as he grinned a broad smile. He thought her engagingly pretty. "I'm sorry, I was far away. Can I help?"

"Is this seat taken? May I sit here?"

"By all means," he said.

She settled herself into the seat opposite him and laid out her tea things from the tray. "I'm sorry to intrude. My name is Marian Mason, I'm one of the senior lecturers on the nursing course. Just finished my PhD at Allminster last year. You looked very deep in thought. Maybe I shouldn't have interrupted you."

"Not at all," said Dr Power. "I'm glad to see a friendly face. I've just endured an interrogation by charm."

"I saw you fleeing the Dean's Office."

"Did you? Was it so obvious I was 'fleeing'?"

"I often see people fleeing from there. I have an office that looks down that corridor. I once even saw the Vice Chancellor bustling away from her den. Between you and me, she's a monster. I recognised you from your picture in the University magazine. The new starters' section. Are you settling in?"

"It's an interesting place, isn't it?" said Power. "I joined here with one aim really, Marian. And that was to add a medical school to the University. I knew it would be a difficult task. All I can say is that, after meeting the deans, I think it will be even more difficult than I imagined."

"Well, I hope you stick with it," she said. "Really I do. I think most of the staff who have heard about your plan support it. The real staff I mean, – the ones who actually do the teaching and the research here, we think it's a brilliant idea." She poured herself a large cup of tea from her pot. "I did wonder what I'd done when I started here when I began my PhD – I was a sister on the neurosurgical ward. My research is on cross-infection. It's got real meaning on the wards and clinically. But no-one here seems to understand the clinical world – it's all about the dean's pet hobbyhorse – pedagogy. Not nursing at all, 'pedagogy' is the Word round here. The Faculty of Health is all about educational techniques and qualitative research. They don't do numbers, anything about compassion or care, or anything that is clinically relevant. Their relevance to the clinical world is . . . academic."

"Well, I have kept my foot in the clinical world," said Dr Power. "And I may be going back to it quicker than I thought."

"Ah, don't give in to them," said Marian Mason. "They'd be only too pleased if you left. Keep on going, Allminster needs to evolve. It can't be all pedagogy and coffee shops." She tried to pour another cup of tea, but she had drained the pot dry. "Well, I'd better be going," she said. "I've got essays to mark, and they won't mark themselves. Although my PhD supervisor, Dr Willems, was so lazy she used to mark them by throwing a pile down the hallway and awarding the highest marks to those that travelled furthest." Marian Mason stood up. "Have you noticed how many coffee shops there are at this University?"

"There does seem to be a café in every building."

"Every hundred yards precisely," said Marian. "The Vice Chancellor can't waddle further than that, so he dots them around and goes from one to another across campus, like a fat bumblebee flitting from flower to flower. See you!" And with that, she was gone.

Having chatted to Marian Mason, Power felt better about the world. Unlike many of the senior staff he had met, she had at least had left him smiling. For once he hadn't felt he was being sneered at or used. He pushed the remains of the lemon cake aside. He no longer felt hungry. "Empty calories," he chided himself. "You were just comforting yourself."

Power was drinking the last of his Americano, when his mobile went off.

Alarmed at the sudden noise, some of the drink went down the wrong way and he was spluttering and coughing as he answered.

"Andrew Lynch here . . . are you all right?"

"Coffee . . . down . . . wrong way," Power gasped eventually, his voice cracking, throaty and breathless.

"Take your time," said Lynch. "Do you want me to ring back?"

"No, no," said Power. "Just you talk for a bit I'll . . . listen."

"I'm aware this is an open line. Where are you?"

"A café. There's only me though, it's late in the day." Power was alone amongst all the tables, the staff having receded and retreated into some distant recess far beyond the kitchen.

"Very well," said Lynch. "Pardon me if I speak somewhat elliptically, and don't reply or speak out any names. I wanted to tell you that I spoke to my source about a certain person." He was referring to his call to the case officer at SIS about Felfe. "The source wouldn't tell me anything about the individual in question. But he responded so quickly that it was clear that he knew exactly who we were talking about. He didn't need to refer to any files. He knew instantly. That means that this person is also an employee, if you see what I mean, or he is a person of interest to my source. Whoever he is, Carl, they advise you contact this person again. He pretty much said that he can be trusted. I thought you should know that sooner rather than later, especially in view of the last thing my source said before he broke contact. He said that the situation is dangerous. And I'm really phoning to say I want you to take a deal of care. His implication was that the University is not merely a nest of backbiting prima donnas, but something altogether more worrying. So be careful, please."

"It would be useful to know what," said Power.

"I think the key person to talk to is the individual himself," said Lynch, by whom he meant Felfe. "I'm going to try some different avenues to find out more about him, because the source would give me no more information."

"Should I contact him," Power found it markedly difficult to not say Felfe's name out loud. "Contact . . . the individual . . . myself?"

"If we want to find out what's going on, yes," said Lynch. "The individual signalled they wanted to talk. So hear them out."

After the phone call, Power sat in the café, alone, musing over Lynch's news and the meetings he had engaged in through the day. There was so much to think about, balance and plan, both at work and at home. The world of his clinical work and the world of his home life seemed real and solid, but this academic realm seemed altogether too speculative at the moment and he knew it was occupying too much of his attention. He tried to focus just on the medical school again. Power reasoned that he needed some reassurance and decided that the one person he needed to talk to about the medical school was the Vice Chancellor.

He picked up his mobile phone again and dialled the Vice Chancellor's secretary.

"Hello," he said. "This is Professor Power."

"Good afternoon, Professor, how are you this afternoon?"

"Rather anxious actually, would it be possible to speak to the Vice Chancellor, just for a moment?"

"He's not here," said his secretary. "He's taken a few days off to go to his cottage in Abersoch. He'll be back soon. Can I make an appointment for you later this week?"

Power tried not to sigh in disappointment. "Thank you, that will be great."

* * *

Power went back to his office at 4.45 p.m. He let himself into the building with his magnetic ID card. Power only had access to certain buildings according to his role and security clearance. The University chose to preserve a strict, layered hierarchy for such things. A select few senior staff, like Shacklin and the Vice Chancellor, had cards that could admit them to any University building. The November evening was dark and chill and Power had been shivering crossing the campus. The drive home would be busy, through the red brake lights and glaring white headlights of Chester's evening traffic.

Only a handful of staff at the University tended to stay beyond 4 p.m. Academics began sloping away from their offices around 3 p.m. Secretaries stayed until 5, librarians who kept the University Library open for study remained till midnight, and security staff plodded the grounds thereafter, checking doors were locked, and students safe. And so at 4.45 p.m. when Power walked through the corridors of the downbeat building where he was afforded his office, everywhere was virtually empty. He needed to return to his office to retrieve his briefcase, laptop and coat.

Power unlocked his door and scooped up his belongings from the chair. He was about to leave, but a small white card caught his eye. It had been placed strategically against the keyboard and screen of the desktop computer.

The card bore a short, handwritten note. The writing was small, well formed and crisply black against the white card. The message read, 'We should meet. Your diary indicates you are free to meet next Friday – at 11.30 a.m. – in St Anselm's Chapel at the Cathedral. Felfe.'

Chapter Seven

Sometimes human places create
inhuman monsters.
Stephen King, The Shining.

Margaret had been tasked with arranging all of Power's appointments with the deans, in a very short span of time. So far Power had met most of them, but it had been with some difficulty that Margaret had tried to arrange an appointment with Professor Ann Teesdale. Margaret had managed to get through to Professor Teesdale on the speakerphone just at the moment that Dr Power walked into the secretary's office on Wednesday afternoon. Margaret was in mid-conversation as he entered her office and Power noticed immediately that she was upset.

"I'm sorry you feel that way, Professor Teesdale," Margaret was saying. "I'm just doing what Professor Shacklin asked me to do – arrange appointments for our new professor."

"If you think I'm wasting my precious time speaking to that idiot, then you've another think coming. Swaggering in here and boasting about how he's going to start another shrine to the medical establishment..."

Margaret looked up at Dr Power and, mortified at what she was hearing, mouthed, "I'm sorry!" to him. Power in turn indicated that he was happy to take over the call. Margaret looked relieved. Power sat down on a chair by the speakerphone and waited until there was a gap in Professor Teesdale's tirade and spoke, "Ann? I was just passing Margaret's office. It's Professor Power."

"How long have you been eavesdropping?"

"I have just walked into Margaret's office. You seem very angry?"

"I am. I don't need to waste another moment on you or your schemes. I don't need secretaries taking up my time asking to speak directly with me either. Who does she think she is? Deans don't have time to speak to other people's secretaries." Margaret raised her eyebrows, and turned away to arrange some papers on another desk. She didn't want Power to see she was crying.

"I wanted to speak to you," said Power. "Margaret was trying to arrange that. I thought we got off on the wrong foot at the deans' meeting and I wanted to see if we could resolve things." He was tempted to add 'like adults', but he sensed that would only trigger more ire.

"I'm not sure there is much point," she bristled. "There's too much that separates psychologists and psychiatrists."

"I'm not really talking from the viewpoint of a psychiatrist, I wonder if we can set that aside. Like you, I'm a scientist, and I'm trying to develop an additional course to teach at a University. The new course will provide chances for research. The course will need to feature psychology in terms of human development, and health psychology. There's a chance to build a new culture for medical students, one that is holistic and takes the best from all that Allminster has to offer."

"I've heard it all before," said Teesdale. It sounded as if she was calming at first, and then her anger started, incredibly enough, to escalate again. "You'll never ditch the 'medical model'. It will just be another temple to disease with the doctor as the sacred priest. Doctors take the skills of women, like tending the sick and dying, and helping people give birth – you take them and you turn them into a male profession that spins white male privilege into gold!"

"The new curriculum could be adjusted . . ." said Power, somewhat wanly, as he was losing hope and also the will to remain professional in manner.

"Psychiatry too – that takes subjects and medicalises them! It took Rational Emotional Therapy from the Psychologist Ellis and Dr Beck turned it into Cognitive Therapy."

"I'm not sure that's quite fair," said Dr Power, and wondered about whether he should point out that the fathers of psychotherapy, Freud and Jung, were both medically qualified. He decided that mention of the good doctors would only inflame matters. "Talking therapies have been around for thousands of years – the ancient Greeks used to try and rationalise with delusional patients . . ."

"Bullshit!" interrupted Teesdale angrily. "You're just trying to undermine my profession."

". . . and Defoe, when he wrote *Robinson Crusoe* in 1719, describes a kind of self-generated Cognitive Therapy that Crusoe uses on himself. He writes down his 'evil thoughts' on one side of the page and then turns them round into 'good thoughts' on the other side . . . as if he was reframing them . . ."

"You're wasting my time, you're just a bigot," and, with that, Teesdale slammed the phone down on Power.

Power looked bemusedly at the now silent speakerphone. Margaret turned around to face him and raised her eyebrows. "I'm sorry about that," he said. "Please can you tell Professor Shacklin that I *did* try? I don't think I'll be trying again. Ever."

"I don't blame you," said Margaret. "You won't be surprised to learn that the personal assistant post to Professor Teesdale is vacant. It's been vacant for the last six months. None of the current administrative staff want to work with her."

Margaret went on to alert Power to the presence of another dean at the University, one who had not been mentioned by anyone at the dean's meeting. It seemed, in a way, that this other dean, Professor Erin Marsh, had achieved the remarkable feat of almost disappearing entirely from the conscious memory of any of the deans of other faculties. If she had known that she was so little remembered, Professor Marsh would have been greatly pleased, for if she was not easily recalled, then she would not likely to be called upon to volunteer or serve in any capacity. Professor Marsh was not reputed for her enthusiasm for work of any kind.

Margaret arranged a meeting for Power later that week.

Erin Marsh was the head of the Faculty of Business, which was based in a half-timbered mock Tudor bank in the heart of the city. Her office, which had once belonged to the bank's county manager, was a grand affair overlooking the Roman city walls, with polished mahogany panelling, parquet flooring and a high, intricately plastered gothic ceiling. From this office in the centre of the city, it was a gloriously short step to any one of the city's stores and restaurants. Marsh was so centrally placed that everyone came to her, and she rarely stirred herself to visit the campus itself. Her secretary had given Dr Power the dean's first appointment of the day at 10.00 a.m. on Thursday. Marsh had grumbled when she learned about the appointment as it was the only one that morning, and if it had not been for Power she could have had an extra lie in. She had asked her secretary to try and delegate the meeting to her deputy dean, the spry and wiry Dr Allen. Margaret had insisted on the appointment however and had not accepted Professor Marsh's default plan, which was always to delegate any possible work. Marsh's favourite business saying was, 'Surround yourself with the best people, delegate the work and don't interfere.'

Accordingly, Dr Power had turned up at Professor Marsh's office promptly at 10.00 a.m. She herself arrived at 10.15, slightly incommoded by having to walk briskly from the car park at the rear of the building to avoid appearing even more late. She grunted at him as she passed him in the waiting area outside her room and mumbled, "Come on then, doctor," before slumping into her chair. Her personal assistant arrived with tea without being summoned. Marsh waved a hand feebly and the assistant poured her a cup of tea. She pointed to the spot where she wanted the cup placing in front of her. "Do you want a cup, Dr Power?" she asked as a slight after thought. Power demurred.

The assistant left and Marsh stirred her tea. She even made the stirring look like a superhuman effort. She laid the spoon down wearily, as if it were made of lead.

"Good morning, Professor Power," she said. "It was an exhausting commute today. Nevertheless, I suppose we must address the business of the morning. I gather you want to open a medical school. What makes you want to do anything so . . . tiring?" She shook her head at the thought of the sheer effort involved.

"There is a great need locally. It may be easy to recruit good doctors in city centres like London and Manchester. It's less easy here in Chester, or in mid Cheshire or in North Wales. They had to advertise a recent A&E consultant vacancy three times in Chester, and another A&E post in North Wales had no-one apply to any of their advertisements. A medical school here would ease that problem by generating the county's own doctors. The bulk of a medical school's graduates want to work and settle within forty miles of their chosen University. And there are a hundred equally good other reasons."

"All very worthy, I'm sure. Well, I'm sold. You want my support? You need my vote? Well, you've got it, **if** they remember to ask me. I do have to go to Senate though and if it comes up on the agenda then I will support it, of course, but really it's all up to the Vice Chancellor, you know. He has all the say in this place. The deans all sob and sigh and make a song and dance. They rush all about, all day, tiring themselves out, but their noise and clamour mean nothing."

Power was surprised that gaining this dean's approval was so easy. He expected that Marsh would attempt to negotiate, to lever an advantage, or finesse a deal to her profit. But to look at Marsh now, overweight and sessile, he sensed that, more than anything, she could no longer be bothered. At what point in her life, Power wondered, has she simply ceased to care?

"I'm grateful for your backing," he said. "If I, or the medical school, can ever repay that support . . ."

"Look, Professor Power, even out of the mainstream here, I get the sense that you face opposition for a proposal which could actually save this University. If you view Allminster as a business it needs the extra revenue stream to survive. Its existing products are tired, sad affairs. Relying on the sad, old cash cows is just bad business. But you face opposition from some very tiresome individuals. I don't need to name names, you've undoubtedly met them. If the Vice Chancellor had any sense he'd have fired at least ninety per cent of his management team a couple of years ago. Don't tell them I said that. You can keep a confidence, can't you? You're a doctor after all. You can have my vote. Just keep my confidence, that's all I ask. I just want a quiet life. Now . . . are we finished?"

The meeting had taken about five minutes. Power had achieved all he had wished, in the most pointed meeting he had yet had at Allminster, and Marsh did not seem inclined to converse further.

Power said his goodbyes, and as he left, Marsh sighed with relief and closed her eyes for a nap.

* * *

His secretary had arranged Dr Power's urgent meeting with the Vice Chancellor at 12.30 p.m. in the University Chapel after Holy Communion. Plans for the Chapel had been drawn up in the nineteenth century by a veteran of the Anglo-Afghan war, Major Louis Cavendish. The Major had famously lost both his left arm and his right leg to a pulwar, (an Afghan sword), wielded by Abdur Khan himself. As architect of the Chapel, Cavendish was assisted by a team of thirty masons, joiners and bricklayers who built from his plans. This team of men all came from the Kabul Field Force that Cavendish had kept together after the conflict.

In the stone porch there was a sepia-tinted photograph of the amputee architect seated at a drawing board with the plans for the Chapel displayed upon it, with his ex-soldiers gathered round him. The photo had been taken by Charles Dodgson himself, and the source of the funds for the Chapel had been Dodgson's pen, writing as Lewis Carroll. The Chapel was a grand red brick affair, larger than was strictly necessary, with four side-chapels, a colonnaded nave, and a lofty vaulted roof with sturdy and solid oak timbers.

A service had just been held in the Chapel, as it was every morning. Usually this was conducted by one of the theologists or a lay reader. The services were a sparsely attended tradition. Participation was usually limited to a few theology students, and elderly lecturers. Today there had been a communion service where the Vice Chancellor himself, as a canon, had assisted a minister from the Cathedral in administering the sacraments – consecrated bread and sweet syrupy wine – to the communicants.

The communicants had left the Chapel some minutes before Power entered, and he found the Vice Chancellor quite alone sitting on a wooden chair in a side chapel dedicated to St Christopher. The Vice Chancellor was robed in purple and munching on the last few morsels of a BLT sandwich that he had concealed beneath a pew before the service started. He looked up at Power with the merest hint of guilt on his face. Armitage finished the last crumbs with a certain grace, and greeted Dr Power warmly.

"Professor Power, Carl, please come in and do sit down," he pointed to a chair opposite him. "What do you think of Allminster's Chapel? It's quite fine. I sometimes assist here, and also at the Cathedral. Canons are usually attached to a Cathedral, you know. I help the Cathedral, the Cathedral helps us." He gesticulated to the architecture around them. "It's a design by Cavendish you know. Pevsner wrote about it in his architectural guide to Cheshire. And we have two paintings by Millais on display here; *Christ and the Moneylenders* and his posthumous portrait of our founder's father, also called Charles Dodgson, who was an Anglican cleric in Daresbury. His son commissioned it for the building of the Chapel. Have you seen them?"

"I'll be sure to look them out," said Power, and settled himself on a seat opposite Canon Armitage. He wondered quite how to begin. The Vice Chancellor made it easier for him by saying, "I want you to tell me how you've been getting on with the deans. I gather it has not been plain sailing. I didn't think it would be, but tell me how you got on, please." He bestowed the most benign smile he could contrive upon the doctor.

"I met with the Bursar, Hamish Grieg. I wanted to know about the University's capacity to invest in the project."

"And did he tell you that I have an unparalleled track record of locating money for new projects?"

"Yes," said Power. "Yes, he did, actually."

"Good, so leave that particular anxiety to me. Don't worry about that. And the deans? How did they behave themselves with you?"

"Well, I have met them all. I didn't expect them to be so . . ." Power wondered how he might diplomatically describe his reception. ". . . I found them divided."

"They're a spiky lot, aren't they? You'll have to grow a thick hide to survive them, and grow one as swiftly as you can. Tell me who was most positive?"

"Well, Sir Robert was very enthusiastic."

"I thought he would be. He usually is about everything. Although he can sometimes subside into despondency. It upsets him to say no. He seems to find it difficult to disappoint."

"And I saw Professor Marsh. She could see the economic benefits," said Power.

"She wouldn't see any point in expending energy to oppose you," said the Vice Chancellor. "And I expect that most of the others were non-committal or neutral except two in particular, who would inevitably be antagonistic. Am I right?"

"Yes," said Power, impressed at the Vice Chancellor's insight.

"Professor McFarlane would be, I think, envious of your new project. Jealous that she hadn't seen the opportunity for herself. She will try and wrestle the project off you. And Professor Teesdale is just . . . well toxic, I suppose. You just need to write her off. That's what I do."

"I can't tell you how much of a relief this is. Your accurate assessment of what I faced last week is spot on . . ."

"Did you find it a stressful week then?"

"Very."

Armitage chuckled. "At least you are only part-time here. I have to live with these people full-time. You can go off and be a doctor and see your patients, or do your forensic work with the Foundation, advise the police or whatever it is. I have the deans morning, noon and night, phoning me, emailing me, or ambushing me in the café and giving me raging indigestion."

Power relaxed once he learned the Vice Chancellor saw things more or less as he did. In his relaxed state Power became more candid. "I can't understand why you have surrounded yourself with these people. Surely they're more of a hindrance than a help to you?"

The Vice Chancellor paused and assessed whether Power was about overstep the mark. "They are who they are," he said. "I believe in their autonomy and I, by and large give them free rein, just as our Lord gives us free will." He waved his hand around to perhaps invoke an idea of the deity who dwelled there. "But it is a quirk of the University system that the Vice Chancellor has almost total control of the University. *Particularly at this University.* So my academics at Allminster are free agents here, up to a certain point. And no further than that." He smiled cunningly. "Are you familiar with the philosophy in *The Prince,* Professor Power? That a Prince 'must learn how not to be good', though a Prince should maintain the appearance of virtue and indeed behave virtuously when the cost is low? That is to say, I can afford to overlook the little evils that my academics do, in order to maintain the greater picture. You see, I've always believed in adults having free will, and as long as they don't do too much harm, well they're there aren't they? I mean they are there in post, like those Foreign Legion soldiers manning the battlements against the approaching hordes . . . they are bodies who serve a purpose . . . they are presences who, one way or another, get the main things done and so the University goes on, and survives to another day? Can you see things from that perspective? From the Prince's point of view? I don't condone all their actions, and for goodness' sake I don't even like half of them. They are simply 'there', for now."

Dr Power frowned. He thought he had best explain himself, even if he risked the Vice Chancellor's displeasure. "But they would worry me if I was Vice Chancellor." Armitage raised a cautionary eyebrow. "The anger that burns in Professor Teesdale. Secretaries won't work with her, because she's a bully. Bullies bring law suits, cases at employment tribunals. McFarlane is so ambitious and wants to control everything and Kneale would do anything for money. In a way they are a danger."

"I suppose our respective definitions of danger might differ. These people represent small evils, and their dangers are known to me. Don't worry yourself. You have a very pronounced sense of right and wrong and it is causing you some distress, I can see. Maybe Professor Shacklin can guide you more when he returns from Malta. He is a day or so late I believe. We haven't had word from him, either. Probably enjoying the flesh pots of Valetta. I expect you've heard various tales about him, but he is basically good." Power wondered if the Vice Chancellor and he had the same knowledge of Professor Shacklin. "He likes a gamble does David. The casinos of St Julian may have got the better of him. He once had to borrow money from Professor Kneale when both of them were away at an academic conference in Istanbul. A conference on 'Research Integrity' I think it was. That caused a big falling out between them. Kneale is very attached to his money, and there he was being asked to bail Shacklin out for what were illegal gambling debts. Kneale has never forgiven Shacklin, even if I did turn a blind eye." Armitage sighed. Power waited and said nothing. He sensed that he had come close to violating the Vice Chancellor's sense of propriety about what a relatively junior academic could say to a Vice Chancellor.

Armitage smiled, however, and looked Power in the eye. "I will take on board what you say, though. You mean well, I know, and from your viewpoint maybe you see some things that I don't see. Maybe you think they all need taking in hand," suggested the Vice Chancellor. "You think they need a good talking to and if that doesn't work *correcting*, and if they don't like it then maybe *correcting* some more! Well, the message has been heard, Carl.

"Now, anything else?"

"I have arranged some external meetings," said Power. "I told Dean McFarlane about one of them, but I've arranged one or two others as well. I don't think Dean McFarlane was impressed – I hope I haven't overstepped the mark. She seemed to want to come along to them."

"Tell me, what meetings have you arranged?"

"One meeting at the General Medical Council in London to talk about the principle of starting a new medical school. The GMC regulate medical education in the UK as well as strike errant doctors off the register. Another meeting with the Chief Medical Officer, and some others – with the national Postgraduate Dean who allots medical training numbers for the UK."

"These are high level meetings," said the Vice Chancellor thoughtfully, a note of caution in his voice. "And you arranged them by yourself? And they agreed to meet with you?" Power nodded. "This is progress indeed. You seem confident of the way forward. These are all medical people, in medical settings?"

"Yes, I thought I could speak with them as colleagues," said Power.

"Such is the medical fraternity," said the Vice Chancellor. "And you know the way Medicine does things. Well, you must go. The University will stand you first class train tickets, taxis and hotel accommodation. Ask *my* secretary to arrange it for you please, as Professor Shacklin seems to be delayed."

"And Professor McFarlane? Should I . . ."

"Leave her behind I say. If it was a University mission to the Nursing and Midwifery Council, I'd send her on her own, I wouldn't send you. Horses for courses, as they say. Don't worry, I will smooth things over with her. Unruffle any ruffled feathers."

* * *

The night was carbon black. Low clouds had snuffed out any prospect of light from the moon and stars. Lynch had tried, and failed, to find some rest in the double bed beside his wife. He wandered downstairs so as not to disturb her sleep. Some anxiety, or foreboding, gnawed at the pit of his stomach. Warm milk, and a bowl of banana porridge, could not soothe this knot of dread. Lynch wondered how much of his intuition was rational and what was animal fear; baseless, formless, primeval. He supposed Power might advise and dispense some reassurance for his friend, but it was too late to phone him to ask. Lynch searched his mind for the root of his fears and isolated the phone call with the Intelligence Service. It had been the warning that there was danger at the University. But the risk had not been named or explained in any useful detail. How could he react appropriately to an altogether unknown danger? How could he protect his friend against a nameless evil? He supposed he must wait to hear what Felfe said to Power at their appointment. Lynch knew the service would use their own slang term to describe such a meeting, and call it a 'bump'. A stupid name for a conversation, Lynch thought.

As he usually did to settle his mind, Lynch turned to the Bible. He read the words of psalm 140 and then he prayed:

> *May the cross of the Son of God,*
> *which is mightier than all the hosts of Satan,*
> *and more glorious than all the hosts of heaven,*
> *abide with me in my going out and my coming in.*
> *By day and by night, at morning and at evening,*
> *at all times and in all places may it protect and defend me.*
> *From the wrath of evildoers, from the assaults of evil spirits,*
> *from foes visible and invisible, from the snares of the devil,*
> *from all passions that beguile the soul and body:*
> *may it guard, protect and deliver me.*
> *Amen.*

And after that prayer, against the day, Lynch climbed the stairs to bed and slept until the morning light crept into his room.

Chapter Eight

*My heart is a cathedral. Widows, ghosts and lovers sit
and sing in the dark, arched marrow of me.*

Segovia Amil

The red, sandstone cathedral at Chester is named after St Werburgh, who was the daughter of a seventh century king, Wulfhere. Lynch had worshipped here on Sundays for most of his adult life. His faith had once been seen as a reasonable part of a staunch police officer's personality, and almost something to be admired. Later in his career, as society became more secular, his faith had been regarded with some suspicion by his superiors and with derision by his juniors who mocked him as 'the dinosaur'. Lynch saw no reason to apologise for his faith or reduce his attendance at church.

Occasionally Lynch attended the Cathedral during the week for Morning Prayer, or to meditate. This Friday he was there to allay his anxieties about his friend Power and his meeting with Professor Felfe. It was very difficult to imagine anything dangerous happening in the hallowed precincts of the great Cathedral. All through the centuries its walls had withstood famine, plague, and war.

The meeting between Power and Felfe was due at 11.30 a.m. Lynch had arrived at 10.30 a.m. with a plan to attend the morning Holy Communion, which coincidentally, was also held in the twelfth century St Anselm's Chapel. Lynch presumed that Felfe planned to meet Power in the Chapel when the congregation had dispersed, after receiving their communion. Lynch's idea was to attend the Communion, leave when Power arrived, and be elsewhere in the Cathedral, close enough to react immediately if Power called on him.

However, Lynch had not checked the timetable for the day's services, and unbeknownst to him the timetable did not follow the usual routine this week. When Lynch walked up to the archway in the West cloister leading to the Chapel's stairway there was a red velvet rope strung across to prevent access. A warden nearby came over to Lynch and told him, "There is a service going on in the Chapel, it will be open again at eleven."

"What time did it start?" asked Lynch. "The morning communion in Chapel is usually at ten thirty."

"It started at ten, sir."

Lynch nodded resignedly. He retreated to a seat in the nave to watch the stairway and meditate. He thought how it would have been preferable to meet Power beforehand and perhaps have had breakfast at a café somewhere, but Power had had an inpatient to review. Lynch found himself unoccupied and looked around to see if Power had arrived early, or for any glimpse of Felfe.

There was a guide taking a school party of Spanish adolescents around the nave. She spoke English in a Bolton accent, making no concession to their limited facility with the language. She entertained them with sheer force of Northern personality, and transfixed them with her large oval glasses and long red hair. "Up the stairway is St Anselm's Chapel which dates from the twelfth century. It has a white Gothic plaster vaulted ceiling. St Anselm was born in Lombardy in the year ten thirty-three, before the Battle of Hastings, when King Canute was king. You know. King Canute who failed to command the waves? St Anselm was a philosopher priest who used logic to reason that there must be a God. Anyway," she looked at the velvet rope that prohibited access. "Unfortunately, it appears the Chapel is closed for a service. I think the timetable must have changed." Lynch smiled. He felt some satisfaction that he was not the only person who had been thrown by the change in routine.

At around 10.35 the warden went over to the entrance to the stairway and moved the rope barrier to one side. One by one the members of the small chapel congregation gradually came down the stone stairway. The warden stood by the bottom of the stairs, assisting the more elderly of the congregation to negotiate the steps. Lynch counted four men and three women as they pottered down the stairs in dribs and drabs, and either over to the Refectory for elevenses or to exit into the City. Several minutes after the very last worshipper had descended Lynch made his way over to the warden.

"Is the Chapel empty now? Can I visit it?" Lynch wanted to check the Chapel before Power ventured upstairs and thought he could also revisit the painting of the *Raising of Lazarus* that he liked.

"May I just check that the Chapel is clear after the Service, please sir? If you just wait here, I'll go and see if it can be re-opened to the public."

"Yes," said Lynch, "of course, as you wish." He drew back and waited as the Warden placed the velvet rope across the chapel archway and slowly climbed the stone steps up to the Chapel above. Lynch listened to the warden's feet as they clicked and clacked up the stairwell. He could hear the footsteps receding into distance over the floor of the Chapel overhead. The steps ceased. There was a pause, and Lynch felt it was an anxious silence. And then there was a scream.

Lynch ran up the stairs, two at a time.

In the second of the three bays in the Chapel stood the Warden, her hand to her mouth. Her scream had evolved into an anxious, whimper. Her startled eyes watched Lynch move from the head of the stairs into the space where the service had been held. Two of the chairs had been knocked over, and in their wake was a body lying on the Chapel's grey stone floor."One of the worshippers," said the warden. "Didn't come down with the others."

Lynch knelt by the old man's side and felt his neck for a carotid pulse. There was none. The man's lips were a purplish blue. Lynch hesitated. He didn't know if he should start resuscitation or not. The body had probably been lying on the cold stone floor, lifelessly, for several minutes and Lynch knew from experience that the chances of a successful resuscitation were to all intents and purposes practically nil.

There were other reasons. The man had convulsed and retched before he fell. There was yellow vomitus on the floor, between the seats. Thick strands of clear mucus were strung between the man's lips and the floor. The old man's furrowed brow still looked heavy with beads of perspiration. His open eyes looked shocked and wild as if in life's last seconds he had witnessed a demon or glimpsed the very mouth of hell itself.

"Shouldn't we do something?" asked the warden. "Hit his chest, call for the defibrillator?"

"He's been dead too long," said Lynch, standing up slowly and deep in thought. "Do you recognise him?"

"No, no," she mumbled. "Should we get an ambulance?"

"He used to worship here occasionally," said Lynch, without reproach. "His name was Professor Felfe. He was due to meet someone I know. Trust me, we do not need an ambulance at the moment. We probably need someone like the police. But let me make a phone call first. I know what I'm doing. I was a Superintendent. There's a certain protocol we follow, especially for someone like Professor Felfe. Can you close off the stairs down below, please? We don't want people seeing the crime scene here."

"Crime scene? What do you mean? Surely he's had a heart attack."

"I know all this must be a great shock to you. Please trust me." She looked up at his face, marvelled at how calm he looked and felt immensely reassured by this man. "I don't believe this was a simple heart attack, all you need to know is that this is a crime scene. I will make an urgent phone call now, if you can just attend to closing off the stairs and letting the other Cathedral staff know there has been a critical incident and it is being handled. Don't let anyone up here, no-one – except someone of authority, like the police or a colleague of mine called Dr Power. He should be turning up any moment. I'd like his help, so please send him up. No-one else, though, as we must preserve the scene. And please try not to touch anything on your way downstairs." She stared for a moment at this man who assumed mastery of the situation, before she moved. He seemed to know precisely what he was doing and she decided that he was implicitly trustworthy. Lynch watched the quietly tearful warden as she descended the stone steps, determinedly avoiding any touch of the handrail.

The night before, Lynch had been afraid of danger, but had not foreseen this. Now, in the nexus of everything, Lynch was alone and surrounded by taciturn stillness.

Alone with Felfe's corpse, he was enveloped by the hushed silence of this moment.

This was the *Golden Hour*, and everything pivoted about this moment. The *Golden Hour*, as Felfe the criminologist would have known all too well, was the hour after a crime, when the trail is most fresh, when witnesses recall everything and when the scene of the crime and its environs are at its most vibrant, when the murderer is still reasonably close at hand; never again will the scene be more liable to yield vital clues.

He turned to the inanimate mortal remains of Professor Felfe and quoted Ecclesiastes, *"And the dust will return to the earth as it was and the spirit will return unto God who gave it."*

Here in the Chapel, at this precise point in time it was Lynch who held the cards to be played, could affect the outcome and choose what would happen next. About this fulcrum ventures might be won or lost, events were still in flux.

The golden rays of afternoon sunlight played about the frozen features of Felfe's face, the warmth of the light contrasting absolutely with his cool, stiffening corpse. Lynch pulled his mobile phone out of his jacket and weighed up what words he would say, and to whom. Once he cast these words to the winds of time, events would tumble and fall about him – moving automatically like a rippling row of dominoes standing end on end, clattering and chattering to the floor.

Lynch rang the number he needed, not the police, not the ambulance, and when the line was picked up he spoke, "Hello. My name is Dovedale. There's been a personal loss, repeat, a personal loss." He paused and listened to the question at the other end of the line and answered succinctly. "Yes, a friend of yours. I am in attendance, and I am alone. No other service yet involved, but this is a most public place." A pause for a question and Lynch's response. "St Anselm's Chapel. The Cathedral, in Chester. I'm requesting immediate assistance. Yes, immediate. Code black."

Lynch folded the phone away. The urgent nature of the call had required the one-time use of an unencrypted line. He knew that the Service would wish to be present and immediately in control of their deceased asset, Felfe. Lynch correctly surmised that Felfe was still one of their agents and that the Service themselves would wish to arrange matters as they saw fit, before the emergency services blundered their way into the scene. There would be no last hospital ambulance journey, or involvement of the local police and coroner, no regular post mortem by a hospital pathologist. Something altogether different would be required.

In the hush of the Chapel, Lynch sat down to wait. He felt he could not disturb the silence by walking about. The silence ate into him. The air itself demanded to be still in that moment of quietude. Above the body, the Chapel's red sanctuary lamp was still burning. Lynch tried his best to focus on the smell of the combustion of its wax and that of the ranks of votive candles still burning before the altar. The focus of his attention on this smell of heated wax and wick was to distract him from the otherwise noisome and acrid smell of the contents of Felfe's stomach, splashed out upon the stone flags.

From his seated position Lynch looked over the body again, trying to observe as much as he could. This would not be his investigation, and he knew he must not disturb the body or the scene beyond that which was absolutely necessary. Whoever did investigate the scene would need to exclude Lynch's fingerprints and DNA from the scene by subtraction. The minutes passed slowly as if that moment of time had stopped and become eternal. Lynch hoped that the Cathedral warden was coping downstairs.

Lynch remembered and whispered a prayer for the deceased:

*Eternal rest grant unto him, O Lord, and let perpetual
light shine upon him. May the soul of the faithful depart and
through your Mercy, rest in peace. Amen.*

At the close of his prayer, Lynch looked up from Felfe's body and saw Power was with him, standing at the top of the stairway, ashen faced.

"What's happened?" asked Power. He walked over from the threshold of the Chapel to where the body of the man lay that he had just been about to meet.

"I don't know," said Lynch. "The service finished. The congregation left, I came up here and there he was. He must have been part of the congregation, but... this happened."

Power knelt and felt for a pulse. He was always surprised by how quickly the body cooled after death. Underneath his warm fingertips the moist, pale skin of Felfe's neck was already leathery and cold. Power shivered involuntarily. He saw the excess of saliva pooling from Felfe's mouth and the splatter of yellow-green vomitus near his crumpled body. Lynch had noticed a wild look about Felfe's eyes. Power's differently trained mind perceived bilaterally dilated pupils. He felt the back of Felfe's head to exclude any skull fracture. He remembered once doing the same and feeling a gooey morass of pulped flesh and bone and brain at the rear of the head of a man who had been felled by an iron bar. Felfe's skull was mercifully intact.

"Has he been poisoned?" asked Lynch. "I mean it's not a normal death, is it?" Lynch had suddenly wondered if his instincts had let him down and he had summoned the wrong people on the phone, and how upset they would be.

"It would be an incredible coincidence," said Power. "To arrange to meet someone to tell all, and then to unexpectedly meet a natural demise, just before that meeting. I mean, it *could* have been a heart attack. Some people do feel nauseated and vomit. But the eyes . . . such dilatation, suggests something else. I wonder about atropine . . . it could be atropine. Atropine would give the dilatation. Slow the heart right down, trigger a ventricular fibrillation..."

"An injection maybe?" Lynch remembered the case of Georgi Markov, who had died on a London street, having been felled by a drug injected into him through the stab of an adapted umbrella, by a passer-by. Markov had been waiting at the bus stop to go to his job at the BBC. He had felt a jab or sting in his thigh, turned to see a man picking up an umbrella from the ground. The needle had been concealed therein. "Could it be ricin?" Lynch asked.

"It could be. Ricin would take several hours to work." said Power, reconsidering his earlier suggestion. "And, now I think of it, it wouldn't be atropine, because his skin is damp, and his mouth is full of saliva. Atropine dries the mouth. It would be something else."

"And we'll find out exactly what that is, thank you gentlemen," said a deep voice from behind Power and Lynch. The voice sounded vaguely familiar to Lynch.

The tall stranger with coal black eyes had made his way up from the nave without a sound. He was about to extend a handshake to them both, when he reconsidered the movement and withdrew his hand. "Have either of you touched the body?"

"I checked his pulse," said Power.

"So did I," said Lynch. "As anybody would. Who are you, please?"

"Commander Farrell, Regional Officer, SIS." He showed them a photo ID cursorily, but would not let them touch this. He nodded to them. "You're Professor Power, of course, you were just about to meet Felfe. And you are ex-Superintendent Lynch. Unfortunate circumstances for our first meeting. We need to get you both away from here as soon as possible. There is a team waiting to come in and investigate the scene, take the body away and decontaminate. We need to take you away for decontamination yourselves, and then a short interview, separately of course. Debrief you, as it were. And then, I hope, you'll be free to go home." He smiled. "Well, let's get below. Follow me, there's separate transport waiting for each of you downstairs. Try not to touch anything or anyone as we leave, follow me." There was no question in his voice. Farrell was not seeking their consent. His words were a velvet command, issued politely, but firmly, and neither Power nor Lynch felt like rebelling against Farrell's implacable will. Afterwards Power would only remember fragments of his walk from the Chapel to one of the Land Rovers waiting on St Werburgh's Row. He recalled two soldiers standing either side of the archway that led up to the Chapel. He noticed the extreme crispness of the crease on Farrell's trousers and remembered musing as to whether Farrell had been, or still was a naval officer. When he had arrived there had only been the harassed-looking Cathedral warden, trying her best to keep people at bay. There was no sign of her now. The South Porch had been unlocked and the public and Cathedral staff were being evacuated that way. The huge West Door had been opened to allow access for Farrell's team. Hazmat suited scientists waited in a huddle near an unmarked green ambulance to extract Felfe's body. Power noted, with unease, the white Tyvek body suits, full-face breathing apparatus, blue chemical-resistant gloves and steel toe boots. One was carrying a video camera; another was carrying a single black body bag for Felfe. Power wondered what biohazard they imagined might have killed Felfe and felt a twinge of fear. Farrell had chosen not to wear a Hazmat suit to greet them, though. Perhaps he didn't believe in a blanket submission to protocol, perhaps he thought himself too senior to be bound by it? On the other hand, Power had noticed how very scrupulous Farrell had been not to touch anything in the Chapel or Cathedral, and recalled climbing into one Land Rover with a driver and a minder, while Lynch had been bundled into another. And they were driven off, at speed through the city streets. Power remembered his minder turning to him and telling him to put on a disposable blindfold as they headed out of the city towards Broughton.

That evening, when Power and Lynch had been deposited back at Lynch's home in Handbridge, they had switched on the news for any word of what had happened. The story was not covered by national or local reports and Lynch muttered something arcane about a 'D notice'.

"What did they tell you?" asked Power of Lynch, over a mug of coffee. "It was as if they didn't trust me. That was when I became worried that they might be holding us responsible for the death. They made me sign the 1989 Official Secrets Act, as an 'occasional employee'"

"It was a more of a case of what they did not say," said Lynch. "I will tell you, because I would trust you with my life, but we can't speak about this with anybody else. Not my wife, Pamela. Nor your Laura."

"*We* need to talk though, don't we?"

"Yes, yes we do," said Lynch. "Very much so. But in this case they did not tell me half as much as they might and I am left looking 'between the lines' as they say, looking into the white space between their words. I think that they do not, yet, wholly trust us. The Foundation I mean. We are granted what information we receive on sufferance."

"Why would anyone want to kill Felfe?" asked Power.

"I think we must first ask ourselves the question, 'Who was Felfe'?"

"Professor of Criminology, that's all I really know, said Power. "Probably German-born from his accent and phraseology. He used lots of German idioms in his speech, which, when I come to think of it, may mean that he probably spent most of his formative years in Germany, and was here only lately."

"That would certainly fit. From what they said and didn't say, and from what I have been able to find out myself, Felfe was born in East Berlin around nineteen-thirty. The city was devastated during the World War, which he only just missed fighting in. After the war he was taken under the wing of the *Ministerium für Staatssicherheit,* the infamous M.f.S."

"Infamous?" said Power. "Surely to be infamous you have to be well-known, I've never heard of M.f.S."

"It was later known as the Stasi, and you will have heard of them?"

"Well, yes, I've heard of them, but Felfe? In the Stasi?"

"The GDR found a role for everyone. The communist state boasted of full employment for all citizens, at a time when West Berlin was on its knees. Felfe's first role was apparently keeping dossiers on his neighbours in the streets around Friedrichstrasse. Who lived where, when they left for work, what their wives bought at the shops, which friends called to their houses . . . that kind of thing."

"He was still keeping his dossiers on colleagues at Allminster," said Power. "Some habits die hard."

"If he was, then Farrell and his colleagues haven't found them. They swooped on his office and home within a few hours of Felfe's death. They found nothing. Emptied either by Felfe himself as a precaution or by somebody else."

"What was Felfe going to tell me?" wondered Power. 'If only I'd stayed at the Grosvenor restaurant to hear him out."

"It's a compelling argument for always having a dessert," said Lynch, smiling.

"He seemed such an unassuming man," Power said, remembering Felfe's quiet and humble manner. "Here we are, talking about him in the past tense. Remembering him." Felfe only existed in somebody's memory now. "Was there anyone else who would remember him?" asked Power. "A family?"

"He once had a family," said Lynch. "But that was decades back. He left them behind."

Power wondered how Felfe would have described his own life. Would Felfe have talked to him about growing up in East Berlin? The grey subdued apartment blocks decorated only with huge posters promoting socialism and the greatness thereof. East Berliners described a particular smell of their portion of the divided city, an aroma blended from the fumes of People's Cleaning Fluid, impure petrol, and the reek of brown-coal briquettes and ragged, rancid tobacco.

His adolescence would have been played out against a backdrop of the jagged wrecks of buildings in the city centre. And any walls of the buildings that survived intact were begrimed by layers and layers of soot from the burning of filthy coal. Pavements filled with the police and soldiers strutting. The public were routinely harassed for their papers at every street corner. The average citizen would spend hours sitting in ramshackle huts to have day-visas stamped. But Felfe never wasted his time in windowless huts or dim corridors waiting to get his passport papers back. One look at his M.f.S. staff card would ensure swift onward passage by any State police. Even the food shortages which led housewives to queue for hours for bread outside the grocery would not affect Felfe on his ascent through the ranks of the M.f.S. As Orwell said, in his critique of Stalinism, '*All animals are equal, but some animals are more equal than others.*' Whereas his neighbours would shed tears of joy at a gift of some oranges from the west, Felfe never went hungry, and never lacked any fruits.

It would not have been wise for him to boast about his ability to get any food he wanted, nor would it have been prudent to show off how easily attainable furniture and clothes were for him. Felfe took care to wear clothes that looked very like his neighbours apparel, but if you looked closely, whereas the cotton or wool of their grey cloth was coarse and harsh to the touch, the cloth of Felfe's drab, grey cotton trousers was fine Egyptian cotton woven with strands of silk within, soft and smooth to the touch. Felfe had always liked the good things that life had to offer.

"Felfe was a paid informer, then," said Power. "He was a spy, betraying his neighbours to the State?"

"His first job was, yes," said Lynch. "Then he rose through the ranks. In the nineteen sixties he met a senior officer, Erich Mielke, and they got on well. They rose together. Promotion after promotion. As Mielke prospered in the M.f.S., so did Felfe. And Mielke took him home to meet his family in the Mansion he owned near a lake in Potsdam. It was a grand house, although it was just called an old hunting lodge, built by the Elector of Brandenburg. It was considerably grander than a 'lodge'. Anyway it was there that Felfe met Mielke's daughter, Ingrid."

Felfe had enjoyed the privilege of a grand apartment in the City Centre, one of the last remaining buildings near the ruins of the Gendarmenmarkt, just south of Unter den Linden. Even in the nineteen seventies, the East German government had not begun to clear the rubble from the wartime devastation in the square. Felfe and his new wife Ingrid lived in the square and started a family. The Felfe family watched the latest colour TV programmes from *Fernsehen der DDR* and on Saturdays Felfe would take his children for a currywurst lunch as a treat at *Konnopke's Imbiss.*

"Felfe was promoted again and again when his father-in-law became the head of the M.f.S. He had made a lucky marriage, but there was a strain within it. Through his world Felfe had glimpsed what the West could offer. East Germans envied the goods that West Berliners could buy, and Felfe also smelt freedom over the wall, and he wanted that. Felfe had an even greater exposure to Western culture when Mielke directed him to spy on the British Embassy."

Felfe ingratiated himself with the Embassy staff when they left their offices to shop or buy lunchtime cigarettes or sandwiches. In those days he was still a young man and he could charm, and he could flirt with secretaries. His unlimited expense account could buy them ever more lavish meals and alcohol, trips to exclusive nightclubs that the East German citizens could never hope to grace. And Felfe would buy and wheedle secrets from those he grew to trust and who grew to trust him. And then in the early nineteen eighties he realised that, somehow, ineluctably, he himself had begun to trade secrets with the staff, and finally found that he was engaged in a two way trade, and selling genuine East German secrets. Almost imperceptibly, he had been turned, as the spy fraternity would put it, and he had become a double agent.

"It was said in London, that Felfe's double dealing helped avoid the cold war becoming red hot," said Lynch. "There are even rumours that Felfe prevented a military exercise from escalating into a nuclear conflict. We might even owe Felfe our lives. Who knows? At any rate the British Government was eternally grateful. When the Wall came down they gave Felfe a choice – exile in the West or retreat further into the East with his wife and family. Exile in Moscow, or exile in Britain. Well, I gather that the escapades with the Embassy secretaries he slept with never sat well with Mrs Felfe despite his protests that he was purely doing it for the GDR. Being patriotically unfaithful, if you like. She went East with her elderly father and Felfe's children."

"She went East while his marriage went west," joked Power.

"Precisely," said Lynch. "And besides all that, when the wall came down, some opportunistic journalist exposed him in *Der Spiegel*. Then Felfe had to contend with the idea that remaining loyal Russian agents would take revenge on him for the years he'd spent betraying the socialist dream. Zealots who still believed in Lenin and Stalin. Felfe scurried to England as fast as his feet could carry him. And he was found a place at Allminster by the last Vice Chancellor, who himself had some dealings with the Service."

"Suppose that Allminster wasn't far enough to outrun the Russian agents? That his luck eventually ran out and they caught up with him today?"

"It's possible, I suppose," said Lynch. "But then again it's been over a dozen years since the Wall came down. Felfe never changed his identity entirely. If anyone held a serious grudge against Felfe and was going to avenge his betrayal they've taken their time. I think it's possible. It all depends what Felfe had found out, what he was about to say to you."

"Farrell asked me this afternoon what Felfe *did* say."

"And what did you tell Farrell?" asked Lynch, who reached for a notebook and a pen. "Force of habit," he said. "What use is a police officer without a notebook?"

"Well," said Power. "Over lunch at the Grosvenor, I just thought that Felfe was gossiping. I think now, he did mention being appointed by Armitage's predecessor. He talked about the medical school and said my principal opposition was Bridget McFarlane, the Dean of Healthcare." Lynch made a note. "And then he started talking about her sexuality, and I thought he was being a gossip, and that when he talked about Shacklin he was just being salacious. A lay-person might imagine that academic conversation was erudite and worthy of the Ivory Towers, but their preoccupations are just the same as anybody else. But what if he was telling me something that **was** relevant?

"He said that in the University everybody was sleeping with somebody. I suppose he meant that it wasn't always easy to discern allegiances. He said McFarlane was sleeping with her assistant dean, Caroline. And then he mentioned Shacklin, Armitage's Anglo-Asian second-in-command, and his sexual scandals. He even said he had taken sworn statements about these indiscretions. For his Stasi like dossiers, no doubt. It was unpleasant to listen to. I felt . . . sullied."

Lynch thought about Felfe's past and how he'd advanced using his neighbours' secrets against them in East Berlin. "If Felfe had been a younger man, I would have suspected him of blackmail," said Lynch. "But we have the benefit of hindsight, and I don't think that money or advancement was his motive. He didn't need money for anything. He was comparatively rich. He lived alone. He didn't crave betterment. He wouldn't want to gain any higher position. That might attract attention, and he was content to hide behind his cover for the rest of his life. So what was he collecting this information for? Did he mention anything else?"

"I can't recall," said Power. "I'd stopped listening to him."

"If he wasn't terminated today by his old employers in the communist bloc, then something he said, or was about to say to you, was the thing that cost him his life."

"Farrell said that too," said Power. "I feel guilty that I didn't pay more attention. How do they square all this? The service?"

"What do you mean?"

"Well, today the Service winged in. Took over the Cathedral. Removed Felfe's body, the body of their historical double agent. They will investigate. And all with no recourse to the local hospital or police? Presumably they are avoiding the local coroner too?"

Lynch paused and thought. "Carl, this is how it works. They have *carte blanche*. The Government wrote the rule book for *them*. There are Statutes allowing the Service a considerable degree of latitude. And successive Governments of every colour have always signed up to them. The 1996 Act gives them a role in serious crime, terrorism, sabotage or threat to our economy. That's how it's squared. He quoted the Act, 'it shall be the function of the Service to act in support of the activities of police forces and other law enforcement agencies in the prevention and detection of serious crime.' Incidentally, the Foundation comes under 'law enforcement agencies' for their purposes. That's why they described you as an 'occasional employee', because of your role in the Foundation with me.

"So if they want a post mortem and investigations, they can arrange them. They can bury Felfe if they want, together with all his history. If they want to hold an Inquest, they will wear the Coroner, like a glove. The Coroner may not even realise they are controlling him, their control is light and deft, but quite, quite sure. And if the service eventually finds they want to prosecute someone for Felfe's murder they will arrange it to their design. At that point the service will simply the Crown Prosecution service like a glove.

"And us?" asked Power. "The Foundation – is that a glove to be put on and taken off as necessary?"

"Maybe," said Lynch. "It rather depends if we let them, I think."

Chapter Nine

*Half of the harm that is done in this world is due to people
who want to feel important. They don't mean to do harm.
But the harm does not interest them.*

T. S. Eliot

Power emerged from the lecture halls with a trail of four nursing students following him, asking him about his thoughts on psychosis, or hints for their module assignments. He paused outside the 1960s, red-brick University Refectory to attend to their concerns one by one. The November day was chilly, despite thin, fragile sunshine. Power pulled his winter Chesterfield coat tightly round him as he talked.

Eventually, the students were satisfied and Power gratefully ducked into the Refectory café. It was busy for mid-morning. The atmosphere inside was warm and steamy. He loaded his tray with plum cake, and bought a cafetière of decaff coffee to go with it. He looked around for an empty table, but there was none. He threaded his way to a table for four where only two people were sitting. He recognised Marian Mason's head of curly brown hair. She was chatting animatedly to another lecturer.

"Hello," said Power, as he approached their table. "May I join you?"

Marian Mason looked up. "By all means, Professor."

"Please call me Carl," he set his tray upon the table and sat down.

"This is Professor Power," Marian said, introducing him to her colleague at the table. "He's a psychiatrist, so watch what you say. He's the one with the plans for a medical school."

Mason's colleague was a thin, nervy woman with hair tightly wound into black braids. Her eyes were obscured behind sunglasses, which she obdurately continued to wear despite the season and despite her being indoors. She was dressed in a white dress with loud yellow sunflowers stenciled all over it that again defied the season. She introduced herself to Power, "I'm Ann McGovern, Head of Social Care. The Department of Social Care is a hostage in the Faculty of Health. And so, if you've got plans for a medical faculty can we join you, please?" Power sensed she was in earnest.

"You welcome the idea of a medical school?" Power had become so used to a hostile reaction he was taken aback by any sign of enthusiasm.

"We'd switch to a Faculty of Medicine in a flash. Bridget McFarlane has no idea how to manage administrators, academics or students. *And* I think that pretty much encompasses all the people in her faculty. And I don't care if you tell her I said that. She knows precisely what I think of her. She can't get rid of me, because she doesn't understand the subject and can't recruit anybody else. For that matter, I'm not really sure she understands nursing. Goodness knows what she teaches her students. She knows nothing of care or compassion. It's not a thrilling prospect for me as I grow older, to be looked after by any nurse she's trained . . ."

"Ah," said Dr Power, not quite sure how he should reply to open mutiny.

"Carl was worried that the deans didn't want a medical school," said Marian. "I tried to tell him that the deans' reaction to his plan was not necessarily shared by the rest of the University." She looked at his plate. "You *do* like cake don't you?"

Power nodded assent.

"I'll bake you a plum cake if you let Social Care move into the medical school," said Ann McGovern. "I'll bake one for you every week!"

"There's an offer," said a booming voice behind Power.

Sir Robert Willett sat down in the last remaining space on the table. "You see, Professor Power, the people who matter want your medical school. The people have spoken!" He looked over to a seating area on the opposite side of the café and his voice dropped to a more tactful level. "I'm avoiding the Vice Chancellor over there," he whispered. Power looked round, just as Willett said "Don't look round."

The Vice Chancellor sat in a distant corner, surrounded by the clutter of a stack of empty dishes left from food he had so far consumed throughout the morning. Seen at a distance, Armitage's red face was unsmiling. He imperiously summoned an employee from a nearby table with a surprisingly delicate beckoning wave of his hand. Power thought Armitage's demeanour was reminiscent of a displeased Eastern potentate summoning a slave to their fate.

"Well," said Marian Mason. "If the Vice Chancellor is holding court and has taken to beckoning staff to his table . . . we'd better go. Anybody in his orbit could be beckoned next. And that means us. Good to see you again, Carl."

"And make room for Social Care in your plans," said Ann McGovern, patting Power's shoulder as they left. The two lecturers carefully chose a curving trajectory through the café that was as distant as possible from the Vice Chancellor's table.

After the others had left, Power saw that Willett had lost some vitality. His normally inflated and bumptious manner seemed to have quite deflated. His persona had diminished now he was alone with Power.

"Is everything all right," asked Power, wondering if he was seeing the real Rob Willett. "You look a bit glum, if you don't mind me saying?"

"I am glum, as you put it," said Sir Robert, mournfully. "Seeing the Vice Chancellor has reminded me of something. And perhaps anyone would be glum if they had no option but to work for that man." He nodded his head in the direction of Canon Armitage. "Goodness knows how I keep presence of mind with his ideas for the University and me. But I suppose that I've had plenty of practice." Willett said very gravely. "Plenty of practice. But how much does he really care about any of us? I suppose you heard the news about Felfe?"

Power nodded agreement, but chose not to say that he had been planning to meet Felfe in the Cathedral where he died, and that he had examined, albeit cursorily, Felfe's corpse as it cooled on the stone Chapel floor.

"A quiet man, Felfe, inoffensive in many ways, and completely overlooked by his peers. Dead, suddenly, in harness. And you see the

Vice Chancellor over there carrying on as if nothing had happened. Look at the empty dishes all around him."

At this, two members of the Refectory staff arrived at the Vice Chancellor's burdened table. One to carry empty crockery away, and the other to place a tagine of Moroccan stew and rice in front of him. "Perhaps that is an early lunch," Willett speculated. "I wonder if there is any separation between the Vice Chancellor's meals? Or does breakfast merge into brunch, and does brunch just blur into lunch? And does lunch accrue into afternoon tea? Certainly, his appetite doesn't seem to be impaired by Felfe's death. It puts me in mind of that colloquial poem about the difference you make to the shape of water? Do you know the one I mean? It goes:

> *Take a bucket and fill it with water,*
> *Put your hand in it up to the wrist,*
> *Pull it out and the hole that's remaining*
> *Is a measure of how you'll be missed.*

"That is a sobering thought, Rob," said Power.

Willett thought for a moment, "Or there is that line by Hesse:

> *No permanence is ours; we are a wave*
> *That flows to fit whatever form it finds.*

"Well," said Power. "At least *you* are remembering Felfe. It sounds as if you miss him, even if some don't.

"Maybe you're right," conceded Sir Rob. "I hear he died of a heart attack, just dropped dead. In the cathedral, of all places."

"Is that what they're saying?" asked Power.

"Human Resources said so in an email statement this morning. Why, is that wrong?"

"No, no . . . I mean I don't know," said Power. "I haven't seen the statement. I was giving a lecture. I haven't logged onto my emails today."

"And then another reason I'm glum and *avoiding* the Vice Chancellor – don't tell anyone! – is because I'm just working out whether the University's latest prized possession is a fake. I don't want to have to tell the Vice Chancellor. I can't face it." He looked shocked at the words that had escaped his own lips. "I'm sorry, I shouldn't have come out with that, please forgive me. Please don't mention I said anything."

"I can keep a secret," said Power. "If you want to talk anything through – I'm used to confidentiality."

"Can you?" asked Rob, looking round the dining room. "It would be a relief, to confide in someone. There's honestly not many here you can confide in and be sure they will honour that confidence." There was a buffer zone of empty tables, between them and the Vice Chancellor. "I don't think anybody can hear," said Rob. "There is a cloud of unknowing between us and the Vice Chancellor. OK, have you ever heard of *The Wasp* manuscript?"

"No," said Power. "I don't think I have. Tell me about it."

"Well, as you know, Charles Dodgson was a great benefactor to this particular University. They named one of the original Halls of Residence after him – Dodgson Hall. He endowed the original Chair of English at the University. The one I now hold. He endowed a chair in maths too. A chair in English because he was an author and a chair in maths because he was a mathematician. And of course, you know he wrote the wretched Alice ... those books and their tiresome characters crop up again and again across Cheshire."

"You're not a fan?" Power observed.

"Once upon a time, maybe. And I suppose I should respect him because my specialty is Victorian Literature. But when you are required to be joyously enthusiastic about a writer by dint of your employment, it has the opposite effect," said Sir Rob. "Well, you might just remember that in the nineteen-seventies there was a great furore and excitement about a missing chapter by Lewis Carroll or Dodgson, rather. The so-called 'lost' chapter from *Alice Through the Looking Glass.* People always suspected that there was a lost episode as we have a document from Tenniel, his illustrator. Tenniel wrote a letter to Dodgson refusing to illustrate *The Wasp* chapter, and in so many words, said the chapter wasn't up to scratch. And then these 'lost' galley proofs appeared with this supposed chapter in them, about Alice meeting a new character. A wasp in a wig, for goodness' sake! Well, this text they were meant to have 'discovered' in the proofs was drab. Wooden. Pedestrian. The galley proof episode includes familiar elements – Alice traipsing through a wood, stumbling on this wearisome creature – this time a wasp who is apparently sad, and then she moves on. The chapter just doesn't go anywhere. Everything in a decent narrative has to have a purpose. The author should not expose his reader to irrelevant nonsense."

"Well," said Power. "Excepting that Carroll deliberately wrote nonsense."

"I can't agree," said Sir Robert, with just a hint of resurgent pomposity. "Everything in his books has a mathematical necessity, a logical place. And this galley proof fragment seemed tired. It disappeared into private hands as suddenly as it appeared. The galley proofs with the chapter in have never been seen since, and more importantly never been verified forensically. No tests on the paper, the printer's ink . . . blah, blah, blah . . ."

Willett sighed.

Power finished what he thought was the last morsel of his plum cake, then he espied a plump raisin on the plate that had somehow escaped. He pinched it up between forefinger and thumb and popped it into his mouth.

"And now," said the Professor of English. "Thirty years later, the University has acquired, (and nobody will tell me how much it paid, or where it came from) . . . *another* competing candidate for the missing episode from *Through the Looking Glass*. Another version of Carroll's story about Alice and the wasp. This one is quite different, though. This fragment does drive the story along, and the wasp is a bit more than just a depressed old insect skulking in a wood. This version of the wasp is active – it flies for God's sake, like you'd expect Carroll would make it do. The University's text is supposed to be Carroll's, I mean Dodgson's, own handwritten manuscript. And it does look like the other handwritten manuscript of *Wonderland* that we know for sure is genuine and which is kept by the British Library. Except . . . I'm not quite sure about it . . . I don't trust this text . . . so how do I tell the University that? I'm bedevilled if I say its genuine now (and it turns out later it isn't) and also I'm politically screwed if I turn round and say it's a fake! Everyone wants it to be real. The University is champing at the bit wanting to announce the discovery of the manuscript to the literary world. Headline news guaranteed across the globe for the University. Suddenly, without me bargaining for it, my reputation is on the line . . . through no fault of my own," Willett paused, thinking. "I wonder, can I ask you, please, will you come and look at it. Or a copy anyway?"

"I'm no literary expert . . ." said Power.

"The opinion of a well-meaning, lay person would be as welcome to me as anybody's at this time . . ." said Sir Robert.

Having drained his cafetière, and full of curiosity, Power followed the Professor of English across the quadrangle towards the Faculty of Arts.

Sir Robert's office overlooked the roof of the University chapel, and from here he had a perfect view of a small gargoyle seated at the North West corner of the steep, leaded roof. Or rather, thought Power, as he entered the office, the gargoyle had a perfect view of Sir Robert. It had a facetious, leering expression and one eye seemed to stare, unremittingly, into Willett's office.

The office was panelled in dark Victorian pinewood that had blackened over a century. The ceiling was in white plaster, arched and vaulted in a Gothic style. Leather bound first editions sat on heavy oak shelves and jostled with twentieth century classics in paperback. A first edition of *Lyrical Ballads* rubbed covers with a 1975 edition of *The History Man* by Malcolm Bradbury. The shelves were home to a complete set of *The European Journal of Victorian Literature*, the academic journal that Willett edited. The journal was bound in a garish, neon orange and the solid block of orange binders stood out uncomfortably from the wall of leather-bound books. On the plaster wall between the heaving bookcases was a Fagin-like photographic portrait of Tennyson, with beard and wide-brimmed hat. The photograph was juxtaposed with a large poster advertising the University's 2001 Conference on 'Literary Reflections of the Anglo Afghan War' that Sir Robert had chaired. Near this was an alcove, closed off by a floor-length purple velvet curtain. There was a heavy desk with a roll-top wooden shutter that could be pulled over the desktop and locked for the night. Power wondered what secret drawers and compartments might be hidden within. On a simple desk by the window was an Apple computer, with piles of glaringly white A4 paper scattered around it.

Sir Robert gestured silently to invite Power to sit down in any one of a large semi-circle of armchairs. It was here that the Professor of English held weekly tutorials for his students.

Power settled in a wingback chair, upholstered in maroon velveteen. The room smelt of dust from the books and something else, perhaps sherry.

In the centre of the spread of armchairs was a heavy-looking, low table. The table had a glass box, framed in wood, upon it. The lid of the box was padlocked, and from a clasp at one corner it had a chain attached to the heavy table, as if the box or its contents were imprisoned.

Power looked inside, through the glass, and saw that there was a shallow, rectangular shape with a black silk cloth draped over it.

"That is the manuscript which has become the bane of my life," said Sir Rob. "The black cloth symbolizes how I feel about it, but its practical purpose is to shield the handwritten manuscript from the light. The University's insurers insisted on the padlock and the chain. Just like a medieval library. They used to chain their books up . . . but then I suppose this manuscript *is* worth over a million pounds. I was given the task of verifying it and writing the first academic paper on it. How I wish I'd dodged that silver bullet. I have accepted a poisoned chalice."

"A million pounds?" said Power.

"At least," said Sir Robert. "If it's unique, and if it's the real deal, of course. The only copy of a lost chapter from one of the all-time classics of Victorian literature? In nineteen twenty-eight the first manuscript of Alice, which was then entitled *Alice's Adventures Under Ground*, sold for fifteen thousand pounds. Calculate what that would be now, with inflation, and then factor into account just how many world billionaires there are who would bid for it. It would attract dozens of wealthy Russians, Arabs and Chinese. Alice is so *very* popular in Japan too. All those bidders would simply drive the price sky-high. I say a million, but it could well be worth millions. Original paper, sepia-coloured writing in Carroll's own hand, three of Carroll's own amateur pen and ink illustrations as suggestions for his usual professional illustrator Tenniel. It has everything you'd want, it has the lot." Sir Robert crossed to the roll-top desk and pulled open a capacious drawer. He extracted a bottle and poured out golden Fino sherry right to the brims of two tall sherry glasses. "It's driving me to drink." He laughed and handed a glass to Power. The glass was filled to such an extent that the surface of the sherry formed a convex, curved meniscus at the brim.

"Can I see the manuscript?" asked Power, as he sipped carefully at the dry sherry. Sir Robert offered him a packet of Nairn's seeded oatcakes to go with the sherry and Power took a couple of the biscuits and placed them on the arm of his chair.

"I'd like you to read it, but it is only a typescript of the text I can offer you. It's easier to decipher than Carroll's scrawl anyway . . . and

I don't want to see the real manuscript ever again. I can only bear it in the room with that cloth over it. I hope you understand." Sir Robert fetched a folder from the window desk and handed it over to Power. "There, have a read. You are familiar with the plot of *Through the Looking Glass*, I suppose."

"Well, it's a strange coincidence – I've been reading *Through the Looking Glass* to my son, over the last couple of weeks" said Power. "Though, I must say that he preferred *The Hobbit.*"

"I don't blame him," said Sir Robert. "Tolkien was a Professor of English and Carroll was a mathematician. The professions of the authors show through. I'll look through some of my emails while you concentrate on it. So you don't feel I'm watching you for your reactions. To put this chapter in its proper context, it's meant to slot into the middle of the book, just after a chapter where Alice has been a train passenger crossing the chess board."

Power took the proffered typescript and began to read.

The Wasp

Alice turned a corner in the path through the great wood and came into a clearing between oak and sycamore trees. The noonday sun shone directly down into the clearing, illuminating the greenery. "It seems to be summer still here," said Alice, "and it was winter when I left home. Time does seem to be different here."

The sunlight sparkled on the glossy carapace of an enormous black and yellow wasp that was basking in the very centre of the clearing.

Alice was more than a little taken aback and she stopped in her tracks and wondered whether she had been spotted and whether it might not be altogether prudent to retreat as best she could.

But the wasp's black eyes glittered as it turned its gaze upon Alice and she did not wish to appear impolite to the wasp. She did feel that she should not anger it. She saw the wasp's tongue flickering in and out of its mandibles and wondered if it too, like the other insects through the looking glass, had the power of speech.

She felt strongly, in any case, that it would not do at all to vex the creature. Alice had had a most unpleasant experience with a wasp. She had been stung before. Whereas she was reassured by the fuzzy sound of furry bumble bees that buzzed around the flowers in the conservatory, the sharply pointed hum of a wasp made her go pale with fright. She remembered, all too clearly, that she had fought with a wasp over afternoon tea on the terrace. Their battleground had been the sticky icing of a chocolate éclair. Cook had just got the recipe from Paris and Alice had been loathe to let the insect rob her of her pastry, but as she dismissed him with a wave of her tiny hand the wasp had claimed the éclair as his rightful domain and sought his stinging vengeance upon Alice.

The glossy black eyes of the wasp gave no clue as to its thoughts upon the matter of Alice trespassing in his sun trap. Alice found this most disconcerting.

"You seem startled, child," said the wasp, eventually. His tongue flickered in and out as he spoke in a slithery, slippery way. He went on to hum a tune, in a vibrant tone and rubbed his two front legs over his triangular head, as if checking he was appropriately tidy to receive a visitor. "You are quite safe," he reassured her. "I do not choose to sting. I much prefer to help gardeners with their pests. I endeavour to lead a beneficial life."

And Alice remembered that in this Looking Glass world things were never how they might first seem.

"Are you a *girl*?" asked the wasp reflectively.

"I am a girl and I am a white pawn," said Alice. "We're playing chess."

"Hmmm," buzzed the wasp. "Girls are not so sweet as they imagine." And he broke into verse:

> *What are little girls made of?*
> *What are little girls made of?*
> *Larks, and Quarks,*
> *and Puppy-Dog Barks,*
> *That's what little girls are made of.*
>
> *What are little boys made of?*
> *What are little boys made of?*
> *Aphids and Lice and*
> *Everything Nice*
> *That's what little boys are made of.*

"That's just wrong," said Alice, affronted.

"Buzz! Buzz! Buzz!" bridled the wasp angrily, and reaching forward suddenly, he swept Alice from her feet, held her within two legs and took off, all in the blankest blink of an eye.

They shot upwards together and Alice was frightened the wasp would drop her from the height of the trees, but the wasp did not let go of her and held her gently and firmly as he gathered speed and ascended into the blue sky.

The wasp called out loudly to her over the noisy buzz of his wings. "You mention chess. And you called it a game."

"Yes," said Alice. "Queen Victoria plays chess. Chess is from far away India, where she is Empress."

"Empressive," said the wasp. "But chess is war. Look down there."

The wasp had taken Alice to a valley three squares to her left. The board was bordered by a narrow grassy valley, and at the bottom of this were an untidy heap of white wooden lumps.

The wasp asked Alice what she thought they were.

"Rubbish, I should think," said Alice.

"Perhaps that's what you think from this height," said the wasp, and he flew lower down in the valley. "Now can you see?"

"Oh!" said Alice, surprised. "They are pieces!"

"Yes," said the wasp. "Pieces of white pieces. There is the head of one of the white knights. And over there the hats of two white bishops. They must have lost their heads. And the broken white wall of a castle, can you see? The pawns are just rubble, I think. This is the valley of fallen comrades."

"Oh," said Alice. "They lie so still. Is there . . . is there . . . another valley for the red pieces?

"What does it *matter*? Chess is a model for battle," said the wasp.

"There have to be casualties." He whirred his wings faster and they took off again, leaving the trench far below.

"Oh," said Alice, a tear coming to her eye. "A game is nothing like a war. A game is a game and a war is a war."

"And a raven is not like a writing desk, I suppose?" asked the wasp, waspishly.

"I don't understand what you mean," said Alice.

"Give it time," said the wasp. "All will come clear."

The wasp soared away from the trench, where the pieces of pieces from Alice's side lay scattered. "If you want peace, piece, for you are a piece, then let me offer you all the peace in the world. I can show you where you can rule the world. If you ruled this world then surely you could make it as you liked?"

The wasp climbed higher into the blue sky above the board and bade Alice look down upon the patchwork landscape of squares beneath. From up here the green wood, the fields, the brooks and the hedges, looked like the squares on the counterpane of Alice's bed at home. Alice could see a tiny train moving like a caterpillar through the grass.

"I was on that train," whispered Alice, in wonder at the land spread out beneath them.

"You can see all the way across the board," said the wasp. "When we met in the wood, where were you headed?"

"Why, to the eighth square, of course. The red queen promised me I should be a queen if I reached the eighth square."

"I wouldn't trust the red queen if I were you," said the wasp. "Promises aren't always kept, you know. People aren't what you think."

"I don't like to think that way," said Alice.

"One day soon you will need to leave this neverland and face reality," said the wasp.

"Who *are* you?" Alice asked the wasp, as she began to suspect he was other than he appeared to be.

"That is what the caterpillar asked you long ago," said the wasp. "And have you worked out who you are yet?"

"I am Alice," said Alice.

"You answer with commendable assurance," said the wasp. "But are you a pawn or a queen or are you a pawnqueen?"

"I'm giddy from being up here," said Alice. "There is not enough oxygen and too much light."

"Ah, said the wasp. "You are lightheaded. Before I set you down back in the greenewood, can I make you an offer?"

"I'm not sure," said Alice, whose governess had always taught her to be cautious.

The wasp began a descent from the heady heights but was still moving towards the line of eighth squares at the end of the board. The air had been cold at the zenith of their flight and became balmy again as they hovered over a castle at the furthest corner.

"That wasn't there before," said Alice. "You've moved it."

"I might have done," said the wasp. "Or maybe I'm just showing you what I could offer you. Do you like the castle?"

"It's very fine," said Alice, as they swooped over the battlements. She admired the shiny red roofs, and as she watched, the castle seemed to unfold and expand to dominate the entire square and beyond.

"I could set you down on the pinnacle," said the wasp, "and because it is on an eighth square you could be queen. Queen of that castle, and more powerful than the red queen, the white queen, the red and white kings; more powerful than all of them. I could do that for you and all you would have to do was thank me, and feed me soul cakes."

"No, I don't know. Not sure. Not sure," said Alice, who was sorely tempted. Her mouth was unaccountably dry and her heart was beating fast. "It wouldn't fit with the rules. I must abide by the rules, surely."

"The rules," spat the wasp. And angrily he buzzed, "The RULLEZZZZ." He swirled round in the air, changing his course with frightening, lightning speed. And down, down, down, his narrow body screamed through the air, through wispy clouds and down over the downs of square six, skimming over the trees of the green wood and for a moment hovering high above the clearing where they had started. "You are sure you want to live by the rules, child?"

"That's what I've always been taught," said Alice. "To always play the game."

"Then you win, but you don't win," said the wasp as they gently descended. "The rules of war are agreed by both sides to prolong the game."

"A game is a game," said Alice. "We must all play fair. I must make my own way to the eighth square."

The wasp's legs gently set upon the ground. "I set you down, but I feel I've let you down," said the wasp. "The raven is war, you see."

"I haven't the faintest idea what you mean," said Alice.

"Yes," said the wasp. "I can see that. You play the game, but you don't understand what it's all about. Perhaps it will come to you in a dream tonight?"

"Thank you for taking me on a flight," said Alice politely, and gave a little curtsey as she had been taught by the Red Queen.

"Thank you," said the wasp. "I see we are back where we started. You will find the path you feel you must follow over there." And his antenna both pointed over towards Alice's right. "Good day to you and good luck."

"And good day to you," said Alice, as she set off again under her own steam.

Chapter Ten

It's a great huge game of chess that's being played
all over the world – if this is the world at all.
Lewis Carroll, The Garden of Live Flowers

"I like it," said Power, putting *The Wasp* chapter down on the table. "It adds to the original story, although I see why Dodgson may have decided to leave it out of the final manuscript. It is much darker than you might expect from a children's book. The image of the taken chess pieces lying broken and discarded in the trench . . . it's not a theme you'd expect in something written for the nursery."

Professor Willett looked up from the PC where he was reading emails. He came to join Power in the comfy armchairs.

"You've finished. Thank you for reading it, Carl. You're right about the imagery of the bodies in the trench. Grim stuff. And yet the wasp does point out that chess is a metaphor (or a *matter for*) symbolising war, so it is thematically appropriate. *Looking Glass* appeared in eighteen seventy-one, six years after *Wonderland*, but it does feel as if the author is describing the trenches in the First World War doesn't it? Although the British Army was constantly at war in the nineteenth century. I'm thinking of the Crimean War, the Opium Wars, the Indian Rebellion, the Boxer Rebellion . . . the list goes on and on."

"But there's something else that jumped out at me," said Power.

"There was a line . . ." Power picked up the chapter again and looked back through the pages to remind himself. "Here we are . . .

> *What are little girls made of?*
> *Larks, and Quarks,*
> *and Puppy-Dog Barks*

. . . It's the use of the word *Quarks*. Is that what's troubling you about it?"

"Exactly," said Sir Robert. "Nowadays we use the word quark to describe a sub-atomic particle. The accepted etymology of the word *quark* is that it's from a quote – '*Three quarks for Muster Mark.*'"

"Yes," said Power. "That's what I remember. *Quarks* and *Muster Mark.*"

"That's exactly what worries me too. Why would Caroll use the word quark? Of course, Lewis Carroll was the king of neologisms and we are grateful to him for words like *mimsy*, and *chortle*, and *burbling*, but '*Three quarks for Muster Mark.*' is from *Finnegan's Wake*, by James Joyce. And Lewis Carroll or Dodgson, published *Through the Looking Glass* in 1871. James Joyce published *Finnegan's Wake* in 1939. That's a gap of nearly 70 years. We have a problem! And even if you think that Carroll got there first and invented quark before Joyce, there's another anomaly."

"Another anomaly?" asked Power, who had only spotted one.

"Yes," said Willett. "Alice talks about Queen Victoria playing chess . . ."

". . . and Queen Victoria didn't know how to play chess?" suggested Power.

"On the contrary, Victoria was excellent at chess. Chess was said to be her greatest solace after her husband Albert died prematurely. No, it's not that, Carl – it's that Alice refers to Victoria as the Empress of India."

"I thought she was," said Power, puzzled.

"Yes, she was, but Victoria became Empress of India in 1876. *Through the Looking Glass* was published in 1871."

"I see," said Power. "But playing devil's advocate . . . what if Dodgson did invent the word quark before Joyce, and what if Dodgson wrote this piece later than the first edition of *Looking Glass* – as if the author had a second go at *The Wasp* segment after Tenniel gave it

138

such poor feedback – and Dodgson planned it as something to be re-instated in a new edition published after 1871?"

"No," said Sir Robert. "That would require both a leap of faith and a defiance of logic. This is a fake, a very clever fake, an entertaining fake, but a stinking fake all the same. Which brings me to my dilemma . . ."

"Dilemmas," said Power. "Anxiety always hangs upon the horns of a dilemma."

"And it's the horns that I worry about, Carl. The horns goring me to death after I reveal my findings. I simply don't know how much they paid for this." Willett pointed to the glass box and fake within, shrouded by the black cloth. "And these people are proud. Vain. They don't like to be proved wrong. This is so typical of the Vice Chancellor. Asking you to do something outside your remit, and you do it as a favour, and then it all goes spectacularly wrong. How I loathe the man. Willett misquoted Shakespeare: *'The fault, dear Professor, is not in our stars, but in ourselves, that we are underlings.'*"

"Better to tell the Vice Chancellor now, and get it done," advised Power. "You would risk your reputation with him and your academic peers if you endorsed this. You're sure that that mistake about the Empress invalidates it?"

Willett nodded soulfully. "But don't say anything to anyone yet, please, Carl. You'll appreciate it would be dangerous for me. The matter needs careful handling. Maybe I can discuss it with the bursar, but I still need to be careful what I say to him. He's a bit odd, he keeps reptiles you know. He's a bit cold blooded himself if you ask me. I don't think he's quite of our world, or our time – you have to watch what you say to him . . . it's always the things you say that can sink you, isn't it? Like in this wretched manuscript. The quark mistake, and the error about the Empress. What a man says can so easily sink him – put a hole in his boat below the waterline as it were . . ."

"Of course. Be careful," said Professor Power. He stood up to go. "I'm so sorry, I have a supervision appointment to get to. A long thesis on Vitamin D and depression to go through with a student. And some potential concerns about minor plagiarism in her text."

Sir Rob nodded. "Thank you for listening to my concerns." He slumped in his chair, deflated and worried. Power was almost at the door when the English professor quoted a final line to him.

I see nothing quite conclusive in the art
of temporal government,
But violence, duplicity and frequent malversation.

"What's that line from?" asked Power.

"T. S. Eliot – making an argument for something more than the venal rulers we suffer on earth – it's from *Murder in the Cathedral.*"

"Ah," said Power nodding, as if he was familiar with the quote, although he wasn't. He said goodbye.

"Fare thee well," said Willett, pouring himself another Fino.

Power closed the door softly and strode down the corridor to make it across campus for his supervisory appointment. He thought about Willett's remark and arrived at his own office troubled and frowning.

* * *

Power spent a long hour with Melanie, discussing her PhD on Vitamin D deficiency and how it might trigger depressive disorder. He went through her literature review and the proposed PhD research protocol she had written, based on the papers she had read. He sipped mint tea and explained how best to avoid the charge of plagiarism when writing a literature review. For the best part of an hour there was little or no sound in the office, but an occasional few words and the scratching sound of Power's *Pelikan* fountain pen striking though words and annotating the margins of her manuscript. At length Power had worked his painstaking way through the entire manuscript, even amending the form of her references. "These should all be in Vancouver, some are still in Harvard style."

"Have we finished?" Melanie asked with a sigh, exhausted with the intensity of the academic concentration of her supervisor.

"You're still at the beginning of this process. I'm sorry if it seems . . . overly rigorous . . . but as your supervisor, I'm just saying that the greater your focus on the detail now at the protocol stage, the clearer your scientific questions will be, so the easier it will be when you write the ethics application, and this is the foundation you build on, and if the foundation is built well, before you know it, you have that final thesis – just as if it had written itself."

"But what do you think? Of my work?"

"Ah," said Power, understanding now that she needed some more supportive words. "Your study is innovative, you know? It's ahead of the curve. It will be a definite contribution when it's finished, whatever your findings."

"Even if my hypothesis is disproved?"

"That's why the preparatory work is important – you demonstrate the basis for your hypothesis, you show the world that it's a worthy question to ask, and then your findings – whatever they are; positive or negative – are a contribution to science."

"But it would be nicer if I found something positive . . ."

Power started to protest, and stopped, chuckling. "Sure, but you must avoid any bias. Play it with a straight bat, OK?"

"Professor Power, can I ask you something?" Melanie neatly folded her work away into a battered Gladstone bag that had once belonged to her late father, and accompanied him on his rounds.

"Ask away," said Power, wondering what she was being so careful about asking.

"Didn't you go on *TopQuiz* once as a contestant?" Melanie asked, with a smile.

"It sounds like you already know the answer," said Power,

"although you're too young to have watched me when it was broadcast. I was a student doctor back then – at Liverpool."

"And your team survived more than one episode?"

"We won one, lost one, and then we were out," said Power. "Why do you ask?"

"We have a team from Allminster competing this year."

"I heard," said Power. "Professor Shacklin was very keen." He noted she found mention of his name distasteful. "*TopQuiz* has always been a bit of a second cousin to University Challenge. A bit *ersatz*." He wondered if he was sounding like the late Professor Felfe. "They started *TopQuiz* when *University Challenge* went off the air, over on the other channel. Opportunism, I suppose. It is a different format though, isn't it? A bit more democratic. Each University gets just one team on *TopQuiz* and so Oxford and Cambridge don't get one for each college, like on *University Challenge*. *TopQuiz* has just three students on a team and special interests according to the students' studies."

"I'm on the Allminster team," she said shyly. "I'm the captain."

"Ah," said Power. "Brilliant. Congratulations!"

"We were wondering if you'd help us rehearse? Tonight?"

"Tonight?" Power smiled, "I'd like that, but I'm afraid I will need to phone home first before making a final decision."

Melanie nodded, "We're in considerable need of some coaching, I think."

"What's the subject mix of the students?"

"Well, mine is neurophysiology, Jason's is English, and Madeleine is a historian."

"The strategy should always be to restrict your specialist subjects," said Power. "If they ask Madeleine questions on history, that's too broad. It needs to be, I don't know, Eighteenth Century History if that's her thing. Otherwise they could give her questions on Viking History in Oslo, and those would be justifiable history questions. Same for English, Jason needs to specify something like the novels of E. M. Forster or James Joyce, and you need to specify what your particular expertise is in the field of medicine."

Melanie agreed, "We're submitting our specialist subjects tonight. They want a few weeks' notice before we film, but I think they've got a big database of questions."

"They have been running *TopQuiz* for years so you're probably right, they have a stack of questions," said Power. "But the final selection of questions is only made the day before filming to stop cheating. And people do try . . ."

"Well, we're in the Students Union bar from six o'clock if you get permission from home to be out, I'd better go," she said, standing up from the table. "There is a man outside your door waiting to see you."

Power looked through the pane of glass set into his office door. There was indeed a figure in the corridor. "That is ex-superintendent Lynch," he said.

"Are you supervising his PhD, too?" asked Melanie.

Power laughed, "I don't think Andrew needs any supervision. Please could ask him to come in when you leave?"

Power got up to greet his old friend as Melanie left. She squeezed shyly past the tall, smartly dressed detective and made her way down the corridor.

"So, this is your University hideaway," said Lynch as he sat down. Power was busying himself boiling an electric kettle, which sat on a tray on the floor, to make Lynch some coffee.

"It's a cubby hole," said Power. "The smallest office I've ever had. If the wider University wanted to show me what it thought of me, this is its message. At least it has some carpet, I suppose. Did you know Universities are very hierarchical places. They even have rules for the carpeting of academic offices? Lecturers can have a six foot rug, senior lecturers can have an inexpensive carpet that reaches to within a foot of the walls and no further. Professors can have a wool carpet that meets the walls."

Lynch pointed at the computer keyboard on the desk. "Is that where Felfe's card was, with his invitations to meet up?"

"Yes, that's where he left his cards," said Power.

"And the door *was* locked?" asked Lynch. "You're sure you left the door locked when you went out?"

"Yes, of course, I always lock my office door, whether I'm based in a hospital, clinic, or here. I'm trained to maintain confidentiality for notes and things." said Power. "But Felfe left his cards on the keyboard, so he must have had a key. I suppose that locks would have been no barrier to him if he was a spy."

"You're assuming that Felfe entered your office and placed them on the keyboard for you to find. That may be an assumption we can't make. Felfe might just have pushed the card under the door. Someone else may have entered your office, seen the card on the floor, picked it up and put it on your desk. A cleaner or a porter might do that sort of thing."

"I suppose," said Power. "But I'd left my office during the day and returned later that same day. The cleaner comes round after hours."

"Well, if it was a third party, whoever it was, they could have read the cards, and found out where and when Felfe was going to be; found out he was going to be at the Cathedral, and murdered him," said Lynch. "I have to ask, why did Felfe send you a card anyway? Why didn't he email you?" Lynch took a sip of the black coffee Power had brewed for him.

"Maybe he never adapted to using email or maybe he didn't trust the email system," said Power.

"As you say, 'maybe'," said Lynch. "But I have to tell you something you won't like."

"Go on," said Power, warily.

"The official story from SIS is that Felfe had a heart attack. I can't get past that version with the Service. The story they wished to impart to us, to you and I, earlier on today was that the post mortem also showed that. Now, I don't know whether that is correct or whether they have just decided that we don't *need to know* the truth."

"But his pupils were dilated and . . ."

Lynch held up a hand. "Please don't shoot the messenger when I say this next part . . . the Service pathologist asked me to remind you that you are a psychiatrist and not a pathologist. She said that the vomiting was merely due to the nausea that people often get with a heart attack. And that after a death from a heart attack pupils dilate anyway. To quote her 'the pupils dilate following cardiac arrest and return to mid position three to twenty minutes after death.'"

"Well," said Power, looking crestfallen. "I've certainly been put in my place."

"Don't worry, they're not critical of *you*. I sense that the criticism is reserved for *me* alone. It was me that called the response team in. It was my 'intuition' that made me call them. But after I did all that . . . when you saw the body . . . didn't you get a feeling this was an unnatural death?" Power perceived his friend was seeking reassurance. "I don't think it was any coincidence that Felfe died when he did. I think he was murdered. You did the right thing, Andrew."

"I'm glad you think so," because I pressed the point with the Service that I *still* didn't think Felfe's death was natural. I think he may have been killed by a foreign agency seeking revenge for his betrayal. Somebody like the GRU or HVA – the *Hauptverwaltung Aufklärung.*" The initials meant nothing to Power, but he said nothing, as he did not wish to appear an ingenu. "I asked SIS to make further toxicology tests – ones that go beyond the basic tests. They were reluctant, but I think they might do them, even if only to have the satisfaction of proving me wrong. And now, can I ask a favour, are you busy?"

"Not till six," said Power. "What do you need?"

"I'd like to see Felfe's office for myself, can you show it to me please, Carl?"

***

Felfe's small department was in a three storey Georgian townhouse; one of an entire terrace in Allminster village that the University had taken over in the nineteen-nineties.

It had taken Power and Lynch fifteen minutes to walk there across the campus and the village. The terrace was fronted by black iron railings and granite steps. Each townhouse had an elegant cream-coloured portico supported by Tuscan columns. Most of them were occupied by History and European Languages. Felfe's entire faculty was crammed into one townhouse and his Criminology department shared facilities with Sociology, Politics, and Probation Studies. A brass sign on the brickwork announced that this was the '*Faculty of Social Sciences and Criminology*'.

"We'll see if this works," said Power, waving his electronic identity card against the security pad near the glossy black door. Lights flashed green on the box indicating he did have access, but there was no sound of the latch unlocking. A student passed Lynch and Power on the steps and simply pushed the door open wide. She smiled at them both. "Come on in, it's always open."

"The Department of Criminology!" muttered Lynch.

Power navigated their way across the ground floor to the secretaries and asked if he could take a look at the late professor's office. Without any further conversation the administrative assistant handed over the key. "You aren't the first to come prospecting," he said. "There was an investigation team, and then we've had a series of senior lecturers and professors traipsing in to see if it would suit them for an office."

Power felt compelled to say that he wasn't there to step into a dead man's shoes, but reasoned that this attempt to save face would only lead to a need for alternative explanations, when he had already achieved what he sought; namely, access to Felfe's office.

The secretary pointed through the door to the graceful Georgian staircase. "It's on the first floor, at the back of the building. Please can you show yourself upstairs? And please do bring the key back. I must warn you, though, the office is a bit poky. Nobody who has seen it wants to move in . . ."

Lynch was already climbing up the stairs, two at a time, when Power began to follow him. Lynch was greatly amused by the absence of security in the criminology department and ascended with a wry smile on his face.

In the end, Felfe's office door was not even locked. There was a battered white plastic sign on the door with Felfe's name seared into it in black. It announced him as 'Dean of Faculty'. The door itself was wide open.

Felfe's room was even smaller than Power's office. A single wooden sash window looked out of the rear of the building over the brown waters of the Dee. A boat with day-trippers on board was chugging upriver as Power and Lynch looked out. "The view would be nice in summer," said Power, looking out of the window at the river. "Felfe was a pretty unassuming man in committees. He dined in style though. I guess he just didn't want to make any ripples at Allminster. He was maintaining cover and not seeking to ascend the academic ladder."

"You're putting a nice spin on the office," said Lynch. "I've seen bigger broom cupboards." He looked around the bare walls and the empty shelves. "And someone has stripped the place bare," said Lynch. The desk and chairs had already gone. The ancient grey carpet had pale dints in it where the furniture had once stood. A lone telephone sat on the floor near a computer jack. Of the PC there was no sign.

"Bar his name on the door he's been completed erased in only a few days," said Power.

"I had hopes there might be some traces of him left," said Lynch. "But the wholesale erasure of the dean tells us more than anything."

Lynch knelt and, on his knees, went round the room's periphery pulling the carpet back from the edges of the room to see if anything had been slipped under.

"Nothing there," said Lynch, and sprung to his feet in a remarkably spritely fashion, considering his middle years. "Shall we lock up now? Let's leave the Department of Criminology in a slightly more secure state than when we arrived."

* * *

On his way to the Students' Union, Power took a short cut through the corridors of Senate House, the building where the Vice Chancellor and Professor Shacklin both had their offices. It was after five and Power was not surprised to find Senate House devoid of any staff, apart from a couple of cleaners arriving for their evening's work. Power had passed Shacklin's empty office and was hurrying through the corridor to the side entrance when, through a glass panel, he caught sight of somebody sitting on their own in the senior staff dining room.

It was Canon Armitage, the Vice Chancellor, reclining on a green velvet-covered bench near the wall, his plump hands folded across his stomach and head back against the wall, eyes closed, mouth open. His portly face looked bronzed and his rotund and relaxed body exuded a sense of deep satisfaction with life. Even though there was a glass door between them, Power could discern the purr of his rhythmic snoring. In front of the Vice Chancellor on the crisp, white, damask tablecloth were the scant remains of his first evening meal; grilled salmon, potage of leeks, potato dumplings and French sausage. His facial expression was one of benign contentment.

For a moment Power pondered what kind of dreams a sleeping Vice Chancellor might have. Dreams of ample suppers and speechmaking at lavish dinners given to persuade the affluent to part with their money to benefit education and research, of control over the lives of students and staff. A Latin phrase from Power's schooldays came back to him as he watched the snoring principal: *'Esse est percipi'*. *To be is to be perceived.* Power mused philosophically on the somnolent Vice Chancellor. Was Armitage dreaming of the University? Was Power and his plan for a medical school a figure in those dreams? Was the Vice Chancellor perhaps dreaming Power and the University into existence?

"He'll go home to his wife now," whispered a voice in Power's ear, making the doctor start with surprise. It was Sir Robert Willett. "He'll go home to her and he'll have the supper she's cooking right now for him at home. He employs a chef here – full time – to run this Senior Dining Room. He's just about the only one who uses it. He entertains people here of course, hosting dinners for visiting dignitaries, schmoozing the councillors and wining and dining Cheshire's elite donors, but he is most interested in the dining room being open for him whenever he likes throughout the day."

"I see," said Power. "I'm just on my way to the Students' Union to help the team practice for *TopQuiz*. I saw him in there, and stopped."

"Did they manage to get a team onto it this year?" asked Sir Rob. "They are such ninnies that they usually don't qualify in the audition stages."

"I'll see what they are like in a few minutes. I was just passing when I saw the Vice Chancellor and was curious."

"Curiosity often leads to trouble," quoted Willett, peering in at the Vice Chancellor, who was now snoring gently. "I came to see if I could tell him about *The Wasp* manuscript. But I think I'll go home instead. I don't want to shock him out of whatever reverie he's having. It would stop his heart. Let sleeping Vice Chancellors lie, I say. Goodbye!" And with that Sir Robert hurried away down the corridor to the deans' car park at the front of Senate House.

The Students' Union Bar was welcoming, warm and smelled overwhelmingly of beer; the woodwork of the bar seemed to wear layer upon layer of yeasty beer smells acquired over the years, like the rings of wood in a tree trunk. The carpet itself had been marinated in waves of spilt lager. It was, above all, a reassuring smell that Power recognised from the Students' Guild Hall at his own University. The aroma cocooned him in a reassuring alcoholic fug the moment he walked in. "Mysterious Girl" was playing on the bar's loudspeakers.

At the far end of the bar, in the zone where bands often played acoustic sets on a Friday night, Melanie, Jason and Madeleine had set up a long trestle table with three chairs for the team. The University audiovisual department had provided microphones and buzzers. Near the trestle table was a small desk and a single chair for the question master.

Melanie waved to Power and wended her way through the crowd

of early drinkers to welcome him. "Hello, Professor," she grinned. "Can we buy you a drink?"

"That's very kind," said Power, looking over at the cheery Union bar. "But as I'm in work let me buy you three some drinks instead. Have you eaten? Do they do food here?" After seeing the Vice Chancellor replete at his dining table Power was feeling rather hungry. It didn't take much to stimulate Power's appetite.

"They do bar food; hamburgers and chips. That sort of thing," said Melanie.

"Ah," said Power, scanning the menu chalked on the blackboard behind the bar. "Can I order anything for anyone else? My treat?"

"We're all right with a drink, thank you, Professor," Melanie said, beckoning the others over so they could tell Power what they wanted to drink.

"If you don't mind I'll order the felafel salad for myself then," said Power. "It was the only vegetarian option."

After ordering felafels and four drinks, Power joined the *TopQuiz* trio on the stage area. The bartender followed with a tray of two pints of Cheshire Cat blonde ale and two lagers and set this down on the trestle table. Power took a sip of his beer and asked, "What's on the program tonight then?"

"We're going to practice as a team, and hoping you will be the question master," Melanie handed Power a copy of the 2002 *TopQuiz* question book. A photo of the long-term host of *TopQuiz*, Giles Masefield, leered out from the front over.

"Very well," said Power. He took a second gulp of beer and sighed with pleasure. "This takes me back to student days at the Guild bar," he said dreamily. "Except of course the atmosphere was mainly cigarette smoke. People smoked dozens of cigarettes a day. You couldn't smell the beer, only smoke."

"The Students' Union stopped all smoking in here last year," said Melanie. "An act of solidarity with the staff. Risks of passive smoking."

"They should do that across the country, it would save lives," said Power, settling down with the quiz book at the quizmaster's chair. "Will we have an audience then?" He nodded at the chaotic jumble of students in the bar, who were milling about and seemingly unaware of the team or Power.

"We thought if we had an audience there, it might prepare us," said

Jason. He wasn't so sure about the idea now. "Perhaps we can keep the sound down and they'll just ignore us?"

Power chuckled at the team's obvious nerves. "Well done for setting this up and facing your fears. I'll just say a few words to you first, and then we'll see what the audience does when you switch the microphones on." The team took their chairs behind the trestle table and looked expectantly towards their quizmaster, Professor Power.

"Please can you swap seats, Melanie? The captain should be in the middle, and just sit a little bit back, so you can see both your teammates. You need to be able to see if they know the answer – you need to be aware of their body language." The team moved round. "You know the format of the quiz presumably, but I'll just run through it again. Every general knowledge question can gain a minimum of five points. And also each team gets six minutes on their specialist subjects." Power glanced at the *TopQuiz* book. Thankfully there were questions divided into subject areas. "Choosing a specialist area is easiest when you're doing a higher degree like a PhD or Masters and if you can specify a smaller area within that and it is accepted, it narrows things down and gives you more of an edge. Should you be unable to answer your specialist question, anyone else on your team can try, but beware, you only have five seconds to answer it or it automatically goes to the other side. It means that all the team needs to be thinking about every question all the time. You can't nod off when it's someone else's specialist question – if they don't know the answer you might."

"If an unanswered question passes over to you from the other team your captain should be the one who either takes it or nominates another team member. The technique in this game, the co-ordination – is as important as what you know." Power looked around the set up and couldn't see a clock. "You'll have to get a timer that's set to five seconds and can be reset repeatedly. And practice with that timer.

"The loss of a specialist question over to the other side is particularly bad news, because if they get your lost question right they get *ten* points.

"Then, there's the quickfire general knowledge free for all, that fills the rest of the show. You need to buzz in quick, but if you mess up the other side gets a go, so you do need to know the answer before you buzz."

- MURDER AND MALICE

Power looked at the team and thought they looked a little glazed over. "Let's try some specialist questions. I have my thumb here in the bioscience section of the book for Melanie. Now Jason is English and Madeleine is history. Let's try five questions of each." He pulled a wad of paper from his pocket to note down their scores. "Shall we switch the mikes on? Go live?"

Power cleared his throat, clicked his mike on and said, "OK." His voice boomed loudly round the bar and everybody in the bar stared at him. Someone, somewhere, lowered the sound to an appropriate level at which the quiz rehearsal would be audible to those who wanted to follow. Power thought he should include his audience, such as it was. "Good evening, my name's Professor Power and here is your Allminster team for this year's *TopQuiz*. They deserve your support. So can you please give them a big round of applause?" There was a smattering of applause around the room. Power feigned a look of disapproval. "Allminster, you can do better than that! Let's hear some noise. Let your team know you're here!" There was a further round of applause, thankfully much louder and more enthusiastic. "This is a rehearsal, so please don't call out the answers. Help the team concentrate and focus. First of all, I will ask the team to introduce themselves as they will on the program." And so Melanie, Jason and Madeleine duly, and nervously, introduced themselves and their subjects.

"Let's try the Specialist round now for questions in biomedicine, English and history. Five questions on each as a practice." And, one by one, Power read out his questions.

"What is the name of the tough membrane that covers the brain and spinal cord?"

"Which English physician published a work about the circulation of the blood in 1628?"

"Who won the Nobel Prize in Medicine in 1999 for work on protein signals that govern the organisation of the cell?"

"What is the name of socket of the hip joint?"

"Who discovered and developed the beta-antagonist drug propranolol?"

Power turned his attention to Jason and selected the quizbook's section on English. Jason was a tall, lanky red-haired student wearing a T-shirt celebrating the Black-Eyed Peas band. Power fixed his gaze on Jason's pale blue eyes. He saw anxiety clearly, and began Jason's questions in English.

"What was James Joyce's final novel published in 1939?"

"What is the name of Shirley Jackson's campus novel published in 1951?"

"Which US author wrote the works *Absalom* and *The Sound and the Fury*?"

"Which Shakespeare play features the characters Cassius, Casca and Cicero?"

"Which English author from Lichfield, Staffordshire, wrote both *The Lives of the Poets* and *The Life of Mr Richard Savage*?"

At first Jason's voice had been distinctly jittery, but as he proceeded, answering question-by-question correctly, his voice became bolder and more confident. With Jason's questions over, Power turned his attention to the last member of the team, Madeleine. Power smiled at her reassuringly. Madeleine had tightly curled red-brown hair that glistened under the bar's lights. She looked confident and smiled back. "Onwards, said Power. "With History."

"For how long, after her marriage in 1540, was the niece of the Duke of Norfolk the Queen Consort?"

"What is the name of the likely organism that caused the Black Death?"

"What year in the 20th century was the global pandemic called the Spanish Flu?"

"What year did Premier Gorbachev and President Reagan first meet?"

"Where did the Velvet Revolution happen?"

As he went through the questions with the team, Power corrected any of the wrong answers throughout the quiz and with the round over, he signalled to the bar staff to switch the microphones off. Power turned to the team. "How was that? How good was that? Quite a good start; ten questions answered right out of a possible fifteen, so at five points a question that's fifty points won. But when you answer incorrectly in this round the question passes to the other side, and so five questions would have transferred over and if they answered all five right they'd have earned *ten* points apiece, as there's a kind of penalty involved, so they'd have equalled your score.

"I think the lesson is that you specify your expertise clearly, answer most of your questions correctly and hope the other team doesn't share your area of expertise. OK, shall we have a break? We will do part Two of the Quiz in ten minutes." The team offered to buy him a drink and Professor Power calculated whether he could have another pint of Cheshire Cat. Reluctantly, he decided against a further beer. He needed to be safe to drive. Melanie and Jason went to fetch a round of drinks and bought Power a black decaffeinated coffee.

A student from the audience drawn to their rehearsal came over from her table to speak to Power. "Professor Power, the psychiatrist?" He looked up and smiled a bit warily at the slight, green-haired young woman in front of him. Her brown eyes stared at him through pebble glasses. "You're new to Allminster aren't you? I'm Natalie, I'm in archaeology, the third year Union Rep."

"Do you enjoy it?" asked Power, trying to deflect any conversation away from himself and wondering if, like some other strangers who approached him, she wanted to discuss his forensic cases. "Do you enjoy archaeology, I mean?"

"Sure," she said. "We've been unwrapping an Egyptian mummy at the Grosvenor Museum today. I'm one of the team working with Professor Morrison. It's his speciality. You don't get many mummies to unwrap these days."

"I suppose as far as mummies are concerned demand does exceed supply. They're not making any new ones, after all," said Power.

"Do you know Professor Shacklin?" asked Natalie, abruptly shifting the subject of conversation.

"I work with him," said Power. He was suddenly aware that the tone of his voice seemed to lack enthusiasm and communicated a reticence to discuss the man. When exactly had he lost faith in his line manager at the University? "I don't know him very well."

"Well, he's not welcome here, in the Students' Union. There's a kind of informal ban on him coming in here."

"Ah," said Power, wondering what conversation would follow. He felt that he was expected to ask why, and dreaded the answer that would be forthcoming. "A ban?"

"Since last year. He attended the teaching awards in the Union. The students nominate their favourite lecturers annually."

"We never had anything as progressive as that when I was a student," as soon as he said this he reflected that the comment made him seem antediluvian.

"Shacklin attended on behalf of the University senior team. He wasn't nominated for anything. I mean no-one would consider him an actual academic. He's an administrator."

Power was mildly irritated by Natalie, but he felt he should not be – that wouldn't be fair. He paused and then asked the only question the situation demanded. He was dreading the answer, "What did he do?"

"He made advances to a friend of mine. Under the table, if you see what I mean. I'm wondering what should happen?"

"Did the Union make a complaint? Did the student make a complaint to HR?"

"You know how difficult it is to jump through those hoops. They're too formal. How can she complain when he oversees everything?"

Like many people in such a position, Power was reluctant to be embroiled in the issue. Nevertheless, Power had a strong sense of right and wrong and felt a duty to do something. "I could talk to her," he offered. "See what could be done, maybe accompany her to speak to the Vice Chancellor?"

Natalie's tense face relaxed as if some anxiety inside her had been dispelled. "Thank you for the offer. I think you probably do listen. People say that. They say you are the doctor who listens. I mean I know someone who was a patient of yours, and she said you listened and heard her. No, really I just wanted to warn you about the people you're working with."

"I think some deans are aware of the problem . . ." Power was thinking of McFarlane. An image of Felfe also came to him. In his mind's eye he saw Felfe talking to him at the table in the Grosvenor Hotel, over that ridiculously expensive lunch. Heard his words about Shacklin again, spoken in his Berliner accent, "I have plenty of evidence on Shacklin, but the time to act against him is not now."

"It doesn't matter for now," said Natalie. "You'd better get on with the second half. I'm sorry to disturb you. Thank you, though."

"You can come and see me another time if you like?" offered Power.

"Shacklin needs castrating is all. That would solve the problem." Natalie turned away and walked through the crowd and out of the double doors at the far end of the bar.

Chapter Eleven

Though it be honest, it is never good
To bring bad news. Give to a gracious message
An host of tongues, but let ill tidings tell
Themselves when they be felt.
Shakespeare, Antony and Cleopatra

That morning, Professor Power was due to have a telephone discussion with the General Medical Council about the new medical school. The GMC regulated all medical education in England and Power knew that some approval by the GMC was crucial for his project. No matter what insults and jibes various deans had thrown at him, Power was undeterred and quietly determined to complete his great work. Before he made his telephone call Power dived into one of the many campus cafes to get a coffee to take back to his office.

The queue of students and academics, shuffled *en masse,* like a thirsty caterpillar, towards a harassed catering employee battling with a capricious espresso machine. Power stood at the back of the caterpillar, waiting his turn and in due course was joined by Rob Willett.

"Good morning!" he said. "How did the rehearsal for *TopQuiz* go? I hear our faculty has a student on the team?"

"Yes, I met him." said Power. "Jason. He did well."

"Jason's a bright chap," said Willett. "When is the real contest? The recording, I mean."

"It's only a few weeks away," said Power. "Ideally we should have had a few months of rehearsals. I need to get them to practice their buzzer technique. Speed is essential."

Sir Rob laughed. "Buzzer practice! If you want a real advantage you should give them something to put in the other team's coffee in the green room. LSD or something. That'd make things interesting, wouldn't it? You could get something, as a doctor, couldn't you?" Power was momentarily appalled, and seeing his expression, Sir Rob back-pedalled. "No need to look so affronted Professor P., I am joking, of course."

"Of course," said Power, wondering if stress was making Willett careless in his choice of wording. "But this is Allminster, not Porterhouse." Power was referring to the campus novel, *Porterhouse Blue*, by Tom Sharpe.

Willett chuckled, but his laughter was strained by anxiety and he wondered whether he could presume to ask Power's advice and help again. He did not do so, however, and instead watched Power leaving with his coffee, and collected his own green tea, before walking slowly across the Memorial Garden in the centre of the University towards the Senate House. The bursar eked out his existence in a cold office on the northerly side of Senate House. Willett moved slowly between the frosted twigs of the leafless shrubs. The wintery sun shone on him as he experimented mentally with different phrases he could use to explain himself to the bursar.

Michaelmas term was drawing to its close. The students were making plans to go home for the Christmas holidays. Willett felt that with the prospect of the end of term he should be feeling happier. He resented the invidious burden of *The Wasp* chapter. Poetry from Larkin ran through his mind. *'And so it stays just on the edge of vision, A small unfocused blur, a standing chill, That slows each impulse down to indecision'*. He mumbled to himself, "A horrid poem: so grim, so real." Trying to shake off his gloom he strode more purposefully along the garden paths towards Senate House.

Hamish Grieg's office was just down the corridor from the Vice Chancellor's, but it was a world away in terms of comfort. A single, narrow window opened to the dull, dim light of northerly skies. The floor was unadorned parquet, worn pale grey with time. Grieg's double pedestal desk had been a utility design from the nineteen-fifties. And as it still functioned as designed Grieg saw no earthly point in parting with it.

The bursar stood up and bowed as Sir Rob Willett entered his domain and invited him to sit in one of the leather tub chairs.

"Good morning, Bursar!" Willett said in as jovial a manner as he could muster. He wore a grin on his face, like a rictus mask. He shook hands with Grieg. Willett refrained from squeezing the bursar's claw too much as he felt if he applied just a mite too much pressure the bones inside would crack and crumble to dust.

"Good morning, Sir Robert," said Grieg. "What can I do for you? I must warn you now that there can be no faculty budget negotiations until March 2005."

Sir Rob looked into the two deep orbital pits that held Grieg's piercing blue eyes and saw no joy there. There was a whiff of something medicinal about the man, as if he had been infused with embalming fluid already. What was the smell? Something about it reminded him of the school nurse's office. The nurse once tended his cuts as a boy, and there had been this very smell, but Willett still could not identify it.

"I thought I might see you about something. Ask you for your opinion first. You know the Vice Chancellor well, don't you?"

"I report to him daily, he maintains a close eye on the finances," said Grieg automatically.

"Ah," said Sir Rob, aware that the bursar had neatly evaded the essence of his question. "But you see other colleagues on a daily basis; the secretaries and so on. What I mean is . . . you get on with the Vice Chancellor, don't you?"

"I see a lot of people very often," said Grieg. I see my pets morning and night, but if you ask me whether I know their minds and feelings? I should say not."

Sir Rob wondered whether the effort of conversation was worth the struggle. He had jokingly described Grieg as like a robot to Power, and now wondered if his jest had been more accurate than ever he knew. "You still keeping reptiles then?" Sir Rob threw out this ill-considered question, driven by a feeling of impending panic as he tried to find some strain of humanity in the calculating machine that was the bursar. "What kinds?"

Grieg frowned. "Slow worms. (They're like a legless lizard). Some salamanders. A few snakes."

Sir Rob struggled for any kind of sociable rejoinder upon a topic so alien to him. "When they die, can you eat them?" As soon as he asked this, he realised the absurdity of his words and how he risked seeming even less human than the bursar himself.

Hamish Grieg did indeed seem perturbed by Willett's last remark. "I wouldn't describe any great warmth or deep affection for my collection," said Grieg. "But I wouldn't describe myself as being cold or callous towards them either. You think I eat such strange flesh?"

"Not at all, not at all, please forgive me. I don't know why it came into my head. It was an unthinking remark to make. I just heard that some people do eat reptiles. I'm sorry about the remark, it was ill-judged. To tell you the truth my morale is as low as a badger's arse."

Grieg frowned at the use of such language and thought it best ignored. "I feel it is imperative to emphasise that I don't eat reptiles," said Grieg, looking heavenwards and surreptitiously scratching at a terrific itch below his shirt.

"Look," said Willett, uncomfortably. "Maybe I should just cut to the chase. The Vice Chancellor has asked me to verify the status of a manuscript the University bought. *The Wasp* chapter by Lewis Carroll. Are you aware of it?" Grieg nodded impassively. "Can I confirm with you, as bursar, how much the University invested?"

"I am not at liberty to divulge exactly how much the Vice Chancellor invested. It was one of his personal projects. I may not know him as closely as you might seem to wish, but I know he feels very deeply *indeed* about the Carroll manuscript. The University will, no doubt, be very grateful to you for verifying it. There will be a budget for a press launch and so on, new money for the promotion of courses in your faculty."

"But how much did the University actually pay for it?"

"I cannot confirm to you the price that was paid. The seller insisted on a non-disclosure agreement. I can't even confirm to you which budget paid for it, or indeed if the University did pay for it. My lips are sealed. Sealed for me, I might add. It is not in my nature to be obstructive, or unhelpful."

"Five hundred thousand?"

"I really can't say," said the bursar, but he pointed up to the ceiling implying that the costs had exceeded this.

Sir Rob Willett groaned. "I think there's a problem with it. I can't put my hand on my heart and say I believe it is one hundred per cent genuine."

"Ah," said the bursar, and his eyes were gimlets probing Willett's soul. "That would be very unfortunate indeed. May I ask, have you told anyone of your concerns?"

"No, no," said Willett, not altogether truthfully, as he had spoken to Professor Power.

"I wouldn't tell anyone if I were you. The value of the document lies precisely in the *possibility* it is genuine. If you destroy that possibility then it becomes worthless, and thus an asset becomes a liability. Worse still for the University, a reputational liability. What analyses have you done that support the possibility it is genuine?"

"It incorporates words and ideas that Carroll wouldn't have used," blustered Sir Rob.

"With the greatest respect for you as a knight of the realm, that's not quite what I asked, is it? I asked you what analyses you had done that *support* the possibility it is genuine?"

"Well, we have run the chapter through a computer text analysis program and compared it to the original *Looking Glass* text that we know Carroll wrote. It has the same analytical elements such as language complexity, use of adjectives, words per sentence and expressive style as Carroll."

"That all sounds pretty convincing to me."

"But it isn't genuine. It isn't this 'new idea' that the Vice Chancellor wants."

"Well, an absolutely new idea is one of the rarest things known to man, isn't that what they say?" Grieg scratched himself under his ribs on account of the burlap vest concealed beneath his starched white shirt. He looked forward to six o'clock when he could walk back into his flat in town and shed the vest. He always put a bottle of witchhazel to cool in the fridge to apply to his irritated skin at night.

"It's a fake," said Sir Rob, desperately. "I need to commission a chemical analysis of the ink and paper to confirm it, but I already know it cannot be real."

"But Sir Robert, if you haven't done *those* analyses, you don't *know* for sure that the manuscript is not genuine."

"I wonder if you could tell the Vice Chancellor? And maybe intimate to him that, the manuscript isn't all he had hoped?"

"Ah, that's why you wanted to see me, I see now, hmmm," Hamish Grieg pursed his lips and put his hands together and sighed. "You wished me to see the Vice Chancellor for you to cushion the blow as it were? Insulate you from his displeasure maybe?"

"I was hoping it might come better from you," said Sir Robert.

"But it is the bearer of bad tidings that necessarily incurs the master's wrath," said the bursar. "I rather think this news may be best delivered by your good self. You are sailing your own vessel here, and you wouldn't abandon your ship now, because of ill winds would you?"

Sir Robert stared glumly at the parquet floor, marveling in a dissociated way at how the pieces of wood intersected with one another in a neat herringbone fashion. He had hoped so very much that the bursar would help him.

"I can see that it's troubling you greatly," said Grieg. "I must admit I am also something of a coward where the Vice Chancellor is concerned. I couldn't bear to upset the man you see. He has a weak heart. Two years ago he collapsed in his office. The secretaries called me in. There he was – face all purple and bloated. 'Call the ambulance' I told them. And I watched the paramedic re-start his heart with the defibrillator. I accompanied him in the ambulance to intensive care. I handed him over to his wife when she arrived. You understand me? Do you understand now, and, forgive me please, understand why I am such a coward in this regard?"

"I didn't know he'd been so ill," said Willett. "That he'd nearly died."

"We chose not to broadcast the collapse," said the bursar. "The succession planning issues we faced made us cautious . . . we would have had to install Professor Shacklin as acting Vice Chancellor. We thought it best not to make too much of the Vice Chancellor's collapse. And that proved to be the right decision, because he was back in his office within a fortnight."

Willett wondered what group of people were subsumed within the bursar's use of the pronoun 'we'. Clearly the 'we' included the bursar but did not include Shacklin, the Executive Pro Vice Chancellor, ostensibly the Vice Chancellor's second-in-command; had the bursar schemed with Mrs Armitage, to maintain her husband's authority?

"But if *you* can't tell the Vice Chancellor . . ."

"Because of his heart, you see," said Grieg apologetically.

"Then how can I tell him?" asked Sir Robert, who did not relish the idea of slaying the Vice Chancellor with the truth.

"Can I advise you, then?" asked Grieg. "Will you perhaps consider my poor advice?"

"Go on. What consolation have you got for me?" asked Willett.

"From what you have told me," said the bursar, "you can still make some positive remarks about the manuscript that respect the possibility it is genuine."

"But it's not," protested Sir Robert. "It can't be genuine."

"You issue an *interim* report. You praise the story in the manuscript. You describe it as heartwarming, fun, likeable, a lost gem. All that might be true, yes? You mention that the research you have done – the computer analysis you did – supports the theory it is just like something else written by Lewis Carroll – *Through the Looking Glass*, I think you said. You maintain the possibility it is real without committing yourself. By maintaining that possibility you are maintaining the value of the asset. You cover all eventualities, however, by saying that this is an interim report and your opinion *is* provisional. You would like to see a chemical analysis of the ink and the paper, if the University Trustees will allow this, you understand there is some reluctance to interfere with or damage the manuscript but you look forward to the analysis in due course. Everybody's face is saved. The Vice Chancellor will be pleased he spotted the potential in the manuscript, when he sanctioned its purchase. The press have themselves an interesting story of a lost chapter found; and the story in the chapter itself can go in the Sunday supplements for the children. Everyone is happy. The value of the asset is maintained. And at the end of the day, I am happy, because the accounts are square." Grieg held up a hand before Sir Robert could speak. "Don't say anything now, please. Think about my advice."

"But I need to see the Vice Chancellor," said Willett. "Surely I must warn him."

"I would counsel you to mull over what I have said for a few days at least before you approach the Vice Chancellor. I think you will find that my solution satisfies everybody, and still maintains your academic credibility."

"But when they chemically analyse the manuscript, when I have to make my final report . . ." said Sir Robert.

"For all you or I know at this very moment, the manuscript might well be the right age, it might already have the right ink, already have the right paper."

"But when they test it . . ."

"*If* they test it," said the bursar. "And maybe they never will test it. Perhaps the Trustees will never give permission for chemical testing. Maybe we will just hang on to the manuscript like some Cathedral relic; the skull of Becket or something like that."

"You know, I wish the Vice Chancellor had never asked me, I wish I'd never seen the wretched manuscript," said Sir Robert.

"Ah," said the bursar. "Old manuscripts inevitably involve dirty hands."

* * *

Power got up before dawn, after an uneasy night's sleep. The house was still dark and as he shaved and washed in the bathroom the December morning's chill made clouds out of his breath. He dressed quickly to get warm; a neatly pressed shirt and newly laundered suit. He ate hot porridge with honey, and sipped black coffee in the warmth if the kitchen.

By 6.30 a.m. he was at the station in Alderley Edge, and by 7.30 a.m. he was getting off the train at Crewe. There was a scurry up and across various stairs and gantries to reach the platform for the London train. At 7.40 he was joined on the platform by Andrew Lynch, freshly arrived from Chester. Two minutes later they were seated opposite each other in the Pullman coach to Euston.

"You're looking smart," said Lynch, admiring his companion's black Jaeger coat, and the brilliance and sheen of his blue silk tie. It was usually Lynch who dressed to impress.

"I didn't sleep much last night," said Power. "Anxious. Not every day you meet the Government's Chief Medical Officer."

"Well, well, what is this? Anxiety in a psychiatrist?" asked Lynch teasingly. "Physician heal thyself . . . but, to be fair, it's quite a thing you are doing isn't it? Starting a medical school from scratch. We're very proud of you, Carl. Pamela tells everyone in Handbridge village that you're bringing a medical school to the city. I'm very proud of you. There's no need to be nervous. Just talk straight to the CMO. You're both doctors. There'll be an understanding, I'm sure. If you like . . . although you may not share exactly the same beliefs as I . . . and few do these days . . . I will pray for your mission today. Prayer is more effective than you may think. Especially when many pray, great things may be accomplished in the Lord's name."

"Thank you, Andrew. I've had the arguments for a new medical school running through my brain all night. In this country we only have three doctors per one thousand people. In Argentina they have four, in Germany and Belgium they have five. The population of the UK is increasing. More doctors work part time and are retiring early. A proportion of trainee doctors never finish their training. It's difficult to recruit doctors in North Wales, Shropshire and Cheshire, and finally, there are five hundred thousand people local to Allminster not covered by a nearby medical school. Having one will drive up the quality of local healthcare and fuel new research. I've got dozens more figures and percentages whirling through my mind."

"What time is your meeting?" asked Lynch.

"Eleven," said Power. "I'm glad you're with me on the journey there, anyway."

"A happy coincidence that we both needed to travel to London on the same day. My meeting at the Crown Prosecution Service is at ten thirty." Lynch brought out his battered copy of the *London A to Z*, and flicked through the pages for the CPS HQ Queen Anne's Gate in Westminster. "You'll probably need the underground station at Elephant and Castle."

"For Hannibal House, yes," said Power. The Virgin rail steward arrived and took Lynch's order for tea and what the menu promised to be a 'Great British Breakfast'. Power wondered whether to have a second breakfast and decided he would drink apple juice and munch jam and toast to settle his jittery nerves.

"And you," said Power. "How do you feel about your meeting with the Prosecution Service?"

"I don't know quite how I feel. I have done my work as best I can." Lynch patted the fat bundle of papers he had been reading. "This is the distillation. A report that sums up the evidence I've collated over the last six months on the case. The sworn statements of witnesses. Men and women who were abused. Enough to charge and convict ten men. Probably more. That fat slug of an MP included. Beresford has worked tirelessly. The Foundation has done all the legwork. It's a case they just need to run with. I should be feeling . . . satisfied. And I am not. Maybe the Lord is forewarning me. I have prayed, myself, for the success of my errand, but I am full of foreboding and I don't know why."

"Well," said Power. "If you cannot reflect, let me be your glass."

"It would be a case of through a glass darkly, I think," said Lynch. "We both started the Foundation because we thought that justice wasn't being done – that cases that deserved justice weren't being investigated, or even if they were investigated, not properly. And here I am with one of the fruits of that labour, going down to London to persuade the 'powers that be' at the CPS about the merits of the case. The facts are here," he gestured to the bundle. "Why must we lobby so hard to see justice done for these young women? Why must *we* encourage others to see what is in plain sight in front of them, and why must *we* then have to press them to do their jobs?" Lynch sighed and looked out of the window. "Too many people protecting that slug. And the newspapers tell us that the Director of Public Prosecutions, the DPP, has never even prosecuted a case in his life? He is said to care more about defending the human rights of the accused. A DPP that has never been a prosecution lawyer? Have you ever heard the like, Carl? It would be like having a Chief Constable who had never made an arrest. Or a doctor who'd never seen a dead body."

Power nodded. "I heard that he works with the Prime Minister's wife."

"So, you can appreciate why I'm glum," said Lynch. "The Lord taught us to be wise as serpents but as harmless as doves. Sometimes I'm tempted to think a more robust line is necessary."

Power thought about the quote. "Is it more about being wise to what's going on around you? Being aware, but not necessarily responding in kind? Not meeting corruption with corruption, or bullying with bullying?"

"I would agree, but it doesn't mean you should just accept what's dished out to you. It just means you shouldn't necessarily fight fire with fire."

"So, if you're being bullied? I appreciate you might say don't retaliate with similar behaviour, but what would you suggest someone does?"

Lynch looked out of the train window at the green, rain-soaked hills careering past. "When Jesus was slapped by the High Priest, he did not accept it. He questioned the basis of why the priest slapped him." He looked more closely at his friend. "Are you being bullied?"

"They have tried to bully me. I know every school has its bullies. And really a University is just a school writ large. Academics just use different tactics. Sly comments, attempts to destabilize and undermine. I was just interested in how *you* might tackle it."

"Call it out," said Lynch. "The principle being, that in naming the demon you gain control over it."

They separated at Euston to make their solo journeys to their meetings.

Later they met in St James's Park at a restaurant called *Inn The Park*. Power ordered garlic and spelt risotto, and Lynch chose rump of lamb with pea puree. Afterwards, well-fed and replete, they shared a taxi to Euston to catch the train back to Chester. Lynch made appreciative comments about Power's success with the Chief Medical Officer, who had welcomed Power's notion of a new kind of medical school, which emphasized a more holistic care for the mind as well as the body. The training numbers made sense and he was encouraged to make his bid for funding. If Lynch felt dispirited at being rebuffed by the Crown Prosecution Service he did not show it. He merely made one comment when Power asked him about how much he minded the apparent waste of months of work. Lynch had shrugged, "I predicted as much. They will not act, even though the truth is laid out before them. Sometimes I wonder if the sin of omission is as bad as the sin of commission. To do nothing?" he shook his head sadly. "It is a measure of how inept the system is, or how deep the corruption lies. That route is closed to us for now, these people do not care; we must think again and pray for guidance."

They arrived back in the early evening. Lynch set off from the station in Chester to walk home to Handbridge village. Power took a taxi to the University, where invited academics were assembling outside the Lecture Halls for an inaugural lecture.

The ritual of the inaugural lecture is an academic hurdle for every newly appointed professor. Most Universities expect all their professors to pass the rite of expounding for an hour or more about their particular field of research in front of their peers. The lectures usually have some form of humorous twist. This evening Power had been invited to a biology professor's lecture amusingly titled;

What liquid costs £30 million per gallon?
or
Why you should own a scorpion farm.

Power's taxi arrived just as the audience was filtering into the lecture theatre. He found a seat on the back row, sat back, and relaxed after his long day. The Vice Chancellor rose with some difficulty to introduce the professor with a few *bon mots* and sat down wiping his brow with a voluminous, starched, white linen handkerchief. Armitage was wearing full academic regalia, all red piping and plush, purple velvet, and the lights were hot. His face was puce-coloured. The lecture was entertaining, bright, and Power enjoyed it. At one point the newly-minted professor touched on philosophy and biology and made a loosely related joke, which amused Power, saying, "A horse walked into a bar and ordered a pint of bitter and a side order of oats. The landlord said, 'You're in here pretty often these days, do you worry that you're an alcoholic?' The horse disagreed and said, 'I don't think I am,' and promptly disappears from existence. The joke is about Descartes' famous philosophy – cogito ergo sum, but to explain that part before the rest of the joke would be putting Descartes before the horse."

As the general audience drifted away, invited guests trooped across the quadrangle and into the Refectory for a reception and five-course dinner. As he had been invited to the reception Power nibbled asparagus canapés and sipped a small glass of plum-red Rioja. The Vice Chancellor, in less formal and altogether cooler attire, glided serenely over to him, with a seeming grace and élan that some overweight men can achieve with practice. He was carrying an Elgin glass with a thimble-full of sherry in it. Despite his huge appetite for food the Vice Chancellor deplored people who drank. "Good evening, Professor Power, are you dining with us tonight?" Armitage already knew he was not, for he loved spending time planning every aspect of the formal dinners he hosted.

"I'm afraid not, Vice Chancellor, I must get home to see my son before he falls asleep."

"Admirable," said Armitage nodding wisely, "a family man, good, good. And you've had a long day in London, I know. I remember these things. Went the day well? Were you successful?"

"The Chief Medical Officer gave Allminster's bid for a medical school his personal seal of approval," said Power, with just a hint of pride in his voice.

The Vice Chancellor beamed. "I knew you could do it, where others could not." He indicated with his eyes towards the small cluster of people around Dean McFarlane. "Well, you must come and tell me more about it in the next few days. Please make an appointment. I must go and congratulate the professor on his excellent lecture. Who knew arachnids could be so valuable? It will be your inaugural lecture soon. You'll have to think of a title. And my chef and I will have to plan the menu. You're vegetarian aren't you?" Power nodded. "Well, we can plan the entire menu to reflect that. Good evening, Professor Power, and keep me informed." Canon Armitage drifted off towards the biology professor who had given the lecture. He had brought his family with him to share in the dinner.

Power stood alone for a moment, feeling as awkward as ever at such a social occasion. The happy sound of other people's conversation bubbled around him, leaving him untouched. He wondered for a moment what topic he could possibly choose to entertain an audience of his peers at his inaugural lecture, and already felt a knot of anxiety gripping and twisting his stomach. Power looked again at the group of women around McFarlane. She was telling jokes and laughing. On the edge of the group was her assistant dean, Caroline. Seeing Power unattended she peeled herself away from the group and veered toward him, selecting a beef and horseradish cracker from a tray, as if to justify her leaving her group. Power felt uneasy as she approached, glaring silently into his face as she munched the canapé. She continued to stare up at him with angry brown eyes as she finished her mouthful. "It's all food with the Vice Chancellor," she said. Power wondered if she was about to make a joke, but there was no humour in her face. "There's a five course dinner planned. And I saw him eating a full plate of sandwiches on his own, in a room by the lecture theatre, just before the lecture. It's all appetite with men isn't it?" She stood up on her tiptoes so she could push her face into Power's, and hissed at him. "Stay away from her," and then, just as abruptly, turned and walked away.

Power stood perplexed for a moment wondering if this latest unpleasant experience really had happened. The moment felt unreal.

Before he could respond or process what had just been said to him, there was another voice at his shoulder. This time it was a familiar voice from times past, and altogether welcome, "Dr Power? Is it you?"

"Graham Allen!" said Power. "Last time I met you we were both at the Royal Liverpool."

"That it was," said Dr Allen. When Power had last known him, Allen had been a thin, medical student who dined on Pot Noodles and worked late into the night, fuelling his studies with caffeine. Power had been his tutor. "You have an astonishing memory, Dr Power." Dr Allen was now a portlier version of himself and dressed in country tweeds. He, in turn, noticed that Dr Power, now elevated to Professor Power, was slimmer, and greying slightly at the temples.

"What are you doing now?" asked Power.

"I'm a GP in the city centre," said Allen. "I actually look after your Vice Chancellor, although I shouldn't say that. He invited me along. What are you doing here?"

"Would you believe that I'm trying to set up a medical school?" said Power. "I should probably come and see you and your partners officially, I need to get support from local doctors. You know, I thought I'd face opposition from national bodies like the GMC and the Department of Health, but, no, to my surprise the opposition I face is all internal."

"We'd love to have students in our practice," said Allen. "Really. Do come and see us. But I can't believe that you're finding opposition at the University itself?

"What I'm finding," said Power. "Is a dish of murder and malice."

Allen frowned, "That bad?"

"I shouldn't complain," said Power, although the outburst from McFarlane's assistant dean made him want to complain, bitterly, to his old acquaintance. He realised that politically he must present the University in a good light to gain the support the medical school would require to succeed. "The Vice Chancellor is very keen on a Faculty of Medicine."

"And why wouldn't he be?" said Allen. "It would be a huge income stream for the University. Medicine is traditionally a course that's always full of students – over a five-year course that's lucrative. And there's the research medicine would attract. Pharmaceutical companies. Big money."

Power exchanged his University card with Allen's own and began preparing to leave as the drinks party was beginning to move into the dining room for the evening's meal. Power made his way, as unobtrusively as possible, towards the cloakroom to get his coat. Bridget McFarlane stood in his way, caught hold of his arm and prevented his progress. When she spoke, her breath smelt heavy with alcohol.

"The Vice Chancellor told me just now about your scuttling off to London. Without me. You're a bit of a snake, aren't you?"

"I'm sorry," said Power. "I don't know . . ."

"Oh, you know very well," sneered McFarlane. Her sing-song voice was slurred with wine. "You may think you have got a win, but it's an easy win, and you'll need real experience when it comes to developing a curriculum and negotiating with the Region for the revenue to run your school. And that's exactly what you lack, experience, *and* integrity. Do you want to know what will happen? When you've got it all set up, the Vice Chancellor will just cast you aside in favour of an experienced hand. He might have promised you the dean's role, but you'll never get it." She repeated her point in a taunting tone. "You've been taken in by empty promise, Doctor. You'll do all the spadework, the heavy lifting, and he'll turn round and give the medical school to a dean to run." She pointed to her own chest and sniffed at him. "Someone with a proven track record.

Power, more annoyed than he ever liked to get, took a deep breath, sighed, and smiled at her sardonically, "Ah, Bridget. Under the influence of both the demon drink and the green-eyed monster I perceive. That's the second time you've made a comment like that. You're repeating yourself. Demeaning behaviour for a faculty dean, don't you think, and completely unjustified on my account. The fact of the matter is that I am the one who has been asked by the Vice Chancellor to bring the medical school to Chester and I fully intend to succeed. It is set in motion; the ball is rolling, and you won't stop it. Your bullying tactics won't work with me."

"Oh, my!" McFarlane feigned shock. "I'm no bully."

"That's how I perceive what you are doing," said Power. "Forgive me, but you're treating me as some insignificant pawn."

McFarlane gawped at him, open mouthed, then gathered herself to threaten him. "I'll finish you, nevertheless. Your career at Allminster is over."

"I don't think so," said Power, "and if when you sober up in the morning you have a change of heart perhaps you can ask yourself why you *need* to behave like this towards people? And if you can bring yourself to act in a civilised manner, and better still, if you find yourself able to support the medical school, then I would be willing to overlook this insulting behaviour. But in any case, an improved attitude on your behalf would make life more pleasant for all of us." He glanced at his watch, "I really do have to go now. Good night to you. Try to enjoy the rest of your evening."

McFarlane was gathering her words as Power began to turn away and just about to launch into a tirade when her partner pushed her way between the pair of them.

"Leave it, Bridget! What are you doing? He's not worth it!" Caroline grabbed her arm and dragged her away towards the dining room. The Vice Chancellor could be glimpsed inside saying grace. The dean and her partner were the last to sit down at table. As Power shrugged on his coat, he saw that Caroline's hand gripped Dean McFarlane's bare upper arm so tightly that her flesh was dimpled and blanched under the glossy, dark blue, painted talons of her lover.

Chapter Twelve

The pursuit of the good and evil are now linked in astronomy as in almost all science. The fate of human civilization will depend on whether the rockets of the future carry the astronomer's telescope or a hydrogen bomb.

Sir Bernard Lovell

At 5 p.m. on a Monday evening, in the third week of December, Power found himself standing on a chilly pavement outside the TV studios in Quay Street, Manchester. Laura and Jo huddled close to him for warmth. The street was dark, and the moon was a waxing crescent in the night, but the lights of the TV studios blazed behind their plate glass frontage. The queue for the filming of *TopQuiz* stretched back 200 yards down Atherton Street. Power and his family had travelled into the city centre by car. They had dined early on endless pizza, much to Jo's satisfaction. Clutching their tickets, the queue gradually inched its way into the lights and warmth of the entrance hall. Jo was excited that audience members had to be patted down and have their bags checked.

"Why are they doing that?" he asked, watching the Vice Chancellor being frisked some yards ahead of them.

"To see if he's smuggled any pork pies in," muttered Power under his breath.

"It's security," said Laura, addressing Jo's question more

appropriately than his father. "There was a year that students in the audience had sneaked in Roman Candle fireworks and let them off in the studio. Another time they brought in bags of flour and threw them at Giles."

"Who's Giles?" asked Jo.

"The quiz master, Giles Masefield." said Power, pointing to signs that adorned the foyer with Giles's grinning mug on. The signs announced:

TopQuiz,
Number One University Quiz

Filming tonight:
Allminster v Cor Christi
and
Manchester v Liverpool

"Giles looks like an idiot," said Jo disparagingly.

"Well," said Power, noting that his son could be very forthright sometimes. "Keep your voice down. We don't want to affect Allminster's chances. They need all the help they can get. We're up against Cambridge's best team. Out of all of the colleges at Cambridge it was Cor Christi College that won through to compete for them. And that's who Allminster have their first match with. What an unfortunate draw!"

"Cor Christi are on top form," said a voice behind Power. He turned round to see a middle-aged man with a crisp powder-blue suit, silver curly hair, Zeiss spectacles and green eyes. His wife stood by him, clutching his arm. "I'm sorry, we couldn't help but overhear. Our son, Glyn Roberts, is on the Cor Christi team. They are all superb quizzers. Allminster have as much chance of winning as a hedgehog under a steam roller."

"But nobody did ask your opinion," said Laura, as she and Power made their way to the checkpoint. They followed the queue of people in front of them as it wound through a corridor and into the main studio where assistants checked their tickets. There was a single tier of seats, raked at an angle facing the set. At the far end of the seating the production team, director, producer and announcer sat in an area separated from the audience by only a waist high screen. A young girl with a headset and microphone seated Power and family at the end of a row adjacent to this production zone. There was a reasonable view of the set where the teams would sit, but Jo was thrilled that if he peered over the low, black canvas screen he could see the mixing console and screens in the production booth. "That's where the director and producer sit when they mix the programme together," Power told his son. Jo was fascinated by the screens and consoles and at being so close that he could, if he wanted, reach over and touch the production equipment. Power looked around the studio.

The audience were all seated in a steeply raked tier of seats that overlooked a square studio, surrounded by black, noise deadening curtains that stretched from the shiny studio floor to the concrete coffered ceiling. The studio floor was painted a glossy black. Aluminium gantries crisscrossed the lofty space and Power saw a wiry young man adjusting the spotlights that shone on the two desks where the contestants usually sat. He crossed to a ladder in the darkness of the far right corner of the studio and slid down it. Other technicians were affixing the Perspex signs that read 'Allminster' and 'Cor Christi' on the front of the teams' respective desks.

On the right, some yards in front of the production booth, was the quiz master's desk. A slim girl, called Annie, a brunette with a pony-tail that swished about as she moved, was sorting out seven stacks of questions on the quiz master's desk. Power thought she looked nervous and pale. He noticed her hands were shaking.

Power scanned the audience around him. The pompous father of one of the Cor Christi team had thankfully been seated far away from them on the left, down on the front row. To his surprise he found that the Vice Chancellor had been seated on the row behind his, slightly to his left. The Vice Chancellor nodded to him and smiled, "I hope the team does you credit, Professor Power."

The floor manager, an elegant middle-aged woman with long blonde hair, moved to a central point in front of the audience and beamed at everyone. "Good evening, ladies and gentleman! Thank you for venturing out on a cold December night. Welcome to Studio 12 where we always film *TopQuiz*. It's the largest studio here. Larger than Studio 2 where they film *University Challenge*. We have a larger live audience too, so . . . let's make some noise to greet our presenter, *TopQuiz* quiz master, Giles Masefield!"

The audience duly erupted into applause as the star of the show, Giles Masefield, skipped blithely onto the set and beamed at the audience. "There you are!" he shouted and the audience began a second round of applause for his catch phrase. "Ha ha, yes, *there you are* and *here we are* in Studio 12. As Sammy said, we have a larger live audience than Jeremy Paxman, and not to boast, with syndication, we have a larger global audience too, particularly in Australia and the USA. *TopQuiz* on Channel 4 beats anything on BBC 2," he laughed. "We've been Number One since 1990! And this is our fourteenth season as the premier academic quiz. And please folks, be kind to me, I've been filming episodes since Friday and if my voice seems a little hoarse you know why! These are the last episodes we are filming for a few weeks. We film the episodes in bursts you see. We'll complete the first round tonight and we will film the rest of the series in the New Year. We might see some of you returning then, if your team survives tonight! OK, I'll leave you with Sammy. I have to go put on my scarf!" The audience cheered.

"Why did they cheer, Dad?" asked Jo.

"It's his thing. Like his inane catch phrase – 'There you are,'" said Power. "It's just that he wears a different coloured scarf in every episode. He's . . . very . . ." Power struggled for the right word. "Flamboyant. He's very flamboyant."

Sammy, the floor manager, took over again and introduced the director, producer and announcer as they entered the production booth next to Jo. Then she asked the audience to stand and give an ovation to the Allminster and Cor Christi teams as they emerged from the green room into the studio. Power dutifully stood up and clapped enthusiastically as the two teams made their bashful, blushing way onto the set and took their seats. Technicians scurried around adjusting the height of the contestants' seats to raise the smaller students and lower the tallest ones so that their eyes would appear at the same height on the TV screen.

Jo was leaning over the side of the production booth watching the production crew at work. They didn't seem to mind and smiled good-naturedly at him, explaining what they were doing and pointing out which screen was fed by which particular camera on the studio floor. Two cameras provided close ups and medium shots of the contestants. Another was trained on Giles Masefield throughout. "My dad was on *TopQuiz* once," Jo volunteered spontaneously. "Before he was old that is." His father sighed.

Power scrutinised the Cambridge team to see if they were as confident as the father of one of them had implied. There was a female contestant, with long orange hair, who was fussing about the placement of their mascot, a Valentine's heart with black eyes, a toothy grin and sprouting droopy arms and legs. In the middle of the trio was a blonde, crew-cut man with a jutting jaw. He wore a blue and white Chicago Cubs shirt. On the right of the trio, facing Power directly, was a sallow youth with long brown hair which fell all over his shoulders, brown eyes, and horseshoe moustache. He wore a Grateful Dead T shirt and looked as if he had been sucked through a time tunnel that stretched from 2004 back to the 1970s. A makeup assistant was fluttering about him trying to comb his hair. He waved her away irritably. Power felt reassured that the Cambridge team did not look relaxed. By comparison the Allminster team, Melanie, Jason and Madeleine looked at ease and seemed to be enjoying the attention of make-up technicians. The floor manager was admiringly arranging their mascot, Allminster's fluffy Cheshire Cat, on the desk in front of them.

Presently all was ready in the studio. The lighting was perfect and all the students were present, groomed and aligned. Power thought the quiz master and star must be delaying his entrance for dramatic effect, but the director in the middle of the production trio seemed concerned. He overheard him whisper to the announcer, "Not another Tequila Monday, I couldn't take another."

Power remembered one of his patients namedropping that once upon a time she had been in rehab with Giles Masefield.

The director waved frantically at the administrative assistant who had been lurking in the distant shadows and whispered. "Annie, can you go and winkle his lordship out of his dressing room." She made a face about this unwanted task, but was starting to head out of the studio when the star of the show launched himself into the studio, nearly colliding with her.

"Sorry everyone," Giles announced to the audience. "I was just taking delivery of my new scarf for tonight's episode." He held the silk scarf aloft, showing off its purple paisley pattern. He shouted his catch phrase triumphantly to more sycophantic applause, "*There you are!*" He collapsed into his seat at the quiz desk, slightly out of breath.

He beamed at the six contestants, "We'll do photos together in the green room later." Power wondered if Giles had indeed been drinking. His smile seemed to verge upon being an inebriated leer.

Jo leaned over to his right to see how Giles's profile appeared on the video monitors in the production booth. He moved cautiously, anxious not to draw any attention or cause embarrassment to his father.

"Shall we do some practice questions? Get you warmed up?" Giles turned first to the Cambridge team. He pointed at them. "From my left to right. One question each, but for practice sake and for our cameras, please buzz in before you answer, and wait until our announcer has said your name before you give me your answer? OK?" He pointed to the first student, with orange hair. "What is the capital of India?"

She buzzed and waited to be announced. "Durrell, Cor Christi," came the anticipated, deep sonorous tones of the announcer, clearly heard but not seen – the Voice.

"New Delhi."

"Correct." Giles pointed to the captain, with the buzzcut. "What is the name of the US Presidents Wife?"

He pressed the buzzer. "Gore, Cor Christi," announced the Voice.

"Laura Bush," said the captain, with a discernibly American accent.

"Correct." Giles pointed to the pale, long-haired student. "What is the name of George Lucas's dystopian fantasy film starring Robert Duvall?"

He buzzed. "Roberts, Cor Christi," said the Voice. Power deduced that this was Glyn Roberts, the son of the arrogant parent they had encountered in the queue to enter.

"THX 1138," said Roberts.

"Excellent," said Giles. "A clean sweep. That augurs well for you Cor Christi." Power groaned and simultaneously felt a twinge of annoyance, wondering if Giles was biased against Allminster from the very outset. "And now," said Giles. "The Allminster students." He gestured at Jason. Power inched forward on his seat.

"What is the legislative capital of Sri Lanka?"

Jason buzzed in as requested. "Bennett, Allminster," proclaimed the Voice.

"Colombo."

"Wrong. Oh dear. It's Sri Jayawardenepura Kotte. Has been since 1982." Masefield pointed at Melanie.

"What is the name of the last film Akira Kurosawa ever directed, released in 1993?"

Melanie dutifully buzzed. She looked worried. "Hughes, Allminster," the Voice announced.

"I'm sorry, I don't know."

"*Madadayo.* Oh dear." Giles Masefield's bronzed face wore a sneer. He pointed at Madeleine.

"What was the name of the only British Prime Minister to be assassinated?

Madeleine reached for the buzzer. "Khan, Allminster," intoned the Voice.

"George Canning?"

"Are you asking or telling me? It's wrong anyway. Spencer Perceval. Shot in 1812. Oh dear, Allminster. Never mind, at least we tested your buzzing skills."

Power frowned. On his left, Laura whispered, "They gave Allminster more difficult questions. That wasn't fair."

"Yes," agreed Power. "It's meant to be an easy introduction to build confidence, not destroy it." He could see anxiety building on the faces of all the Allminster contestants. In contrast the Cor Christi team now looked more relaxed and were laughing happily amongst themselves.

"Any water?" barked Masefield. "Where's Annie?" The floor manager, Sammy, shimmied over to his desk carrying a bottle of spring water, which Masefield snatched without a thank you. "Annie should have put out water along with the question cards. It's not a difficult job, even for an intern." He sighed and turned his attention to the production crew and pointed at the producer. "How's the hangover? Quite a night last night. Did you get home to the wife?" Power could see that the producer was formulating a response, but Masefield wasn't really interested in whatever the answer was going to be. He had already turned his attention to the announcer. "At least the names are pronounceable tonight. Even for you!" he laughed. "Are we ready for a run through?" he asked the director. The director made the OK sign.

"I hope the autocue works today. Did we sack the girl on Sunday?" The producer ducked and hid his face to avoid answering his star's unprofessional comment. "OK Allminster and Cor Christi," said Giles. "It's time to do a take. I like to go straight through the half hour. Non-stop. See you on the other side."

The studio lighting shifted. Cameras moved to set positions. The annoying opening music began and the floor manager faced the audience, smiling and bouncing to the music. Towards the end of the thirty second burst of music she put her hands together and started clapping. The audience followed her cue and the house lights came up. Giles, presenter of fourteen years, blonde-haired, but greying on top, be-scarved survivor of tabloid maulings when he had come out a dozen years before, and renowned substance abuse patient of the Priory, beamed into the camera as if all was well with the world.

"*There you are!*" He roared in welcome. The audience began a second round of applause for the catch phrase. He held up a hand to steady them. "And *Here we are!*" A brief ripple of applause. "An excited audience here tonight as we move towards the close of the first-round matches. Tonight we have Cor Christi College representing Cambridge University and for the first ever time on *TopQuiz*, Allminster University." Polite applause from the audience cued by the floor manager. The Vice Chancellor, Canon Armitage, clapped madly and went purple with pride. Power feared he would burst like some burgeoning blackcurrant. "*TopQuiz* audiences are always the most excited!" Giles grinned, flapping his scarf. "Tonight's scarf is a gift from the fine folk at the silk factory at Macclesfield – thank you guys!"

There began a montage of scenes from Cor Christi and the announcer described the College. "Cor Christi was founded by Thomas Wolsey in 1520 and filled the new Library with books from his sacking of the monasteries. The first Master was an abbot that Wolsey had recycled from Glastonbury, who fell foul of the Protestant Queen Elizabeth who had him beheaded in the College Library, where his blood is still said to stain the flagstones in front of the librarian's desk. A grim reminder to all those who have overdue books and must pay fines."

Then there was an introductory film featuring Allminster and the announcer read, "Allminster was founded in 1875 after a sum of £25,000 was endowed by the author of the Alice books, Lewis Carroll. Allminster has grown significantly since the 1960s and researches topics that Carroll would have been familiar with such as mathematics and theology, but is planning 21st Century teaching and research into subjects like quantum physics and medicine that would have been 'through the looking glass' for their founder Lewis Carroll."

"Let's meet their teams!" said Giles, in markedly avuncular fashion.

The TV screens set above the audience showed what the TV viewers would finally see and they focused on the students, and their names respectively. "First off Allminster – special subjects Medicine, English and History. Then Cor Christi – special subjects Astrophysics before 1960, American State Governors between 1980-2000 and The Fantasy World of J. R. R. Tolkien's novel *The Hobbit*."

Power groaned inwardly. He had advised his team that Allminster's best strategy would be to make their specialist subjects as specific and niche as they could. Cambridge had taken the strategy to the limit by making their fields as narrow as possible.

"As you know, *TopQuiz's* unique structure has two teams of three, with the captain in the centre. A first round where each team gets six minutes on their nominated subjects. And then a second, final round with as many general knowledge questions as we can get through.

"First off, the team from Cor Christi. The clock starts with the first question."

"Bennett, Astrophysics before 1960," intoned the announcer as the house lights dimmed and the spotlight fell upon the vivid, orange hair of the contestant. On the TV screen above Power's head the entire screen was taken up by a close up of the screen. A six minute countdown clock sat in the bottom right of the screen.

"Who was the radio astronomer who founded the Jodrell Bank Observatory in 1945?" asked Masefield. The clock started ticking down on Cor Christi's specialist question section.

"Sir Bernard Lovell," said Bennett.

"Correct. Quasars were first discovered in the late 1950s. What is the term quasar short for?"

"Quasi-stellar radio sources," Bennett said with a trace of smugness.

And so it went on. The Cambridge team had learnt their deliberately narrow fields well and their knowledge easily encompassed the questions leading to a maximum score. Jo groaned as he had so dearly wanted his father's team to win. Power thought he was glaring at the Cambridge team a little too fixedly and whispered to him, "It's just a game, don't get too upset."

"It's Roberts," said Jo. "He doesn't know anything."

"But he must do," said Power. "He got all his questions right." Although when he thought about it, long-haired Roberts's eyes had looked like a rabbit's caught in the headlights more than once or twice.

Allminster's specialist round was not a complete disaster. But several questions on the Lakeland poets, Jacobean kings and the ventricles of the heart had eluded Power's team. When the questions were necessarily passed over to the opposing team Roberts answered them correctly every time. Accordingly Cor Christi college came out of the specialist round 45 points ahead.

Jo stared very hard at the Cor Christi team.

"And now, with Cor Christi in the lead, we turn to the quickfire General Knowledge round," said Masefield.

And the quickfire questions began, "Who invented the hovercraft? What is the highest peak in England? Who composed the Sinfonia Eroica? In which two countries is Lake Titicaca?"

Allminster did their best, with Melanie answering as many as she could. But Roberts was quickest on the buzzer, so quick that at times he looked bewildered by having offered to answer. Giles was just about to censure him for failing to answer immediately for one question, but just in time Roberts seemed to summon the answer and his expression of dull incomprehension was replaced by sudden activity as he spat out the right answer. Cor Christi's lead was extending inexorably and everything now pointed towards a crushing victory over Allminster.

Power felt he wanted the earth to swallow him up. He closed his eyes against the spectacle of defeat. Indeed he closed them just at the moment that Jo stood up and leaned over the barrier into the production booth and prodded the producers' shoulder. "It's not fair," he whispered. The producer turned round and initially tried to wave Jo away. But something about Jo's sincere and urgent expression made him pull the headphones from his ears and lean in towards him and listen.

When next Power opened his eyes he was mortified to see that Jo was seemingly distracting the producer by leaning over the barrier and whispering into his ear. "Sit down, Jo," Power hissed, as quietly as he could. Jo was pointing at the contestants and then up into the murky darkness of the shadows beyond the well-lit stage. The producer nodded.

Jo sat down and looked at his puzzled father. Jo folded his arms defensively and whispered, "I had to say something. What's happening isn't fair." Power frowned, and perplexed by his son's behaviour, saw the producer seemingly responding and whispering into his microphone.

The producer stood up and, half crouching, moved out of the production booth into the shadows to speak to the floor manager.

Having listened to the producer's instructions, the floor manager, Samantha, stood up. All this time she had been sitting unobtrusively between the audience and the contestants.

Meanwhile Masefield was still firing questions at the teams, and he continued to do so, but out of the corner of his eye he had glimpsed the floor manager standing up. He kept going, although he felt a vague apprehension and irritation at the distraction.

Samantha sidled gracefully within the shadows, across the studio to a place on the edge of the studio lights, just out of camera shot. When she heard a new instruction from the producer in her earpiece, she strode purposefully into the glare of the studio lights and stood right in front of the Cor Christi team.

"What IS going on?" shouted Masefield, annoyed that his single take had been interrupted. "I'm working here!"

"Sorry. Security alert, Giles," said Samantha, without turning round. She stood defiantly confronting Roberts. She wasn't about to take her eyes off him for a second. "Don't be alarmed ladies and gentlemen. Everything is under control. Lights please." The house lights came up and the shadows in the studio were dispelled with brightness.

Masefield threw his question cards onto his desk in disgust. "Will somebody have the decency to explain to me what's going on?"

Power looked at his son, who was standing on his seat. He saw an expression of pale excitement on his son's face. "I hope I'm right, Dad," Jo said. His soft voice was tinged by anxiety.

"Everybody, please keep calm and stay exactly where you are," said the floor manager. She leant across the contestants' desk and looked straight in Roberts's eyes. "Mr Roberts," she said softly. "Would you be so kind as to lift your hair up so I can see your ears please?"

"I'll do no such thing," he said, and stood up intending to exit the studio.

"Let's not make any more of a scene, shall we?" said Samantha. She gestured to the burly security guards that had appeared at the studio exits. "YOU are on camera, and there's no way out. Lift your hair. I want to see your ears."

Sheepishly Roberts lifted the curtain of hair from around his face and tucked it over and back behind his ears. In his left ear Samantha immediately saw what she had been instructed to look for. She turned to look at Giles Masefield. "It's an earpiece with an aerial, Giles."

"Oh," sighed Masefield. "My God." He sank back in his chair.

Power now saw where the producer had gone after leaving the production booth. The producer had dived elsewhere into the shadows of the studio and now the lights had been brought up he could be seen at the bottom of the ladder leading up into the lighting gantries crossing the ceiling of studio 12. He was waiting at the bottom of the only route down.

Jo pointed up into the ceiling space to a place on the gantry where a young woman with a pony-tail had hidden during the recording. Even now, Annie, the assistant, was reluctantly climbing down the ladder. She clutched a copy of all the *TopQuiz* questions in her hand. One security guard led her away backstage. Two other guards separated the Cor Christi team and led them away, one by one, through another exit.

There were shouts of protest and several parents in the audience stood up and tried to follow their offspring, but their way was barred.

The producer and the floor manager took central stage in front of the audience. "Hello guys," said the producer. "Something pretty unusual has just happened and I'm afraid we can't continue with any filming this evening. An eagle-eyed member of the audience," he gestured to where Jo stood, "alerted us to something that was going on right in front of our eyes. A member of the Cor Christi team was wearing an earpiece with an aerial and the answers were being whispered to him by an accomplice on the gantry above the studio. As there is a cash prize at the end of the series, I'm afraid we will need to give the video evidence to the police."

"That's all slander. You can't say any of that!" Mr Roberts, who had interrupted Power in the queue was standing up now, shouting and spitting with rage at his son being so publicly accused.

"We all saw the earpiece with our own eyes," said the producer. "It's all on video. I suggest you sit down and say nothing more. In fact, if I can ask, can I implore you, ladies and gentlemen, to keep your own counsel about this evening. We have a security inquiry to complete now. You are all potential witnesses, so you must not tell anybody outside this studio what you have seen. We are involving the police, we must be mindful not to prejudice any legal proceedings. In order that the inquiry is not prejudiced, please, please, *please* can you refrain from telling friends, family or the media about this? So we can manage the situation and act fairly towards all concerned?"

"What do we do now?" asked Masefield, plaintively.

"Just give me a minute, please Giles," said the producer. "Can I ask please if there are any senior staff representatives of the two Universities here? If there are can the most senior individual from each University join me for a moment?"

Vice Chancellor Armitage and the Deputy Master of Cor Christi stood up simultaneously, but whereas Armitage looked empowered and noble, despite his dumpy appearance, the deputy master of Cor Christi seemed to stoop over and look away, as if he did not wish to be associated with what had just transpired in the studio. They made their way down to the producer who drew them over into a huddle near the Quiz Master's desk. Masefield looked mournfully into the distance. It was inevitable that the scandal of the cheating would hit the press and he dreaded dealing with them. Masefield had avoided newspaper reporters for years. But the PR people for the studios would want him to help maintain the programme's image in any way possible. It would be a case of 'all hands on deck'. How could they avoid the stain that scandal would bring? Giles Masefield, past Chancellor of Queens University, Birmingham, ex-MP for the Lib Dems, darling of daytime television, mime partner of Lionel Blair and loquacious contestant on *Just a Minute*, and *Countdown* was currently lost for words.

Power hugged his son. "Well done for spotting that. I'm sorry I didn't understand what you were doing. How did you know?"

"I saw the long-haired student giving the right answers, but when he was listening to the questions and buzzing in, I could see he didn't know. He seemed as surprised by the answers he gave as anyone. Then I looked up there and saw her shadow and the glow of her torch as she read the cards."

"You've got good eyes," said Power. "Well spotted."

"You're a good detective, Jo." said Laura. "But what's going to happen now? The filming can't go on."

Power looked at the Allminster team. They looked lost and very alone. Power beckoned the floor manager over and said, "I'm Professor Power from Allminster. I've been mentoring the Allminster team. Can I go and speak to them, please? They look a bit upset."

After some consideration she nodded. "We will probably need statements from them."

"Surely not?" asked Power.

"I'm afraid so," said Samantha. "What's happened is fraud, you see. It's a very formal process now."

Melanie's team was shaken, indeed. In the adrenalised heat of the contest they hadn't noticed anything and now suddenly the adrenaline was gone and they felt flat. Tearful even. Power had to explain that it was his own son that had alerted the producer to what was going on. Melanie gasped, "I thought it was us. I thought we were just incredibly bad. They were getting all the answers right."

"You were playing against cheats. Anybody can look good if they're being fed the answers," said Power. "Look, we will meet back at Allminster, OK? I'll buy you all lunch and we'll talk it through. Everything will be all right. I think I'd better go back now, but don't worry. It's OK."

Power could see the Vice Chancellor breaking away from his meeting with the producer and making his way over to where Power had been sitting. Power hurried back to where Armitage was now talking to Laura and Jo.

"I believe that this is the young man who saved Allminster," said the Vice Chancellor. He reached out and shook Jo's hand.

"My son, Jo," said Power, effecting introductions. "My partner, Laura. The Vice Chancellor, Canon Armitage."

"Well, you did some sterling work tonight, Jo. You're as clever as your dad." The Vice Chancellor grinned at Power. "Well, tonight was a surprise to everybody, I think. This episode between Allminster and Cor Christi is cancelled, of course. Cor Christi has been disqualified. I felt sorry for the Deputy Master. He has to deal with the fall out back home – the extremely negative publicity that will inevitably follow for the College. Mr Roberts will need to be expelled and depending on the results of the investigation maybe the others on the team too. How much did they all know? It seems difficult to believe they knew nothing. Why did the TV assistant help Roberts? That's yet to be established. Is she a relative? A lover? Does she hate the programme? Was she motivated by money or exacting revenge?" Armitage held his hands palms upwards in a gesture of puzzlement.

"And what happens to our team, Vice Chancellor?" asked Power.

"They are treated as if they won tonight and pass straight to the second round. Allminster lives to fight another day!" He patted Power on the shoulder. "Will you come and see me tomorrow, Carl? Must get off, I'm feeling a bit tired. It's all been a bit draining. There's something worrying me, and I need to ask for your help."

Chapter Thirteen

Sooner strangle an infant in its cradle
than nurse unacted desires.
William Blake, The Marriage Of Heaven And Hell

Margaret, Professor Shacklin's secretary, had been effectively covering for him during his protracted absence in Malta. There is not much that an efficient secretary cannot do in the absence of their employer. In fact the office of Professor Shacklin, Executive Pro Vice Chancellor, was arguably more efficient without him. There were no long meetings to minute, no appointments to run, and no waiting for decisions. Anything she deemed particularly problematic could be referred upwards to the Vice Chancellor, to whom Shacklin himself would have inevitably referred it in any case. Comparing her working life when Shacklin was there to how it was now, Margaret much preferred the current state of affairs.

Professor Power put his head round the corner of Margaret's office door and said, "Good afternoon". He had been in clinic all morning and had come in to the University expressly to see the Vice Chancellor as he had been asked to.

Margaret beamed at him, as Power was one of the few senior figures at the University who spoke to people as if they were, well, people. As he entered he placed a cardboard tray of two coffees on the desk. "Would you like a coffee?" he asked.

"Thank you, I would, please have a seat. What brings you here today?"

Power produced a sheaf of papers. I have emailed these to Professor Shacklin, but I brought some hard copies for the files and for the Vice Chancellor. They are accounts of my meeting with the Chief Medical Officer last week, and also some details about the meetings I've had with the Chief Executives of hospitals round the county. Getting their agreement in principle to having Allminster students on their wards."

"All positive?"

"Yes, I'm delighted to say they were," Power replied, as he peeled the top off one of the coffees and offered it to Margaret. She reached in a drawer for a sachet of sugar for herself. Power continued, "People outside the University are considerably more enthusiastic about a medical school than the people inside the University."

"I heard about the quiz last night. Your son saved the show, I believe."

Power nodded. He assumed that the Vice Chancellor had been talking, despite the TV producer's plea to stay silent about the program. "I was amazed by him," said Power. "He just stood up and boldly tapped the producer on the shoulder and told him they were cheating."

"That took some courage from a boy," Margaret said. "I'd be too frightened to say anything. But the student from Cor Christi had an earpiece and somebody was reading him the answers?"

"That's right, a TV assistant hid herself on the walkway up above and was whispering the answers to him."

"It sounds dangerous work. I've no head for heights myself. She must have hated the programme to do that."

"Any sign of Professor Shacklin? I'm concerned to discuss progress on the medical school."

"Not a word from Malta. Not even a postcard from him," said Margaret. "But I was thinking just now that I can cope with most things without him. If I need a signature on anything I just ask the Vice Chancellor. Some thing's I do need advice on though. This morning I had a phone call from Biology. They did an equipment audit – their first since two thousand and one, would you believe? – and found that their biology archive was missing some items."

"Biology archive?" queried Power.

"I don't quite understand what it is, myself. Biological specimens I think. Like pickled nematodes, or foetuses in jars. As far as I could make out it was some specimens in an old collection from the nineteen-sixties. Something about the reptiles at Chester Zoo. You know we have links there like other universities. Anyway, Biology wanted to know if they should report the loss to the Home Office, or the police. That little dilemma I took to the Vice Chancellor."

"And what did he suggest?"

She shrugged her shoulders, "He said, 'Leave it with me'. So I did."

"But involving the police for some reptile stuff?" Power mused. "Well, they were going to involve the police about last night's quiz. The studios classed the cheating as fraud, because *TopQuiz* earns the winning Institution a fifty thousand pound cash prize. What a headache for everyone!"

"Still, Allminster lives to fight another day. The Vice Chancellor was very pleased with your boy. How old is he?"

"Jo is seven going on seventeen. I know I'm his dad and his biggest fan, but I do admire the way he put two and two together yesterday evening. He couldn't sleep last night. He was so eager to tell his friends about it, but nobody's meant to say anything, I had to ask him not to tell anyone." said Power.

"I don't think the studios can stop it getting out," said Margaret. "Too many people know. And the Vice Chancellor certainly hasn't kept it to himself."

"Could you check if he can see me now, please?" asked Power. "He told me to come and see him today."

"I'll phone his secretary," offered Margaret, and dialled through to the Vice Chancellor's office. There were a few exchanges and then she put the phone down. "He can see you in half an hour or so. The dean of healthcare has just gone in."

"Bridget McFarlane?"

"The very same. I think she's asking for a few days off." Margaret looked at Power, wondering if she should say something or remain discreet. "Can you keep a secret?"

"Confidentiality is my middle name," said Power. "It goes with the profession."

"Bridget wasn't in this morning. Hasn't been in all this week. She drove up to the Senate building and dived straight inside his office. I glimpsed her outside his office, only for a second. Wearing huge sunglasses again."

"I'm sorry?" Power was initially confused about the mention of sunglasses, as the heavy, rolling sky outside was that of a dour December day. "Oh . . ." he said, as light dawned.

"Left eye. Blue. And not a fetching shade of eye shadow. And a nasty pinch mark on her arm. She covered it up as soon as I glanced at her. I pretended I hadn't seen. It's not for me to say anything. But it's not the first time. The Vice Chancellor is aware. She's asked for time off before, until it's all healed, or can be hidden by foundation."

"You never know what people have to contend with at home, do you?" said Power softly. "I didn't know." But he had noticed how McFarlane's lover had gripped her arm at the Inaugural Lecture. He had noticed that. He felt some guilt that he had been beginning to hate McFarlane for her words alone. "What does the Vice Chancellor suggest she does?"

"We don't know," said Margaret. "We just hope he advises her properly. What would you say to her if you were him?"

"Go," said Professor Power. "Don't wait. Save yourself and go."

* * *

Despite what must have been a difficult interview prior to seeing Professor Power, the Vice Chancellor looked remarkably chirpy. He was seated in an armchair with an assortment of tea things on various tables.

His chef had just delivered afternoon tea and was, even now, descending the stairway that led back to the Refectory. Power's stomach rumbled as he had not had time for lunch between his clinic and driving over to the University. Armitage offered Power his choice from a plate of sandwiches and poured him a cup of tea. "There you are, Carl." He stopped himself. "I'm sorry, I've been inadvertently using that wretched man Masefield's catch phrase all day. *There you are. There you are.* What does it even mean? A very good effort by the team last night, I thought. A shame for the deputy Master of Cor Christi, but what else did they deserve but disqualification? And we get free passage to Round Two."

"It would have been nice to win in competition, though," said

Power, trying to find a vegetarian-friendly sandwich on the Vice Chancellor's various plates. He settled for egg and cress in granary bread.

"In evolutionary terms, success is success," said the Vice Chancellor. He started munching a ham sandwich. When he swallowed the last mouthful of the ham he fixed his eye on Power. "Difficult interview with McFarlane," he confided, and reached for a pate and tomato sandwich. "She won't take advice. There's only so much you can do as an employer. Be understanding. Give her time off. But time off won't solve a recurrent problem."

"I could talk to her," offered Power.

"Would you? That's kind – more than kind of you," the Vice Chancellor paused and thought, sipping black tea with lemon in. "No, on balance, no, I won't ask you to do that. I must respect my dean's privacy and I can't ask you to do too much."

"I have brought these papers for you," said Power, offering the file of reports on his meetings with the county's hospital Chief Executives and his London meeting with the CMO.

"Please put them on the desk for me, will you, while I finish this repast."

As Power walked over to put the reports on the desk, he passed the chess set near the window. He noticed that the pieces had moved, but before he could analyse the exact state of play, the Vice Chancellor offered to pour him another cup of tea.

"I'm fine, thank you," said Power, resuming his seat.

"I'm glad your meetings about the medical school went well. Green lights all the way?"

"All the way," said Power. "I do expect other established medical schools like Manchester and Liverpool to raise some objections, but the case for more home-grown student doctors is so compelling . . ."

"You have faith in your own good arguments. Not everyone will share that faith, I'm just warning you. Things can take surprising twists. I'm glad for your minutes though. It's a vital dictum to 'always write things down'. As they say: 'Always speak the truth – think before you speak – and write it down afterwards.'

"Now I have something of a favour to ask of you, a big favour, I know you are busy on the medical school project and I know you have patients in clinics elsewhere, but can I please ask you to take a few days out from that daily routine? I wouldn't ask, but the matter is pressing and urgent."

"If I can help, I will, of course," said Power.

"There's something I'd like you to investigate. This is touching upon your expertise and your other work – with the Foundation. I have heard a lot about the good work it does. The University would like to commission you and the Foundation to investigate something, or someone."

"Felfe?" suggested Power.

The Vice Chancellor furrowed his brow. "Felfe? No, not Felfe. He just dropped dead of a heart attack. Poor old man. Reputation for wining and dining to the extreme."

Power struggled not to comment or raise an eyebrow at such a statement about overindulgence issuing from the Vice Chancellor's plum tart stained lips.

"He was taken on by the University as a favour by my predecessor, and probably kept on our books for too long. No, I don't want you to investigate him. I want you to investigate Shacklin."

"I'm sorry if I jumped to the wrong conclusion," said Power, knowing he had said the wrong thing.

"It's all right," said Armitage, offering him a spare plum and Armagnac tart. Rain lashed the windows of the office, and wind crashed and blustered its way around the walls of Senate House, but there was a fire crackling brightly in the grate, and Power felt warm and comfortable.

"I sent Shacklin to Malta to shore up our relationship with the University there," said Armitage. "We exchange students with Malta via Erasmus. We have joint research programmes. We offer external examining services to them too, and modules on some of our postgraduate programmes. We derive considerable revenue from the partnership. Like all relationships this one needs care and attention to survive. I've been over there myself. They visit us. I've sent Shacklin a few times. He likes it there. Swimming. Good food. He may enjoy a flutter in the casino after he's done with business. I don't know. I sent him out for a few days. But he's gone AWOL. I made several phone calls, and according to airline and border control records, he flew and arrived there. Shacklin checked in to his hotel. He ate his breakfast on two days. He met people at the University on two days. On the third day? We don't know. No-one saw him at the University. He didn't eat breakfast. He didn't check out of the hotel. He did not fly home on his scheduled flight. He was not treated in the hospital. He was not found by the police dead on the streets of Valletta and taken to the mortuary. He has not phoned home, or sent an email. His University credit card was not been used after the second day. And that is the sum of all my investigations."

"Your investigations sound very thorough," said Power.

"I thought it was worth investing some time. But my investigations are at a distance, made remotely, you understand? Now, I think that the University's reputation is worth protecting, and I am worried about what Professor Shacklin may have got caught up in. He may be at risk, need help, or the University may need to take steps to limit any . . . scandal. However, telephone enquiries can only achieve so much. An enquiry from someone actually there in person counts for far more. And we would invest in the Foundation to cover all costs, whatever you consider the going rate to be? Would an initial allocation of ten thousand pounds be sufficient to begin inquiries?"

"My colleague, Andrew Lynch, could advise on that sort of thing," said Power carefully. "It sounds a perfectly reasonable amount to me, but he's an ex-Superintendent and would know better."

"I know exactly who he is," said the Vice Chancellor. "I believe in due diligence and always ensure I know precisely who I am dealing with." He reached in his pocket and removed a credit card. He noted that his fingers were leaving a greasy residue on the plastic and he wiped it delicately with a linen napkin. "I'm assuming you will take the commission on as you haven't yet said anything to suggest you are not interested." He finished cleaning the card and presented it to Power. "The bursar has issued you with this, at my request. It's a credit card for basic expenses on top of the overall ten thousand pound commission. Meals, travel on the island – a hire car to track Shacklin round the island. Try not to put any alcoholic beverages on the card. The University is not keen on subsidising alcohol." Power looked at the credit card. It had his name in silver on the lower left corner: Professor Power, Allminster University. "We'll book your flight and hotel. The University has its favourite travel agency. We might as well book you into the same hotel as Shacklin – the Hotel Phoenicia in Valetta. Have you ever been to Malta?"

"Never," said Power, "I wonder – the Foundation would wish to send Lynch with me. I think his skills would be valuable."

"I was hoping you'd say that," said the Vice Chancellor. "Of course, of course, he can go. And if it's all agreed by you both that you're going, please let my secretary know as soon as you can. I'd like you to head out today, or tomorrow at the latest. Shacklin's trail will be cooling even now."

Power was thinking how he would cover clinics and ward rounds. His Specialist Registrar would have to act up again. He would need to ask Laura to take Jo to school for the last few days of term. His University sessions had some appointments with potential GP and Consultant tutors which could be re-arranged for the next year. "I think I can cover it. I have some appointments with potential medical tutors over the next week to postpone. I wanted to build up a bank of Honorary Professors to act as advisers."

"Don't postpone them. Leave a list of their names with my secretary. I'll invite them to a grand lunch in the Senior Dining Room so I can talk to them all at the same time. And I have asked her to type up what information I was able to gather on Shacklin's activities on Malta, that will give you both a start."

Power finished the last of a cream scone and drained the last drops of his cup of tea. The Vice Chancellor surveyed the state of the table after their afternoon tea. They appeared to have done the chef's work justice. "I think we've finished everything," said Armitage. "It's important to get a resolution on Shacklin one way or another. If he's away for a while, then the automatic protocol is that the position of acting Executive Pro Vice Chancellor goes to the next most senior dean, and that is Bridget McFarlane. And she would be acting Executive Pro Vice Chancellor until we could appoint a substantive successor to Shacklin, which may take months. And whatever her good points, and whatever her problems may be, I couldn't bear the thought of that *inter-regnum.* From your point of view, Bridget would not favour the medical school in any way. No, she wouldn't, not at all. She'd sooner strangle an infant in its cradle."

Chapter Fourteen

The secret services are the only real measure of a nation's political health, the only real expression of its subconscious.
John Le Carre; Tinker, Tailor Soldier, Spy, 1974

The next afternoon Power and Lynch flew to Malta. Power had felt a sense of excitement as they neared the island. He had read two guidebooks and pored over the enclosed maps whilst sipping Cisk lager on the plane. He had read of the fabled Knights of St John, repelling a naval siege in 1565 and defeating the concerted might of the Ottoman Empire. He had read of the stone temples at Tarxien and Ħaġar Qim, from the third millenium BC. He had looked out of the oval cabin window at the glossy deep blue of the Mediterranean, and in his enthusiasm he had almost set the purpose of their mission to one side. He had read of the unusual language of Malta, the honey of Gozo and other sweet delights such as 'qaghaq tal-ghase', and vegetarian dishes derived from Moorish cuisine such as Kapunata. However, the mention in one guidebook of Maltese rabbit stew unsettled him.

The warmth of the Mediterranean sun enveloped Power as soon as he stepped off the plane onto the baking concrete of the terminal apron. The brilliant sunlight flooded his eyes, temporarily blinding him with its white intensity. Nevertheless, as his eyes adjusted to the light, the warm glow which bathed him made Power sigh in contentment.

Lynch hired a rental car from the airport and they drove to Valletta, their vehicle jostling in the midst of impatient traffic. Just outside the massive citadel walls they drew to a halt in the driveway of Shacklin's erstwhile hotel, the Hotel Phoenicia. The five star hotel took pride of place by Valletta's entrance gate. A hotel doorman offered to park their car for them. They had been afforded palatial rooms with glossy tiled floors and magnificent views across the Grand Harbour. Power could not resist the temptation of taking an immediate dip in the pool and arranged to meet Lynch for dinner later. Lynch frowned in mild disapproval at his friend prioritising hedonism before duty. Lynch's first care was to introduce himself to the hotel manager, a short, tubby man, dressed smartly in black and sporting a pencil-thin moustache. Lynch explained their mission to find the missing academic.

"Of course, we are eager to help you, Mr Lynch. We were very distressed at Professor Shacklin's sudden disappearance. He went out one day in the morning and did not return. He was not at breakfast the next day – the day he was meant to check out – and when the chambermaid went into his room at noon – after the time guests are meant to check out – his bed had not been slept in and all his things were scattered around the room."

"Scattered?" asked Lynch. "Had his room been broken into perhaps or been searched by someone?"

"Maybe the word I chose was improper. I meant his things were not packed away in his suitcases. His clothes were in the wardrobe. His shaving equipment was by the basin in the bathroom. I meant, he had left everything behind, you know. No-one had searched his things or trashed the room."

"Is there anything else you remember about Professor Shacklin?"

"I must check something with you, sorry, your visit here is 'official'?"

"Yes, we are making an official inquiry on behalf of Professor Shacklin's employer, Allminster University. Your reception has details of my passport and Professor Power's. Professor Power is employed by the University. He has a staff card. If you wish I can give you the number of the University so you can check our credentials?"

"No, that won't be necessary. I am just checking. The nature of what I have to say . . . we would not wish to bring anyone into disrepute, or ourselves be associated with . . . you are not a journalist? Or his wife's private eye?"

"No," said Lynch. "Nothing like that. I believe his wife divorced him long ago."

The hotel manager sighed. "I am afraid that I remember him clearly enough. How shall I put it? Professor Shacklin did stand out as a guest. He was out during the day at his work, but at night – at night, he was even busier."

"How do you mean, please?"

"He was here for three or four nights and each night there was a different woman with him. Sometimes two. One he might dine with and then take out to the casino. Then later he might return here for the night with another. He was always most charming to the staff, especially if they were young and female. He tipped well. One night he came back from the casino, alone though, shaken and drunk. Reception thought he might have been in a fight. He complained that he had been set upon on his walk to the taxi home. A watch had been stolen. We were concerned, our guests' safety is a priority, you know? We asked if he wanted to involve the police, or see the hotel doctor, but he said no."

"Which casino was this?"

The hotel manager shrugged. "There are three or four in Valletta; or maybe the Dragonara in St Julian's. I don't know. They seem to be opening up all the time now with our joining the EU. There is a lot of new money coming into the city. Russian billionaires, Italian 'Ndrangheta nobility, dare I say. Great yachts in the harbour with their own helicopters. People buying citizenship here to become citizens of the EU. Many new people. People you don't want to upset, if you see what I mean. That's why I checked twice about your mission in case . . . always we must check. Maybe Professor Shacklin won some money from someone it was wiser he really should have lost against. There are some people that it is better to lose against than win. If your luck is such that you win their money, well then, you may lose your health, or even your life."

"And Professor Shacklin's effects – his clothes and luggage – do you still have those?"

The hotel manager nodded. "I assume that next you will ask me for them? And I would say that you can have them, as long as your colleague from the University can give me a written receipt. It was the University who paid for his stay. Professor Shacklin just never checked out."

Lynch obtained a receipt form from the manager and traipsed out to the pool where Power was doing a butterfly stroke up and down the length of the pool, surging through the clear, sparkling water. Once Lynch had attracted Power's attention and got his signature, he returned to the manager with the damp receipt form, collected Shacklin's bags and took them upstairs to his own room to search them for clues.

Shacklin had brought three suits. Two of these were sharply cut evening-wear suits. There was an underlying scent of aftershave – bergamot and clove – but there were also traces of women's perfume, and each suit had a different blend of aromas. There was a long, straight blonde hair on the shoulder of one suit and two dark brown hairs on the back of the second evening suit. There were crumpled, worn shirts which smelled stale, and there was blood on the collar of one. The stain didn't look like the small blood mark that occurs with a shaving accident, and in any case, Shacklin's bathroom kit contained an electric razor. The blood stain on the collar was more extensive. There was a cardboard ten pack of durex condoms. Two remained. Lynch sighed softly. There were three cards from casinos in Birgu, St Julian's and St George's Bay. There was an electric phone charger for a Nokia phone, but of the phone itself there was no sign. There was no wallet. Presumably they had both been with Shacklin when he left the hotel that final time.

In terms of Shacklin's official mission to the Island, Lynch found his document case containing correspondence between the University of Malta and Allminster; Memoranda of Agreements, a campus map, some scribbled notes of meetings he had attended at the University on the day after he arrived. Lynch wrote down the names of three professors – Savona, Malarbi and Costaguti – that Shacklin appeared to have met. There was a scribbled note on a telephone pad relating to a fourth, Profesor Xuereb, but more than his or her name there was no more detail.

Lynch continued to search through the belongings, wondering absent-mindedly how he might identify the perfumes. The aftershave in Shacklin's bathroom kit was Armani.

* * *

Power climbed out of the pool just as the sun was setting. The water ran from his body, glittering like molten gold in the light of the setting sun. He showered at the poolside and went upstairs to change for dinner. When he descended to the lobby, he found that Lynch was sitting patiently in an arched alcove making notes on a pad of stark white paper. Lynch was smartly dressed in chinos, a crisp white shirt and cool, navy jacket. The fronds of a potted palm stretched over his head and he was sipping his way through a cafetière of coffee. Lynch stood as he saw Power strolling over the tiled lobby.

"Are you ready to get something to eat?" Lynch asked. "We need to erase the memory of that airline food."

"I'm always ready to dine, you know me," said Power. "Although, I may struggle to find any vegetarian food here. I was looking at the guide book and it was championing the local fresh fish, lobster, rabbit and Maltese pork."

"We'll find somewhere, don't worry," said Lynch. "I've spoken to the hotel manager and he recommended a local Italian restaurant, with Maltese wines and produce. Italy is only ninety miles away after all. The restaurant is called *Papannis*. How does that sound?" Power nodded agreement appreciatively. "Shall we be off then? He gave me directions." Lynch reached down and gathered all his papers together. "I'll bring a bit of work with us."

They walked across the Art Deco tiled floor of the hotel atrium and out through the triple-arched portico. The evening was cool and mild after the warmth of the day, and the soft breeze was scented with salt and spice. They crossed a large roundabout with a Triton fountain in the centre, weaving a path through dozens of yellow, white-roofed buses that circled the fountain. Hoardings behind the nearby bus station still carried faded posters advertising the Play Back Concert at Fort St Angelo in the Grand Harbour to mark Malta's accession to the European Union. Beyond was the Valletta City Gate, a narrow breach in the solid and vast reinforced limestone walls that surrounded the city. They passed through the Gate walking companionably, side by side, along brightly lit streets, past innumerable, tall, narrow church fronts. They walked past open church doors that released perfumed clouds of incense and offered views of worshippers treading bright red carpets, within glossy, icing sugar white marble walls, festooned with legions of tapering candles, their flames reflecting and flickering on golden-framed icons and towering gilded, carved altars. From every street corner statues of the Virgin Mary on high, looked benignly down on the pair as they made their way past mahogany-countered pharmacies and glittering ice cream shops. They passed the great Co-Cathedral of St John, and the Grand Master's palace, before turning left and encountering a branch of Marks and Spencer, a dear remnant of Malta's English colonial past.

On a street called Triq id – Dejqa, (Strait Street) they found the restaurant they sought. The street was immersed in the quiet of the evening. Many years ago the street had hosted the red light area of the capital, but with the leaving of NATO and the British Fleet the drunken din raised by noise of rabble rousing sailors had been replaced by a sombre peace. Papannis was a small and informal restaurant with limestone walls and arches, their stone façade lined by gloriously full wine racks. They ordered starters of crab and lobster ravioli for Lynch and fried cheese with honey for Power, followed by seabream and roast potatoes and ricotta and pistachio ravioli. Power insisted on trying a wine from the Island called Medina Girgentina. "The guidebook mentioned this – it's a grape only grown here," he said. "And it's been growing here since 500 AD."

"I hope the vintage of the bottle is a bit more recent," Lynch said.

Inevitably the conversation drifted to their mission on the Island. "You spoke to the manager about his restaurant recommendations. Did you talk about Shacklin, too?"

"We did," said Lynch, trying the wine. "It's a very light wine, nice, I could drink quite a lot of that."

"Probably you could, it's only ten per cent proof," said Power. "So what did the manager say? I expect he wouldn't recall Shacklin."

"On the contrary," said Lynch. "I'm afraid that Shacklin made quite the wrong impression and was certainly remembered."

"Oh," said Power, frowning. "Do I take it that he let the side down?"

"Well, the manager was relatively polite and restrained about him, but clearly your colleague let Allminster down, badly – womanising and a possible fight at the casino. As Shacklin never checked out, his luggage was left in the room, and I've gone through his effects."

"Effects?" said Power, pouncing upon the word. "As if he were dead? 'Effects' sounds so final." He rested his knife and fork for a moment, suddenly moved by the gravity of what they were discussing. The luxury of the hotel, the golden sun as he swam, the sumptuousness of the food before him – everything had lulled him into a feeling that he was on holiday. Perhaps Shacklin had felt the same way and been lulled into softness, and failed to appreciate all the dangers in his environment. Or perhaps he had just lost himself and meandered into some hedonistic binge. Perhaps he had travelled into the Island's interior, and was distracted from his University duties and embroiled in some intense Dionysiac orgy of the senses.

"What Shacklin left behind at the hotel does help us a little. He has, or had, his mobile phone with him, but he left his charger behind at the Phoenicia. He probably also has his wallet with him."

"We know when he last used the University credit card," said Power. "It was the evening before he was meant to fly back."

"Yes, I remember the Vice Chancellor's information," said Lynch. "From the bursar, I think."

"If you can let me have all the details I will go through them tomorrow. We may be able to follow him round the island using the purchases on the credit card."

"But why did Shacklin stand out to the hotel manager?" Power pressed for an answer. "You didn't say in any detail."

"Let's say Shacklin surrounded himself with different women," said Lynch. "The manager implied he took at least two different women to bed on different days. And he visited at least one casino, and was either mugged or got into a fight on his way back. I mean, to be honest, we are building up a number of reasons why someone might have taken exception to Shacklin. A jealous lover? Someone that he'd lost money to? Alternatively, someone who targeted him because he'd won money?"

The restaurateur cleared their plates away, and proposed the dessert special of the evening, a homemade tiramisu. They both accepted.

"We've got limited time here on Malta," said Power. 'How should we approach this?"

"I've thought about that," said Lynch. "I've pieced together Shacklin's itinerary for his official work here. Although I'm surprised he even had time to work. He's a man who clearly burned the candle at both ends. He had several meetings at the University and we can track his last days and hours of official work. Shacklin kept fairly good notes. I wondered if you could take the car tomorrow and interview the University people he met? Try and get a feel for what he was working on?"

"OK, said Power, accepting the file that Lynch had collated and passed across the table. "What will you do?"

"There's a resource we have on the Island. I didn't mention it before, but there is a Service office I've arranged to visit tomorrow. They should help us track Shacklin's various interactions on the Island."

"Involving the Service . . . that sounds very . . . covert of you."

"I can't say very much in here, but I'll walk you past the office on the way back and tell you more." Lynch paused, and sighed at the first taste of the tiramisu. "This has been a blissful meal."

"I can legitimately put it on the University's credit card, too," said Power, showing the oblong of plastic to Lynch.

Lynch frowned, "No, I rather think we should pay for it via the Foundation. The card will track us just as it tracked Shacklin. You know I'm always cautious about using expenses. It's often the first thing an employer looks to use when they want to dismiss you. I'm sorry, we can cover the meal as part of the overall commission."

Power felt he had been mildly reproved and he put the card safely away. "I suppose you may be right," he conceded.

"Cheer up," said Lynch. "Of course we should be grateful that someone else is paying for dinner. It's just a matter of how we want them to pay for it, and how much we want them to know about our whereabouts. Let's keep the card for justifiable emergencies."

They walked back through Valletta under the cloudless, starry sky. On Republic Street the Christmas lights of Valletta – bright yellow, green and red stars – twinkled under the heavens. They turned left and passed an outpost of the University then the church dedicated to the shipwreck of St Paul. All at once, in a side street, far away from the lights, Lynch stopped. "This is it," he said.

"What is?" Dr Power looked around at the dilapidated buildings where they had paused.

"This is the office of the British SIS," said Lynch. They were by an abandoned building, with a shabby green double door. The green paint was peeling. Dust and grime lay thick upon the step. Two ghost signs sat either side of the double entrance. White letters sitting on curved verdigris-covered plaques read 'Degiorgio and Azzopardi, Merchants and Agents'. "The office was once used by agents for steamships, insurance and an oil company, long before the Second World War. When Malta became Independent in 1974, the SIS retreated here. This is one of only three bases left in the Med. The others are in Gibraltar and Cyprus. The last listening posts of Empire."

"It looks empty." said Power. "No security at all. Look at the locks. Nobody works there now."

"You're not looking properly. I counted at least four security cameras tracking us on the approach here," said Lynch. "Anyway, I'll find out tomorrow and let you know what happens when you knock on the door."

They resumed their journey back to the hotel, past the Auberge de Castile and around the Triton Fountain. "When you see the people at the University tomorrow," said Lynch, "Please can you keep a look out for two women?"

"What?" asked Power. He paused under the *porte cochère* of the Phoenicia.

"Shacklin was, erm . . . 'intimate', with at least two women. A blonde woman who wore Flowerbomb perfume and a woman with curly brown hair who wore Flower by Kenzo."

"How on earth do you know all that?"

Lynch tapped the side of his nose, with a knowing look. "Well, I think I was quite resourceful. I found a receptionist who knows her perfumes," said Lynch. "And most obligingly, in the interests of justice, she agreed to smell the jackets of Professor Shacklin."

"She certainly deserves a tip," said Power. "I will keep my eye out for anyone rash enough to succumb to Shacklin's charms, but I tell you now, I'm no good at perfumes."

"Hmm," said Lynch, as they parted company before bed. "Maybe we will need to buy a couple of bottles in Valetta, early tomorrow, for you to compare?" Power shook his head doubtfully as they got into the lift. "We could take them home as presents, if that doesn't make me a cheapskate," mused Lynch.

"Maybe leave them here for your olfactory friend in reception," said Power.

* * *

The morning sun was low in the sky, dazzling Lynch as he walked into the walled city. He wended his way between the ancient buildings towards DeGiorgio and Azzopardi's. He looked admiringly at the dry wooden façades lining the narrow streets. Above the shops were apartments where dozens lived, with glazed balconies up high called gallerija, where children played and old people rocked their remaining years away, looking down and watching passers-by on the streets below.

Lynch stood alone on the paviered street outside the dilapidated, but elegant, Georgian entrance of DeGiorgio and Azzopardi. The tall, sculpted double doors had been painted green, but were faded and cracked from decades of Mediterranean sun. The stuccoed walls on either side of the doors were yellowed and flaking. Lynch felt, standing here, in this space, that time had stood still for so many years.

There was no bell or intercom to provide any concession to twenty-first century communication. There were twin door knockers, prancing porpoises, fashioned in bronze. After weathering decades of rain the copper in the alloy had oxidised into a duckshell, green patina. Lynch lifted one of the porpoises with purpose, knocked politely on the door and waited.

There was an almost imperceptible click and the left-hand door swung gently open. He moved forward and the entrance swallowed him quietly and discreetly. The door closed itself behind him, as if moved by invisible hands.

Lynch was in a small, high-ceilinged atrium whose walls were painted a stark white. He estimated that the space was perhaps six foot square, dimensions that would be much smaller than the original architect's design for a hallway. He tapped the oh-so-solid wall beside him. It felt cold like solid concrete. The sole way out of the atrium, besides the wooden doors behind him, was a single, white steel door. In the ceiling, Lynch observed a camera and a grille for a speaker. A disembodied voice spoke through this. "Good morning, can you oblige by identifying yourself, please?"

"Andrew Lynch. I have an appointment at nine a.m."

"Of course you do, Superintendent Lynch, sorry to be so formal," the voice gave him his old title, presumably as a courtesy. "Mr Azzopardi will be down to see you shortly."

The steel door slid open swiftly and silently, and Lynch was admitted into a much larger space, with a Victorian Minton tiled floor and marble columns. This was the original entrance hall. The white concrete box was some sort of blast-proof containment device to thwart armed entry by aggressors. In front of Lynch a graceful stairway ascended out of sight to distant floors. A set of high-grade stainless steel bars rudely separated the elegant entrance hall from the stairs.

A scrupulously dressed young man, wearing an ochre-coloured three-piece suit skipped down the marble stairway. His face was closely shaven and framed by curled brown sideboards. He smiled in welcome to Lynch, and reached in a waistcoat pocket for a transponder fob, with which he unlocked the gate in the steel bars and invited him through.

He locked the gate shut and swung round to shake Lynch's hand vigorously. "Good morning, I'm Mr Azzopardi."

"*The* Mr Azzopardi of Degiorgio and Azzopardi?" asked Lynch.

"He is long gone, maybe a lifetime ago. It's my working name, Mr Lynch. I'm not really called Mr Azzopardi; except when I'm here. Come with me, please. I'm sorry about the entrance. It's just security. You won't believe how many tourists give the doors a knock. We don't usually acknowledge any callers. But we expected you of course, and we had already identified you walking down the street outside. I say 'we', but there's just me here today, the rest of 'us' is overseas. SIS is spread pretty thin in the Med these days. I'm the duty officer for this station today."

"You must be busy," said Lynch, as they climbed the wide stairway together, side-by-side.

"Moderately," said Azzopardi guardedly. Lynch noted that his skin was deathly pale, as if he hid away from the Mediterranean sun. "I'm writing an economic report for the Foreign Office. Malta became a full member of the EU this year. I'm asked to brief the FO on the immediate economic impacts."

"And are there any?" asked Lynch.

"Rather," said Azzopardi, as he led Lynch up to a two man office at the front of the building. The gallerija was open and a welcome breeze was ruffling the papers on the desk by Azzopardi's computers. "I've set myself up in here today," said Azzopardi. "I move round the offices as I like on different days. It can get a bit lonely. Have a seat. You can log on to that computer on the desk if you need to do some work. I've set it up with a guest account for you." Lynch nodded gratefully. "Your GCHQ contact emailed asking me to extend all possible assistance, etc. That means you can use the kitchen and have as many coffees as you like." Azzopardi grinned and sat down. The document he had been working on was partially hidden by a moving screen saver. "Yes, it's all change for Malta. I'm not sure that they know what they've taken on, to be honest. The people will feel the wind of change, to be sure. It's not going to be just a new currency on the way. All their major public works will need to be tendered across the EU, and of course, Italy will want a share. Free movement of goods means that cheap mass produced Danish bacon will replace expensive local bacon. Free financial movement means that any money coming into Malta can be laundered and sent anywhere in the EU. So Libyan oil can be imported and re-badged here. Pharmaceuticals can be imported and re-badged with an EU logo. And rich Germans can buy up villas and drive up property prices. And local politicians will make millions from turning a blind eye. Gonzi's Government has already opened up the gambling regulations, and do you know what's really hot here? Online gambling. It's been legalised and even has tax incentives. Companies from outside Malta running the online casinos pay just five per cent corporation tax. By the end of this financial year ten percent of Malta's GDP will be online gambling."

"I wouldn't have thought of such a thing," said Lynch. "Online gambling – what's the point?"

"It's big business, that's the point," said Azzopardi. "The regulations are lax here, and hardly enforced. Deliberately so I'd say. Have you seen all the yachts in the harbour? Beautiful, sleek craft, reeking of money"

"I can see them from the hotel window," said Lynch. "Gleaming white monsters – so big they have helicopters sitting on them."

"And much else aboard too," said Azzopardi. "More gadgets than a Bond film. Scramblers that detect and disrupt mobile phones that come too close. Sensors that are sensitive to electronic signals given out by digital cameras. Try and take a photo of the yacht, and they detect the surge in the camera's battery and they fire an electromagnetic pulse back at your camera. The photo in the memory of the camera is corrupted. Now, tell me, if the owners of the yacht have nothing to hide, why do they need such impressive toys?"

"Where do these yachts come from?" asked Lynch.

"Some are Russian, although the Russians prefer Cyprus, to be fair. Others are 'Ndrangheta. Italian. The successors to the Mafia, you know?"

"I know of the 'Ndrangheta," said Lynch.

"Malta is attracting them like syrup water attracts wasps," said Azzopardi. "The Maltese Government is falling over itself to have their shell companies develop casinos, restaurants, pharmacies . . . and some of these companies have not filed a set of audited accounts since they were dreamt up years ago. The money, once it's laundered, can just about flow anywhere in the EU." Azzopardi laughed. "It's so transparent what is happening. It's blatant. A yacht arrives in the Grand Harbour. The owners dress up and visit the casino. The casino accepts their money – huge bets, huge stakes, tens of thousands of dollars – the casino takes their bets. The yacht owners lose everything. The yacht owners leave. You might think it's a sad story, no? But everyone is very happy. Because the yacht owners meant to lose the money."

"Meant to lose the money?" asked Lynch incredulously. "What if, by some quirk of fate, their bets won?"

"Then they just keep on playing until they do lose," said Azzopardi. "Everybody loses everything if they keep on playing in a casino. So when the 'bad' or illegal money has been 'lost' and belongs to the casino. Suddenly the 'bad' money is converted, like alchemy from lead to gold, to 'good money'. That is called *'placement'*. It is the most dangerous phase, as the money could be intercepted on the way to the casino, but once it is in the casino's treasury, it is theoretically good. So that is 'placement'. The next phase is *'layering'* – the casino – or the legitimate company that owns it then disperses the money in a series of investments. The money is broken up and channelled to different countries. That's where the lack of borders in the EU – the freedom of movement of money – is so crucial to these people. The sums are moved and moved again and again to confuse detection. Finally, the money has reached the third stage of money laundering, which is called *'integration'*, where the sums are fully assimilated into the legal economy."

"But the yacht owners who are losing all this money . . ."

"You don't understand me. No-one is really losing money," laughed Azzopardi. "Don't you see? It's a circle. It's the same people all along. They are merely losing to themselves. Processing the money. I admit it's a bit like a perpetual motion machine, but I assure you it pays. These people have 'bad' money that they can't spend. From drug operations, smuggled oil from countries that can't sell it legally because of sanctions against their country, or because it's the profits from organised crime. These people lose it deliberately in the casino, but they also, (through shell companies and intermediaries), own the casino. They own every bit of the chain. They are losing and winning at the same time."

"But why doesn't somebody do something?" asked Lynch. "Europol?"

"Because somehow everybody is involved in this game of running to stand still; in both winning and losing. The politicians lose their country's reputation and sovereignty, and they also win by joining in the big property deals, by being incorporated in offshore deals. And me, I write all this down in my report, and I send it off to HMG in London."

"And what will happen then?" asked Lynch.

"I lose my time and my life's energy writing the report. But I gain nothing," said Azzopardi. "My only prize is a headache."

"I have cases like that too," said Lynch. "I've just invested three months of my life collecting evidence on a series of abuse cases. I took it to the DPP, and I just know they will do nothing."

"Poor us," said Azzopardi. "We work and we slave, eh? And nothing happens! Nothing happens unless there is political will. And if the people (I mean the public) if they do not care, (because the people are never told anything remotely important so how can they care?), then if the people don't care why should any Government act?"

"Exactly so," said Lynch. "We are the same, you and I."

And on this point of identification, Azzopardi grimaced, "There's no appetite in HMG for listening to either of us." And then he asked, "So, we are aligned. How can I help you Superintendent Lynch? I'm all ears."

"I work for The Foundation, an independent organisation that takes up causes, investigates crimes and rights wrongs, if you take my meaning. We were commissioned to find a man, an academic who disappeared in Malta two weeks ago. I'm here, with a representative of the University who is also a founder of The Foundation, Professor Power. He's a forensic psychiatrist."

"I've heard of him," said Azzopardi. "I read about his cases in the press, The Ley Man, and Cannibal Jo."

"Yes," said Lynch, only slightly hipped that Azzopardi remembered Power's role in solving these cases, and not his own. "That's him."

"And ... don't tell me ... the local police have been less than useful?"

"They established the basic facts of the case when our client, the University of Allminster, phoned them. Professor Shacklin attended three meetings with the University here, was meant to check out of his hotel on a Monday and fly home. He wasn't in his room that night, never checked out in the morning and never left via the airport. He's not in a hospital, or in jail. And that's all they were prepared to establish until he turns up again, dead or alive."

"Well, he could always have been Shanghaied and left on a yacht with a few Russians," chuckled Azzopardi. "But you know how difficult it is to disappear nowadays, unless you are totally incapacitated. We leave traces in the ether wherever we go – bank cards, mobile telephones, CCTV – all that."

"He stopped using his University credit card the day before his flight home. I know he has a mobile phone because there was a charger in his room amongst his belongings."

"That's quite useful, because the phone might still be on him. We could help you track that."

"I have also established from the hotel manager that Shacklin had, er, female guests in his room and slept with them." Azzopardi noticed Lynch's discomfort at the mention of casual sex and smiled to himself. "There are some hairs on his clothing," said Lynch. "And he visited a casino, where he allegedly got himself beaten up. Professor Power is interviewing Shacklin's contacts at the University as we speak."

"If you're thinking of having a forensics lab check his belongings out don't use the police labs, I warn you. Bring the clothes here. We can have them analysed instead, much quicker. And," he rummaged in a drawer and withdrew some small packets, rather like those sachets containing scented towels in Asian restaurants. "You can screen some patches of his belongings if you like. These are a new innovation we have. They test for cocaine dust. Wipe them on the surface you want to touch – lapels, cuffs of the suit, whatever – and the wipe goes blue in the presence of cocaine dust."

"I'll try it, of course, and I'll bring the belongings in tomorrow," said Lynch. "But I doubt forensics can isolate anything. The stuff has been lying in his room, then collected by hotel staff, stored by other staff, then passed from another person to me . . ."

"We'll have a go for you, Superintendent Lynch. Don't worry."

"Why did you focus on the cocaine?"

"You mentioned the casino," said Azzopardi, as if that was all that needed to be said. "Now, do you have the demographic details on Shacklin – full name, date of birth, place of birth, home address – as much as you can, really?"

Lynch ferreted in the document file he had brought and took out a page with Shacklin's basic details and handed this to Azzopardi, who inputted them into a file. He finished with Shacklin's employer, the University.

"Allminster University," Azzopardi mused on the name. "I know you mentioned it before, but the word Allminster rings a bell. Let me think about that. Right we're good to go. You've got his University credit card details. But he must have a personal bank card, no?"

"I suppose so," said Lynch.

"Let's look for it," said Azzopardi. We use a program called PRUDENCE. It will give us the last thirty days of transactions of his bank cards."

Lynch was about to protest that surely banking details were

confidential, when he realised such a comment would make him sound an Intelligence *parvenu*.

He began shuffling his chair round to look at the screen Azzopardi was using.

"It's OK, stay at your desk there, I'll mirror the screen I'm using to your computer so you can see what I'm looking at. Look, I've brought up Shacklin's Gold Card. You can see the transactions. A car service. A meal in Chester, probably for two given the price. Another meal out. Petrol. A home delivered pizza? They're usually disgusting. Then we move to Malta. Presumably these are the things he didn't want to put on the company card for the University's financial controller to see. Entry fee to a club. Bar bill from the club. Difficult to tell with club drinks whether he was buying for himself or a score of people. Club drinks are expensive!"

Lynch was writing down the dates and places of the transactions. "I'll print this off for you," said Azzopardi helpfully. "And here's something interesting. "An evening at the casino, documented in four unhappy transactions." Azzopardi mentally added them up. "He spent thirty thousand pounds in one night at one of the new casinos in St Julian's. He wasn't winning so he topped up his account at the casino, not once but three more times. Did you know your man has a gambling problem?"

"I think Carl did mention that," said Lynch. "But who has thirty thousand pounds to waste on gambling?"

"No-one with any sense, in my book," said Azzopardi. "Looking at the balances on the rest of his bank accounts, he was in a desperate position financially. Have you considered suicide as an explanation for his disappearance?"

"I don't think we've ruled anything out," said Lynch, slightly despondently. "And if he owed too much to the wrong people, maybe it's possible someone took their pound of flesh to settle the debt?" Lynch wondered if this explained the mugging that the hotel manager had described.

"Was the casino debt a surprise?" asked Azzopardi. "You look surprised."

"I shouldn't be, I know," said Lynch. "A long-term police officer should never be surprised by the human condition. But he was a senior academic."

"So? Maybe he was just good at controlling his appearance, like a chameleon."

"This last transaction is interesting," said Lynch. "Fifteen Maltese Lira to Malta Cabs. It's dated the day that he was supposed to fly out. Maybe he did take a cab to the airport after all."

"The fare is high though," said Azzopardi. "The fare to the airport from Valetta would be half that. Hold on," he punched some keys on the keyboard and up came a new screen in front of Lynch. "Luckily Malta Cabs has a computerised dispatch system. We can link the transaction number like this, and . . . *ecco* your man took a taxi at seven a.m. from Valetta to Dingli Cliffs. That's on the Southern coast, about seventeen kilometres from here. Odd to go sightseeing at that time in the morning, but I suppose he could still have made the journey there, seen the cliffs, which are spectacular by the way, (you should try to see them) and then got back to the hotel to check out in time for the plane?"

"So we know from his card transaction that he was alive for another day after the last University credit card transaction, possibly," said Lynch. "And it's a one way journey? No return?"

"He took a one way express to the cliffs. No return. You do know it's a suicide spot, don't you? Spectacular, but also perpendicular."

"That would make sense, sadly," said Lynch. "We have Beachy Head in the UK. Is there anything else? Any idea of where he might have been headed in the despatch?"

"Nothing," said Azzopardi. "From what I know of there are a few farms, a weather station, I think. A café? Look," he brought up a recent newspaper story from the *Times of Malta* on the screen. He read the headline. "Girl from Gozo Crime Family Kills Herself at Dingli."

Lynch glanced at the story about a young woman who had plunged over the cliff edge and dashed herself to death on the rocks below. She had been thirty-three, and mourning the deaths of her father and brother, who had died in tragic circumstances. Her name was Savina Daidalos. Something about this name seemed familiar, but Lynch couldn't work out what it was. "Who was the crime family," he asked Azzopardi.

"Daidalos? The family dealt in cocaine. Not a big player in the global scheme of things, not now we're in the EU, but still, the family was hideously wealthy. The father and son died in a plane accident."

Something again struggled to find its way out through the thickets of Lynch's memory, but failed and remained tangled and lost to him."

"Let's have a look at his mobile calls and messages," said Azzopardi. "There's a record of his phone right here." He clicked on it. "But don't go quoting all this to others. This is FVEY technology courtesy of the NSA. The director, Alexander, believes in the policy of 'collecting it all' – every message, every email. I'm using TEMPORA. That will give us the last thirty days." Up came a list of who had called Shacklin and *vice versa* plus all his text messages. The last text message he sent was 'Where are you?" sent at eight a.m. on the day Shacklin disappeared. "It's sent to an unidentifiable number," said Azzopardi. "They should ban pay as you go phones. Everybody needs to be on a contract so we can identify them. The message location was the South Coast of Malta. So he went to meet someone who wasn't there. You don't go to meet someone if you're going to kill yourself. It's a pretty solitary activity, suicide."

"Usually," said Lynch. "I have seen suicide pacts though, and assisted suicides." Lynch remembered, with an involuntary shudder, being called to a house in the early days of his career. An elderly couple had taken an overdose a month earlier and a police officer was summoned to break in, by the postman on his rounds, because of the smell through the brass letter box.

Azzopardi was scrolling through the text messages. "He was having an affair with a student," he announced. "Look – there are messages where he asks to meet her after her lectures. There's stuff about a trip with him to a hotel in York. And another exchange where she's worried about her essay grades and he promises she will pass her end of year exams. And here, she says she's late and he replies he will take care of everything."

Lynch put his head into his hands and groaned profoundly. "This man! Every discovery about him just leads to another set of questions."

"Like the Hydra," said Azzopardi, grinning at Lynch's discomfiture. You cut off one head and another two grow back."

"Mmm," said Lynch, not looking up.

"I'll print it all off for you," said Azzopardi. "It can be a problem, all this information. Maybe some of it is just noise. I expect you'll filter out what's important in time. An affair in England might have nothing to do with his death here in Malta."

"Death?" queried Lynch. "Why do you say that?"

"Because the all traces just stop there. At the cliffs. And you know yourself that, on the balance of probabilities, when someone has been silent for so long . . . and the data analysis shows that Shacklin's phone never left that cell – the one on the coast there. So I'm betting that Shacklin is no more. If that comment is in bad taste given Shacklin's gambling problem, I do apologise."

Lynch felt unable to make a counter argument against Azzopardi's assertion that Shacklin was probably dead.

Azzopardi was keen to change the subject, and said with some enthusiasm, "I can use PRISM, if you want? There may be some extra data there for you?"

"What does PRISM do?" asked Lynch, somewhat weakly. He needed a cup of tea. He was no longer concerned about appearances. He no longer cared if Azzopardi knew that all these programs and their bewildering acronyms were news to him. However, Azzopardi didn't mind. He was enjoying showing off his technology.

"PRISM is in its infancy, of course, but it is a program to survey and collate all internet communications. It results from US demands on corporations like Microsoft, Apple, AoL and Google. They collaborate with the NSA and the Government leaves them alone to make a profit. As a bonus, British Intelligence also gets to use PRISM. Shall I print off all Shacklin's emails for you?"

"Please," said Lynch. "Look, can I go and make a cup of tea for us both? While you're helping out with all this? It's the least I can do." Azzopardi pointed Lynch in the direction of the kitchen and Lynch walked there through the silent, empty building. He wondered at the unoccupied rooms, once presumably busy with clerks and secretaries working secretly for the Empire, and now run by a single duty officer, seemingly with the world at his fingertips.

* * *

The same morning, Power had driven to the University of Malta's main campus at Msida. The official car parks were overflowing and so he parked the hire car on a narrow side road and wondered whether there was any University, anywhere in the world, that didn't have a parking problem.

In his slightly compulsive fashion, Lynch had provided him with

214

a list of people to interview, and had even gone so far as to make the appointments in advance, all while Power had been swimming up and down the pool at the Phoenicia the day before. He consulted the list as he got out of the car and started walking to the campus:

10.30 a.m. Professor Savona, University Rector (Main Administration Block)

11.45 a.m. Professor Malarbi, Dean of Medicine and Pro Rector for Science (Faculty of Science) (Enquire with both about any females Shacklin may have had contact with at the University – long blonde hair, or short, curled brunette. Enquire too about a Professor of (possibly) Physics called Xuereb).

2.00 p.m. Professor Costaguti, Head of External Enterprises and Erasmus Programme (Valletta campus)

When Power was admitted to the inner sanctum of the University for his first appointment, Professor Savona proved to be a short elderly man. A few remaining wisps of grey hair hung like clouds above his ears. His copper-coloured eyes were watery with age. Savona dispensed tea with lemon and a dose of sympathy about the disappearance of Shacklin. As the sympathy was dispensed, Power sipped the weak tea thoughtfully and listened. The Rector's spoon clinked against the porcelain of his teacup as he stirred it, seemingly endlessly. They sat in the shade of Savona's office. Thin slivers of sunlight shone through the window's venetian blinds. The light made waving patterns on the wall as a breeze wafted the blinds to and fro.

Professor Savona continued. "Naturally, we were all most concerned and sorry to hear of the disappearance of Professor Shacklin. I do hope he is found, safe and well, as soon as possible. It is so distressing for Allminster, and of course, his family."

"I think his parents are deceased," said Power. "And he was divorced, but as you say, it is all most unsettling. I've been sent by the Vice Chancellor on a commission to see if I can find Professor Shacklin. If you can shed any light on his last few days it would help us considerably."

"Of course! Well, I met Professor Shacklin one morning to discuss refreshing the memorandum of understanding between us, to renew our agreements about Erasmus, and he was charming. We discussed his new project to develop a medical school, his negotiations with the local hospitals, his plans for the curriculum and so forth. Very enterprising of him, I thought." Power raised a solitary eyebrow in surprise, but refrained from making any comment. Professor Savona continued, "I agreed the renewal of our agreements, and that was that. It was a formality really. He had appointments with others. I understand he was staying at the Phoenicia. Very expensive there. Allminster must have some money! He could have saved your University hundreds of pounds by staying in our University accommodation." Power nodded, but thought that Shacklin prioritised his social life, and might not have wanted these activities observed.

"Did he have any friends at the University here, any . . . friendly or even close relationships?"

"To me he seemed focused on his work. I did invite him to dine with my family," said Savona. "But he explained he was working on a document in the evenings and had a deadline for it when he got back." Power inferred that Shacklin would deem that dinner with the Rector lacked the kind of excitement he craved. "Professor Shacklin wished to give me the impression he was focused on his work. Tell me, are you having any success in tracing your colleague?"

"We have some leads," said Power. "Whilst he was with you did he ever mention meeting a Professor Xuereb?"

"I honestly can't say I've ever met anyone of that name," said Savona. "Professor Power, if I can enquire, what is your role at Allminster?"

"I've been appointed by the Vice Chancellor to create the new medical school," said Power. "To develop the curriculum, liaise with local primary care and hospitals for student placements, that sort of thing. In more normal times I'd probably wish to discuss a reciprocal relationship with your medical school."

Savona diplomatically did not mention the conflict with the narrative given to him by Shacklin. "I gather you are meeting Professor Malarbi later. She is our medical dean and I think that a future reciprocal relationship, swapping elective students maybe, would be very welcome. I think you are also seeing Professor Costaguti in

Valletta?" Power thought the Rector had been very well briefed. Power also deduced that Savona was in the process of dismissing Power from his presence. "You will see the old campus building in Valletta then, it dates back to 1595, when it was a Jesuit college. This University officially came to existence on 22 November 1769, when Grand Master Fonseca signed *Pubblica Università di Studi Generali*. We have grown from a handful of students then to nine thousand students this year." Savona stood up. "Will you be seeing any of the Island while you are with us? It is a very ancient and beautiful place." Matching the Rector's non-verbal cues Power got up and shook Savona's hand.

"Do you recommend I see anywhere in particular?"

"The prehistoric temples," said Savona. "All of them, but Qrendi and Hagar Qim in particular. Visit them. Imagine the people who built them. We don't know who they were but we can surely appreciate their exquisite taste and their sense of design."

"Thank you for your time, Rector," said Power, and slipped out of the Rector's offices and strode purposefully across the campus. The campus was expansive and built at the turn of the century; rectangular flat-roofed blocks, three or four storeys in height, and fashioned out of light, salmon-pink bricks. Power spotted a student canteen and dived in to buy a drink. The day was warming up and so he bought a can of Kinnie, a local fizzy drink, to try. From its appearance he thought Kinnie would have a bright orange flavour, but it was made from bitter oranges and extracts of wormwood, and was not to his taste. He went back to the counter and bought some mineral water instead.

Professor Malarbi, was a blonde-haired haematologist. Power gauged her to be in her early forties. She wore no make up, but had steel-blue eyes, with smile lines around them. She was enthusiastic in manner. Her handshake was surprisingly firm and her gaze direct. They met in her office in the Faculty of Science where she directed both the science faculty and the medical school. As Power explained his mission to her he noticed that she betrayed no emotion at all, even when he told her that Shacklin had failed to return home to Allminster. When he had finished his explanation, she merely commented on Power's profession. "You're a psychiatrist, aren't you?"

"I am," he said.

"I enjoyed my psychiatry attachment as a student at St Thomas's Hospital. In those days Malta sent her students to London. The

Government still sends patients to London for specialist treatment, but less so nowadays. We have developed our own medical service here. I'm pleased to say it's very decent."

"Did you meet Professor Shacklin?"

"He wanted to talk to me about medicine. I don't know why. He's no doctor and it was clear he knew nothing about the subject."

"How did he seem? In his mood?" asked Power.

"Are you asking me if he was depressed? Do you think maybe he killed himself? I would say he seemed the opposite of depressed. He was very full of himself and clearly his libido was intact." She paused. "You look surprised."

"I didn't expect you to say that, that's all," said Power.

"We're both doctors," she said. "No point in talking in code. And don't go thinking I accepted his offer. I sent him away with a flea in his ear."

"I don't quite follow," said Power.

"He asked me out. And I declined," she said. "I know that type of man only too well and I can't put up with any of them. I'm sorry if I'm being so direct about one of your colleagues, but he had no respect for me." She held up her left hand and Power noted the wedding ring. Power felt instinctively that Professor Malarbi was telling the absolute truth. The blonde hairs and perfume on Shacklin's clothing were not hers. "Why should I respect your Professor Shacklin? Even if he is dead."

Power felt that whatever the circumstances, Professor Shacklin was not *his*, but he focused on the word she had chosen to use last. "Dead?" said Power. "Who said he was dead?"

"I checked the options out when I heard he was missing. There was no Professor Shacklin admitted to any of the Island's hospital beds. He's not lying ill anywhere. He never left the Island. He hasn't made contact with his employer. *Ergo* he's dead. Sorry to be blunt, but was he the kind of man that goes on a drug-fuelled binge for weeks at a time, disappears from society and fails to tell his employer? He didn't seem that type."

"Do you know anybody else that did go out with him whilst he was here?"

"No," she said. "I can't imagine anyone I know lowering themselves to his level. But then, he would only continue to behave the way he did if his methods had had some previous success, wouldn't you say? Did he have a reputation in England?"

Power noted her use of the past tense again. "He has a reputation," he admitted. "I'm afraid to have to say that about him, but yes."

"I don't know why you're 'afraid' to say it," said Professor Malarbi. "It would help many more people if such things were acknowledged, rather than people being 'afraid' to speak out."

Power wondered about whether he should mention the new medical school, but he felt that any new ideas he raised at this meeting would be tainted by the impressions that Shacklin had left in Malarbi's mind.

"Do you know anything else about Shacklin's visit? Did he say anything about his plans that might help us find him?"

"He thought he might make a trip to Gozo. It's a small island a few miles away. He said he'd never been there," she said. "But I advised him that to be worthwhile it would need a full day and he said he didn't have that much time left. Seems he was right." She raised a quizzical eyebrow.

"We're not sure he's dead at all," said Power, but he was aware his voice lacked conviction.

Malarbi fixed him with a disbelieving stare. "I'm sorry if I'm not more sympathetic towards your colleague, but I'm not a natural diplomat, I can't switch on a sympathetic face and pretend an emotion I don't have. I hope you find him alive, of course, but he didn't strike me as the kind of person I'd ever want to be in the same room with again."

"I appreciate your candour," said Power. "You have been more helpful than you think. As per medical research negative results can be as useful as positive ones." She nodded. "One last question, Professor Malarbi, do you know Professor Xuereb? We think Shacklin may have met them."

"I have never met a Professor Xuereb."

"Possibly Professor Xuereb is a physicist?" asked Power.

"Not in the Faculty of Science. And I'd know if he was here or not, as it's me who signs off the salary list every month."

Power drove as swiftly as he could back to the capital and right up to the *porte cochère* of the Phoenicia to hand the hire car, a Subaru, over to the doorman to park. He hurried into the walled city seeking lunch and found *Caffe Cordina* on Republic Street. Power chose a bar seat in the busy, but splendid interior, and admired the arched ceiling and gilded walls. He ordered a bagel filled with tomato and grilled aubergines, a rum baba and a Maltese coffee. He was surprisingly hungry and knowing his next appointment was only minutes away he demolished his lunch with a rapidity that did not guarantee good digestion.

The Valletta Campus building was thankfully just a short walk down Old Theatre Street, onto Triq it-Teatru l-Antik and then left onto St Paul Street.

When he arrived, a secretary at the compound entrance informed Power that Professor Costaguti was teaching, and showed him to the board-room on the first floor, up an elegant and grand flight of stairs. Power took a seat at a massive mahogany table and looked round the wood-panelled walls. The ancient casement windows let in just a fraction of the hubbub from the tourists on the street below.

Power waited and waited, and after twenty minutes was about to conclude that he should go, but he knew he had no other appointments for the day, and Costaguti might have the vital information they needed.

Eventually the heavy boardroom door swung open and a diminutive young woman peered round the room to see whether Power had left. Her face registered some surprise that Power was still sitting calmly and attentively at the table. She was, Power thought, in her early thirties and for a moment he wondered if this was another secretary come to relay news that the good Professor had left the building. Power stood up for politeness' sake and asked, "Have I missed the Professor?"

'No, no," she said. "I am Professor Costaguti."

She made her way over to the table and took the place opposite Power, who resumed his seat. A wide field of shiny, polished wood separated them. Power could get no eye contact with her. She fiddled anxiously with her hands. Her face was pallid. She wore no make-up or perfume. It was as if she simply wanted to melt away into the wainscotting behind her.

"Well, hello," said Power, knowing he may need to work on creating any rapport with her. "I'm pleased to meet you. I'm a doctor from England, from Allminster University." He judged it best to omit that he was a psychiatrist. "A professor from Allminster, who was here a few weeks back, has disappeared. The police haven't found him. He's not in any hospital." Power checked himself and fell silent in case he was speaking to fill the void left by Professor Costaguti. Her silence was profound. Normally he had a hard time stopping professors from professing. He needed to draw Costaguti out. "What do you teach here at the University, Professor Costaguti?"

She spoke seemingly automatically, and in a monotone, looking down at her hands, "I look after enterprise. I ensure that our courses fit our students for the real world. Put business skills in accountancy. Project management into architecture. Health management into medicine. I liaise with business, and set up new projects."

"Oh, I see," said Professor Power, moving slightly to see if she would attend to him. "I could definitely have done with some business skills when they made me a clinical director in the NHS."

She rewarded him with the faintest of smiles. Power wondered if she had always had low self-esteem and if she was particularly vulnerable at this time. Had Shacklin scented vulnerability as well? Power thought he would test her reaction to his name.

"What did you and Professor Shacklin find to discuss?" The reaction was immediate. The smile, faint as it was, vanished abruptly and Costaguti's head lowered.

Power felt a sinking feeling in his belly.

"You know, Professor Costaguti . . . can I ask you your first name please?"

"Abigail," she said in a whisper.

"Abigail. If you wanted to tell me anything about Professor Shacklin, anything at all, you need to know that I would believe you." She looked into his eyes just for a moment to judge his sincerity. Power continued, "I'm interested in your truth about Professor Shacklin. I'm not Shacklin's defender. I'm certainly not his friend."

There was a long pause. Power surmised that Abigail was weighing up whether she could trust him. Telling him what happened could just lead to further hurt and loss. He could see she was on the cusp of telling him. This was a critical pause. If he spoke too soon or too late the likelihood of her disclosing would simply evaporate.

"Did he ask you out? From what I know of him, that's what I think he might do." Power held his breath and waited.

After a moment's more reflection she nodded. "Yes," she whispered. Power breathed again.

"What happened?" he asked. "Did you go?"

Shacklin had asked her to dinner when he met her on campus. He'd arrived at her flat in Sliema and walked her to a casino in St Julian's. He had been superficially charming and she had put her head on his shoulder when they danced. But he drank and he drank and, after dinner, roughly pulled her outside into the gardens at the rear of the casino, and there his hands had become more than explorative, and more invasive. She had protested vigorously. She had pulled away. But he was relentless, assaultive. She had been very frightened and nothing she said made any difference to his lust. He was clutching at her in a frenzy, his hand between her legs, penetrating her with his fingers. She had reached for and hit him with a silver jug from a nearby window ledge and when this fell clattering to the floor she had scratched his face, because he still wasn't letting go of her. He seemed to waken when he raised fingers to his torn skin and saw his blood on his fingers. He mumbled that he was sorry, but by then she had begun to run back into the casino, and through the excited fug of dancers and gamblers. She fled out into the night to the taxi rank. She was ashamed. She had told no-one at work. Since then she had stopped wearing make-up, somehow the feel of it on her skin made her feel guilty. She had stopped wearing perfume. She had started wearing dresses that covered every inch of skin from the eyes of men around her. She had started going to bed very late, being afraid of what dreams might come. In recent days she had hurried home from work every night and kept every door and windows double locked when she was indoors.

"Have people noticed you are acting differently?"

"I think so," she said. "I don't eat with people any more."

"Have you told anybody at all what happened?"

"I told a friend. A boy I've known since school. He works away. On Sicily. He said I sounded different when he phoned me. I regret telling him, I don't think he took it well. He went so quiet on the phone. I haven't heard from him since."

"When did you tell him?"

"He phoned. Just by chance. The morning after," she said.

While Shacklin was still on the Island, thought Power. "I'm sorry," he said. "So sorry – that Shacklin behaved the way he did."

"You believe me then?"

"I believe you, of course I do," said Power. "And it's something that needs to be taken seriously by Allminster and by your University. When we find Shacklin I will make sure he is held responsible. Will you tell your employer? Get help from them? They could assist you if you wanted to talk to the police. Or I could help you now, if you preferred."

"I don't want to tell anybody else, for now. It was bad enough getting the courage to tell you. I feel a bit better for telling you."

"Does it help you to know that you are believed?"

She nodded. "Can I go now?" She needed to remain in control. "I need to go."

"There are ways you can be helped. If you want, that is." Dr Power plucked his card out of his jacket pocket. "This is my card. You can call me. Any time. And the University here will have its own occupational health service."

"Thank you," she said, looking back only once as she swiftly left the room.

Power let out a long sigh and sank back into his chair. He felt he had worked so hard and yet he realised that he hadn't asked nearly enough about anything that might help them track Shacklin. He hadn't asked who the friend in Sicily was. He hadn't asked what Shacklin had talked about at dinner. Had Shacklin ever mentioned a Professor Xuereb? Did Abigail herself know a Professor Xuereb? What if her male friend had sought revenge on her behalf?

He wondered how long it would take a ferry to cross the ninety miles or so from Sicily to Malta. Maybe a couple of hours?

Power felt he couldn't go back and ask Abigail anything else now. He got up from the board-room table feeling drained and made his way downstairs, hoping to go back to the hotel for a swim during which he could reflect on the case. He was crossing the entrance hall, his brow furrowed in thought, when he heard a voice booming out after him, echoing through the marble and stone atrium.

"Dr Power! It's you! Here!"

Chapter Fifteen

Gambling can turn into a dangerous two-way street
when you least expect it. Weird things happen
suddenly, and your life can go all to pieces.
Hunter S. Thompson

The Phoenicia Hotel is always less busy in December than in the summer months, but as the days crept towards Christmas, Power and Lynch saw more and more people arriving to weather their Christmastide in Malta.

When Lynch got back to the hotel he was burdened by the sheer volume of new information Azzopardi had unearthed about Shacklin. To ponder the new facts he decided to walk in the grounds at the rear of the hotel, beyond the swimming pool that Power had enjoyed so much. The Phoenicia was an old hotel, a remnant of colonial rule, of Empire, and it seemed benignly riddled with the ghosts of history. The hotel grounds included shady pathways between palm trees and deep emerald-green, fat-leaved shrubs with half-hidden trunks through which hoses wove their snake-like way, irrigating the easily parched gravel beds, with hissing water. He wandered through the historic terraces around the marble-white fountain that played in the very spot that Churchill, once a guest of the Phoenicia, had sat under a parasol to protect his pale and wrinkled skin from the Mediterranean sun, and daubed at a canvas on his easel. Lynch dissected all the new facts about

Shacklin, weighing up which particular set of events might have triggered his disappearance. Facing a fear of being overwhelmed, Lynch prayed silently as he walked, seeking divine guidance. As he paced the same paths a third time, he noticed that where the hoses had been playing on the verdant undergrowth, they had stopped, and the water which was still a sheen of moistness on the hot ground steamed gently upwards, while hoses elsewhere in the gardens took their turn to play upon bushy blue agapanthus and bougainvillea. Lynch strolled prayerfully along the paths, between bay and lemon trees, and fragrant oleander and sweet jasmine. The sun looked like an orb of pure honey in the sky, spreading a sweet golden light on the world below. Even so, the sun was sinking in the afternoon sky, its afternoon heat had become a mellow warmth, and so Lynch went indoors. He climbed the elegant stairways slowly and thoughtfully. Alone in his room he showered. The cascading hot water revived Lynch's spirits, which had flagged under the tawdry complexity of Shacklin's life. Refreshed, he dressed quickly and found he was looking forward to re-uniting with Power to learn about Shacklin's business meetings at the University.

Lynch knocked on the door of Power's suite, but as there was no response he wandered through the hotel looking for his friend. He found Power at a table by the azure-blue swimming pool, drinking local Cisk beer. Power smiled at him in greeting and pointed to a second pint of beer he had ordered for Lynch in advance. The beer shone golden in the late afternoon sun. The glass was dappled with condensation and accompanied by a couple of dishes with crisps and olives.

"Splendid," said Lynch. "I need a beer. We've got so much to talk about. How was your day?" Lynch looked at Power. "What did you find out?"

"Well, I went to the University, as you suggested, Andrew. I saw the Rector for instance, and I think he knew more than he was willing to say. And the dean of science, well, she was frankly scathing about Professor Shacklin. He actually tried it on with her. If you wanted any evidence that he was a poor judge of character and circumstances, that would be it. Shacklin clearly has little emotional intelligence." said Power. "It doesn't take a genius to see that Professor Malarbi – that's the dean – is not a person to be trifled with. She is very direct, very forthright, and bruisingly honest. And the third person I spoke to, Professor Costaguti, well she had an even worse experience of Professor Shacklin when she went out with him to the casino. I have to say, quite bluntly, that he sexually assaulted her. Just now she's so traumatised that she couldn't tell me much more than the fact of his assaulting her. Somehow it felt wrong to pull any more information out of her than she had already given me."

"He assaulted her at the casino?" mused Lynch. "I dislike him more and more. I have another tale of Professor Shacklin and the casino myself."

"So your investigations were successful?" asked Power.

"I have a wealth – an abundance, a veritable glut – of information generated by Mr Azzopardi at the Valletta SIS branch office. I have spare copies for you to read through later. Azzopardi is the branch officer for the office. That's not his real name by the way. He helped me research all the digital details of Shacklin's life. The process was sobering. I hadn't realised how transparent our lives have become. I gave Azzopardi just the briefest details of Shacklin. He clicked buttons invoking this programme then that programme, and within seconds up came everything – Shacklin's bank accounts, Shacklin's text messages from his lost phone, Shacklin's emails; basically every trace and essence of the man in the digital world.

"I learned that Shacklin lost thirty thousand pounds in just one evening at the casino, probably placing successive bets. He was, or possibly still is, desperate for money, because in general his bank accounts are threadbare. A University apparatchik cannot afford to lose thirty thousand pounds a night if his annual salary is one hundred thousand.

"And also I learned that the professor was having a long-term affair with a student at Allminster."

Power groaned. These latest facts suggested a desperate man, someone who had become wildly impulsive and was damaging everyone around him. Power wondered what had triggered this loss of control and a string of sexual and monetary improprieties. Had Shacklin fallen ill and become disinhibited through a frontal lobe lesion or mania? Or had he always suffered from a gambling disorder and been sexually untamed?

Lynch continued, "I found that Shacklin was probably alive on the morning of his planned flight home. There are transaction records for his own credit card. The University bursar didn't have access to Shacklin's personal card details. Shacklin booked and paid for a taxi to Malta's southern coast himself, to a suicide spot called Dingli Cliffs. He was due to meet someone there according to his text message log (you see how much information the Service has access to – at the click of a button), and so if Shacklin went there to meet somebody I'm not convinced his motive for that trip was to throw himself off a cliff, even if he had impoverished himself through gambling." Lynch looked at Power. "But the information – and there are reams – still doesn't tell us exactly why the man has disappeared. We have no body. We don't know where he is, except his mobile phone never left the Southern coast. Azzopardi tracked Shacklin's mobile phone to a mobile communication cell on the southern coast. The phone never left there. Whether the phone became separated from Shacklin, I don't know.

"And seemingly now there's a tapestry of people with reasons to harm Shacklin with a dozen or so threads to unravel. Did he fall foul of the casino? Was he corrupt, was he siphoning money from Allminster? Did he fall foul of a jilted girlfriend from home? Or was he involved in buying or selling drugs?"

"Drugs?" Power looked puzzled. He was genuinely surprised and he had never imagined Shacklin would be involved in anything like that. He wondered if perhaps he was being naïve.

"I haven't got to that part yet. But drugs may also be involved. Azzopardi gave me a kit to test Shacklin's clothing. I wiped his suits with chemical swabs and the swabs came up a delightful peacock blue. So his clothing tests positive for cocaine. Of course that could be a false positive. Maybe his clothes were handled by someone who uses cocaine, or maybe he took his jacket off and put it behind him on a chair whilst he played poker at the casino and someone brushed past him. The test showing positive for cocaine could be nothing – a red herring amid a shoal of clues."

"Well, perhaps we've done all we can today," said Power. "When things get complicated, perhaps the best thing to do is set them aside and think about something else, or better still sleep on the matter." He looked at his watch. "And maybe we can set them aside for a while, because I met somebody on the University campus in Valletta this afternoon. Someone we both know. And I've invited him to dine here with us tonight."

"Who?" asked Lynch, puzzled.

Power gestured to a figure making his way out of the hotel's garden entrance and ambling towards their table. A grey-haired man in a spruce white linen suit of startling brilliance, with a small, pink rose in his buttonhole. Lynch noted his hair was long, but neatly groomed and tied into a pony tail. This was accompanied by an equally long white beard. Power extended his arm and waved animatedly to the man, to draw his attention. Although he could not quite place who it was, Lynch thought the man looked familiar. His memory slipped into gear and he finally recognised the man who was now walking over to their table.

"Well, Carl," said Lynch. "It seems we do have an old friend in Valletta." He stood up and extended a hand of welcome to the distinguished old man. "Good evening, Ramon. It's a while since we walked the Way together."

The old man laughed and shook his hand. "Buen Camino. We met then, yes. But once you walk that path together, you always walk that path. It just unfolds before us, does it not?"

Ramon Calleya had once been a fellow pilgrim walking the St James's Way with Power and Lynch some years before. The start of the pilgrimage can be defined differently, according to who and where you might be. For instance, it could be said to start at your own front door. But the main walking path stretches 790 miles from Le Puy-en-Velay in the Haute Loire region of Southern France into Northern Spain and finishes at the cathedral in Santiago de Compostela. Ramon Calleya had told them he regularly walked the route during his annual leave in the University holidays. It would take someone eleven days of solid walking, day *and* night to walk the entire Way, so modern pilgrims often start at points along the way, and stop intermittently at hostels and paradors – state owned and run hotels, often in picturesque castles or monasteries. For most pilgrims though a bed in a hostel is all that is required to rest their weary bones for the night. They fall into a deep sleep and are scarcely aware whether their surroundings are a gothic palace or a wooden hut.

Power and Lynch had met Ramon, camping in a tent, when there was no room in a hostel. Together they had watched the billions of stars of the Milky Way, as they danced, exquisitely bright in the Galician sky.

"And have you walked St James's Way this year?" asked Lynch. He remembered Ramon talking of making annual pilgrimages.

"No, my ancient hip told me I was not to walk this year. Maybe I will have it replaced for insubordination, and next year I will march along the Camino on my shiny new metal hip?"

"We walked the way with you at the very start of the Millennium," said Power, drawing out a chair for Ramon. "What about the between years. Did you walk it another time?"

"Twice," said Ramon proudly. "Guzzling wine and painkillers along the way." He looked guiltily at Power, "I know I shouldn't have mixed the two, Doctor." Ramon winked at Lynch.

"And what are you doing here in Malta?" asked Lynch. In asking this question, Lynch perhaps betrayed the quality of his memory, for once upon a time Ramon had told him.

"I work here," said Ramon, looking reproachfully at Lynch over his gold rimmed spectacles . "I don't expect you to recall, but I am a Professor at the University of Malta."

"Of course you are," said Lynch. "I remember now. Please forgive me, Ramon. It has been four years."

"Perhaps I can take you to dinner?" said Ramon. "We can re-forge our friendship."

"We were hoping to buy you dinner here at the Phoenicia," said Power. He signalled to a white-jacketed waiter for more Cisk beers for the trio. "Do you agree, Andrew?"

"Of course, please join us, Ramon." said Lynch. "Do you know why we are here on Malta?"

"I did mention it," said Power. "And Ramon is happy to help us; I thought he could advise us – from a local point of view."

"And I assured Professor Power that I am the soul of discretion," said Ramon.

"I hope you won't find our conversation about the missing man unpleasant," said Lynch.

"I'm fascinated by a mystery, and it's a small island," said Ramon. "If I can help you find him I will."

"Then it's settled, we'll be your hosts tonight. Is dinner here any good?"

"It is the best," said Ramon. "Five star. A rare and expensive treat for an ancient and impoverished professor like me."

The waitress from the bar who had arrived carrying their three beers giggled at Ramon's overheard comment about the immoderate expense of dining at the Phoenicia. "Oh, Professor Ramon!"

"You know the Professor?" Lynch asked the waitress.

"Everyone knows the Professor at the Phoenicia. He is a television star. A good tipper too. He's very rich." She went off, chuckling to herself.

Ramon shrugged. "I may have done a few educational programmes on TVM2. She's probably referring to that." His modesty belied the fact that he presented a weekly magazine programme that blended twin themes of philosophy and astronomy.

"I know you are the soul of discretion, Ramon, but you won't reveal anything we have to say about the missing man on air?" said Lynch. "I am sorry, but I have to check."

Ramon feigned an expression of mild offence at the implication he might be indiscreet. "My lips are sealed. You can trust me. But my programme is not topical – on air I only talk about subjects that range from Pluto to Plutarch. Any confidence will be respected."

After their drinks, the trio moved from the poolside to an elegant table in the grand bay window of the grand restaurant. All was mock Edwardian splendour, with silver cutlery and crisply starched linen tablecloths and napkins, under a soaring ceiling. In the centre of the room was a dance floor where the young Princess Elizabeth had waltzed with her new husband, the Duke of Edinburgh when they lived in the Villa Guardamangia in Pieta just outside Valletta.

It was early evening and the dining room was not so busy that the *maître de* could not afford to lavish his attention upon them. He attempted to press upon them the most expensive wines, but Ramon held up his hand. "We want the best wines, and quality does not always equate with cost." Instead of a bottle of Screaming Eagle Sauvignon, Ramon steered them towards a particular wine, native to Malta; a bottle of Isis Chardonnay from the Meridiana vineyard at T' Qali.

They ordered starters of Butternut Squash Veloute for Power, Avruga Caviar and Smoked Eel for Lynch and Ramon, and main dishes of Stuffed Local Rabbit, Swiss Chard with Morels, and 'Café de Paris' Cauliflower, Capers, Raisins and Oyster Leaf. The trio sat back expectantly with an aperitif of Zeppi's Bajtra poured over ice. Ramon explained the aperitif was distilled from the pulp of the leaves of the prickly pear. Power looked at the pink liquid with interest. It had a sweet, delicate flavour. As he drank it he tried not to think about the prospect of watching Lynch and Ramon dining on rabbit.

"How is life on Malta?" Lynch asked Ramon.

"For an elderly widower it is perhaps better than I could hope for," said Ramon. "I sleep well, I bask in the sun, I tend my garden, I write papers on physics, and philosophy, and I teach – the questions of the young keep me thinking – and they gave me a platform on the television where I can spout my opinions on the stars. What more could I want? When I was a young man you know physics was a part of philosophy – natural philosophy. Then physics became consumed by maths. And now, with quantum physics, suddenly things have taken a philosophical turn again. Erwin Schrödinger who pioneered quantum physics had a great passion for Indian philosophy."

"And young ladies too," said Power. "He got his wife's maid pregnant in Dublin."

"There's an interesting story there, almost about quantum entanglement. Schrödinger was a Professor of Quantum Physics. His work inspired work in so many fields, including DNA, the molecule of life. The pregnant maid was taken away by her angry family and Schrödinger's illegitimate daughter was brought up in a foreign country. She was never told who her famous father was. When, in turn, her son was brought up, he too was never told who his grandfather was. That son became a Professor of Quantum Physics. I see it as an allegory of quantum entanglement." He took a sip of the aperitif and looked at Power and Lynch with some satisfaction.

"God works in mysterious ways," said Lynch. "I remember you telling us about the mysteries of the heavens. It is a shame that we do not meet in better circumstances."

Ramon sighed, "Times have changed. The island was a simpler place after the war, safe, God-fearing, cherishing its peace after bitter times, but these days there is a danger about it again. Little Malta glitters like a jewel in the Mediterranean Sea, but a new undercurrent flows in our daily life. And it is all to do with money."

"There is great wealth on show in the harbours," said Lynch. "Superyachts jostling in the water, as far as the eye can see. I met a

Mr Azzopardi today and he told me of the money rolling in from places like Russia and gangs on Sicily."

"If your Professor Shacklin was involved with those people go home now and stay clear," warned Ramon. "If you're thinking of tackling anything that overlaps with N'drangheta business, my advice is don't. Just don't. To tackle N'drangheta business you would need your own private army." He frowned. "They come in boats. No need to go through customs or board planes. We're just a two hour boat ride from Pozzallo or Portopalo di Capo Passero. Bring over a briefcase stashed with cash and re-invest it. Launder it. No one asks questions. No one dares to." The waiter arrived with their chilled wine and whilst he poured their glasses, Ramon held his tongue. Once he had gone Ramon resumed his warnings. "This quest of yours is dangerous. I am an old man, my life is over, but you are young men. You are charming, intelligent, and as far as I can judge, both in prime health. You were engaged in a dangerous matter when I met you first, in Northern Spain. If the N'drangheta are involved then do know that you are dicing with death – what puzzles me is why the two of you need to do this? You chance your lives with every challenge? Is it for the thrill of cheating death or for the feeling of a doctor who denies death by treating disease? You are playing a game of chance with the highest stakes – a bit like Bergman's chess player in *The Seventh Seal*? If you win you can return home to your wife and family. If you lose . . ."

"I appreciate your concern. We both do. But I always put my trust in the Lord. Carl went to your University today to see if they knew anything that would help our investigation, but besides Shacklin being a pest to your female colleagues, – well he was more than a pest to be honest. His bank accounts and his mobile telephone logs tell us a story – of a loss of thirty thousand pounds in the casinos of St Julian's, and affairs with students. We even found traces of cocaine on his jackets."

"Your professor was very 'sex and drugs and rock and roll', wasn't he?" said Ramon.

"He assaulted a Maltese colleague of yours . . . and she told an ex-partner about the assault . . . a man who lives on Sicily . . . which as you say, is only a couple of hours away," said Power. "And we are wondering whether the ex-partner arranged to meet Shacklin on the morning he disappeared."

"You see Ramon – there are complications upon complications!"

said Lynch. He turned back to Power. "When you were at the University did you ask about Professor Xuereb?"

"I did," said Power. "They all denied knowledge of such a professor. The Dean, Professor Malarbi said she signed all the salaries off, and so she was sure he wasn't on the payroll."

"And where precisely does Professor Xuereb come into all this?" asked Ramon gently, mopping up the last of his rabbit's sauce using a morsel of bread.

"The name – Professor Xuereb – was written on a telephone pad in Shacklin's hotel room," said Lynch. "Written there as if it was information he'd just found out and noted down. But we don't know who Professor Xuereb is?"

"And there I can help you," said Ramon. "I can pay you back for this splendid repast. I know who Professor Xuereb is."

Chapter Sixteen

*If you want to find the secrets of the universe, think in
terms of energy, frequency and vibration.*

Nikola Tesla

The trio finished dinner and sat replete, drinking cafetieres of coffee in the lounge. Power and Lynch had been anticipating that Ramon would tell them all about Professor Xuereb at the dining table, when he was approached by three teenage girls and their mothers from Valletta, who had just arrived to dine in style. They had recognised Ramon, and his autograph was required by all three girls. They flashed their brown eyelashes at the professor and said effusive thanks as their mothers whisked them away for dinner.

Power, Lynch and Ramon had taken refuge in the lounge in a secluded alcove by a leafy palm tree, and ordered a large plate of almond krustini and sesame ottini to accompany steaming, aromatic black coffee.

Ramon occupied a plush, gilded, crimson couch. He spread out on it, revelling in stretching out his arms and legs along the back. He sighed happily.

"Now we are suitably alone and no-one can overhear us," he said. "I can tell you the story of Professor Xuereb. First of all though, can I ask you, Carl, to tell me exactly what words my colleagues at the University used to describe him?"

Power thought back over the conversations of the morning at the University, trying to recall the exact phrases the academics had used. "Professor Savona, the Rector, said that he'd never met anyone of that name, and Professor Malarbi said she'd never met a Professor Xuereb and never signed a salary for a Professor Xuereb in the Faculty of Science."

"Academics! You can always depend on them to choose their words with absolute care!" He looked at Lynch as the sole non-academic there to see if he would agree. "Our University grew from the *Collegium Melitense,* which was founded in 1592 by the Jesuits. And I think the traditions must have continued as those answers are most Jesuitical." Ramon chuckled to himself.

"So, were they lying?" asked Lynch.

"They were telling the truth," said Ramon. "From a certain point of view."

"I don't understand," said Power.

"The Rector and Professor Malarbi were only appointed in the last few years. And you will know that a University is quite a big organisation. You can work in one faculty and never meet a colleague from a different faculty. So, yes, it's possible that the Rector never met Professor Xuereb, and it is also probably true that Professor Malarbi has never signed off the salary for Professor Xuereb. But the truth you sought and were not given is that Professor Xuereb did work in physics at the University. *I knew him.* I worked alongside him. But Xuereb might not have met this particular Rector, and Malarbi certainly arrived after he had left. But I'm sure they both would have known of Xuereb. He was infamous at the University. Fancy them not telling you about him! I am surprised by them. It goes to show how much you can trust your academic colleagues." Power nodded thinking about his own colleague, Shacklin, at Allminster and recent revelations.

"So, now we know he was an academic here in Malta, please tell us everything you can about Professor Xuereb," said Lynch. "What does he look like?"

Ramon imagined his colleague's features and tried to describe them. "He is in his late forties. He has a commanding air. The Xuereb family had a long and noble tradition on the Island. They fought in the Crusades. He has curly brown hair, brown eyes, square-ish glasses. A goatee beard. But he never makes eye contact, and as a result people tend not to trust him. When he was young I told him to look at people and if he couldn't bear looking at their eyes, to look at a point here, above the nose." Ramon pointed to just above the bridge of his own nose.

"You've known him a while then?" asked Power.

"Paul Xuereb, yes I've known him for many years. His mother asked me to tutor him in physics when he was at college. He was a very able scientist, as if to the manner born. He was born in Naxxar in the sixties and went to study at Stella Maris College, which was run by the De La Salle Brothers. That was when I first met him in the senior school, although his mother also engaged me as a tutor to give him extra lessons at home. She thought he was particularly gifted in mathematics and physics, and she was right. Mothers usually are, aren't they? In other subjects, like English and art, he was almost clueless though. I wrote his reference to UCL in London where he did his Masters and won the Jackson Lewis Scholarship. His mother went with him to keep house for him in London. Then he did his PhD at Cambridge in quantum physics and phonons. For his doctorate he developed a mathematical model to describe how phonons could trigger an 'excitation' among superconducting quantum 'bits' causing shifts in a superconducting circuit's frequency."

"I followed you for most of that, but I lost you there," said Power. "You mentioned phonons. What is a phonon. I've never heard of one?"

"I'm very glad you asked, Carl," said Lynch. "Are they like photons?"

"In a way," said Ramon. "It's all to do with quantum physics. Both sound and light behave like waves, but wave phenomena can also behave like particles. Photons are light particles and phonons are the equivalent quantum particles for sound. Paul's choice of an area of study is of course highly ironic."

"How so?" asked Power.

"He cannot bear noise of any description," said Ramon. "One of the earliest stories his mother told me about him was that when he was an infant at his mother's knee he was so sensitive to sound he would protest about the loudness of the bells of the cathedral in Valletta, over eight miles away. He refused to let his family have a television or a radio in the house. He insisted that heavy curtains should be hung over windows and doors to keep out the noise of the birds in the fields around the house."

"He lived only with his mother, till she passed away. His father could not tolerate a son who was consistently telling him not to eat or breathe and make sounds."

"Xuereb sounds as if he might have been autistic," said Power.

"Well," said Ramon. "When his father protested one day about being made to live like a Trappist monk, his mother inevitably sided with her 'brilliant' son and the father left to live a life in town where he could eat a packet of crisps and cough without having to go to the shed outside."

"And she moved to London to be with him when he was at UCL, you said," prompted Power.

"He was young and unworldly and couldn't have gone abroad without her," mused Ramon. "I was pleased he came back though. I liked him once. I was even more pleased he got a job at the University, in my own department. But he never . . . he never settled . . . do you know what I mean? People were always suspicious of him, because he stood out. For instance, he was always railing against the noise that students made. They weren't making any untoward noise, but he perceived them as deliberately trying to annoy him. He wore noise-cancelling headphones when he walked about the faculty. That looked odd to everybody! He didn't look at anyone, he didn't like to listen to anyone. But his work was brilliant. Ten, fifteen years ahead of his time. He wrote some papers on sasers that were astonishing."

"Sasers?" asked Power.

"Saser is an acronym, it stands for Sound Amplification by Stimulated Emission of Radiation. Like a laser is for light, a saser is for sound."

"You're teasing me," said Power. "There's no such thing!"

"Maybe it sounds bizarre to the lay person, but I assure you it's a very real thing, a saser produces an intense beam of uniform phonons on a nano scale that move through tiny super-lattice structures, ping-ponging between lattice layers until they form an ultra-high frequency phonon beam."

"And what does that do?" asked Power.

"Paul said he wanted to develop sasers to use in medicine. He was interested in the effects of sound on the human body, perhaps because of his own extreme sensitivity to sound. The sasers would, he said, revolutionise medical imaging, provide high precision devices for measurement of tumours.

"He had high hopes for his postdoctoral research and expected the faculty to greet his work with the same enthusiasm that he had always come to expect from his mother. Well, as you know, the academic world can be cruel." Power nodded thoughtfully. "He bid for faculty money to fund his brilliant research – he wanted to start an institute to develop these sasers. He believed his work was of global, even historic importance.

"As you might have guessed, the faculty did not wish to invest in his genius, although I had advised them that he was ten to fifteen years ahead of his time. He was a visionary, (or at least the sonic equivalent of a visionary). It is an unfortunate truth in this world that even if you are a genius – if you don't, or can't, rub along with your peers – they won't support you."

"And he was a genius?" asked Power.

"Undoubtedly," said Ramon. "But after they turned him down he didn't give up straight away. His mother insisted he should never give up. So, with his mother's unwavering belief behind him, and without being given any University backing he went to the private sector to negotiate funds for his research. And he returned in triumph, so he thought. He managed to convince some institution or benefactor and he brought back a promise of eight million dollars! Enough to found his Institute and more."

"I sense there is a 'but'," said Power.

"You are absolutely correct, Carl. The University quibbled. They asked where does this money come from? He wouldn't say." Ramon poured himself another cup of coffee and went on. "As you know, the research grants are supposed to be accepted by the University and administered at arms length from the researcher – the University takes its cut for housing the research, providing the equipment, employing support staff and so on. Grants are the lifeblood of a University – they help it prosper and enlarge itself. But they wouldn't accept this huge amount of money. The University administers the grants to ensure probity, so it can all be audited, and the University couldn't take on money from an unknown donor, it was against it's principles. Paul didn't seem to understand the nuances of this process. He had acquired the money he needed, so why wouldn't they co-operate? It was a second humiliation at their hands. More than he could bear. Paul became embittered, isolated. He was silent and uncooperative with students and colleagues, even with me." Ramon sighed. "There was a false rumour in the faculty that this was mafia money to develop weapons for them to defeat drugs enforcement officials and customs officers. Another rumour spread that this was a military project on behalf of the Israelis. I don't know where the promised money came from, because he had stopped talking to everyone." Ramon paused. "Then his mother died. Suddenly. The very next day he tendered his immediate resignation from the University. He left to found his Institute alone – he certainly had the funds to do this! He called it The Jericho Institute. And I gather that whereas he had had peaceful intentions at the beginning of this process, the purpose of the new Jericho project was to develop weaponry. Sonic weaponry."

"The name being a reference to the city of Jericho in the Old Testament?" asked Lynch.

"Exactly," said Ramon.

Power shook his head, not quite understanding the allusion. Lynch explained. "Jericho was a city to the north of the Dead Sea. It was said to be the oldest city in the world. The army of the Israelites, under the command of Joshua, used trumpets and shouting to bring the walls of Jericho down. '*When the trumpets sounded, the army shouted, and at the sound of the trumpet, when the men gave a loud shout, the wall collapsed*'. It shed new light on the verse. I never imagined that there could be sonic weapons. Are you sure that sound can be used like this?"

"Assuredly," said Ramon. "A focused beam of sound could be a powerful weapon to project sound – the military has already applied the technology – you can project concentrated sounds at 155 decibels for over a mile. Your ears feel pain at 120 decibels, so you can imagine that is a weapon in itself. Or you could use the sound projector to send a command to your troops across a beachhead, or use it to disorientate enemy troops by playing them battlesounds or screams. Other sound weapons cause autonomic bodily responses in humans – dizziness, panic, palpitations, internal vibrations, nausea, even a feeling of overheating. And if I know Paul Xuereb, he is ahead of the technology I've read about in the research journals."

"Could he be working in the area around Dingli cliffs?" asked Lynch.

"There's nothing really round there that I remember," said Ramon.

"The cliffs themselves are stunning. Apart from that, there are goats and sheep, some wildflowers like general's root and henbane, a few pig farms. There's a navigation beacon, for aircraft to triangulate their position. But the station is automated now, unmanned, and I don't know, I would guess it's going to be replaced by satellite navigation. It used to be an RAF station in the Second World War – there was an underground radar installation that fed information to the Lascaris War Room in Valletta. The Italian planes would fly in from Sicily to disable the airstrips here by bombing them into massive craters and shattering our towns to rubble. The radar gave early warnings of the incoming Italian bombers. But that was over fifty years ago – I don't think that is the modern infrastructure that Paul needs – the underground radar rooms were damp and derelict."

"But he does have eight million dollars to buy what he needs," said Power.

"How dangerous is Paul Xuereb?" asked Lynch.

Ramon frowned. "I've known him since he was a boy and until now I've never thought of him as dangerous. He was always aloof and distant, but I never thought of him as a risk."

"Maybe not," said Power. "I can see what Andrew is worried about though. Xuereb may be very self-focused. His mother may have instilled a sense of uniqueness, a sense of superiority. To have his dream of success burst by the University, must have hurt him immensely."

"I stood up for him, recommended the University support him," said Ramon.

"But he has turned his back on the University, and moved away from conventional peer approved research into weapon innovation," said Power. "His actions speak to me of hurt through bereavement, and anger towards the world. And in his isolation, who knows what direction his lonely mind is taking."

Ramon looked upset. "He was my pupil. I feel a sense of guilt. Do you, in your professional capacity, really think he may be dangerous?"

"It would seem that he has renounced the past. All that is left to him, unless he can be redeemed, may be to harm others."

"Oh," said Ramon. "I feel I have failed him somehow. Is there anything I can do?"

"Would you come with us to see him, if we can find him?" asked Lynch. "If I can locate him, maybe we can see how he is?"

"I will, if you can find him," said Ramon.

"I have a few ideas," said Lynch. "I will see Mr Azzopardi in the morning, and ask for his help."

Chapter Seventeen

One great use of words is to hide our thoughts.

Voltaire

"There you go," said Lynch, as he handed Azzopardi a sealed and tagged plastic bag full of Shacklin's clothes and shoes. They were standing in the marble hallway of the Service's Malta office, behind the ghost-like façade of DeGiorgio and Azzopardi.

"I must thank you for the swabs you gave me," said Lynch. "One of Shacklin's suit jackets did test positive for cocaine, so a forensic analysis of all his clothes will be very welcome."

Azzopardi held out the plastic bag of Shacklin's effects away from his body, his face wearing a look of disdain. "If Shacklin was at the casino, then the cocaine traces could just be cross contamination, but the labs will tell us more. I'll put the bag in the old concierge's office."

Azzopardi ducked under the stone staircase and into a cubbyhole with *Ssorveljar* painted on a ghost sign by the entrance. He emerged wiping his hands together.

"I will send the effects off today, I see you remembered to label the bag carefully. It wouldn't do to lose the evidence. Now, are you coming up for a cup of tea again? I would welcome the company. There's nobody else in till tomorrow when the Station Commander is in for my handover and to greet a field agent. There are no other visitors expected today."

"Of course," said Lynch, sensing Azzopardi was somewhat lonely. "I wanted to ask you about something."

They climbed the stairs to find which of the many offices Azzopardi had chosen for the day. "I expect you'd rather be off seeing the Island," said Azzopardi. "Are you going to spend any time sightseeing?"

"My colleague, Dr Power, is doing the sightseeing for both of us this morning. But it's not all work for me, we had a good dinner at the Phoenicia with a Maltese TV star from your T channel last night. That was the highlight of yesterday."

"And who would that be?" wondered Azzopardi as he made them a pot of tea.

"Ramon Calleya," said Lynch.

"I've seen him," said Azzopardi. "He does a stargazing programme, late at night on Channel T." Lynch nodded. Azzopardi poured Lynch a piping hot cup of tea and offered him an Ottijiet biscuit from a porcelain jar. The biscuit had an aroma of fennel and cloves. "I have some new information to feed back to you. Yesterday we worked to try and find Professor Shacklin, of Allminster University, yes?"

Lynch nodded.

"Last night I remembered something," said Azzopardi. "I love a mystery, of course, but this one was playing on my mind. I couldn't sleep. I kept thinking over and over that there was some detail I'd forgotten. Then I remembered what it was – there was an enquiry that was passed to us by London station a couple of months ago. It was from a Professor at Allminster."

"Shacklin?" asked Lynch.

"Not him. A different name altogether," said Azzopardi. "It was an email request for information from a Professor Felfe."

Hearing Felfe's name, Lynch edged forward in his chair, "What information did Felfe want?"

"Three things he wanted to know about. He was asking if three words meant anything to the Service here. If they rang any bells with anyone. All the Malta Station staff were asked and we had to say whether or 'no' they had any resonance with us."

"What words were these?" asked Lynch.

"Felfe had, we inferred, overheard some conversation or intercepted some communication that linked these three words with Malta. I will give you the three elements he was asking about, but whether they are codewords, passwords, symbols of some kind or actual things, we never found out. They are:

Wanderlust   Sannik Law Co   The Banker

Now, do they mean anything to you, Detective Lynch? We checked for a Law firm called Sannik. There is no such firm on Malta or on Sicily. Does any term mean anything to you?"

"Not much, I'm sorry to say. The last one, The Banker, maybe. I'll come back to that. But, tell me, the Service entertained his enquiry because Professor Felfe was a Service asset?"

"At one time he was a considerable asset," said Azzopardi. "A key source of intelligence. He was dormant for years, though, and the Service thought he was extinct, like an extinct volcano, and then this communication out of the blue. Wanderlust, Sannik Law Co and The Banker. Inexplicable."

"You do know Felfe is dead?" asked Lynch.

"I checked his file only this morning," said Azzopardi. "You found his body, it said. It seems a meaningful coincidence. You found him in the cathedral?" Lynch nodded. "Heart attack as the cause of death, it says."

"It says that does it? About the cause of death?"

"It does." Azzopardi's voice had a ring of finality about it.

"My colleague, Dr Power, wondered if it really was a simple heart attack or something else?"

"It's there in the file. In black-and-white. Nothing more incontrovertible."

"Well," said Lynch. I will trade you the three words for the information I have about The Banker. Just like you, I was struggling to sleep last night. So I read all through the hoard of Shacklin's emails." Lynch had them with him in a folder. He started riffling through them as he talked. "Shacklin just couldn't separate his work from his private life. I know more about his sexual liaisons and the inner workings of Allminster's curriculum committees than is good for me. But I did find this," Lynch handed over a sheet with an email thread on it. "It shows that Shacklin was trying to arrange a meeting on the Island with someone called The Banker."

Azzopardi took the paper and read down the page. He took his time and his brow furrowed in concentration as he made a note on a blank piece of paper on his desk. He looked up at Lynch. "Shacklin doesn't say enough here to be useful to us. He merely introduces himself in his Allminster role and asks for a meeting. He has to send three emails in a row before The Banker replies though. It indicates a degree of persistence by Shacklin and a deal of reluctance on the Banker's part. And the reply is just two sentences."

Azzopardi quoted the email, "'I would like to reassure you that all is well. Coincidentally, I will be in Malta when you are and so I can meet you at the research facility myself and answer any questions you have. I will phone you at the Hotel Phoenicia.' There's no definitive information about The Banker, whoever he, or she, is."

"I imagined The Banker to be a man," said Lynch.

"Why make that assumption?" asked Azzopardi.

"Could you work your magic on The Banker's email address for us? Use that program you used yesterday?"

"You mean PRISM," said Azzopardi. "No, I'm sorry, but that won't work with The Banker's emails, whoever they may be. The email address The Banker writes from is not a conventional one. It is a dynamic address, routed through something called the dark net, with quite a different encryption system, something called blockchain. Ironically the dark net is a perversion of our own service encryption systems. Almost unbreakable. Whoever The Banker is they certainly don't want to be identified."

"The dark net?" asked Lynch, fearing that the answer would yield little enlightenment.

Azzopardi took a breath before he embarked on his explanation. "It's like a dark net that overlies the existing web. It uses specific encrypted software to access the net and communicate with other users with similar software. There was a browser that came out a couple of years ago called Tor that helped you access it. The Darknet is a network of spider-like parasites leeching off the legitimate web – the Clearnet – and they can talk to one another without people like you and me being able to listen in. There are new currencies springing up on it. You can understand that The Banker, if he or she **is** an illegal banker might very well like the Darknet to transfer currency between, say, organised criminals – all transfers being unseen and unchecked. These new currencies are called cryptocurrencies."

"I think it's vital we find The Banker," said Lynch. "He, or she, could be the key to finding out what happened to Shacklin. We need to follow any money involved and see where it leads us . . ."

"But this email correspondence between Shacklin and The Banker only tells us that The Banker exists. Otherwise it's a blank wall. It tells you nothing. Which is, of course, precisely how The Banker would want it."

"There's no way to trace it?" asked Lynch sadly.

"None that I have been told of," said Azzopardi, munching on a fennel flavoured biscuit that he had just dipped in his tea.

"There are too many questions in this case," said Lynch. "And not nearly enough answers. We need to resolve something. And so, I hesitate to ask you yet another question."

"Go on," said Azzopardi. "Let's go for peak complexity, let's scatter the jigsaw pieces all over the table, before we start piecing things together."

"When you were telling me that the cliffs at Dingli were a magnet for suicides . . . you happened to mention a woman who had thrown herself to death at the cliffs. You mentioned the *Times of Malta* report and the name Savina . . . Savina Daidalos."

"Yes, I remember, the Daidalos family. Once upon a time Papa Daidalos ran every racket on the Island. But times change . . . the family has become history," said Azzopardi. "What of them?"

"I understand everybody thinks that the daughter, Savina, killed herself after her father died and she was left on her own," said Lynch. "The men of the Daidalos family – father and son – were cocaine dealers who died in a plane crash. I think you mentioned that. Where was the crash? Was it in England?"

"Yes," said Azzopardi. He looked at Lynch and wondered about the reason behind his interest in the Daidalos family. "Do you know some more about that?"

"I think so. I believe that the plane involved was a Cessna 182. It came down in North West England in the night. Dr Power and I were called in, but not to the crash itself, rather to the scene in the farmhouse that the plane crashed into. We never investigated the Cessna crash, the focus of our investigation was into what turned up in the farmhouse. But we saw the crash site, the blackened devastation that was left behind and the wreckage that the Daidalos father and son died in . . ."

"Life is a tapestry of coincidences," said Azzopardi.

"What were the Daidalos family doing in England, though?" wondered Lynch.

"Admittedly, it's a long way to fly, from Malta to England," said Azzopardi. "But these families are happy to fly to Libya, Sicily, France, and Spain. England is just a few hops more. And if you're delivering cocaine or transferring money, what better way?"

"What if the deaths of the Daidalos family were arranged?" said Lynch. "What if the Cessna coming down in the night-time was not a flying accident, and Savina's subsequent death not the tragic suicide of a bereaved daughter?"

"You say you want to simplify the case, to narrow things down, to make it all more manageable . . . and then you go and resurrect the Daidalos family saga!" Azzopardi was patiently amused at the irony.

"I know, and it may not be related at all," sighed Lynch.

"I will tell you what," said Azzopardi. "I will print off the old police files on the Daidalos family and have them couriered over to the Phoenicia. Would that help in any way?"

"Thank you so much," said Lynch. "I am very grateful. I'll leave you be now, I'm sure you are very busy."

"Come back any time, even if I'm busy, it sometimes gets a bit lonely all alone in this big place . . ." He paused. "Although, I am expecting official visitors tomorrow. We are shadowing a Russian superyacht that's sailing from Cyprus. I know you have security clearance, but don't even tell your colleague. There is SIGINT to say it is carrying the female agent who poisoned Yushchenko. She is the chef who cooked him soupe à la dioxin." He chuckled to himself.

Lynch raised an eyebrow in surprise, but refrained from any comment. "One last thing before I leave you to your work," said Lynch. "Where would they have taken Savina Daidalos's body?"

Azzopardi jotted down the address of the Valletta morgue and handed it to Lynch. "Are you thinking of paying a visit to the morgue?"

"No, I think I'll leave this to the doctor."

* * *

Dr Power was at that very moment leaving the gift shop of The Holy Infirmary, a museum that had once been a hospital founded by the Knights of St John in the sixteenth century. He had spent a couple of hours wandering the low, arched corridors where victims of war and piracy and plague had breathed their last. Some survived, depending more on their underlying constitution and good fortune, than the medical care of the day, such as it was. He had read of plague epidemics and the isolation hospitals elsewhere on Malta, read of its use for casualties in various wars fought by the British and seen the entrance to tunnels deep under the Infirmary where frightened citizens of Valletta had taken shelter from the Axis bombardment in World War Two. He had shuddered at the tiny entrance and the narrow tunnel beyond, but had not dared go into the darkness with the other tourists. He had chosen to hurry back to the surface and the bright winter sun.

Power had arranged to meet Lynch for their mid-day meal. He chose an outdoor table with a crimson-red tablecloth at a bright and busy café. He counted himself lucky to have found a table and studied the menu. He ordered a glass of chilled white Malbec to drink while he waited for Lynch. The sun warmed his bones, and he was feeling satisfied after his morning of sightseeing. He was looking through his *Lonely Planet Guide to Malta & Gozo* and wondering what he could visit next when a shadow fell over the page he was reading. He looked up, expecting to see his friend, but instead there were two couples in sunglasses and shorts looming over him. They looked exceptionally clean, dressed in pure white and each carried a camera and a woollen jersey slung around their neck.

"Hallo," the tallest man said. He took his sunglasses off and his green eyes stared emotionlessly at Power, from under sandy eyebrows. "Or is it hello? You are English?"

"Yes? Hello?" said Power. There was something about the man's manner that Power didn't quite like. He stood too close, and there was a definitive air of command.

"We wish to dine here. We are short of time, and we could move these two tables together." He pointed to Power's table and the table next to it. "Be so kind as to move away with your drink. You can sit over there on that wall."

Before Power had time to respond, Lynch had interposed himself between the table and the newcomer. "I'm sorry," Lynch said. "This table is taken. We are having lunch here." He waited until the man had stepped back, sat down opposite Power and picked up the menu to scan it.

The two couples moved away from Power and with scornful expressions slowly walked away from the café. Power overheard one saying, *"Die Engländer hatten ihre Zeit in der Sonne. Wir wird Malta haben jetzt."*

"I think I arrived just in time," said Lynch. "I'm sorry I was a bit late. Have you had a good morning?'

"I visited the Pro-cathedral and then the old infirmary, the one that the Knights used to run. And I bought some gifts to take back, including one for Pamela, as you requested. I hope I chose something suitable." He fished in his pockets. "I bought two different silver Maltese pendants for Laura and Pamela, and a model of a Knight for Jo." He brought out the pendant he had bought for Lynch to give Pamela and handed it to him. "I was just working out where to go this afternoon."

"Ah," said Lynch. He looked at the pendant and thanked Power. He paused to put in his order for lunch – a *tuna Niçoise* and a tonic water. Power put his order for a variant of *Kusksu* soup made with Cannellini beans.

As the waitress walked away Power resumed their conversation. "The way you said 'Ah', just before, when I was wondering what to see this afternoon . . . it sounded as if I might not be sightseeing this afternoon, after all," said Power. "Do you have something for me to do, perhaps?"

"Yes, I'm sorry, but I do," said Lynch. "I'm driving over to the South of the Island to take a look at the cliffs. I know that Ramon thought it was unlikely that his ex-colleague would use the old RAF navigation station, but I wonder if that's where Shacklin was headed. Was he meeting Xuereb there?"

"And so where am I headed?" asked Power.

"Do you want me to tell you after lunch? In case it affects your appetite?"

"Well, you can't make me wait and wonder through lunch," said Power. "Where am I going?"

Lynch reached in his pocket and took out the address that Azzopardi had scribbled down and gave it to Power.

Power stared at the address on the neon Post-It note. "The morgue!"

"Yes. To see if there are any records on Savina Daidalos," said Lynch. "I thought they would co-operate best with a medical man like yourself. And you'd understand the terminology better . . . I will drive to the coast to see the cliffs she allegedly fell from."

Power groaned. He had loathed every minute of dissection classes at medical school and found attending post-mortems in third year pathology a distinctly unnerving experience. "You make a compelling argument," said Power. "But are you sure you wouldn't like *me* to drive out to the coast instead?"

"Nice try," said Lynch. "But at least you had the morning off."

Power shrugged in resignation. His attempt to swap duties had failed. "Did you have a fruitful morning with Azzopardi?"

"I did, if by fruitful you mean growing yet more questions for us to look into." Lynch paused whilst the waitress placed food and drinks on the red tablecloth in front of them. Lynch continued, "We know that Shacklin was interested in Professor Xuereb and that Shacklin was headed to the cliffs at Dingli. Maybe he was going to meet The Banker, or another person entirely. Perhaps Xuereb? We know Shacklin gambled recklessly, and so we can assume he also needed money, badly. A University salary wouldn't cover the losses he was running up. We know that he had come into contact with cocaine; because of traces on his suit. Was he an addict or was the cocaine just a contaminant? He might have brushed against some residue in the casino.

"Now, Azzopardi revealed some other facts to me – some weeks before his death, Felfe, your German professor, had been making enquiries about some terms he had learned about that he thought were important. Three things he asked about – Wanderlust, Sannik Law Co and The Banker. We need to follow these up. Sannik Law Co has already been checked by Azzopardi. There's no law firm on the island with that name."

"Wanderlust sounds like the name of a horse," said Power. "Do you think Shacklin liked gambling on racing too?"

"Nothing about Shacklin would surprise me," said Lynch. "But it did intrigue me that your friend Felfe had been making these enquiries. Perhaps he was just about to divulge his suspicions to you, when he died in the Cathedral."

"Poor Felfe," said Power. "If he had stumbled on some criminal activity and was about to disclose it to me, then doesn't that make it more likely he was killed to prevent him doing so?"

"Exactly," said Lynch. "But even Azzopardi has been fed the SIS line that Felfe's death was completely natural."

"And Savina Daidalos. The poor women who jumped off a cliff. Why am I sent on her trail?"

"Don't you think there is something unusual about her death, too?" asked Lynch.

"She was doubly bereaved, I think you said, that would be a risk factor for suicide." Power thought for a moment. "Although it is an atypical suicide method for a female – throwing yourself off a cliff, I mean. Men are the ones who choose violent methods like shooting, hanging and jumping. Women tend to use overdoses. Nevertheless, the exception proves the rule."

"You know, I've never understood that saying, *the exception proves the rule.*"

"Just because a violent suicide method is unlikely in women, doesn't mean it couldn't or didn't happen," said Power.

"Well," said Lynch. "There's a significant coincidence I discovered whilst I was talking to Azzopardi . . . Savina's father and brother died in a plane crash." Power nodded at Lynch to go on. "The crash was that of a Cessna they were piloting themselves. They crashed in England. The crash site we saw last year, at the farm house. That was it."

"No," said Power, astonished. "Really?"

"The Daidaloses were a rich family who lived on the island of Gozo, just northwest of the island of Malta. The father was a 'businessman' who dealt in drugs and ventures that laundered the cash from the drugs. My suspicion is that someone killed all three members of the family: father, son and daughter."

"Why?" asked Power.

"Money," said Lynch. "They were in the way. Or because they posed some kind of threat."

"We came here to find Shacklin," said Power, bewildered by all the new questions that Lynch had generated. "But this is more, much more. Ramon warned us about the risks we might be taking."

"Don't worry," said Lynch. "I know there are a lot of loose ends as of now, but if we work together we can tie them all up, one by one by one."

* * *

Micallef, the herder, stood with his goats and sheep high up on the clifftop. The animals milled about him as he leant, hands on the top of his staff, chin resting on his hands, staring inland to the road. The goats munched contentedly on grasses, golden samphire, chicory, spurge and salt tree. The afternoon sun was shining upon them all, herder and his flock, but at 12 Celsius Micallef found the day slightly chilly. He wore a jumper and thick waxed jacket against the winter air. The afternoon was blissfully peaceful but for the 'pit pit pit' sound of the robin's repetitive call, the occasional bleat of his flock and the distant repetitive wash of the waves on the shore below.

The road nearby that wove its way along the cliff top had been empty all afternoon. Micallef watched as a grey Audi hire car purred along the road and slowed to a halt in one of the numerous vacant parking spaces. The single occupant got out and stood, his hand to his forehead screening his eyes from the sun, and surveyed about him. All at once he spied Micallef and paused. Then the figure crossed the road and started walking toward him across the scrubland. When he realised that the man's intent was to walk right up to him Micallef was alert, but he did not vary his stance, and maintained his position, head on his hands, hands on his staff waiting stolidly for the man to reach him.

The stranger was tall, with greying black hair. He wore a smart blue, short sleeved shirt, light grey shorts and Birkenstock sandals. That the man did not mind the relative chill of winter's day marked him out as a Northern European visitor. Once upon a time Micallef would have bet on the stranger being English, but these days such a dapper man as this was as likely to be German, or even Russian. Micallef wondered what he wanted, but the answer was coming to him. The sheep scattered from out of the stranger's way as he continued on his inexorable path towards Micallef. When he was about twenty feet away the stranger raised his hand in greeting, smiled and called out, "Hello!" Definitely English, thought Micallef.

Micallef lifted his head from his hands and gave a single nod in the stranger's direction and waited for some further indication of what the stranger might want.

"Good afternoon," the visitor said. "I wonder – can you help me?"

"You lost?"

"No, I'm where I wanted to be, I think. My name is Andrew Lynch. I'm looking for someone."

"Oh?" Micallef raised an eyebrow. "Police?"

"I was a British policeman, but no more," said Lynch.

"Policemen all look the same."

Lynch nodded in affirmation and took off his sunglasses to let Micallef see his eyes. He reflected that although the shepherd was gruff he did not sound altogether hostile. There might yet be a prospect of co-operation from him.

"I am hoping for a local's advice, are you from near here?" asked Lynch.

Micallef cautiously assented, although the question seemed redundant given he was obviously shepherding his animals.

"An English man called Shacklin went missing near here, a few weeks ago. I'm asking people if they saw anything."

Micallef shook his head. "We get a lot of tourists in the summer. I wouldn't notice any one of them. Not particularly. And at any time of the year some come and jump."

He jerked a thumb over his shoulder towards the expanse of sea beyond the cliffs.

Lynch pointed over to his left at the building complex in the distance. "Do you know anything about that building? What is it?"

Micallef narrowed his eyes. He had the feeling that Lynch, or whoever he was, knew precisely what the building was. "It's the navigation station. For the aircraft."

"Does anybody called Professor Xuereb live there?"

"Never heard of anyone called that," said Micallef, and he began to walk away on the journey back home. His flock obediently followed him, leaving Lynch alone.

"Can I get into the Navigation Station?" Lynch shouted after him. "Do you know if it's staffed?"

Micallef halted and turned to stared at Lynch. "I don't know who you are or why you're asking all these questions. I suppose it's something to do with what Zammit found at his farm, but I've got one thing to say to you. Stay away from there. The farmers keep their animals away from there. All the people round here stay away. Stay away! You hear?" And before Lynch could frame a follow-up question Micallef turned and stalked off. His sheep and goats trotted hurriedly along behind him.

Lynch walked back toward the distant Navigation Station. The scrubland was strewn with rocks and this made walking difficult. The station had a high wall around it, with curls of razor wire all along the top. Lynch could see the upper half of a circular stone tower, inside the perimeter. The tower was crowned by a white, geodesic dome. There was a sign on the whitewashed perimeter wall which threatened potential visitors with prosecution for trespassing. Another sign proclaimed this was 'MATS – Navigation Transmitting Site' and below there was a late addition; 'A.U. Jericho Institute Research Station'. Lynch noted the word 'Jericho' and smiled.

He took out a digital camera and tried to take a photo of the sign, but as he pressed the shutter button on the camera there was an ominous hiss and the screen died. Lynch looked at the blank screen uncomprehendingly. He was sure he had charged the camera up before leaving the hotel that morning.

He walked over to a large, wire meshed gate – the only apparent entry into the walled compound. All was as Savina Daidalos had found it when she approached the navigation station several weeks earlier, there was no intercom or bell at the gate.

Lynch wondered if he should press ahead in his mission to try and find Professor Xuereb, or whether he should retreat now and consider his options. The fact that the Navigation Station had a dual label of 'MATS – Navigation Transmitting Site' and 'A.U. Jericho Institute Research Station' told him that Xuereb was probably linked to this building, as Ramon had mentioned that his protégé had developed the Jericho Institute. That was all the link he needed. He could leave the Station and the cliff top now and discuss matters with Power. They could enlist the help of Ramon. It might be best to prevail upon Ramon to approach his old student and colleague for them.

But somehow Lynch could not leave the puzzle right in front of him now. Everything pointed to this place as being important. Shacklin had journeyed to somewhere near here. Savina had died near here. This was the Jericho Institute Ramon had spoken of. Why go back to the hotel now?

Lynch leant forward towards the steel gate and called out for attention; shouting through into the dusty courtyard behind. "Hello! Is anybody there? Can you help me?"

There was a single vehicle parked inside the compound, a silver Toyota Land Cruiser. Lynch reasoned that this meant there must be a human somewhere inside.

He shouted out again and his barked questions bounced and reverberated off the walls inside.

A sash window in the tower, just below the dome, opened upwards and a head shot out of it. The bearded face wore an expression of sheer irritation, "Why all this noise?" he demanded. "Can't you be quiet?"

"I'm looking for a Professor Xuereb," Lynch shouted up at the man in the tower. He thought it prudent to indicate that others knew of his journey there, and so he added, "My office in Valletta sent me."

"I'm the caretaker," the man shouted. His sunglasses glinted in the sun. "The station is unmanned. Everything is automated."

"And yet you are here!" shouted Lynch.

The man frowned as if the noise of Lynch's voice was unbearable to him. "Do you have to be so loud? Please go."

"Have you ever seen the Wizard of Oz?" asked Lynch, smiling grimly.

"What do you mean? Please go now. You're trespassing. I will use force if you remain there."

"The sign says this is the Jericho Institute. Are you Professor Xuereb?" Lynch challenged him directly. "Can you come down and talk to me? I have a message from Ramon."

At the mention of Ramon, the man's face registered a flicker of surprise, and then he retreated inside. The window in the tower closed to.

Lynch waited for ten minutes, pacing up and down outside the gate, until it became clear that he would never be voluntarily invited into the Jericho Institute.

Professor Xuereb watched the bank of CCTV screens inside the tower and saw Lynch turn away from the gates and walk back across the scrubland towards his car.

Xuereb rubbed his beard thoughtfully. The sound weapons he had researched and built had proved themselves before and there was no immediate need to prove their utility again, but the visitor had rudely disturbed him and he was cross. The visitor had had that universal air of authority and fixity of presence that spoke of officialdom. The stranger's stride across the scrubland was steady and assured. Xuereb switched on the sound cannon. Outside the tower the square dish that focused the sound beam moved a few degrees northwards and Xuereb began to track Lynch's progress towards his car as he focused the aim of the weapon on Lynch's head. He flicked the range up to 160 decibels and 19,000 Hz and paused. He fantasized about what he could do to the man. Xuereb could burst his eardrums with the focused sound beam, induce the worst headache Lynch had ever felt, or rupture a vessel inside his cerebral cortex. It was tempting, just a flick of a switch was all that was required and not a trace of evidence would be found at any post mortem to implicate him.

He imagined how he could turn the volume of the sound weapon down to 100 decibels and play the beam along the right hand side of Lynch's head. Lynch would automatically move to the left to avoid the intense noise. He could swing the beam back onto Lynch's right ear, forcing Lynch to move left again. Incrementally he could shift him leftwards towards the cliff edge. This tactic had certainly worked on Savina Daidalos, although Xuereb acknowledged this steering tactic had always worked best at night when the subject, whether animal or human could not see the cliff edge. In daylight, Lynch would not make that error, however unpleasant the noise.

The advantage of ending Lynch would be that another person who had annoyed him by trying to interfere in his life would be gone. The disadvantage would be that Lynch's disappearance would only attract others to the research station. Lynch had specifically said he had been sent there, so others would know he had journeyed here. And he had mentioned Ramon. Other disadvantages now presented themselves to him. There was no-one to help him this time. On balance, the advantages of ending the stranger were outweighed by the disadvantages.

Xuereb switched the sound cannon off and watched Lynch walk away through the scrub cross the distant road and climb into his car.

Xuereb had noticed an unusual police presence round the nearby pig farm when he went out for groceries that morning. There had been police in the village store too, and the police were never usually around this remote place. It made him feel uncomfortable. And now it seemed that Ramon had tracked him down as well. Renting the tower and the research station had been a whim of his. It had seemed a good idea at the time. He had imagined the benefits of the quietness and the solitude. He had completed the first stage of his work though. His plans and research notes were all encrypted on-line. The machines he had developed had been designed to be portable. He could use the Land Cruiser to move everything in just two trips.

He stood up, feeling resolute; it was time to leave this place.

* * *

Dr Power stood in the foyer of the morgue and struggled with his anxiety. He was trying to swallow down a feeling of panic and a wave of nausea occasioned by the sweet smell of disinfected decay that filled his nostrils. He associated this distinctive aroma of mortuary disinfectant with the scenes inflicted on him through his years of medical training. The medical school dissection room he had endured anatomy classes in, the University pathology labs with jars of pickled limbs and organs floating in formaldehyde, the post-mortem suites in district hospitals reeking of the sickly ripe smell of slashed open abdomens and the glistening viscera – all clustered at the forefront of his memory now. Power was almost about to leave and retreat, when a pathology assistant approached him, and the doctor's fate was sealed. The assistant was wearing a hair net, turquoise scrubs and plastic clogs, rather like operating theatre staff. "Are you Dr Power?"

Power nodded, unable to open his mouth, fearful even to breathe in the air around him. "Mr Azzopardi phoned to tell us to expect you and to co-operate as best we can. Can I see some photo ID please?"

Power fumbled in his jacket and silently withdrew an ID card naming him and his role at the Foundation. This was the first time he had used it. Lynch had insisted he have a card a year previously.

"Thank you, Professor Power," the assistant said. "We get journalists trying to get in and take photos. Low-life scum." He asked Power to put some plastic overshoes on and handed him a gown to cover his clothes. He walked part way through two heavy transparent plastic swing doors, holding them so Power could follow. "It's this way, come through, please."

Power had been hoping to be led to an office and to be presented with a copy of the post-mortem report. He thought that they were passing through an air-conditioned area to get to the office, when the technician suddenly stopped and turned to face Power. "Did you want us to put her on a table for you?"

"You mean her body?" asked Power, horrified at the thought.

"Of course, no relative has come forward to claim her. So she remains here. And the inquest isn't for a month. Do you want her putting on the table then?"

"No, no," stuttered Power.

"That's fine then," said the technician and he got hold of a handle that protruded from the grey wall to Power's left and heaved upon it. What Power had taken to be the wall of a corridor was, in fact, a wall composed of drawers from floor to ceiling. The drawer on his left was pulled open, and kept on going until it extended several feet in front of the doctor. He saw a shrouded form on the platen of the drawer in front of him. Without further warning or ceremony, the technician peeled the cold, formaldehyde soaked fabric apart to reveal the naked body of Savina Daidalos.

Power, stunned at the suddenness of the assistant's actions had unwanted thoughts and emotions whirling about in his mind. Part of him, his medical training, took over as if he was on automatic pilot. He became detached and observed, as if from some distance, the abnormal angles of her right femur and right humerus. The jagged shaft of the fractured femur protruded through a bloodless wound in her thigh. On the left side of her face her features were preserved as they had been in life. A finely sculpted nose and high cheekbone, left eye closed, but sunken after death in its socket. Rosebud lips, now purple with deoxygenated blood. Her left limbs were smooth and she had clearly been elegant and tall. Her skin was now pale as marble and along the lower visible edge of her body there was the purple staining of lividity as her blood had settled. He tried not to look at the dark curled hair of her pudenda. The right side of her face was distorted by injury. Rocks had lacerated her cheek to the bone and shattered her orbit. Her right eyelid and skin of her forehead were gone and the white bone of her skull showed through. Her shrunken right eyeball stared dully at him.

Power shivered involuntarily in the necessary cold of the mortuary.

The technician could see that Power was looking pale and suddenly discerned a difference between his manner and the usual demeanour of pathologists who came to do second post-mortems for families and defence lawyers. "You are a pathologist, aren't you?"

"No," said Power, unable now to take his eyes away from the grim sight of Savina's corpse. "I'm a psychiatrist. Really I just wanted to see the report..."

"Ah, said the technician. "I assumed you were providing a second opinion for the Inquest."

"It's all right," said Power, recovering a little after the initial shock. "I am medically trained. It's just I don't usually . . ."

"No, no," said the mortuary assistant. "I'm sorry if I presumed." He mimed pushing the drawer in. "Shall I?"

Power nodded and the assistant draped the chemical ridden shroud back over her body again and carefully closed the drawer with a touch more reverence than he had shown when he flung it open. "Suicide," he said. "She threw herself down a cliff around two hundred metres high. Straight on to rocks."

"**If** it was suicide," said Power. "Are there a lot of suicides at those cliffs?"

"Several this year, and every year," the assistant said. "Would you like a sit down and a cup of tea, Doc? You look a bit peaky." Power nodded wanly. The assistant smiled. "Come through to the office then."

The technician was called Aaron. He seated Power down in the pathologist's office and brought him a mug of strong, sweet tea. He ferreted around in a filing cabinet and extracted a copy of the post-mortem report. "The pathologist isn't here today, but she won't mind you having a copy, I'm sure. What's your interest in our client, then?" He gestured to the drawers in the morgue beyond the office.

"Her brother and father died in England. In a plane crash," explained Power. "We're just wondering if there was foul play in all three deaths." He scanned the report through. The pathologist had noted similar superficial injuries to the ones Power had seen. There had been a large bleed in the white matter of her brain. This was attributed to the head trauma when her skull hit the rocks at the foot of the cliff. There was no alcohol in her bloodstream. Toxicology had found no drugs. Power was slightly surprised as suicidal acts are often associated with ingestion of alcohol. "Were any of her effects brought in with her?" asked Power. "A phone, papers? Anything?"

Aaron looked at a register.

"Just a dress, a pretty white dress. The pathologist even noted the make, 'Hugo Boss cotton dress'. We identified her by a tattoo on her shoulder, in case you wondered how we did that."

"Well," said Power, as he finished the pathologist's conclusions. "I suppose that's it. Thank you for showing me. I'll be going. Thanks for the tea." He stood up and together they began walking towards the morgue foyer.

"As I say, Dr Teare, the pathologist, would have met you, but she's part-time and with her family today. But her work's building up for tomorrow. Two hospital deaths and a find from near Dingli."

"A find from the Dingli area?" asked Power.

"Came in just an hour ago from the police. Found at a pig farm near Dingli. A body part."

Power felt compelled to ask more. "What kind of body part?"

"A hand," said Aaron. "A left hand to be specific. Found outside a pig pen at the farm."

"A pig pen?"

"Just outside the bars of the pen. Actually clawed into the dirt. There's dirt under broken finger nails – probably the owner had been clawing at the ground when he died."

"But where was the body?" asked Power.

"It had been inside the pig pen presumably – at one stage anyway," said Aaron. "But you see pigs are omnivorous and so they would have, erm . . . recycled the body. They will eat anything, you know. The boars can be very aggressive. He may well have been alive when he fell in. Or at least semi-conscious, as maybe he clawed at the dirt to try and escape. But they'd have been on him by then. Vicious they can be. Bit right through his wrist."

Power was speechless for a moment and then was troubled by the idea that pigs could be so minded as to eat a human. The thought both fascinated and horrified him. "You say he fell in, how do you know it **was** a he?"

"Well, it's definitely a man's hand, there are hairy knuckles and the back of the hand is hairy, do you want to see?"

Power paused, the embodiment of ambitendence, and wavered on the threshold of the mortuary. He was just in front of the plastic doors that could lead him to freedom and away from all this accumulated death. "I would normally say no," he said, putting his sense of duty ahead of his instinct to flee. "I don't want to, but just now I have the sudden intuition that I really should take a look. Would you mind showing me please?"

"Not at all," said Aaron, and guided Power back to the grey steel wall of drawers. He pulled another one of the cabinet drawers open and there on the sheet metal platen was a transparent plastic bag, tagged with a police number and details.

"I can't open it before Dr Teare gets here, but you can see it's a man's left hand."

Power peered into the drawer and observed the stump of a wrist where the pigs had gnawed through both the ulna and radius bones. The two bony shafts stuck out, with remnants of shiny white tendons and nerves trailing out of the wound. Power found himself suddenly recalling long-lost terms from his anatomy tutorials like *extensor carpi ulnaris* and *extensor pollicis longus*. He was inspecting the dorsum of the hand, and could see that Aaron had been right about the dark hairs on the back of the hand and the fingers.

It was then that Power saw the ring on the little finger. The ring was exactly as he remembered it. A bulbous, large and somewhat tasteless golden ring, with a plump, crimson ruby set within it.

Chapter Eighteen

*And when long years and seasons, wheeling about, brought about
the time ordained for him to make his way homeward; even so,
trials and dangers, attended him – even in Ithaca, near those he loved.*

Homer

After dinner, and a very long discussion with Lynch, Dr Power sat down in a deserted part of the Phoenicia lounge, gathering his thoughts prior to making an international call to the Vice Chancellor at home.

The Vice Chancellor had nearly finished dining with his wife in the Georgian rectory they owned in Davenham, Cheshire. She had been bobbing in and out of the service door to the kitchen all evening, bringing steaming dish after dish to the double pedestal mahogany table. With each course the Vice Chancellor's pace of eating had slowed, until at last he was lingeringly munching on glistening *poires au vin rouge*. His wife was extolling the virtues of the recipe by Richard Olney and how she had prepared it with cinnamon and zesty orange peel. The Vice Chancellor chewed away stolidly, looking out of the north-facing dining room window into the glitteringly-lit driveway outside.

"Would you like your usual coffee after dinner?" asked his wife, as she was clearing away the plates.

He grunted assent and then qualified this. "Decaffeinated, please. I haven't been sleeping well."

"Maybe your evening meal is lying too heavily when you try to sleep?" she said gently.

He didn't hear, or didn't acknowledge her caring words. "Can you see if there's any Stinking Bishop left? And some of those Swedish crackers?"

"They're very salty," she pointed out. "Maybe . . ."

"Those crackers accompany that particular cheese perfectly," said Canon Armitage. "If you would be so kind . . ." He watched her potter off into the kitchen, and returned his gaze to the long drive outside the window. Beyond this he could just see St Wilfred's Church through the trees.

The sweeping graveled arc of the drive had seen numerous families crunch their way through its pebbles on foot or by carriage. Armitage imagined a Victorian rector driving a horse and gig into the drive after his visits through his parish. There was a list of the rectors' names on a black wooden plaque in the hallway. One of the first clergymen to live in this house had been called Tomkinson. Armitage wondered how many children and servants Tomkinson had had and whether he could find a census record which would tell him. The rectory was too big a house for just Armitage and his wife, but if the rector had had a Victorian brood of ten children, how frenetic his life must have been. The hallways would have been filled with the boisterous shouts and laughter of the children. The retreat to his study to write the weekly sermon must have been a delightful respite from the *melee*.

The Vice Chancellor was musing about the ghosts of his rectory, when he was jerked back to the present by the insistent clamour of the telephone ringing in the timber panelled hallway.

He looked hopefully towards the kitchen door in the expectation that his wife would answer the phone, but all he could hear was her loading the dishwasher and making coffee. Reluctantly, Armitage heaved himself out of his chair and tottered from the dining room out into the hall and across the Minton tiled floor to the telephone on the hall table. His wife had been polishing the woodwork of the panelling with lavender scented beeswax. He sneezed at the smell.

Rubbing his nose with his sleeve, the Vice Chancellor picked up the receiver and sank his bones into a leather, wingbacked armchair before answering, "Armitage here."

"Good evening, Vice Chancellor. It's Carl Power here. I'm phoning from Valletta. I hope I'm not interrupting anything."

"Good evening, Carl. I have just finished dinner, well, except for the cheese and biscuits. And a coffee."

"I am sorry. I wouldn't have disturbed you unless I had news."

"News of Shacklin? Has he turned up at the hotel?"

"No, I'm afraid he hasn't," said Dr Power. Mindful of the Vice Chancellor's heart condition he asked, "Are you sitting down?"

"Yes, why should I be sitting down?" The Vice Chancellor rested his head against the russet, moquette-upholstered wing of his wingback chair.

"The news is not good, I am afraid."

"Go on, please, Professor Power. I rather expected that you would find that to be the case."

There was a pause as Power wondered how best to formulate the news. "We followed David Shacklin's last movements around the Island. I've interviewed the academics he spoke to. We've tracked his mobile phone to the south west of the island, where it stayed. We've looked into his spending at restaurants and casinos." Power heard the Vice Chancellor groan at the mention of the word 'casinos'. "But we have both come to the conclusion that he is not alive. Although that remains to be confirmed absolutely."

"You mean that his trail goes cold and that leads you to conclude he is no longer . . . active?" asked the Vice Chancellor.

"No, it's more definite than that. We have found his remains."

"Dear God," whispered the Vice Chancellor softly. "What do you mean? Where?"

"We do not have a complete body," said Power. "In fact we have only his hand. I identified it personally this afternoon. It was his left hand, with that ruby ring of his."

"He wore a ring?" said the Vice Chancellor. "I never even noticed. But still, I mean, dear God. The poor man. Where was it found? How did he die?"

"His hand was found outside a pig pen on a farm a mile or so from a place called Had-Dingli. I suppose it was very honest of the farmer not to remove the ring."

"The hand was outside a pig pen? This is outlandish."

"I know," said Dr Power. "We are working on the theory that his body was consumed by pigs and that his hand somehow got outside the pen. He'd scrabbled in the dirt. He must have been alive when the pigs set upon him."

"But pigs. They wouldn't . . ."

"They would. They eat anything, and they can be aggressive. We believe it was possible he was semi-conscious when he fell in the pen. He came round during the attack."

"Oh, how dreadful," said the Vice Chancellor. "How utterly dreadful for him. I don't suppose you could be mistaken?"

"My colleague, Andrew Lynch, thought to bring colour photographs of Shacklin with us. Photographs that he had obtained from the Press Office at Allminster before we left. The photos show his hand and the ring. It looks identical to us." He paused. Sitting in the Hotel Phoenicia, Power waited for Armitage to say something else, but the silence just went on. "I realise that this is a shock for you, Vice Chancellor, are you all right?"

"Me? Oh, I'm all right. I'm just wondering what's to be done. There are official channels to go through. It's not for us to notify his family, although I don't think he was a family man. And of course, any official notification would have to be through the British High Commission and the police. And it wouldn't be right for us to issue a press release yet, without absolute confirmation. But I think . . . I think . . . we will, unfortunately . . . have to make Professor McFarlane acting Executive Pro Vice Chancellor. Now, that **is** a shame."

"But what should we do now, Vice Chancellor? Here in Malta there are several lines of investigation we can follow . . ."

"Please come home," said the Vice Chancellor, shortly. "I fear we will need you here if we are to save the medical school project from Professor McFarlane."

"But . . ." Power began to protest.

"I engaged the Foundation to find David Shacklin," said Armitage firmly. "And you have succeeded. I am very grateful to you. To Andrew Lynch and to you. You have both acquitted yourselves and have concluded as to whether Shacklin could be found alive. Not the conclusion that any of us wanted, but a conclusion nevertheless. The investigation into David's untimely death is now a matter for the British High Commission and the Malta police." The Vice Chancellor made it clear he would brook no suggestion otherwise. "I will be expecting you both back in the next twenty-four hours, please. Have a good journey, and come and see me for a chat when you return."

Canon Armitage replaced the receiver on the phone. He heaved himself out of the armchair and went back to his place at the dining room table.

His wife looked up at him expectantly. "The University again?" she asked. "What now? Another cry-for-help student threatening an overdose? Why won't they let you have some peace?"

Armitage sighed, as he picked up his plate of grapes, biscuits, and cheese. "It's Professor Shacklin," he said. "They've found his body in Malta, well, they found part of it." He picked up his coffee cup. "I'm going to the study to do some thinking."

"You shouldn't be working," his wife scolded him. "Home is for relaxing."

"I am going to think about some chess moves, not work," he said. "I'm sorry to leave you after such a fine dinner. But I need some quiet time."

And he shuffled off towards his study, leaving an aroma of the cheese wafting in his wake. His wife wrinkled her nose in distaste. The Vice Chancellor's favourite cheese smelt like a hockey club changing room.

* * *

"What did he say?" Lynch wandered over from the bar carrying two pints of beer and placed one in front of Power.

"The Vice Chancellor said he wants us back tomorrow. That we'd completed our mission, which was to find Shacklin, and to leave any investigations in the hands of the police and the British High Commission."

"Ah well, I'll see what flights I can book for us," said Lynch, sipping at his pint. "You know, I like Malta, it's not bad here. I think I might bring Pamela back for a holiday in the spring."

"You don't sound very concerned that we've been recalled in mid-investigation, and with so much left to do," said Power.

"Well, our mission was to find poor Professor Shacklin, and I suppose we have. The Vice Chancellor is correct, officially the investigation now belongs to the local police. And we also had a fixed fee for the mission, so if we complete it early that is in our favour. And presumably the Vice Chancellor also wants to limit our expenses." Lynch looked around the lounge of the Phoenicia appreciatively and nodded. "A lovely place."

"I suppose so," said Power. "The Vice Chancellor seemed most worried about the negative effects of Shacklin's death on the University hierarchy. He sounded a bit shocked that Shacklin was dead, and then he was immediately thinking about which dean was going to act as locum Executive Pro Vice Chancellor."

"He has a big organisation to manage," said Lynch. "The University will always be at the forefront of his mind."

"You're right, I guess. That responsibility is the reason why he's paid two hundred thousand a year." Power took a draught of his beer and sighed gratefully. "But all the questions are unanswered. I mean, someone must have put Shacklin into the pig pen. Lifted him in, while he was semi-conscious. I suppose he was naked . . ."

"Maybe," said Lynch. "I'm not sure if the pigs would mind if he was clothed. Would they eat the clothes too? That is a point we'd have to check if we were investigating, I don't know, myself. I can't get past the fact that if his hand was found as it was – after scrabbling in the dirt. He must have come round as they were eating him. It doesn't bear thinking about."

"No," said Power. "No, it doesn't." The memory of the severed wrist recurred to him involuntarily – a vivid image of the gnawed bones sticking out. "Who would do that to a man?"

"Whoever it was they didn't check after Shacklin went into the pen. Maybe they were disturbed and ran off or maybe they never went back to see what remained."

"Maybe they knew the pigs well, knew what they were capable of, what they could do," said Power.

"If they had checked afterwards, they would have found the hand," said Lynch.

"I did wonder if it was Professor Xuereb that Shacklin was meeting. Maybe he put Shacklin in the pen. But whoever it was, they were in a hurry. They made a crucial mistake in trying to dispose of his body, they failed to remove his ring."

"I don't know," said Lynch. Maybe the murderer did go back after the pigs had done their work. Maybe the hand was covered by dirt and only later came to light. Maybe it lay in the dirt. Perhaps the farmer

268

hosed the pens down and uncovered the hand which had been previously buried?"

Power acknowledged the possibility. "And Savina Daidalos," he continued. "Does her death fit in with Shacklin's activities on Malta at all? And what was Shacklin involved in? Certainly gambling, but perhaps drugs as well?"

"There's enough here to keep an investigator busy for weeks," said Lynch, musing. "Sannik Law Co? Wanderlust? The Banker? What do they all mean? Was Shacklin meeting The Banker? Is Xuereb, The Banker? You know, part of me is reluctant to leave the case here, and another part of me is glad to let other officers run round after all these leads." Lynch fished his own mobile out of his pocket. "I'll phone the airline and book us some tickets."

* * *

They arrived home in the early evening. Lynch drove through the stormy countryside of the Edge on their route from the nearby airport. The Macclesfield Road outside Alderley House was dark. Branches of the trees clashed together in the wind. Heavy rain peppered its surface and the collected rainwater ran in a stream along the side of the road, chuckling and glugging.

They drove through the stone gates and onto the driveway in front of Power's house. Welcoming lights shone out from the hall and lounge. Power stepped out of the car, relieved to be back at his own home. The front porch had a benign Green Man carved into its stone lintel. The carved face looked benignly down on him as if pleased to see the wanderer's return. All at once, the front door swung open and his family spilled out onto the front step. His son Jo ran joyously up to him. Power reached down and swung him up into a bear hug. "Jo! I missed you!"

"Dad, Dad! Now you are back can we go and see *The Incredibles* at the cinema?"

"Maybe, just let me get in!"

Lynch fished Power's luggage out of the Audi's boot and, smiling at the family's reunion scene, joined them on the threshold. He noted that Laura's baby bump was beginning to show, and he grinned. He knew how long Laura had been trying for a baby. Laura was kissing Power. She paused and smiled over at Lynch as he joined them.

"Hello, Andrew! Have you both been busy?" she asked.

Lynch nodded. "Mission complete," he said. "A frantic few days."

"Fully occupied?" she asked, as they moved inside the entrance hall and closed the door against the stormy night. "No time for any fun?"

"We divided tasks. Carl interviewed all the people at the University. And found Ramon, an old friend, who led us to a sonic weapons expert. And Carl did the . . . er . . ." Mindful of Jo's presence, Lynch tailored his words. "Carl went to the hospital and that visit concluded our task."

"You found your Professor Shacklin, then?" asked Laura. "Was he . . .?" Her words tailed off as she noticed Lynch's frown. Power shook his head. Their looks told her everything.

"I'll tell you all about it later."

"Let us talk of other things, then," said Laura. She turned to Lynch. "Won't you come in for a cup of tea? I have baked a plum cake."

"How could I refuse?" said Lynch, and he followed the family inside.

Chapter Nineteen

I had a dream, which was not all a dream.
Byron, Darkness, 1816

Laura teased Power for bringing presents home so close to Christmas, but he had insisted it was a necessary rite. A traveller must bring presents home to their family. Power had never thought of holding the presents back till Christmas Day. When he gave her the present of a Maltese cross from Valletta she became tearful and kissed him. Jo went off playing with the model of a Knight of St John and a treasure box that Power had seen at the airport.

Over plumcake and two pots of tea, Power and Lynch described some of their stay on Malta. Laura was horrified at Power's tale of being at the morgue on the day the farmer found Shacklin's hand lying in the dirt.

"Just his hand?" she asked.

"His body was no more," said Power. "Recycled into bacon or sausages. Another very good reason to be vegetarian." He looked at Lynch.

"I will never be a vegetarian," said Lynch staunchly. "But I take your point."

"Poor Professor Shacklin," said Laura. She paused, thinking things through. "But if his hand was found after it had been scratching and scrabbling in the dirt . . . doesn't that mean he was alive when he was eaten?"

Power nodded.

"I can't bear to imagine it," said Laura. "Surely pigs wouldn't ..."

"Pigs are omnivores," said Power. "Like humans are omnivores. And sows will even eat their own offspring; they call it 'savaging'."

Laura shuddered. "It sounds as if you have both been very busy. Definitely not a holiday, then."

Lynch shook his head. "No, but now I feel I *need* a holiday. We worked hard; made very rapid progress on the case."

"But now we have to drop it," said Power. "The Vice Chancellor recalled us the instant he learned Shacklin was dead. He insisted we leave everything to the Maltese authorities."

Lynch looked thoughtfully at Power. "He said come home, because he wanted to save money on our expenses. When he sent us there, all he wanted to know was whether Shacklin needed help, or what had happened to him. And, yes, he can justifiably stop paying our expenses, now. But you know me, Carl, I don't like to leave a case with so many loose ends."

"What do you mean?" asked Power.

"I mean that the case might not be funded by the University anymore, but that I won't let it go. I'm going to keep my ears open. I can't abandon it."

"No, I didn't believe you would," said Power.

"And now, I think I must go," said Lynch. "My wife is waiting at home, and we have quite finished the sticky plumcake." Not a crumb was left on the blue willow pattern plate. "Thank you, Laura."

Laura laid a hand on Lynch's arm before he could stand up from the table. "Before you go, Andrew, there's something that has been troubling me." Her voice caught. She sounded stressed and on the verge of tears. "I know you have both been working so hard, and I trust you both. I do."

"What is it?" asked Power, moving round the table to put a comforting arm around her shoulders.

"I had a phone call last night, from some woman, an angry woman who was making accusations."

"Was it a patient of mine?" asked Power. He had, like all psychiatrists at some time or another, been the focus of a patient's delusions or paranoia in the past.

"I don't know who she was, Carl," said Laura. "She just said that

272

you'd gone away with a woman. That you were in Malta at the same time for a holiday together."

"No," said Lynch. "Carl was only ever with me, or interviewing people at the University, or visiting the morgue. There was no woman. There wasn't even any holiday."

"I know I shouldn't have got so upset. I know I shouldn't have listened to her for a second," said Laura, sobbing now. "I'm sorry, sorry to both of you."

"There's absolutely no need to apologise," said Power, glowing with new found anger that someone had seen fit to upset his partner. "I just wonder who it was."

"It was a spiteful thing to do," said Lynch. "To worry you, in your condition."

"She just said that one thing – that one hateful thing – then rang off," said Laura. "I pressed the code to get her caller number, but it said her number was not available."

"I'll see if I can find out anything," said Lynch. "Maybe let all calls go to the answerphone now, if they leave a message ring back any person you want to hear from. And if she calls and says anything spiteful, well then we have a recording of her."

Lynch stayed a little longer, until he knew Laura was comforted, and then he drove away, westwards, towards his home in Handbridge village.

* * *

Hamish Grieg, Allminster's Bursar, arrived at his office just before 6 a.m. He was used to spending an hour or so quietly to himself before any other staff arrived in the Administration building. He liked the silence. He could concentrate on the precious columns of figures in his spreadsheets. He could watch their dance as they moved from column to column, formulas and column totals whirring and clicking, adjusting to his will like violins in an orchestra conforming to the baton of their conductor. Grieg imagined money in his spreadsheets as stored energy, like a virtual molecule of ATP to be expended to build new estate and motivate the University's academics into action just as ATP drives the biological machinery of the cell, building proteins and fuelling the replication of life itself.

The whole edifice of his rigidly predictable and orderly morning was therefore shattered by the unwelcome occurrence of a solitary figure sitting in an armchair outside his office, waiting just for him.

He mustered his limited social skills and fashioned a watery smile with the features of his pale face. "Good morning, Professor McFarlane, I wasn't expecting you," said Grieg. "I thought you were on holiday." He inspected her, and indeed, her face did seem to have gained something of a holiday tan since he had last seen her. Her close-cropped brown hair had been bleached by the sun.

"The Vice Chancellor phoned me to give me the sad news about Professor Shacklin," she said, without actually greeting Grieg.

"Yes, yes," he said. "Terrible news."

"And he requested I act up as Executive Pro Vice Chancellor in Shacklin's stead, and that is why I am here."

"The University is usually empty at this hour."

"It seems we are both early birds. I expect to catch my worm."

Grieg unlocked his office door, and somehow, (he wasn't quite sure how), McFarlane walked into his office ahead of him, moved the heavy armchair with a scraping sound across the floor and seated herself at the side of his desk. "I can see what you're doing better if I sit here. If you have any other appointments planned for this morning I suggest that you cancel them."

Grieg's mouth gaped as his jaw fell. McFarlane noted his discomposure. "I'm sorry, Mr Grieg, but I do need to see what's going on. And the best way to understand an organisation is to see where the money is and how it flows around the organisation. This is, of course, something you have chosen to keep to yourself for many years. That stops now."

"I assure you that I have done nothing wrong . . . nothing! And I . . . I resent the implication."

"I never said anything of the sort," said McFarlane. "I merely wish to establish an understanding of the organism that is Allminster and where its strengths and weaknesses are. Where it needs propping up and where it needs pruning. So, here, today, I want you to show me every account, every income stream, and every line of credit."

"Oh, I couldn't allow that," Grieg started scratching at the itches that had suddenly cropped up all over his chest.

"**You** couldn't allow it?" McFarlane stood up. She was several inches taller than Grieg and she loomed over him. "For the Executive

Pro Vice Chancellor? The University's second-in-command? I think the Vice Chancellor has been remiss to delegate the finances of this institution without proper oversight. Millions of pounds of public money, without his properly understanding what you are . . ."

It was unusual for Grieg to display anger. His careful rituals were precisely designed to avoid even a modicum of expressed emotion, but he felt his legs and arms tremble and his voice went high and strained. "The Vice Chancellor understands the state of the University's finances perfectly well. You speak as if I conceal things from him, as if the accounts are unaudited by independent firms. I can assure you that everything that I do is subject to the most detailed analysis."

"Well, I don't understand the University's finances. And that changes today, this morning."

"I . . . I'm sorry . . . it can't be this morning. Professor Shacklin's death has only just been announced. Some respect for the departed surely? We thought you were on leave."

"Shacklin is nothing to do with this University now. I'm sorry to shatter your false image of a senior colleague, but he was an embarrassment and a liability. The Vice Chancellor phoned me as soon as he learned of Shacklin. I am the new Executive Pro Vice Chancellor and I intend to discharge my duties accordingly."

"Forgive me, but you are the *acting* Executive Pro Vice Chancellor, this is not a substantive appointment?"

"So? I don't intend to be passive caretaker for the role, Bursar. If I am 'acting', as you so carefully put it, I shall act."

"Please forgive my choice of words. You have taken me a bit by surprise this morning, I didn't expect anyone to be here. I meant to say it would take a few days for us to prepare the accounts, to get them in a state you could easily assimilate to . . . get reports collated and so on."

"I'm happy with the raw data, Mr Grieg. My father was an accountant. I was practically taught to read using spreadsheets. And I have a Master's Degree in Healthcare Management and Finance. I got a distinction for my thesis on Fraud in Healthcare Commissioning. I want to see who has been spending the money, and where. I want to see the figures for every faculty, every department, every professor, every investment, the income from every student, every rent we earn, every council rate, every electricity bill. In short, I want . . ."

". . . everything," sighed the bursar.

"Everything," she agreed.

"Dean McFarlane, I am sure you will understand that I need to check with the Vice Chancellor, first. That would be accepted etiquette."

"That isn't necessary at all. He has promoted me, and the email announcing my promotion was sent to all the Executive Team."

"I remember Professor Felfe once asked to see the books. And look what happened there."

"What do you mean, Mr Grieg? He died naturally, didn't he?"

"Yes, yes, I just meant that the Vice Chancellor refused his request, but only after he'd persuaded us to give him the data. Felfe could be very charming and insistent if he wanted something. Not following the correct protocol proved inconvenient for me. It put me in a difficult position with the Vice Chancellor." He recalled the self-punishment he had felt compelled to inflict upon himself.

"Felfe was always pushing his nose in where it wasn't wanted and he wasn't the Executive Pro Vice Chancellor. I am."

"But I am sure you can understand my position. I cannot forgive you this sudden intrusion . . . I can't grant it. You spoke before of duty. I must check with the Vice Chancellor before I allow you such detailed access. That is **my** duty." He scratched himself irritably.

McFarlane glared at him. "Very well. I will be back here just after nine when the Vice Chancellor usually gets in. I expect you to have cleared my access by then."

She left in a whirl of perfume and Grieg slumped into his chair, his inner calm dispelled and ruined for the day, and perhaps for the entire week.

* * *

Professor Power was waiting patiently in a queue, hoping for a decaffeinated latte. The University café was full, Power was behind a long line of students and his attention was wandering. Over in the corner, the Vice Chancellor was holding court at a large table, laden with a stack of empty breakfast plates from food that he had already consumed. He had been joined by the bursar who was talking animatedly and whereas the Vice Chancellor was continuing to sip coffee and munch on a *pain au raisin*, Hamish Grieg had no mind for such earthly consumption. Grieg's tiny espresso remained untouched. Power wondered what had upset the bursar so much.

Power's attention was taken away from the Vice Chancellor by a hand upon his shoulder. "Good morning, Carl. There's a terrible queue today. Can I offer you a drink in my office?" It was Sir Robert Willett, Professor of English.

"That would be kind," said Power. He had only intended to grab a takeaway coffee to sip whilst he spent half an hour on a review paper about viral encephalitis. However, when he observed Willett's sunken and red-rimmed eyes, he realised he should not refuse the offer. Willett clearly needed to talk.

"I gather you have been in Malta," said Willett by way of conversation as they made their way up to his office. "I won't ask you about Shacklin. I don't want to know and I expect you won't wish to talk about it anymore. I guess you were busy on Malta, because you don't seem to have caught much of the sun."

"There was not much sunbathing done," said Power, sadly. "Mainly interviews."

"I went to Malta once," said Willett. "As a student. In the nonsensical footsteps of Edward Lear and limping Byron. Lear loved it, Byron hated it as it was a military stronghold." He paused to unlock his study door. "I wouldn't mind retiring to one of the islands myself. And writing the great twenty-first century English novel. Like Monsarrat, who retired to the island of Gozo. Did you go there?"

"No, no," said Power. 'There was no time."

"Ah," said Willett. "You missed out." He invited Power into his study and set about filling a kettle with water and washing out some dirty cups in a sink near the window. He opened the window to let some fresh air in, for the room smelled fusty and warm. "The little islands of Gozo and Comino are very atmospheric. Nicolas Monsarrat – you know him surely – the son of a Liverpool surgeon who wrote *The Cruel Sea*. He retired to little Gozo and wrote himself to death." He chuckled at the thought and quoted the author. *"'Let me end my days somewhere where the tide comes in and out: leaving its tribute, its riches, taking nothing. Giving all the time: pieces of wood, pieces of eight; seaweed for the land, logs for the fire, sea-shells for pleasure, skeletons for sadness.'* That was from his very last novel."

"I never crossed to Gozo," said Power. "I suppose there's a ferry?"

"Gozo was the island of Calypso. Ulysses was imprisoned there by Calypso for seven years."

Power looked around the office. Papers and books were scattered everywhere. The manuscript of *The Wasp* still sat in its square, protective box, squatting malignantly on its table, shrouded in black material. At one end of the room, furthest from the window was an alcove shrouded behind a long, purple and gold velvet curtain that trailed upon the floor. Power wondered what was in the space behind the curtain. Maybe a set of bookshelves or a store of clothes?

Willett brewed black coffee, and set a mug down on the table in front of his guest. Seemingly exhausted by his effort at hospitality, he sank into an armchair, and slumped. His eyes stared emptily at Power. For a moment his naturally ebullient persona had evaporated and he was suddenly lost for words, bereft of any enthusiasm.

Power sipped his coffee and gave Willett time to collect the energy to express his thoughts.

When next he spoke, Willett quoted Byron:

I had a dream, which was not all a dream.
The bright sun was extinguish'd, and the stars
Did wander darkling in the eternal space,
Rayless, and pathless, and the icy earth
Swung blind and blackening in the moonless air;
Morn came and went—and came, and brought no day . . .

"Bleak and beautiful words," said Power. He looked round the office and noticed that the couch had a tousled blanket upon it and a dimpled cushion that Willett had used as a pillow. Over on the windowsill near the sink Power noticed a soapbox, razor and toothbrush.

"How are you feeling, Rob?" asked Power.

"As bleak as Byron," said Willett. "Would you fancy a sherry to go with your coffee? Cheer us both up?" He felt down by the side of his chair for the sherry, but when his hand returned it held an empty bottle. "Ah," he said. "Maybe there's another in my desk."

"It's all right, Rob. Leave it for now. Maybe a bit early in the day for a sherry?"

"What time is it, Carl?"

"Just after quarter past nine."

"Maybe you're right then," said Sir Rob. "I stayed here last night. Thought it best not to drive under the circumstances."

"Taken too much sherry?" asked Power.

"You know, I can't quite recall what happened last night."

"This is not like you, is it? What's the matter?" Power gestured at the black swathed manuscript. "Is it still this? Have you managed to tell the Vice Chancellor?"

"I told the bursar and he refused to tell Armitage, he implied it would kill the old duffer. That's a whole new layer of guilt he laid on me."

"It's only money," said Power. "The Vice Chancellor can't care that much."

"You don't know the Vice Chancellor," said Willett. "And then there's Shacklin dying."

"Ah," said Power, looking down at the floor. "Poor Shacklin."

"I gather he was at the pig farm when he got the chop," Willett smiled apologetically at the taste of his own joke. "Shacklin's hardly cold and McFarlane has jumped into his shoes and scurried off to the bursar to see the books. She'll find out I'm paid twice what she is, and realise her faculty has been subsidising mine for years. English is taught at every University in the world these days. As a result we get fewer overseas students here in England. That's where the money is – overseas students. She will see how much the bursar has siphoned from her faculty to keep the arts afloat. Then she'll find out how much the University squandered on this fake manuscript and she'll have found the final nail to put in the coffin of my career." He laughed. "No wonder I'm looking for my way out. Writing on the Island of Gozo sounds like bliss."

"You seem more than a bit down," said Power. "Unlike your normal self."

"Maybe I am," said Willett. "There's no hiding it from you. It started with this," he gestured at the black-clothed manuscript box, "and my mood has just slithered downhill."

"It wouldn't do any harm to see somebody about your mood," said Dr Power. "Get some treatment. Take some time off – perhaps a holiday to get some perspective on things that seem overwhelming at the moment?"

Willett sat silent, staring at a spot on the floor. His face was devoid of emotion and for a moment he was wholly immobile. If he was breathing then his breath was almost imperceptible. "Maybe," he said slowly. "I've been thinking about Felfe. I'm reading a lesson at his memorial service. The University will always do the thing that's formally right. But did anybody here really care about him? One day he was here and the next day he was gone, and who really cared?"

Power could feel Willett's depression hanging heavily in the air, like something solid pressing down upon him. It was a struggle to find something to say, the conversation dragged upon him like he was swimming through thick oil. "People do care, Rob. But when you are feeling depressed it's more difficult to see the good in people and situations. Maybe you need to see your doctor?"

Willett didn't seem to have heard. "Felfe – nobody liked him. He sat in all those meetings over the years and he said nothing. Sometimes, when it was an important decision and a vote was called, Felfe would abstain. He'd say that it wasn't safe to have an opinion that was extreme, so he'd abstain. It was infuriating. And all he'd do in a meeting was have a cup of tea and a single digestive biscuit. And all he'd say in the meeting was '*Verdauungskeks*' as he addressed the ruddy biscuit." Power nodded as he listened. "He changed a bit in the last few months though," said Willett.

"Did he?" asked Power. "How did he change?"

"He seemed more animated. You'd see him in the Library, pulling down books off the shelves, and running computer searches. That was new. He even came up to me once and asked me about my brother. That surprised me. He'd remembered I had a brother. I was surprised. He reminded me that I'd mentioned my brother at one of the Vice Chancellor's interminable dinners. He'd noted it down that I'd said my brother was a pilot. He wanted me to ask him about flight routes."

"How odd," said Power. "Can you remember what it was he wanted you to ask?"

"Yes, I remember. I remember because it was unusual for him to say anything at all to me. He wanted to know whether a small plane, a Cessna 182, could fly from Malta to the UK"

"I wouldn't have thought so," said Power. "That sort of small plane could fly a hundred miles and Malta is what? Over a thousand miles away."

"I think that's what Felfe thought too. My brother said a Cessna with long-range fuel tanks could manage it with two or three stops to refuel. Flying at fifteen thousand feet with oxygen masks on and re-fuelling at places like *Les Eplatures* in Switzerland, Bergamo airport in Milan, and *Ajaccio* on Corsica. So I passed my brother's message on to Felfe, and Felfe looked highly satisfied. He said thank you, and he made a scrawl in his little notebook, but he never volunteered exactly why he wanted to know."

"Did he ask any other questions, or say anything else?" asked Power.

"Not a thing. That question he asked of my brother – that must have been one of only three or four conversations I ever had with him. That's why it stuck in my memory, I suppose."

"How odd. And rather poignant, I think," said Power, standing up. "I must go Rob, because I have an appointment with the Vice Chancellor and I can't be late." He went on to make an offer. "Do you want me to say anything? To broach the subject of the manuscript?"

"It's kind of you, but I'd rather you didn't," said Willett. "I will try and get the courage to do it myself, soon."

Power looked at his academic friend, slumped on the faded couch. "Don't forget you can always talk to me. Anytime you need, Rob. And make sure you take care of your health. See your doctor."

Willett nodded. "Thank you, Carl. I'll certainly think about it."

Power took his leave of Willett, slipped out of the door and ran down the stairs to his appointment.

* * *

Only the Vice Chancellor was not there when Power arrived at his office as arranged.

Power thought back to the professor he had worked for when he was a lecturer at the Royal. The professor abided by a strict hierarchy of waiting times; he never failed to make a senior lecturer wait fifteen minutes, a junior lecturer wait thirty minutes and anyone else wait an hour to see him. He did this to show that he was, at all times, in control.

Armitage's secretary was apologetic and made Power a cup of thin, watery coffee. She herself sipped at a glass of boiled water with a slice of lemon in it. "I'm sorry he's late. He thought he had time for a quick haircut at the barber's across the road." Power thought of the Vice Chancellor sitting waiting for a trim.

At length, the door to the Vice Chancellor's office opened and he stood there, solemn and newly shorn. "Good afternoon, Professor Power, will you come in, please?"

Power followed the rotund Vice Chancellor into his office and sat down in the armchair that Canon Armitage indicated.

Whereas on his previous visit the Vice Chancellor had plied him with food and drink, this time there was none to be had, and the Vice Chancellor's demeanour seemed uncharacteristically austere, even mildly irritable. "Carl, I wanted to assure you that the University is most grateful to you and your detective colleague for your endeavours in Malta on its behalf. You succeeded where, I am sure, many other people would have failed. And although we could have hoped for a better outcome for Professor Shacklin, you both concluded your mission with great expedition. I find myself with the unhappy task of organising two memorial services for your professorial colleagues. Professor Felfe's will be before Christmas and Professor Shacklin's will be in the New Year. I wonder if I can ask you a favour in that regard. Will you, perhaps, read a lesson for Professor Shacklin's memorial service?"

"Of course," said Power. He recalled that Willett had said that he was going to read a lesson at Felfe's service.

"Thank you," said Armitage. "Is there anything else you would like to tell me about David Shacklin's activities on Malta? Any explanation you can offer as to why he died there in such a macabre way?"

Power thought about the details of their investigation and all the questions that he and Lynch had churned up in the waters surrounding Shacklin's disappearance. There were the tales of Shacklin's untoward conduct with female academics at the University of Malta, his spectacular losses at the casino, the cocaine on his suit, and the unexplained contact with rogue scientist Professor Xuereb. Still more questions concerned Professor Felfe's request to the Intelligence Service for information about Sannik Law Co, Wanderlust and The Banker. All of this he could legitimately report to the Vice Chancellor and ask his advice, but something in the Vice Chancellor's icy manner irritated Power. He only had questions to report, and because the Vice Chancellor had peremptorily summoned Lynch and him back from Malta; there had been no chance to find conclusive answers. Power discovered he was nursing a simmering resentment and instead of discoursing about the puzzling misdemeanours of Professor Shacklin and the multitude of loose ends still left in Malta, Power said instead, "What exactly Professor Shacklin was up to on the Island, we don't know, and we have no firm answers."

The Vice Chancellor scrutinised Power with some care, having detected the petulant tone in Power's reply. "I think you are being cautious in what you say and loyally protecting the vestiges of what dubious reputation Professor Shacklin had left. That is perhaps kind of you, but I am perfectly aware of David's peccadilloes. He gambled. He had debts. He was . . . uncaring and manipulative with the opposite sex. He was, to put it bluntly, a reputational liability to this University. I think that if you had stayed in Malta you would no doubt have found out much more regarding his nefarious activities. But I have to ask you what profit to the University would accrue from funding a long investigation that would only jeopardise the University further? I know you may have wished to ferret out Professor Shacklin's motives and deeds, but if there is anything to find we shall leave that to the official agencies, and issue any necessary damage control press releases when, and if, we have to."

"I understand," said Power, feeling somewhat chastened. "I absolutely understand."

The Vice Chancellor nodded acceptance, and moved on, "Shacklin's departure raises various difficulties. As soon as I learned of David's demise my immediate duty was to fill the void he left in the University structure. Nature and Universities abhor a vacuum." He sighed, and Power theorised that one potential cause of his unusual brusqueness might be this particular stress. "Protocol dictates that the most senior of the remaining deans acts up to fill the Executive Pro Vice Chancellor role until a substantive appointment is made. And McFarlane knows that very well. In fact, she reminded me of this succession plan only a few weeks ago, before anything was . . . certain . . . about Professor Shacklin."

"Before we even knew he was dead?" asked Power.

"Exactly so," said Armitage. "The very day after he failed to return as planned."

"Sir Rob Willett would appear, to me anyway, to be the most senior dean," Power said hopefully, knowing that Willett had been an advocate of the new medical school.

"Wishful thinking?" suggested Armitage. "Seniority here is defined in terms of number of years employed by this University. McFarlane has been here ever since she was a very junior lecturer. She's been here longer than all of us, even me." He sighed. "I was appointed Vice Chancellor when she was a new dean. I'm afraid I've always sought to keep her away from the levers of power. No pun on your name intended. I quite forgot that she has a Masters in financial management. She's been down to the bursar already today, throwing her newly acquired weight about, pulling rank, asking for the keys to the financial kingdom. She could do a lot of damage to causes we both hold dear. She will not suffer a medical school to be built, or even planned, I am afraid."

"Are you telling me that's that, then?" asked Power. "Game over?"

"In her position she can wreak havoc," said the Vice Chancellor.

It was Power's turn to display irritation. "I can't abide politics. I left the NHS once because all my colleagues – nurses and doctors and managers – they all had their own agenda, and not one of those agendas was about patient care. I am here to do one thing really, Vice Chancellor. That is to start a medical school. And I've been down to London to the Department of Health, and the General Medical Council. I've seen Chief Executives, and General Practitioners, and all sorts of external bodies. There's been no opposition *outside* the University. I've had green light after green light from people outside. The only opposition I've faced is from twisted individuals *inside* the University, who would cut off the University's nose to spite their own face. They should be supporting a medical school. I don't have time to waste on this dissent. I can find other work outside the University – no end of patients to care for, rewarded by knowing I'm doing a worthwhile job treating people, and if I was motivated by making money then there are more efficient ways of earning it. These senior academics – it's like hitting my head against a brick wall. And I am beginning to think . . . to realise rather, that I simply don't have to go on playing this game. I can simply walk away."

The Vice Chancellor glared at Professor Power, because none of his other employees would ever dare to speak to him this way. Armitage managed to bite back the words he might have spoken reflexively, and assumed a friendly demeanour and a smile. "Come, come, Professor Power. I have been playing this game a little longer than you. You just need to persist a bit longer, play your part and let the game unfold. Listen to me," he leant forward, and said in a confidential way, "This is my next move. I will be seeing McFarlane later to brief her on her new responsibilities and emphasise the limits to the role of an acting Executive Pro Vice Chancellor. When Professor McFarlane says she will assume the role of Chairing the Medical School committee I will tell her that I, personally, will chair this committee. This will neutralise any damage she can do in terms of delaying the project. And I shall tell her that I have put the substantive appointment out to advertisement. The advert for the substantive Executive Pro Vice Chancellor post – the job description, and minimum criteria – go live on the University website today. They will be on the Times Higher Education website tomorrow, and the European websites by the end of the week. Closing date strictly in thirty days. We must suffer McFarlane into Hilary term, and no later."

He sat back and watched Power to see what effect his words had made. "You let me deal with McFarlane. Don't let her affect your thinking on the medical school." He paused. "You can help me though. By putting together a list of regional stake holders in the medical school project. The people we need on our side regionally – Chief Executives, medical directors, top GPs. And then we'll invite them all to a dinner in the middle of Hilary term. Push the boat out a bit. You can bring your wife, and your colleague, Andrew Lynch, as a thank you for his work in Malta."

Mollified by the Vice Chancellor's skilful set of words, Power nodded his agreement.

"Good," said the Vice Chancellor. "Now come with me, I have an artwork on approval from Bonhams I want to show you. It's over here." The Vice Chancellor heaved himself out of his armchair and toddled over to a lectern in the coldest corner of his office, right away from the heat of the fire. The lectern had a blue velvet covering over it. "To keep out unnecessary light," he explained to Professor Power. "Do you have any expertise in art and antiquities? Drawings?" Power thought about this, remembering a time, years before, during an investigation, he had pretended to be just such an expert. And he also thought about how expertise had proved a double-edged sword for Sir Rob Willett.

"I have absolutely no expertise at all," Professor Power declared as definitively as he could.

"What a shame," said Canon Armitage, sadly. "I would have valued your opinion on whether to invest in this piece." He whisked off the velvet. "It's a print from 1559. Ostensibly an etching by Heyden, after Breughel. *La fete des fous.*"

Power looked at an etching of townsfolk and peasants dancing and whirling about outdoors, cavorting, laughing and tweaking each other's noses. In the foreground a jester was cocking a snook at a violin player. In the top right corner Power saw what might have been a colonnade, somehow reminiscent of a flying saucer.

"They're asking five hundred and fifty thousand," said the Vice Chancellor. "It might be a suitable addition to our collection."

Professor Power made appreciative sounds, but declined to vocalise a single sentence that might suggest he had an opinion either way. The thought of Willett alone in his study agonising over another of the Vice Chancellor's purchases, the manuscript of *The Wasp,* forestalled him from making any further comment.

Chapter Twenty

D r Power sat down in an oak chair, one of a row of four, next to the
centre aisle. He watched discreetly as a few other mourners, who
had been behind him, drifted into the Lady Chapel. They sat and
distracted themselves by admiring the patterned red Minton tiled
floor, which looked like a series of Turkish carpets rendered in stone.
Trying to avoid thinking about death and mortality, they turned their
attention from the tiled chapel floor to the carved wooden panels of
the walls.

The day was bitterly cold and the tiny cast iron radiators of the
Cathedral's thirteenth century Lady Chapel were struggling to make
any difference to the chill. Instead of wrapping a comforting blanket
of heat about the mourners, the feeble radiators exuded nothing more
than a few tepid threads of warmth. As he exhaled, Power was sure he
could see his breath steaming in the frigid air. He wrapped himself
closer still into the dark wool of his overcoat.

The black-suited academics and solemn-faced friends settled
across the aisle from him. Power picked up a copy of the 'Order of the
Memorial Service for Professor Johann Felfe', printed by the University

printers and laid on each of the Chapel's seats. He flicked through its pages and drifted into reverie. Dr Power disliked funerals, and the recent experience of burying his father was only too fresh in his memory for any comfort. Power glanced through the choice of hymns in the order of service and found no sense of Felfe's past, his long exile in a country other than his own. There was only the present. Power found he was remembering a fragment often recited by his father, '*Hold to the now, the here through which all future plunges to the past.*' He wondered where it came from, this paean to the present moment. He realised that he had never asked his father where the phrase came from. He could never ask now. All of a sudden grief washed over Power and he felt small, and very alone, in the vastness of the Cathedral chapel.

Just before 10.30 a.m. when the service was about to start, the stone-vaulted Chapel was still only a quarter full. Power studied the sparse congregation which composed a few secretaries, several University deans, a few strangers and a handful of postgraduate students. He didn't notice that someone had occupied the seat next to him, and it was not until Andrew Lynch said, "Good morning, Carl," that Power realised his friend had joined him.

"I didn't know you were coming," said Power.

"I wanted to see who showed up," said Lynch. "There are a few representatives from SIS here. The rest I presume are University employees. Felfe had no close family, and few friends. A loner. A small congregation. Just as you might expect of the requiem for a spy."

"It's bitterly cold," said Power.

"Maybe we can go for an early lunch in a pub with a log fire after the ceremony," suggested Lynch.

"And forego the Vice Chancellor's funeral do in the senior common room with mince pies and sherry?" asked Power. "Tsk tsk. Seriously, how could I?" He winked at Lynch. "All right then, you've twisted my arm. Let's go for an early lunch in the warmest pub we can possibly find."

Almost as if Power's comment about his sherry and mince pies had summoned him, the Vice Chancellor now appeared by Power's side, standing in the aisle of the Chapel.

The Vice Chancellor was dressed as a Canon of the Cathedral. Power remembered now the tradition that the Vice Chancellor of Allminster was always made a Canon of the Cathedral. Armitage wore a stark white surplice over a black cassock. Around his portly neck he wore a clerical white collar adorned by starched preaching bands. A purple silk stole, the colour of mourning, was draped around his shoulders.

He leaned in close to Power and whispered. "Carl, I'm so pleased your colleague Detective Lynch can join us this morning." He nodded to Lynch with a polite smile. "I wonder, if I could ask a favour of you?"

"Of course," said Power trying not sound wary.

"I believe I asked you to read the lesson at Professor Shacklin's memorial service in the New Year. Could I possibly ask you to bring forward your reading of a lesson?

Power assented and murmured, "If you wish, of course."

"I think I mentioned that Sir Robert would read today."

"Yes, I believe you did," said Power, aware that Lynch was listening closely.

"Well, I'm afraid it is nearly time to begin the service, and Sir Robert has not deigned to arrive. He is usually punctual, but I am afraid to say that of late, he appears to have become something of a liability in this regard. He was late for a key lecture this week, and not here today. You will find Sir Robert's lesson is already marked in the Bible on the lectern, and this is the verse." He proffered Power a slip of paper. "It's 1 Corinthians 15, verses 50-57. The reading comes after a quote that I will make from Psalm 58. I will look over to you, and if you make your way to the lectern I will be introducing you as you walk."

Power nodded, he felt somewhat nervous now.

The Vice Chancellor was about to turn away, when he paused, cupped his hand round his mouth and put his lips close to Power's ear to hiss, "This Chapel here . . . it wasn't here in *this* chapel that you discovered him, was it?"

Power was reminded of an image of Felfe, deathly still from his final convulsion and sprawled upon the stone flags of St Anselm's Chapel.

"No, no, not this Chapel," he whispered back.

"Good," said Canon Armitage, and walked solemnly to the front of the Lady Chapel.

"It will be fine," said Lynch, picking up on his friend's anxiety. He flipped through the pages of the Bible in front of him, found the verses, and pointed them out to Power. "Just read through the verses and familiarize yourself during the service."

The Vice Chancellor made his way to the dais in front of the altar. He looked across to the mourners and there was a hush. "Welcome to you all. Welcome to this University Memorial Service for Professor Johann Felfe, the late Dean of Faculty of Social Sciences and Criminology. I welcome his academic colleagues, friends and all those who knew him, as we commemorate his life today. Before I begin, you are all welcome back at the University for seasonal refreshments after the service; sandwiches, some sherry, a few mince pies. And before we commence, may I just say that this is also the last day of Michaelmas term for the University, and so this service marks a close to our academic work, our staff and students will be dispersing for Christmas and, as Vice Chancellor, I wish you all to make the most of your Christmastide, and I wish you peace, comfort and joy. But now, let us address ourselves to remembering our dear colleague Professor Felfe who passed away of natural causes, whilst attending a service elsewhere in this Cathedral. He was a private man, but a devout man; loyal to the service of his adopted country and loyal to his University and his students."

And here the Vice Chancellor broke into the words of the service:

I am the resurrection and the life, says the Lord. Those who believe in me, even though they die, will live, and everyone who lives and believes in me will never die.

The Vice Chancellor began reading the rest of the liturgy. Two hymns followed, and then Canon Armitage announced he would read from Psalm 58. Lynch gently nudged Power to remind him it was almost time for him to make his way to the lectern.

Armitage began to intone the words of Psalm 58:

The wicked are estranged from the womb;
These who speak lies go astray from birth.
They have venom like the venom of a serpent;
Like a deaf cobra that stops up its ear.

Power stood, and conscious of all the eyes upon him, began walking in the most dignified manner he could assume to the front of the chapel as the Vice Chancellor introduced him. "And now we have a Bible reading from 1 Corinthians, read to us by one of Professor Felfe's close colleagues, Professor Power."

And so Power read:

I declare to you, brothers and sisters, that flesh and blood cannot inherit the kingdom of God, nor does the perishable inherit the imperishable. Listen, I tell you a mystery: We will not all sleep, but we will all be changed in a flash, in the twinkling of an eye, at the last trumpet. For the trumpet will sound, the dead will be raised imperishable, and we will be changed . . .

On he went to the conclusion of the passage.

Power felt himself blushing as he read. With the reading done, he scurried back to his place by Lynch. Back in his seat, Power felt even colder than before. Shivering in the icebox of the Lady Chapel, Power could hardly wait for the service to end, but it ground on until the final dismissal. Power and Lynch shook hands with the Vice Chancellor as they departed. "Thank you so much for standing in for Sir Robert. I am immensely grateful."

"I'm glad I could help, Vice Chancellor," said Power. "We must give our apologies for the reception, however. I am afraid I must confer with Detective Lynch on a case."

"That is fine," said the Vice Chancellor, patting him on the arm. "I hope your discussions are fruitful. Have a good Christmas, Carl, and you too, Mr Lynch."

Power and Lynch hurried out of the Cathedral and down St Werburgh Street. They walked rapidly to warm themselves up, passing as quickly as possible through bustling Christmas crowds. Power was puzzled by his companion occasionally changing tack however, crossing the cobbled street and pausing to stare into a shop window. He assumed that Lynch's behaviour was related to Christmas shopping, because Lynch was usually very focused in his walking and always strode purposefully ahead.

At length, they strode down Lower Bridge Street towards the river. Lynch paused for a moment outside a tall, half-timbered building and peered up the street.

"Is everything all right, Andrew?" Power asked.

"Of course," said Lynch with a smile, and they burst into the magnificently warm bar of the Bear and Billet. Lynch ordered pints of Okell's bitter for them both and requested plates of sandwiches and vegetable soup from the kitchens. He found Power huddled at a table by a roaring open fire.

"I'm chilled to the marrow," said Power, as he stretched out a hand to take his pint from Lynch. Somehow the chill of the funeral service had seeped into the heart of him. "It's at times like this that you can be grateful that the English serve their bitter warm."

Lynch chuckled and took a lengthy draught of his pint, and when he put his glass down, sighed in pleasure. "I needed that." He looked over at the leaping flames of the fire. "Nice to remind ourselves of the living world again. What did you think of the service?"

"I don't know much about memorial services," said Power. "I try and stay away from such things. I suppose it had the standard elements?"

"There's a range of sentences and readings that are traditionally used, but your Vice Chancellor – I presume it was his choice – well if it was, then he chose oddly. Particularly Psalm 58. What *was* he trying to say?"

"That bit about the words of serpents?"

Lynch quoted the lines again, from memory, and asked, "Was Canon Armitage implying the distinguished Professor was a liar?" There was a trace of indignation in Lynch's voice. "Speaking ill of the dead? I watched the SIS representatives when he used those words. They looked ... uncomfortable." He paused, thinking. "A curious choice, Psalm 58. It is one of six psalms that are traditionally labelled *michtam*, which may mean something 'golden', or even 'secret'."

"Another secret revolving round Professor Felfe?"

"Your colleagues seem encrusted in secrets, like barnacles on the hull of a ship. But even considering Felfe was a spy, he seems straightforward compared to Shacklin. And at least with Felfe's secrets, I am beginning to unravel them a bit."

"Go on, please."

"We have a candidate to explain Wanderlust," said Lynch. "I think *Wanderlust* is a small ship, registered in Panama."

"A ship or a boat?"

"Ah," said Lynch. "I'm told you can put a boat on a ship, but you can't put a ship on a boat. This vessel is a small ship."

"But not a large boat?" teased Power.

"A small ship," said Lynch firmly. "Ninety feet in length with a draft of six feet. Built in nineteen twenty-two. And *Wanderlust* has been sighted twice in Maltese waters in the last month. Azzopardi phoned me yesterday to ask if we thought that Felfe was referring to a ship."

"Do you think *Wanderlust* is the name of a ship then?" asked Power.

"I don't know," said Lynch. "We need more detail, but it was good of Azzopardi to let us know. Do you think we should invest some time in finding out?"

Power nodded.

"I will ask Beresford to work on finding out more about *Wanderlust's* history. And I think we should also ask Beresford to make some enquiries about other loose ends in this case. Could you make a list of all the anomalies you've noticed whilst you've been at Allminster? No matter how small, and then we can set Beresford to work. He's as relentless as a terrier rooting out rats from a drain."

They paused whilst the barman placed two steaming bowls of thick green vegetable soup, a plate of ham sandwiches and a plate of brie and grape sandwiches on the wooden table in front of them.

Power waited cautiously until the barman had left. "Where is *Wanderlust* sailing now?"

"I don't know," said Lynch. He reached in his pocket and brought out his phone.

"That's new," said Power, suppressing a twinge of envy.

"It's a Motorola smartphone," said Lynch. "The A100. It does emails and has a camera. And it has GPS. I have even installed a program that offers AIS."

Power didn't know what the acronym meant and knew that he was meant to ask. "Go on, explain please. You're pleased because you know something I don't – so by all means begin the lecture and enlighten me."

Lynch smiled. "AIS stands for Automatic Identification System. It's a satellite system that can track vessels all over the world. For the last two years sea going vessels with transponders can be tracked in real time." He clicked a few buttons and showed Power the screen. "Here's a fishing trawler, BM27, *Our Miranda*, just off Berry Head, Brixham, latitude 50° and longitude -3.5°, travelling at 7 knots."

Power was impressed. "So, if you have this AIS program, where's *Wanderlust*?"

"Ah," Lynch looked a bit crestfallen. "The requirement to have the transponders put on ships is only for vessels above three hundred gross tonnage. *Wanderlust* is below that level." He put the phone away. "But in any case, if Felfe was interested in this ship, probably the ship's captain doesn't want to be tracked." Lynch paused in his drinking of his soup, with his full soup spoon halfway to his mouth. "I suppose no-one likes to be followed."

"I don't suppose so," said Power.

"Well, just keep your eyes on me, then," said Lynch, as he buttered a piece of bread roll. "And don't look round."

"What do you mean?" said Power, resisting the immediate impulse to turn round.

"Well, we were followed when we left the Cathedral. And we were followed along St Werburgh Street, and Eastgate, and Bridge Street. All the way here."

"Is that why you were dodging around the streets like that?" asked Power. "I thought you were looking out for Christmas presents. Who was following us, then?"

"Well, again I must warn you not to turn round. But they are still following us, or rather you. I say you, because she is glaring at your back right now. She's not looking at me. She is sitting alone at a table across the pub behind you."

Power felt the hairs on the back of his neck stand up. "Can you describe her, Andrew?"

Lynch looked her up and down briefly, appraising her. "I'd say she's in her late thirties, possibly early forties. Dressed in an angry fashion, looks very out of place, alone in a place like this. She has a long, tall drink of water in front of her, and so in no way is she here to enjoy herself. Her gaze is fixed on your back and if looks could kill, you would be dead by now. Her hands are two little clenched fists. Pale skin, and face white with anger. Very definite black eyebrows, and short, green hair."

"Ah," said Dr Power. "That would probably be Caroline Diarmid from the University."

"Well," said Lynch. "I dare say we've found your stalker. Stay here. Whatever you do, don't look round. Don't come over. Don't interact with her. Let me handle this now; right through to the moment when she leaves the pub."

Lynch stood up and began walking as if he were going to the bar, and then changing direction, moved sprightly over to the table Caroline was sitting at. He pulled out a chair and sat down opposite her, in such a way that she could not easily get past. "Hello, Caroline. We need to talk. Don't make a scene, I just need a quick word and then you can be on your way."

"Who the hell are you? Who said you could sit down?"

"My name is Andrew Lynch, I'm a detective." He noted that this information was an unwelcome surprise to her. "Your name is Caroline Diarmid of Allminster University, and you made a recent phone call to Dr Power's home." He saw she was about to open her mouth and he forestalled her. "It's all right, I won't be charging you under the 1997 Protection from Harassment Act today. That is, as long as you can calm down, take a deep breath, and we can have a civil conversation." She looked at the resolute and confident expression on the immaculately dressed man opposite. Where, she wondered, did he get his relaxed assurance from?

"Now, Caroline, perhaps you can explain to me exactly what all this is about?"

'He's the one who's wrecking my life, you should be talking to him."

"I was just talking to him, and now I'm talking to you. Please tell me why you think 'he's wrecking your life'? That will help us both."

Caroline looked at Lynch's steady blue eyes and dark hair, peppered with iron-grey. This was a solid soul who would not brook any outburst from her. She sensed any hostility or feigned offence would merely wash over him, like a wave of sea foam breaking against a granite cliff. A single tear ran from her eye. She sniffed, but Lynch did not waver.

"My partner left. We had had a row. She flew out to the Mediterranean. She said she needed to take a break. Get her mind together. She said she would be on her own, so I let her go." She pointed at Power, who had his back turned to them and was getting on with his lunch. He knew better than to interrupt Lynch when he was dealing with something. "Then I found out about him."

"And what exactly did you find out about Dr Power?"

"That he'd flown out to the Mediterranean on the same day as her. And then I *knew* they were having an affair."

"Who is your partner, please?"

"Professor McFarlane. She's always talking about Professor Power. Professor Power was at this committee. Professor Power said this, Professor Power said that. She's obsessed with him. She fancies him, she's in love with him."

"The Mediterranean is a vast place. Where did your partner go?"

"Sicily."

"Professor Power was working for the University, at the Vice Chancellor's request, on the Island of Malta. A whole different island." She paused as she assessed the logic behind Lynch's reassurance. "He could have got the ferry to see her. It's not far. An hour or two and then they would be together."

"What does your partner say?"

"She denies everything. She always does."

"You've had arguments with her like this before?" asked Lynch.

"She's always looking at other people."

"I see," said Lynch. "You know jealousy can be a terrible thing."

"I've got cause though," Caroline said, seething, with arms firmly crossed.

Lynch sighed. He wondered that an academic could have such poor reasoning skills. "Professor Power was busy investigating the disappearance of Professor Shacklin. You surely know the result of that investigation?" She nodded reluctantly. "Well, you can appreciate that Professor Power was not on holiday with your lover. He was travelling across Malta, interviewing people, and even visited the morgue. He wasn't lying on a beach with your partner. I know. I was with him all the time. He hardly had time to tie his shoelaces, let alone conduct an affair on another island altogether."

"I don't understand why she went there, though. To Sicily. The only explanation I can think of was that it was close to where he was."

"You would have to ask yourself, why your partner wanted to get so far away from you?" He saw she was about to protest. "I'm not going to argue with you. I'm just asking you to reflect. Now, I've said what I needed to. Are you going to leave Dr Power alone, or do I need to press for charges under the Harassment Act and take out a private prosecution for damages – for all the hurt you've caused him and his partner?"

"You don't need to do anything of the sort. I'll avoid Power, for now. But I don't think you'd really do any of that – press charges and take me to court. That's just a bluff."

Lynch laughed at her. "Try me! I know my way round the courts, I know them like the back of my own hand. You leave my colleague alone. And for that matter, leave your partner alone too." His amused smile disappeared as quickly as melting snow on the lawn on a sunny day, and he became stony-faced. Lynch pointed at the knuckles of her right hand. The skin was red. "Did her face collide with your fist perhaps?" There was real anger in his voice.

She stood up and attempted to push past him. Lynch did not budge and she had to retreat and sidle out the other way round the table. She left in silence.

"Mind how you go," said Lynch under his breath. He stood up and walked back to Power. "All done," he said. "I don't think Laura will hear from her again."

Power smiled in gratitude. "I ordered you another pint." Power himself was drinking black decaffeinated coffee. "You're walking back to Handbridge? Not driving?" The village was a short walk from the City Centre, over the Old Dee Bridge.

Lynch nodded. "Thank you," he said.

"How did that go? I tell you, it was all I could do to resist my curiosity. It was so hard to stop turning round and coming over. What happened?"

"Did you overhear anything we said?"

"Some," said Power. "You didn't sound yourself. Your voice sounded harsh. I heard something about charges and court."

"Caroline needs to know there's a limit to her behaviour, and that she's right up against it," said Lynch. "She is jealous, angry, violent. Out of control. And frightened she is losing her partner, who I guess is the main breadwinner. She imagines that her partner is fascinated by you, and you had an affair with her on Sicily."

"But that's ridiculous," said Power.

"It made sense to Caroline Diarmid. The green-eyed, green-haired monster of jealousy has her in its grip. Maybe this jealousy has been going on for years."

"Professor McFarlane is ambitious, and she's just been promoted."

"And that won't make Diarmid feel any more secure," said Lynch. "She rowed with McFarlane. McFarlane had enough and took herself far enough away to get a break, and to let Diarmid simmer down. She decides on a weekend break. She looks on lastminute.com, or whatever, and books herself on the first plane to Palermo, far away, where Diarmid can't just follow. Maybe she phones Diarmid when she arrives somewhere in Palermo – 'I'm just telling you that I'm somewhere in Sicily. I'll be back when you've calmed down. No, I'm not telling you exactly where I am . . .'

Diarmid's jealousy notches up an inch or two higher. Diarmid knows you've flown to Malta. Maybe McFarlane gossiped about you searching for Shacklin. Diarmid looks on a map and notices Sicily is a stone's throw from Malta. She adds two and two together and she makes five. She seethes at home about you and McFarlane in bed. She calls Laura in anger, spite and hurt."

"Morbid jealousy," mused Power. "Also known as Othello syndrome."

"I had to be clear with her," said Lynch. "I sent a warning shot across her bows. I've seen these cases before."

"Hmm," said Power, thoughtfully. "Setting firm boundaries."

"Does she hit McFarlane?" asked Lynch. "I noticed her knuckles were barked and red. She's hit something or someone."

"I once saw Diarmid grip McFarlane's upper arm quite viciously. Really dug her fingers in. That was just after McFarlane had been talking to me," said Power, still thinking.

"I told her not to hit her partner again. She didn't protest, so I assume that I guessed right, and that there is violence between them."

"People always think that domestic violence is a male behaviour. And, of course, males are usually the perpetrators," said Power. "But it's also something about couples, about one's dominance over the other, with imbalance and insecurity in the relationship, with jealousy and anger. We all have those emotions. I didn't like McFarlane before. I probably still don't, but now I feel sorry for her, too."

"Whether you like McFarlane or not, she is at high risk, I think," said Lynch. "But you will know that risk as well as I."

"We can imagine we can control these emotions, but anger is a slippery thing. Anger's difficult to keep hold of, even when you know that's what you must do. It's a sudden beast." Power paused, reflecting on his training at the Royal. "I used to study and work with an old Professor who always used to tell the victim of any jealous, violent patient to leave them, and to leave without any qualms, without any fuss, and immediately. He used to say 'the best defence is geographical', by which he meant getting as far away as soon as possible."

"Didn't that rather break confidentiality?" asked Lynch.

"He didn't care," said Power. "He said that if he was taken to court by the patient he'd just say to the judge that he was trying to save a life. Did you ever hear the tale of the Lady of Llyn y Fan Fach?"

"No," said Lynch. "I can safely say that I have never heard that. The tale sounds as if it must be Welsh, and as we are not far from the Border, I'll let you tell it to me."

Power grinned. "It's a cautionary fairy tale. About a young man who was tending the cattle by a lake. All of a sudden he saw the most beautiful woman he had ever seen, walking towards him out of the lake, combing her hair with a golden comb. In that very moment he saw her, he fell in love with her. He immediately asked for her hand in marriage, and after considering the bargain she agreed, but on one condition. The condition was that if he struck her three times without good cause, that marriage would cease.

"They lived together for many years, the farm prospered and she brought huge numbers of animals into the farm from her home in the lake. They had seven children and when the eldest was seven years old her husband asked her to go with him to a wedding in a nearby village. They got dressed to go, but she dallied and appeared reluctant, so teasingly he flicked her with one of her gloves. 'That is the first blow without cause,' she said. And they got on with their marriage until one day when her eldest son was eight, and there was a Christening to go to. They went, but whilst everyone was rejoicing, his wife, the Lady of the Lake, was sobbing. He got angry with her and took her outside where he asked her why she was crying and she said she was crying, 'because the child has been born into a veil of tears' and he hit her. And she said, 'That was the second blow without cause.' And they went on with their marriage as before until her eldest child was aged nine. Then they were invited to a funeral of a neighbour, and they went to the church where everyone in the congregation was weeping and grieving. However, the Lady of the Lake laughed and cheered loudly and he grew frustrated and hit her again. She stood up and explained herself, 'I am celebrating because your neighbour is free of pain and suffering and has gone to heaven. And now, the third blow without cause has fallen upon me. Farewell.' Without any further word she walked to the edge of the lake, gathering all that was hers, including her animals and their descendants and disappeared into the sparkling water, and was never seen again."

"Each time he hits her it's more violent," said Lynch. "It's just like real life, a progression. And a good example of your advice, that the best solution is geographical separation." Lynch shook his head, drained his pint, and took his leave of Dr Power.

Chapter Twenty-One
Spring Term
10th January, 2005

*Words have no power to impress the mind without
the exquisite horror of their reality.*

Edgar Allan Poe

D r Power had driven twice round the University car park in his battered old Saab. On this frosty Monday morning, the first day of term, every space in the car park was occupied. Power bumped the left-hand side of his car onto an icy grass verge hoping he would not attract the ire of the porters. He got out of the car to find he was standing on the frozen surface of a deep dark puddle, which had metamorphosed into a solid sheet of ice. He slithered his way across the glassy surface to the gravel of the car park. He walked on past students and parents unloading cars to ferry clothes, duvets, blankets, pots and pans and surly Yucca plants altogether unused to the cold of an Allminster winter, to the tepid confines of student bedrooms on campus.

He progressed along a trail of parents and their offspring carrying cardboard boxes and suitcases across frosted paths, and up the gritted stone steps of the Student Halls, remarkably like a trail of leafcutter ants conveying neatly severed green leaves, held above their heads, back to the nest. There were a few clusters of the families around the entrance to the Halls, and their ferrying task complete, the parents were taking their leave. The older generation wanted to linger, while the slightly embarrassed fruit of their loins aimed to speed up the process, lest their parents attract unwanted critical attention from their peers. Allminster was their new adult life, unrelated to older parents, or the childish rituals of Christmas holidays. Here they were forging their new lives, and merely wished to be left to get on with it. Power watched the reluctant parents detaching themselves to commence their journeys back to empty houses in dormitory suburbs hundreds of miles away. He calculated that in something under a decade hence he could be dropping his own son, Jo, off at some University.

The Refectory had a sign outside promoting an offer of full English vegetarian breakfast, with toast and coffee for £3.50, and Power was just considering the merits of this, when a female voice hailed him. Power slowed as safely as he could on the gritted ice, and turned. It was Caroline Diarmid. When he saw that it was Diarmid who had hailed him, Power's face must have fallen, because she hurried to reassure him. "Don't rush away," she pleaded. She walked up to him. "I'm not wanting to make a scene, I have been reflecting on everything, and I actually want to apologise." Power could see she was close to tears. "Do you have time to talk? Just for a moment?" She gestured to the Refectory. "I'll buy you a coffee."

Power did not like to think himself an unreasonable man, but he did not honestly want to spend any time with her. Nevertheless, he agreed gruffly, saying that he had 'five minutes or so' before his next appointment, and followed her into the Refectory. The Refectory was more redolent of a canteen than anything else, with vast steel counters carrying bowls of cereal and jugs of milk, and large, rectangular steel pans with scattered rounds of toast inside. An indifferent staff lurked behind glass-fronted hot plates, ready to assemble plates of hardened fried bread, tinned tomatoes, withered eggs and thin bacon. Caroline ordered canteen coffee, which eventually proved as tepid and bland as Power dreaded. She paid a desultory cashier, before settling at a white formica-topped table near the wall. At a neighbouring table, overseas students were cramming their faces with toast and cereal to last them through the day's lectures.

"So," said Dr Power, who had a vague presentiment that he really should be somewhere else. "We've never really talked have we?" She did not reply. Having successfully initiated the conversation and manoeuvred Power into a fixed position to listen to her she now seemed to be struggling to find words, or else was choked with emotion. There was a vast mirror on the wall behind her. Power could see the whole world of the Refectory reflected behind Diarmid's green-haired head. He mused on the possible word, 'Reflectory', while he waited for her to speak. "Is it difficult to get the right words?" he asked.

She nodded, "It's difficult ... I have to try to ... confess to you."

"I'm no priest," said Power, and from the depths of somewhere he recited a quotation, half remembered, half forgotten. *"'Are you contented with the morning that separates, and with the evening that brings together, for casual talk before the fire, two people who know they do not understand each other ...'"*

"Where does that come from?" she asked.

"I can hardly remember," said Power. "Some dusty corner of my memory?"

"It's almost precisely why I came to see you," she said.

"Is it?" asked Power. The quotation had come to him unbidden. "Does it happen to mean something to you?"

"It's like Bridget and me, nowadays," said Diarmid. "We are not getting on."

"Ah, said Power, and nodded, encouraging her to say more.

"She annoys me," said Diarmid.

"You feel annoyed?" It was intended as a slight correction to her thinking. "How annoyed do you get?"

"Blazing," she said.

"Angry enough to hit out," said Power.

She stared at him for a moment, trying to fathom the man opposite. He had made a statement of fact and not been asking a question. "Yes," she said at last. "Too many times."

"You know," said Power, "Once is too many times."

Power could see that she was, even now, struggling to control her temper with him. "Did Bridget ask you to talk to me?"

"It was ... a condition," said Diarmid. "We ... we ... talked over Christmas."

"I see," said Dr Power, who did not like being used as a bargaining chip in a quarrel and wondered what kind of a Christmas had resulted in Diarmid being forced to seek him out. Power's Christmas had been full of festive traditions – the stirring of plum puddings, the packing of presents in stockings, the squeals of delight from Jo as he opened them at break of dawn on Christmas morning. What had Bridget McFarlane's Christmas been like? Had there been any moments of tender intimacy or had it been a lengthy cocktail of alcohol fuelled rage and discord, mixed with jealous accusations? A tempest of arguments between the two of them, ending in night time violence and tearful expressions of remorse in the morning?

Power asked, "And how might I be expected to help?"

"Take me on for therapy," said Diarmid, bluntly and without enthusiasm or grace.

"I see," said Dr Power thoughtfully. "But only a few weeks ago you imagined I was having an affair with your partner."

"I know I was wrong about that now," she said, although Power heard no conviction in her tone.

"If I wasn't there, then what do you now think was going on with Bridget? Why do you think she went to Sicily?"

"She went for a holiday," she said sullenly. "To get a break from me."

"I've never been to the island, myself," asked Power. "Has Bridget been to Sicily before?"

"I think she's been a few times," said Diarmid suspiciously. "Before we got together. She wouldn't tell me much. She said it was just a last minute booking. Why do you ask?"

In just this short conversation with Diarmid, Power had seen various waves of anger and suspicion ripple through her. He knew that, even with the best will in the world, he could not bear to work with her. It would be exhausting, and he had no sympathy for Diarmid. He would be too harsh a therapist. He reached into his pockets and pulled out a scrap of paper and a pen. He began scribbling a note. "I can recommend a therapist, someone who is much more experienced at this work than me. Someone who could see you alone in sessions, or sometimes together with Bridget. She works with this specific relationship problem," by which he meant domestic violence and anger.

"You're rejecting me as a patient?"

Power noticed a flush of anger bloom around Caroline's neck. He sensed how very difficult it had been for her to approach him, to overcome her basic distrust of him and ask for therapy. Now he was refusing her request and spurning her sacrifice of dignity. Caroline had swallowed much pride to accede to her partner's request that she should approach Dr Power.

"I'm not the right person," said Power quietly. "I don't have the right skills. You deserve someone with more specialist experience. This therapist . . . she is the best in the region. This is her name and the address of her consulting rooms. You will need to ask your GP to refer you to her. You deserve the best therapist, who is not me in this case, and from a practical sense it wouldn't be ethical for me to treat you, I'm a university colleague. I'd be wearing two hats, do you see? You need your therapist to be *your* therapist."

She nodded, slowly, the blush of anger receded. Caroline had accepted the explanation, and Power allowed himself a slight sigh of relief.

"I hope the referral helps," said Power.

"It has to," said Diarmid stonily, as she folded the paper with Power's scribbled note into her pocket. Without any word of goodbye or thanks, she left the table and the Refectory.

* * *

Power walked gingerly over the frosted pavements, and through a deserted rose garden towards his office – the thorns on the pruned stems of the rose bushes glistened with ice. There were few students in this area of campus. At the start of term teaching in the lecture halls and practicals in the labs had barely begun. Indeed, Power had not seen anybody for a few minutes. He pulled his coat tightly round himself as proof against the chill wind that rose up from the rain-swollen waters of river Dee as it flowed steadily past the campus. All at once Power looked up and was stopped in his tracks by the sight of something suspended in the air and moving in the breeze, turning and twisting slowly at the end of a taut piece of rope.

For a brief moment Power had wondered whether the suspended object was part of some heartless and grotesque student prank or protest, but he soon realised that the body hanging from the stone gargoyle outside Sir Robert Willett's open office window was no mannequin or stolen tailor's dummy. The hands and face were all too solid flesh, although beginning to be cyanosed and dusky with death. There was an almost imperceptible jerking of the feet, a remnant of decorticate spasm. Power began to run, sliding erratically upon the ice, towards the Arts building's main entrance. The thought he'd been a few minutes too late nagged at him even now. At the wooden double doorway he slipped on the ice, despite the thin layer of red grit scattered there, his shoulder slamming into the door jamb. Face grazed and semi-stunned by the fall, Power regained his balance and hurried into the heat of the entrance hall. He began a running ascent of the grand marble stairway up to Willett's office. Power's earnest hope was to retrieve the body through the office window and begin resuscitation.

Willett had apparently foreseen any interruption, however, and guarded against it by locking his office door. Although Power rattled the office door handle and repeatedly rammed the door with his shoulder, the oaken door was resolutely stout and would not yield a millimetre.

A secretary from the Faculty office poked her head out of the office doorway and stared at Professor Power in alarm. "What is going on?" she asked.

"Have you got a key?" Power shouted. "It's urgent. There's been an accident."

"Sir Robert keeps his own key," she said. "No-one has a copy. He has valuable documents in there."

The Carroll manuscript, Power thought, and what else? He took out his mobile and dialled the emergency services. As he described the circumstances and the possible need for police, fire and ambulance services, the secretary grew pale, and held on to the doorframe for support.

Power then phoned the central administration. The Vice Chancellor's secretary answered and Power explained himself as best he could. "There's been a major incident," said Power. "I've phoned for the emergency services, but the Vice Chancellor needs to be informed and we need the area around the Arts Faculty cleared. People need to be kept away."

"What's happened?" the Vice Chancellor's secretary asked.

"Rob Willett has taken his own life by hanging. He's hanging against the Arts Faculty building. Keep people away."

"Where are you?"

"I'm outside his office, I tried to get in to save him, but he's locked it from inside. Nobody's got a key and the door is solid. I can't move it an inch."

"It's OK, Professor Power," she had sensed the acuity of his distress. "I will put our crisis protocol into play. You say the ambulance is on its way?"

"Yes," said Power.

"Can I ask you to stay there, until they arrive? Ask one of the secretaries to open both doors in the entrance way."

The police arrived first, clattering up the stairwell. The officers carried up a red 'enforcer' – which was effectively a very heavy battering ram with two handles that could be swung at the door. The door parted company with its lock and, groaning and shrieking, shuddered open. A shreddingly keen wind blew from the wide-open sash window and whistled past Power and the police, hurtling through the doorway and down the stairwell outside, like a screaming banshee. The wind picked up the papers on Willett's desk and threw them up into the air like a fluttering snowstorm. Power would always thereafter remember the alarmed shouts of the police and the paramedics who were now arriving. The tone of their voices, the innate fear.

The paramedics went over to the window and started hauling the body inside. There were inappropriate protestations from a junior police officer that the body should stay where it was for forensics, but he was overruled by the senior paramedic who wanted to attempt resuscitation.

Over the paramedics' uniformed shoulders Power could see Willett rotating on the axis of the rope and saw with despair his lolling, swollen face, its skin blue and contused. All spasms of Willett's limbs had ceased, and at the sight of Willett's deeply cyanosed lips Power gave up all hope for the life of his colleague. Willett was suspended by a grey rope, looped around the neck of the gargoyle and anchored to the heavy cast iron radiator.

The paramedics hauled on the rope and multiple arms of the assembled emergency staff reached out to claw at the clothing of the dean, thus making purchase upon him. They dragged him onto the wooden parquet floor of the office, like fishermen landing a catch of mackerel on the deck of a trawler. Unlike a catch of floundering fish from the ocean, flapping on the deck in protest at their extraction from the deep, there was an absence of movement from Dean Willett.

The paramedics dutifully began their attempt at resuscitating the corpse. Power doubted anything could be achieved. Part of Power wanted them to cease their pointless frenetic activity, and the rest of him wanted to witness a miracle performed, and to have his cynical doubts to be proved resoundingly wrong. He wanted to see Willett jerk back into life; for his body to quicken a second time, to hear the raw, gasping sound of restored life as his lungs gulped oxygen again.

"Oh, my goodness," said a voice at Power's side. "Oh, how terrible."

It was the Vice Chancellor who now stood at Power's shoulder, ashen and somewhat unsteady. Armitage's eyes were fixed upon the body of his professor. Power was startled at the sudden appearance of the Vice Chancellor by his side. Despite being overweight Armitage could move with feline grace.

Power viewed the grey face of the Vice Chancellor with concern. Armitage's blue eyes were watering with apparent tears.

"Perhaps you'd better sit down, Vice Chancellor," suggested Power.

"Maybe so," said the Vice Chancellor, collapsing into an armchair. Power crouched down beside him. The manuscript sat malignly on the table in front of them in its box, covered by the black cloth. The paramedics were still working on Willett's body. "I wondered whether something like this might happen," whispered Canon Armitage. "He hadn't been himself for some time."

Power struggled to find any words to say and there was an uncomfortable pause while he reflected on a host of regrets. The paramedics called time on the resuscitation. Whilst one was writing notes, two others rolled out a black vinyl body bag alongside Willett's body and began shifting him into it. The police officer was preoccupied with a call to his control on the radio. Suddenly he called out, "Where's the rope, I need to preserve the knot."

The paramedic did not look up. "We cut the ligature to try and save his life. The rope's over there," then whispered to a colleague, "I don't know why he's bothering. It's a classic suicide. He even locked the door behind him."

"I have to secure the rope as evidence, and search the scene for a note when the body's gone," said the officer, who had overheard. "Does he have a phone on him?" The officer wanted to check text messages and recent phone calls.

"He's in the bag now," said the paramedic. "We didn't find any phone on him. We looked. Have you searched his desk? We need to get off now and have him certified before the coroner's post mortem. He's a suicide though. Straight and simple."

They bound the body bag to a stretcher and lifted Willett's body for transportation to the ambulance. The officer bagged and tagged the rope for evidence.

As she was leaving, the last paramedic spoke to Professor Power and the crumpled figure of the Vice Chancellor. "We have to be off," she said. She fumbled in a pocket. "There's a support line number on here. I'm sorry about everything . . . he was your colleague was he? We have to be away, the police will attend to you." She looked a little more closely at the Vice Chancellor. "Are you all right, sir? Would you like to accompany us? We can take you to the hospital for a check over."

The Vice Chancellor shook his head firmly, wondering if she really meant him to go in an ambulance with Willett's corpse. He reached in his pocket for his GTN spray, and he administered it under his tongue. Dr Power reached over to take the Vice Chancellor's wrist and measure his pulse, which was full and regular at 80 beats a minute.

The Vice Chancellor gently pulled his arm away from Power. "I'll be all right, Carl, I've just taken some GTN. I'll be fine. Don't worry. I'll just have a bit of a headache for the rest of the day. Side effect, but you'll know that, of course."

"If you're sure," the paramedic said. "A touch of angina is it?" The Vice Chancellor nodded and gave a feeble smile to reassure her. "Well, we'll be going," she said. She held out the card again. Power took it from her hand for politeness' sake and watched her leave.

"Are you sure you're all right, Vice Chancellor?" asked Power. "You look pale."

"The shock," he said. "And some pain . . . here." He held his hand to his chest. "It will pass. Don't fuss over me. It will pass with the spray. It always does."

The police officer was still in the room and seemed eager they leave. "I would suggest that you vacate the room now, I need to close and seal it for the forensics team."

"But it was a suicide," said the Vice Chancellor. "He had been depressed."

"That's not for us to conclude, sir." said the officer. "That's a matter for the coroner, depending on the evidence."

"If you can just give us five minutes, please," said Power. "It's been a bit of a shock for everybody, and I think the Vice Chancellor needs to get his breath back."

The officer nodded assent, but stayed by Willett's desk, ostensibly looking over its surface for a suicide note.

"I'll be ready to move in a few minutes," the Vice Chancellor said. "The pain is passing."

"Would you like me to drive you home?" offered Power.

"No, that won't be necessary. It is very kind of you, Carl, but there are things I must attend to." He turned to the police officer. "Will the police be informing the family, or should I . . ."

"We have dispatched a police officer already to his aunt's house. She is his next of kin, I understand from your Human Resources Department. I gather he was divorced, and estranged from his new partner."

"I see," said the Vice Chancellor. "His children, though . . . I thought he had two."

"They went to live with their mother. She was awarded full custody. No contact for years."

"Goodness," said Canon Armitage. "Rob always implied that he was with them and that they were doing well at school. It goes to show how little I know . . ." he looked at Power. "I feel guilty, all of a sudden. And so the Knight has fallen. I think I will take myself home, you know, I need some time to think. I'm more upset than I imagined I would be." He stood up very gradually, as if the morning's event had somehow preternaturally accelerated the aging process. And just as he had attained his full height, his deputy Bridget McFarlane swept through the doorway.

"Ah, you're already here, Vice Chancellor."

"They have just taken Sir Robert away," he said sorrowfully. "And I . . . I am going home. This has been an awful strain, Bridget. I know there are protocols to follow, but I am sure that everyone will play their part without me for today. I am sorry, but to see him like that. Do you think you can cope until tomorrow? I will be better then."

"Of course, Vice Chancellor. You just go home and rest." She made no eye contact with him or Power. Power watched as she swept the black cloth off the glass box that contained the manuscript. "I have been told by the officers downstairs that the police need to have us out of this room. And this manuscript cannot stay here. Professor Willett cannot exactly guard it any more." She regarded the chain and padlock that secured the box to the heavy table, and to everyone's surprise, withdrew a pair of boltcutters from her capacious handbag, and swiftly snipped through the chain as if it was made of black liquorice. The Vice Chancellor goggled at McFarlane's manoeuvre, aghast at her single mindedness and audacity. She swept the glass box up into her arms. The rapid movement left a swirl of expensive perfume in its wake. She stared at the police officer, who could not quite believe what he was seeing. "It can't stay here. It's worth over a million pounds. It's nothing to do with any police investigation, and if your superiors do want it, it will be stowed away in the University's safe room."

"We would rather everything had been left exactly as it was," the police officer said reproachfully.

"We can't afford to lose it, officer, if your superiors need it, you can tell them it will be in the vaults, ahead of the press conference, and then its contents will be in the public domain," and, before any more could be said, she left, like a whirlwind or other force of nature.

"I must go now," said the Vice Chancellor, patting Professor Power's shoulder. "I don't think I can stand any more of my colleague's humanity today of all days. I hated to ask her to act up in my absence. I don't want to cede any control to her, but it seems unavoidable today. I must conserve my energy for another day. Thank you for your kindness at least, Professor Power."

Power watched as he left, a seemingly diminished man. Power paused at the top of the stairs, watching Canon Armitage plod slowly downwards. Once the Vice Chancellor had left, Power reached into his pocket for his mobile and dialled Lynch.

* * *

"After all that, in swept Bridget McFarlane, pounced upon the manuscript and took it for self-keeping. Not a sign of remorse in her manner, or any concern about what had just happened to poor Rob."

Power was finishing off telling Andrew Lynch what had just happened, on his mobile. Lynch was at his desk in the Foundation offices looking out at the stumpy ruin of the castle nearby.

"Where are you now?" asked Lynch.

"Walking across the campus to my office. That's where I was going when I saw him up there . . . saw Sir Robert."

"Are you all right? It must have been quite a shock for you."

"I've only seen a handful of bodies after a hanging," said Power. "It's a terrible sight. And I feel so guilty about Rob, I spoke to him before Christmas. He was depressed, no doubt about it. I told him to get help, I couldn't treat him myself – that wouldn't be ethical, but maybe I didn't do enough for him. Strangely enough, another member of staff asked me for help only today. Minutes before I saw Rob, and I turned her down too, for the same reason. You can't treat colleagues . . . it opens up all kinds of conflicts of duty and confidentiality."

"You did the right thing," said Lynch. "No, I know you. Don't blame yourself about your colleague, Carl. You did point him in the right direction."

"And that's what I did with the other colleague today," Power looked about him to make sure no one was near. "It was McFarlane's partner, asking for therapy to treat her anger. Maybe Bridget gave her an ultimatum? Get help or the relationship is over, because I don't think Caroline Diarmid would ever come to see me voluntarily. Not even if we waited until hell froze over. It was clearly a case of *force majeure*. I gave her the name of a good therapist though, one who works with domestic violence families."

"And how did the Vice Chancellor take Willett's death," asked Lynch, thoughtfully.

"He was clearly shocked. He almost collapsed and took glyceryl trinitrate under his tongue for angina. I really began to think I might have another death to cope with."

Lynch thought he ought to change the subject, "Beresford is still doggedly wading through all the anomalies you have identified at the University. He pointed out to me that, although she has a nursing background, McFarlane's highest qualification is in health finance. When we are trying to identify The Banker, she must rank high on the list of subjects. And her seizing of the manuscript as a University asset does make her seem more financially orientated than anything."

"Certainly, without compassion for Rob, or the Vice Chancellor. And she seems very hungry for advancement," said Power.

"I think we should meet in Chester for a discussion later, over a pint maybe," said Lynch. "Whatever you planned for today, you are clearly going to need to adjust it. There's been a message left for you at the Foundation office. It could be quite urgent." Power felt a sinking sensation in the pit of his stomach. Lynch hurried to qualify his use of the term urgent. "It's not to do with home or anything. Don't worry. Everyone's fine. It's a message from a firm of solicitors on White Friars Lane – Russell and Jones."

"Is it about a medicolegal report, maybe?" asked Power.

"No, and it's interesting they contacted you here at the Foundation, and not at the University. This firm are solicitors for Felfe. They are processing his will and his effects. Don't get too excited though, he's not named you as an heir to a fortune. But he has left you a letter. They would like you to go and pick it up and sign for it."

"A letter from Felfe," mused Power, thoughtfully. "Some sort of message from beyond the grave?"

"You appreciate it may be important," said Lynch. "He may have discovered what those three clues meant, he may even name The Banker in the letter."

Power had reached the door of his University office on campus as he talked to Lynch on his mobile, but somehow he had lost the will to work any more. "Well, I don't feel able to concentrate now. Not after this morning. I think I'll make my way over to Whitefriars and pick the letter up now."

"Excellent," said Lynch. "And I'll meet you afterwards and we can restore our spirits over a pint." Power felt cheered by the prospect. The events of the morning had chilled his soul to the marrow. The thought of warming himself by a crackling log fire in a pub thawed his troubled heart.

* * *

The small office of Russell and Jones was in White Friars, a cobbled street lined by three-storied, red-brick Georgian houses, all nestling tightly within the city walls. Sometime in the thirteenth century there had been a Carmelite monastery on Whitefriars. The street name itself was derived from the white habits they wore.

Any ceremony within the solicitor's premises was solely perfunctory, and delegated to a secretary behind a high counter fashioned from polished pine. Power had to verify his identity with his University ID card, and the sealed envelope was duly provided. The seal was the most formal aspect of the proceedings, being a blob of shiny, red wax, smeared with carbon from a candle's flame.

Power probably spent no more than three minutes inside Russell and Jones, and then made his way to a nearby Nero's coffee shop to sit with a china bowl of decaffeinated latte and read through the Felfe's letter:

Dear Professor Power,

I chose to talk to you about my discoveries at Allminster, because you seemed like a man who could listen. You didn't seem like my colleagues; blinkered by their own egos and self-interest. You wanted to create something noble – the medical school – just for the sake of creating something good in this wretched world. And when I tried to talk to you, perhaps it was too soon for you to accept what was going on, or perhaps you were unwilling to take on the burden of knowledge I offered. If Adam and Eve had really understood the implications of knowledge, and the burden it imposes on one, then they would never have been tempted by the serpent to bite into God's own apple. *Die Last des Wissens wiegt schwerer als Unwissenheit.*

Nevertheless, you will eventually alight upon the knowledge, so I might as well try again to warn you. A new enterprise such as
Medicine will require heavy investment. The more you pursue your dream of a medical school the more you will realise that the University's *official* income is far less than you might think. Far less, for example, than its expenditure on new student halls, a proposed Faculty of Engineering that was already committed to before you arrived, an impossibly generous staff pension scheme (that will have a shortfall of a billion in a few decades) and its random investments in Art might suggest. I am afraid there are deliberate flaws in the design . . .

If you are reading this, Dr Power, then it is because I am

dead, and my solicitor has seen fit to pass this on to you as instructed. The fact that I wrote these paragraphs is testimony to the possibility that I foresaw my life was probably coming to an end. I no longer have the capability of feeling anything, but I certainly would have felt no surprise at my death, only perhaps in the mode and precise timing of that death.

Your reputation as a keen forensic mind precedes you, and I have no doubt that you will have unravelled the reasons behind my academic post at Allminster. I did my best to maintain an academic façade, to go through the pretence of lecturing and writing papers on criminology as an elaborate cover. The good Lord knows too that I unwittingly managed to surpass the mediocre efforts of my so-called academic peers, who wrote with sincerity and held their Professorial posts in earnest. To speak candidly, I was a spy. I was very useful to your Government for many years. I risked my life for other's freedom. And they rewarded me with a sinecure post at an unobtrusive second rate University. I began to live again, no longer a spy, but still living under cover. I knew that I was always living on borrowed time, *geliehene Zeit*, because I was a double agent, and for many years my name was on a 'kill list' by people still loyal to a despised and fallen communist regime. I suppose my name never quite rose to the top of the list, as I have been in England for years and am still alive. But now I must be near the top, surely?

There are modes of existence – ways of being – that just become like second nature. You wear them like a pair of gloves, slip into them, keep them on for years. I'm talking about spycraft; ways of seeing the world, obtaining information, protecting oneself. And when I came to Allminster I began to leave the gloves off more and more. It was a gradual process. And I nearly forgot that way of being, that *weltanschauung*. But then I began to notice things; discrepancies, secret conversations and meaningful looks between colleagues. I spent time in the bursar's office to trace the money – not easy to do as he arrives fiercely early and stays unfashionably late. You will know that if you wish to find out the story behind anything, you should follow the money. I didn't learn much from the official accounts, but then when did the official accounts ever reflect the real path of money through an organisation, like water percolating through the mountain? And the bursar is so very close about his money and racked with his weird observations and rituals. He tries to control the money as rigidly as he controls his own narrow existence. But the money almost has a life of its own, and trickles through the sandstone of organisations and finds its ways between the strata, trickling and gushing on its own way, its own path. Following the money as it runs away is the knack. All I learned was that the official income from the State – all the official fees and grants – does not cover the expenditure.

I found hints of a secret investment fund in Malta. I found them through the impressions of writing left on blank leaves of paper on a pad, abandoned in a Senate meeting room, I found references to a dead man named Daidalos, a research station, a casino, and three specific terms I could not decipher immediately; The Banker, Sannik Law Co, and Wanderlust. I have drawn a blank with the first two, I don't know who The Banker might be. I assume someone with a background in finance. But now, *Wanderlust*, I think is a ship.

I could burden you further with my suspicions as to who The Banker might be, but I do not wish to obscure your thinking by my surmises and assumptions, which all rely on instinct and intuition. I, for instance, feel that The Banker arranged for Mr Daidalos's death, but where is my evidence? I have tried to cover my tracks so that The Banker does not suspect, because if The Banker killed Daidalos, then The Banker would kill me in the blink of an eye.

I suspect though, that I may have made one or two mistakes along the way. For instance, I removed the note pad with those terms on from the meeting room and took it away. I had to go to my office and analyse the impressions left on the pad from the pens used on the sheet above. It requires a certain finesse and I did not want to be disturbed doing this in the meeting room. I intended to replace the pad afterwards, but when I returned to put it back on the table there was already someone in the room. I could hear them rattling around inside, moving chairs in a fury, looking in drawers, and I assumed they were searching for the missing pad. I panicked. I left without seeing who this was. More importantly, though, I didn't want them to see me.

On another occasion I overheard the bursar talking with Dean McFarlane at some interminable reception for Faculty Nurse of the Year. She was boasting about her distant Italian roots and I thought he seemed very interested to hear that her grandmother was from Palermo and called Bacchi. You may be aware of that family? However, Bursar Grieg is obsessed with reptiles and only wanted to talk about the asp viper, which is found on Sicily and which has a fatal bite. He asked her if she'd ever seen one and talked to her about a zig zag stripe on its back, and collecting poison from it. Ridiculous man. Nevertheless, they caught me listening to their conversation and stared at me, before I moved away.

As I said before, if you are reading this, then I am already dead. My fear was justified. I am fairly fit. My family is long lived. There is no reason I should suddenly die. I am not depressed. I would not kill myself using the method traditionally forced upon spies – defenestration. If I am dead, then I would suggest they probably chose poison.

And if you have read this far and understood even a tenth of my concerns, then I would warn you, Dr Power, that your life is at risk. My death is surety of this.

Knowledge **is** a burden, but if you use it wisely, you have a chance of staying alive.

Johann Felfe

Chapter Twenty-Two

Know ye not that they which run in a race run all, but [only] one
receiveth the prize? So run, that ye may obtain.
1 Corinthians 9:24

Lynch placed a pint of bitter in front of Power. "So you don't think that Sir Robert was murdered, then?"

Power lifted the pint to his lips, smelt the hoppy aroma for a moment and gained inspiration to talk. "Logically everything points to suicide. Rob was so very upset – overly so – about the manuscript that he thought was fake. I urged him to discuss it with the bursar or the Vice Chancellor, but he never did, as far as I am aware anyway." He took a long draught of the bitter. He sighed in contemplation. "I also urged him to see his doctor for some treatment . . ."

"I will ask Beresford to add to the list of anomalies he is tasked with checking up on," said Lynch. "Item One – Did Sir Robert see his GP? Item Two – Did Sir Robert confess his anxieties to the bursar or the Vice Chancellor?"

"Why would you ask Beresford to check up on what seems to be a suicide, unless you also had some doubts?" asked Power. "Everything points to suicide. He was depressed. He was alone, no family to act as a protective factor. And he hung himself behind a locked door." Power took a swig of beer and sighed appreciatively. He looked carefully around the bar of the Pied Bull, a pub on Chester's Northgate, to see if anyone could be listening to them. "No Caroline Diarmid here, stalking me."

"No," said Lynch. "I gather she somewhat delayed you this morning on your way in?"

"Yes," said Power, reproaching himself. "If I hadn't spent those minutes with her I might have intervened."

"Ah," said Lynch. "*If ifs and buts were pots and pans, there'd be no work for tinkers' hands'.* You weren't to know what Sir Rob was going to do, Carl. This kind of thinking does nobody any good. So let me get the order of things right. You speak to Caroline. Leave the Refectory, walk across campus. See Sir Robert suspended, outside the window. You run indoors. The door is locked. You try to gain access. You phone the emergency services and the University administration. The nearest secretary does not have the key – only Sir Robert has this. The emergency services arrive and force the door. There then begins an unsuccessful resuscitation. In the midst of the commotion the Vice Chancellor arrives and, in shock, he himself falls ill. Whilst you are tending to him, the paramedics take the body away. A police officer remains to secure the room. McFarlane arrives and brusquely takes the manuscript that Sir Robert deemed fake, and which, presumably the University still believes is worth a fortune. McFarlane spirits the manuscript away. Then you watch the Vice Chancellor go, and then you yourself depart. Have I got the gist of it? The right order of events?"

"You have it exactly," said Power.

"Three deaths at Allminster," said Lynch, summarising the state of play. "Number One: Felfe, dead of a heart attack. Number Two: Willett, a suicide. These two deaths appear to be distinct, to be separate events, and to look 'natural', (if you can class death by your own hand as 'natural'). Neither of these deaths is necessarily suspicious. Having said that, Felfe writes to us, and announces that he has an intimation of death. He had found something out and disturbed the waters. The old secret agent foretold his own demise. And death Number Three: Shacklin, murdered on foreign land, guzzled by pigs, (probably in a failed attempt to hide the body), leaving his hand behind to point out his murder. Without the hand, and without Felfe's letter, would we ever have linked Shacklin's disappearance to foul play? After what happened to Shacklin why should we assume that Sir Robert killed himself?"

"You have it exactly again," said Power. "I agree we should not assume anything, and yet Rob was depressed, and behind a locked door. It will inevitably look to all concerned that his death is a suicide, and I am left with the feeling that I didn't do enough. Do you know, I wondered something earlier . . . I wondered if Rob Willett was a suicide and that he didn't just kill himself because of the fake manuscript. I wondered whether he was showing remorse. I wondered if *he* was the murderer."

"Why would you think that he was a murderer?" asked Lynch, and he drained his pint of Weetwood ale down to the last drop.

"I was thinking back to a conversation I had with him after you found Felfe's body in the Cathedral. At that stage Felfe was officially thought to have died of a heart attack. And ostensibly – apart from what we have gleaned from Felfe's letter and our knowledge that Felfe thought his life was at risk – everybody who's anybody still thinks Felfe died of an infarction even now. But Rob Willett didn't exactly say that. I wondered if he made a Freudian error when he was talking to me. As if he was making some unconscious admission of guilt. He made a kind of literary bad joke. He was a professor of English after all. He made a reference to a play by T. S. Eliot. And the play in question was *Murder in the Cathedral*. Now why did he refer to the death as a murder? Was it a just a coincidence, a bad joke or a *parapraxis*? Was he telling me something? Was he confessing, then?"

"And you wonder if his suicide was the act of a guilty man?" Lynch paused, and considered the information for a long while. Then he made a note on a small pad of paper in his meticulous handwriting, and restored the pad to his pocket. "It's worth considering. Definitely worth considering. But I still think that the key to all of this lies overseas, in Malta to be specific. And that reminds me, I must phone Azzopardi."

* * *

Caught somewhere between waking and dreaming, an eddying stream of thoughts and images glided oneirically through Power's mind. He lay beside his pregnant partner, Laura, cocooned in a thick duvet. Power's bed was his warm redoubt against the chill of dawn. His flow of thought slowed and faltered to a crawl. On a knife edge between awareness and slumber, it was sleep that finally claimed him. He sank into the arms of Morpheus and dreamed once more. Power was in the countryside, walking alone. In the distance he could see a chess piece, a pawn grown to the size of man, walking away from him and retreating into a bank of fog draped across a hedgerow. And then he was walking arm in arm in step with another chess piece, a castle. Their journey was a companionable one across a lush green field, but no words were spoken between them. They plodded along, side by side. Suddenly, the castle vanished as Power was caught up in a rush of air and was propelled upwards to a vantage point high in the sky, looking down on the castle below. A knight rode past suspended in the air, saddled upon a mighty steed, richly caparisoned in deep purple, its hooves galloping through the clouds. The knight himself was armed, as if for imminent battle.

"Watch out!" Power felt compelled to shout out in the knight's wake. "Be careful!"

"I've had plenty of practice. Plenty of practice," the knight roared back.

Power surfaced abruptly from his dream to find that he was being shaken by the shoulder. The images from his slumber instantly faded into oblivion. He mumbled querulously, "What is it? What is it?"

It was Jo, surfaced from his own bed, who had climbed downstairs from his room above. "I can't sleep," he said. "I'm cold. Can I get in?"

Power shifted across the mattress and lifted the edge of the duvet so that his son could wriggle his way into the bed. Jo snuggled between his father and Laura and settled happily into their shared warmth.

* * *

For the whole of January, Azzopardi had not heard of or seen trace of the *Wanderlust* in the seas round Malta. For the whole of January, Lynch had not heard from Azzopardi. Beresford found no clues about the *Wanderlust* in his investigations at Allminster. Both Lynch and Beresford had worked on other more pressing cases in the Foundation's files. And for the whole of January, Power did not see his dream of a medical school at Allminster progress at all. Power felt everybody at the University, and even the Vice Chancellor in his absence, was stalling him. Where was any sign of the necessary investment in the medical school? Power worked more on his clinics than he did on academia. He would visit the University and occupy his office occasionally, lecture sporadically, mark papers, and try (always unsuccessfully it has to be said) to set up a meeting with the Vice Chancellor. Armitage was nowhere to be seen. The Vice Chancellor's favourite seats in the University cafes and restaurants remained empty. When Power called to his office, Armitage had always either 'just left' or was 'due to come in tomorrow'. There were no weekly meetings about the medical school project anymore and progress had stalled altogether. Professor Power began to feel he was *persona non grata*.

The secretaries kept offering him appointments with Executive Pro Vice chancellor McFarlane in Armitage's stead, but Power would never accept these offers. He did not want to speak with her.

As cold, cruel January edged into February, however, Power changed his mind and accepted the offer of a meeting with Bridget McFarlane, no matter how distasteful that might prove. He needed reassurance about the medical school project and he wanted to know why the Vice Chancellor was hiding away from him. Where was he?

"Maybe Armitage is ill," Lynch had volunteered an explanation when they discussed it the night before. "You said he reacted badly to the hanging of Sir Robert. You said he'd had a heart problem before and that the bursar had covered for him. Maybe that's the case again. Meet her instead. See what she has to say."

An anxious Dr Power arrived at the new Executive Pro Vice Chancellor's suite fifteen minutes before the 4.40 p.m. appointment. He was shown to a pink, upholstered bench in the waiting area, where he perched uncomfortably. In taking over Shacklin's office, McFarlane had enlarged the territory to include two further offices for her secretaries and an enclosed space where Power now waited. Power took out his mobile and phoned home, seeking solace as much as anything. "Hi, Laura," he said, when she answered. "How are things?"

"Fine, we're just making tea. Jo's helping me chop some celery, carrot and onion for the tomato sauce to go with the pasta. He's being very professional. His onion is diced very fine. You're out tonight aren't you? You'll be sorry not to enjoy this sauce. It will be delicious, won't it Jo?"

"I've got this meeting and then there's the function to go to. A Press Conference. It's to do with the Alice manuscript. Three-line whip for all academics."

"The newly discovered chapter?"

"Yes, there's TV news and reporters. Speeches, wine and nibbles."

"That sounds like a party from the nineteen-seventies. Cheese and pineapple on sticks?"

"No, I think the University will do proper canapés, but like all these affairs, the kitchens never make enough vegetarian ones to go round. So can you please save me some of the pasta for when I get back."

"If Jo leaves any, then you can have that," laughed Laura. "He must be going through a growth spurt. His appetite is huge." Laura paused. "Maybe if it's celebrating *Alice* there will be tiny pieces of cake with 'Eat me' on, or pieces of a giant mushroom?"

"I don't think Allminster is that imaginative," said Power.

"Don't be too cynical," Laura teased. "We'll save you some tea, don't worry; would you like to speak to Jo? He's got a new joke for you."

She passed the phone on to Power's son, "Hi, Dad!"

"Hello, Son," said Power. "Have you had a good day? I've got a meeting to go to so I'll be back a bit late tonight, sorry."

"It's all right, I'm making pasta sauce from scratch."

"Are you adding any oregano?" asked Power. "Any basil?"

"It's tomatoes mainly, Dad. You're such a foodie." Jo sighed. There was a note of reproof in the boy's voice.

"Laura says you have a joke for me."

"Yes, Dad. Tom told me this one. Are you ready?"

"I'm ready."

"It's a pirate joke," said Jo, preparing his father for the witticism. He changed his voice to that of a West Country seafarer. "Aharr, how do ye turn a pirate furious?"

"I don't know," said Power. "How do you turn a pirate furious?"

"You take the 'p' off him," said Jo, proudly.

"Oh, that's very good, Jo!" said Power, chuckling. For a moment he had been totally lost in the conversation and only gradually became aware of a presence at his side. He looked up to see Bridget McFarlane wearing a simpering smile. "Excuse me, Jo, I must ring off. There's business to attend to. I'm sorry, I will see you later tonight."

"Oh, don't mind me," said McFarlane, as Power stowed the phone away in his pocket. "Family comes first, doesn't it?"

"I'm sorry, said Power. "As I'm going to the Press Conference later I thought I should phone home to catch my son whilst he's awake."

"Phone home. Just like E.T.," said McFarlane, pretending to a sense of humour as she ushered him out of the waiting area and into her newly decorated office. Power felt a little as if he were being summoned into the web of a spider, but, oh, what a pretty web it was! There was a round oak table set with tea things next to a cerise-coloured bowl of pink and white anemones. The flowers were dwarfed by an evidently heavy geode of purple amethyst quartz, which sat alongside, glistering hypnotically at Dr Power. Underfoot, the lush woollen carpet was watermelon pink. The walls of McFarlane's office were covered in hessian the colour of sugar dusted bubblegum, and a cloying fragrance hung heavily in the air.

"There's a sweet scent in here," said Power.

"I'm glad you think so," said McFarlane. "Do you like the room? I've had the offices re-designed. I had two secretaries to move in, and Caroline of course, to keep me on the straight and narrow." Power nodded thoughtfully, wondering about the cost. "I had to have the office suite redecorated," she said almost apologetically. "The last incumbent didn't leave it in the best of condition." By which remark she was referring to Shacklin. "I have a very sensitive nose. The new fragrance is citrus and a hint of patchouli. Just a hint, though, as too much is sickly. I have to say it, but Shacklin left it smelling of fenugreek and cumin. His sweat reeked of it. Carl, I'm not being racist, please don't think that. But the room smelt of him and his activities, it just reminded me of him all the time, so I said to the Vice Chancellor, it needs clearing out and starting again. New fabrics, new wallpapers. Scent clings on to fabrics, you know." She caught Power's expression. "I really do have a very sensitive nose. I could detect everything Shacklin had been eating. Coriander and garlic and . . . you yourself smell of mallow and sea salt and sage."

Power instantly felt self-conscious. In a conversation you can control your smile, your posture, your facial expression, the tone of your voice, but once you have embarked on a dialogue how do you control your bodily aroma? He decided to press on with his own agenda.

"How is the Vice Chancellor?" he asked.

"I think," said Bridget McFarlane, pausing to offer Power a seat and taking a moment to pour out some Darjeeling tea for them both. "I think Ambrose, (the Vice Chancellor), realises that he has been overworking for many years. He is so, so tired. And he realises that he needs to take a bit of a back seat for a while. The tragic suicide of Sir Robert has really told upon him. And to be frank there is a mountain of work to be done on the University strategy with regard to its finances. The Vice Chancellor is simply not well enough. So I've stepped up to assist." She smiled at her virtuous thought.

"I would be only too happy to see him, in my professional capacity. To help, I mean. I have tried to book an appointment to see him, but . . . is he even here? Will he be at the Press Conference later?"

"Ambrose Armitage has asked me to be Deputy Vice Chancellor. He is only working a few hours each day."

Power took a sip of Darjeeling to cover his surprise at this news. "As I say, I'd be only too happy to see him, if he is not well."

"And I applaud your sentiments, I really do. I will pass them on, but he's not ill, mentally speaking, if that's what you have inferred. He has no need of a psychiatrist. He's just very tired."

Power decided not to quibble about tiredness as a recognised symptom of depression. "I also wanted to see the Vice Chancellor to discuss the medical school – the progress of the plan . . ."

McFarlane sighed irritably, "There can't be any progress in this financial year – the University cannot afford to invest any capital whatsoever. It is struggling to survive as it is. We are looking at dropping courses like chemistry and making redundancies rather than develop new ones."

This bluntly delivered statement rocked Dr Power, but he tried not to show his surprise. Power thought that this approach was short-sighted but suppressed an urge to argue. Instead he said, "The medical places would be valuable to the University. If we made some of the places available privately we could charge at least twelve thousand a year in tuition fees. It could offset other financial demands."

"Dr Power, you are confusing capital and revenue and being, I am sorry to say, you are being financially naïve."

Power did not respond. He knew her antipathy to the medical school was so deep-rooted that by arguing he was merely elevating his blood pressure for no good reason. Power really needed to speak to the Vice Chancellor, but where was he?

"I understand the problem," said Power softly. "But perhaps . . . perhaps if I could identify some funds externally . . . if I could find external funding, then surely there could be no opposition . . ."

"If you can find the funds elsewhere, and there was no conflict of interest, then you will find me a reasonable person, but how much do you estimate a medical school would cost?" Bridget asked this, half believing that Power would not have a clue.

"A full thirty million," said Dr Power crisply. "That should be sufficient to build the school and equip all the anatomy, physiology and pathology labs."

She smiled then, falling back on the comforting thought that Power could never achieve the task he was setting himself. "If you can secure that sum, then I am sure there could be no objection, from me or the Senate."

Power nodded, "Thank you, I'll start looking."

"You're a resourceful man, Dr Power," said McFarlane charitably. "And can I thank you so much for seeing Caroline for therapy? I know you can't talk about her therapy as she's your patient, but she is finding your weekly session very helpful."

Power raised an eyebrow in surprise. He had not seen or talked with Caroline since his coffee with her on the first day of term. Certainly he had not been seeing her for weekly psychotherapy, despite what McFarlane had just said. Not for the first time he wondered just how dangerous Caroline Diarmid was, and also whether he should tell McFarlane immediately that he was not seeing Caroline for therapy. He decided to approach the subject in a circumspect way. "Caroline, yes, did she help with the re-design of her office too?"

"Oh, yes," said McFarlane. "Orange walls to match her hair."

"But isn't her hair green?" asked Power.

"It was," said McFarlane, frowning a little. "It's been orange for a few weeks now."

"Oh, yes," said Power. "Of course. Can I ask, if it's not too much trouble . . . how Caroline got on with Dr Shacklin?"

"She loathed him."

"Was she ever jealous of you and him?"

McFarlane supposed this had to do with an element of therapy, but part of her mind was still troubled that Power had said Caroline had green hair, when she had had it re-dyed a fortnight back.

"As a matter of fact, she refused to let me be alone with Shacklin, ever. Because of his reputation with any woman who still had a pulse."

"And Sir Robert? Did she loathe him too?"

"She avoided him. He was too bumptious; too full of himself, and too full of toxic masculinity for Caroline."

"Not jealous though?"

"What do you mean?" she asked irritably. "What are you asking *me* for?"

"I'm sorry," said Dr Power, realising that either his phrasing irritated her or he had asked one question too many.

"I am glad you are seeing her, of course," said McFarlane. "It's just that I don't like to be reminded of how she sometimes feels about things. She misperceives relationships. I suppose I must bear some share of the responsibility. I can be . . . secretive. She formed the idea I was with someone else when I went to Sicily. What she didn't know, and what I couldn't tell her, was that I had gone to see members of my family who live there. So, I concealed it from her, and she knew something was being withheld."

"Sorry, what did you conceal?" asked Power.

"My grandmother lives there. I am a quarter Italian. I call my grandma Nonna Bacchi. Have you heard of the Bacchi family?" Power shook his head. "Nonna is old, and set in her ways, her *Catholic* ways. She doesn't know about Caroline. She doesn't know about Caroline and me. She would never understand, let alone approve. And so I pretended I was going to Sicily alone on a break, when in fact I was going to be with my family."

McFarlane noticed Power wince. He was weighing up how to tell her that Caroline was not actually seeing him and wondering how he could explain why he had not been frank immediately. Seeing his hesitancy, McFarlane, long used to some people's condemnation, concluded that Power probably disapproved of her

She stood up suddenly, spilling the dregs of her cup of tea. The tea spread across the table, and dripped onto the new Axminster. She swore. Power knelt and patted the damp patch with a paper napkin. "No harm done, I think," he said gently.

She remained standing. "We'd better leave it there. I have to get ready for the Press Conference. I have a presentation to give and the TV cameras are here."

Power stood up and was about to leave, but he realised he still hadn't corrected McFarlane's belief he was Caroline's doctor. He had decided that, on ethical grounds, McFarlane needed to know, for her own safety as much as anything. "I will go and let you prepare. But there is one last thing I need to tell you. I should have told you much earlier, and I apologise. I need to tell you something about Caroline's psychotherapy."

"I thought psychiatrists couldn't discuss their patient's therapy. That would breach confidentiality."

"Yes, I've been thinking about that," said Power. "But confidentiality doesn't apply in this case."

"Oh, and exactly why not, doctor?"

"I think you need to know that Caroline *hasn't* been seeing me for psychotherapy. I don't know what she has said to you, but she has never been my patient."

McFarlane gaped at him and said nothing for a while. Shock gave way to an expression of sheer annoyance. "Why are you telling me now? Now, just before the Press Conference?"

"Because you need to know, Bridget. And when would be a good time to know, except as soon as possible? You can't go on like this, believing that Caroline is having treatment that might stop her being violent to you. I'm sorry to tell you this, believe me. But you need to know what is and what is not. Or else how can you protect yourself?"

* * *

Andrew Lynch had driven through Allminster village on his journey to the University. He remembered Allminster from his teenage years. He had once bicycled to the village to meet a girl for a picnic of scotch eggs and tomato sandwiches, long before he met his wife, Pamela. They had picnicked and kissed in the open fields all through a long hot summer day and in the evening had gone to a supper dance with jugs of lemonade at the church youth club. The University campus was small then, based around the Old Hall that had belonged to Charles Dodgson, but since its expansion in the white heat of the sixties the village had been transformed and swallowed whole by the campus, which surrounded its every quarter.

Lynch parked by the old village church, which had been gutted to house the Department of Performing Arts. Lynch snorted to himself in disapproval and locked his car.

He met Power outside the 1990s conference centre, which

MURDER AND MALICE

squatted on the hayfields where, decades before, Lynch had lost his
virginity to Rosie, aged seventeen.

"There was a village here once," said Lynch reprovingly. "A nice
quiet place –totally consumed by your university."

"I have to say, that it feels less and less like my university," said
Power. "I'm beginning to believe that there is no money for a medical
school."

"But there were funds to buy a valuable manuscript," said Lynch,
flourishing the invitation to the launch event that Power had procured
for him.

"Oh, don't start," said Power, laughing. "Come in, there may be
enough funds left to buy us a free glass of wine and a vol-au-vent."

A thin student with spiky black hair and a tremor to his thin, pale
hands took their invitation cards and ticked their names off a list.
Students from the Department of Events Management were
encouraged to get a direct experience of their subject. (It also met with
the bursar's approval, as this policy saved on the costs of hiring staff).

Banners splashed prominently with Allminster logos, were
hanging from the entrance walls and draped over tables announcing
'The Wasp!' and 'The Lost Alice Chapter Found'.

Students sat at tables laden with *Alice*-themed pamphlets and
giveaways. Behind the students were Pull-up Stands with boastful
phrases like 'Allminster Discovers the Missing Chapter' and
'Alice-minster: The Lost Story'.

Dr Power had underestimated the amount of thought that had
gone into the food and drink. Far from being confined to vol-au-vents,
there was a bounty of food. Waiters in red and white livery mingled
with the guests, carrying trays of glasses of red and white wine, or a
special non-alcoholic Alice punch. Lynch chose the punch which was
in a little bottle with a handwritten label round the neck saying 'Drink
Me' and tasted of rose lemonade. The Vice-Chancellor's favourite
caterers had been engaged.

Power admired a buffet, spread on a long trestle table. There were
silver dishes of cucumber sandwiches, made of white and brown
bread, laid in a chessboard pattern upon the salvers. Predictably, there
were strawberry jam tarts as a reminder of the Queen of Hearts, but
adorned with Chantilly cream. There were porcelain plates full of fairy
cakes with lacy, pink-sugar butterfly wings. A little sign nearby in neat

329

copperplate handwriting said 'Flutterby cakes'. Some crispy taco shells had been draped with bacon formed into saddles and given fried potato heads, wings and tails and were similarly labelled as 'Rocking Horseflies'. As a concession to vegetarians there was a flaky mushroom pie in a great oval dish, with the message 'Eat Me' formed in pastry on its shiny golden surface.

Bemused journalists were wandering to and fro, snatching and drinking glass after glass of Merlot.

In the corner of the foyer sat a grand piano, around which a quartet of music students were performing the sitar and piano suite from Ravi Shankar's score to Jonathan Miller's *Alice*.

The music slowed and paused. Another music student, acting as a trumpeter, and a drama student, both in eighteenth century courtier's uniforms fashioned from ruffled Burgundy silk, took up strategic positions either side of a lecture theatre entrance. The trumpeter trumpeted a fanfare. People turned round and, on cue, the drama student Master of Ceremonies solemnly intoned: "Ladies and Gentlemen, the Queen of Allminster, (Allminster being Cheshire's first and best University), begs your attendance upon Her Majesty in the Meeting Hall." The doors swung open in tandem and the Master of Ceremonies beckoned the astonished crowd of journalists and academics inside.

The Meeting Hall was set up with conference tables, spread with black and white chequered tablecloths, and with trays of steaming teapots, teacups and saucers laid out upon them. There were accompanying plates piled with jam tarts and custard creams with 'Allminster' stamped on them. Each conference table had a press pack with leaflets on the history of Allminster, Charles Lutwidge Dodgson, a proof copy of *The Wasp* chapter, and a promotional booklet from the Allminster University Press. Power and Lynch took up seats at a table in a corner of the Meeting Hall towards the back, which gave them a vantage point to view the whole proceedings. On the stage was a music student, in pastel silk, and white wig, playing psychedelic themes on a 1960s mellotron.

"Far out," muttered Power, as he leafed through the press pack. There was a two-page report ostensibly verifying *The Wasp* chapter, said to be by the late Sir Rob Willett. He read some of the report, with its academic sentences concerning philological word frequencies, syntactical similarities and favoured phraseology. It reflected none of the doubt or angst in Power's last conversation with Sir Robert.

Lynch was reading through Willett's validation of the manuscript, and, when he finished, commented in a whisper, "I may have difficulty deciphering the critique, but he seems to stop short of saying the chapter is genuine."

"Because he thought it was fake," Power whispered back.

"I remember, you said. But did he ever tell the Vice Chancellor?" asked Lynch.

"I don't believe he did," said Power. "He was terrified."

"Over a manuscript?"

"It was about his academic reputation, I think," said Power.

As the hall was filling up, they were joined at their table by two others. Power recognised Erin Marsh, the Dean of Business and Enterprise, as she slumped down into her chair and a gentlemen in clerical dress, a dark suit, purple shirt and dog collar. He introduced himself as the Bishop of Shrewsbury. Lynch had stood up as they took their seats and offered them a cup of tea. "I presume we are meant to serve ourselves," he said, as he picked up the heavy teapot, poured the steaming tea into the waiting cups and passed them round the rest of the table.

The Bishop accepted the tea with thanks, and opening the press pack, put some *pince nez* reading glasses on his nose and started to read *The Wasp* chapter. He hadn't read more than a sentence, before the lights in the hall went down and a spotlight fell on the stage. Into the light stepped Bridget McFarlane, but a markedly transformed Bridget McFarlane.

"And there is the promised Queen of Allminster," said Power.

"Oh, my God," said Erin Marsh, with slack-jawed surprise. She turned to the Bishop at her side and apologised, "Sorry, Bishop." The Bishop nodded benignly at her contrition, blue eyes twinkling at her over gold-rimmed, half-moon reading glasses. The Bishop's beard was fulsome and flowed like a cascade of curls, a waterfall of long, silver-grey hair that played about his chest and which trembled as he nodded his forgiveness.

"Professor McFarlane does look somewhat alarming," he conceded, before re-focusing his attention on the text of *The Wasp* again.

Bridget was wearing a black and white taffeta ball gown; a black off-the-shoulder top with deep plunging neckline showing her cleavage, and an A-line skirt with tendril-like black embroidery around the waist. Resting on her brunette hair was a diamond and jet tiara. Her face was a white circle of *oshiroi* makeup, with stylised black eyes and black lipstick.

Power had noticed the gasp of the audience when McFarlane emerged into the spotlight. She was indeed metamorphosed, and remarkably, Power found her not without charm. Out of the corner of his eye he glimpsed McFarlane's lover, Caroline, at a table to the right of the stage. She was glaring round the auditorium at the audience, nursing an angry jealousy at the crowd's rapt attention to the elegant figure on stage.

McFarlane also sensed how her altered appearance had caught the imagination of the audience and felt unsure of how she should manage this unexpectedly positive reaction. She paused to steady herself, just for a moment, then began her presentation. Her slides appeared on the screen behind her as she spoke. "Good evening, Ladies and Gentlemen, visitors and staff of Allminster alike. '*Who in the world am I? Ah, that's the great puzzle.*' Those were the words of our founder,

Charles Lutwidge Dodgson, otherwise known as Lewis Carroll, as he described the central puzzle of our own personal existence. Who am I? Tonight, I am dressed for the occasion, as the White Queen from *Alice*, but to the staff here I am Executive Pro Vice Chancellor." Power noted that she did not say acting Executive Pro Vice Chancellor.

"Has she got delusions of grandeur?" hissed Erin Marsh, lazily munching on a scone.

"As you all know," McFarlane said, "the White Queen is from *Alice Through the Looking Glass*, our founder Charles Dodgson's second book about Alice, written in eighteen seventy-one, under his pseudonym, Lewis Carroll. And the theme of the book is a vast chess game. Alice, as a nominal pawn, travels across the chessboard to become a queen herself. The White Queen had the vital quality for academic life in that she could believe 'six impossible things before breakfast'. This would be a useful attribute in running any University, as I have found since acting as Deputy Vice Chancellor."

"What does that mean?" asked Lynch. Power could only shake his head.

"At Allminster we revere our founder and his brilliant works," said McFarlane. "We cherish his memory and honour his groundbreaking publications in mathematics and literature. Last year, our Vice Chancellor, who unfortunately cannot be with us today, invested in an important manuscript. He bought this from a distant relative of Charles Dodgson. The descendant of a relative who cleared Dodgson's study at Oxford after his death in eighteen ninety-eight. There were a great many manuscripts and work books. Most were, terrible to report, simply burned. Some of them were kept however, and one manuscript, the Allminster manuscript, was the manuscript for a lost chapter from *Through the Looking Glass*." Lynch had pulled a pocketbook out of his jacket and began making some notes.

"The chapter that we are here to celebrate and publish today, is called *The Wasp*. The original was omitted from the final version of *Through the Looking Glass*, partly because of technical difficulties faced by the illustrator, John Tenniel. A version was said to have been found in the nineteen-seventies, but we have reason to believe that our own, our Allminster version, copyrighted and published in your packs today, that is the true lost chapter. And we publish the late Sir Robert Willett's verification of *The Wasp* alongside the chapter. A computer analysis of the chapters demonstrates, indisputably, that this chapter is the true work of Lewis Carroll. *The Wasp* is to be published this Sunday in *The Sunday Telegraph* magazine. We regard this as a significant coup for Allminster."

Power noted that McFarlane was effectively placing herself at the centre of the winning team, when it was Armitage, the Vice Chancellor and Sir Robert who surely had been the key players. Neither of whom was present to take any credit today, (not that Willett would willingly have been involved at all). Power felt uncomfortable at McFarlane's trumpeting of Sir Robert's opinion, knowing as he did that the English professor had considered the chapter a fake. He wondered if McFarlane would open the presentation to questions from the journalists who were covering the event and filming and photographing her. He fantasised about taking the public opportunity to ask his own pointed questions of McFarlane.

A middle-aged woman, dressed modestly in a sparingly-cut grey suit appeared in the wings of the stage. McFarlane beckoned her forward, but did not cede the microphone to her or introduce her with any intention of letting her speak, merely letting her stand awkwardly there, as some kind of living prop to McFarlane's continued performance. "I am joined by Dr Cherie White, the Head of the Allminster Press. To celebrate the newly discovered chapter Allminster Press are publishing the chapter singly, and also in its appropriate place in a special edition of the *Looking Glass*, exactly as it was intended to be, for the first time ever. The Allminster edition will, of course, will then be the definitive version of the text globally.

"Now, if there are questions from the press about the Allminster *Alice*, Dr White and I would be delighted to answer them."

There was a pause.

"I'm tempted to ask more than a few," Dr Power whispered to Lynch.

"Let's keep our powder dry," said Lynch. "See what the press ask."

The Bishop had finished his reading of the manuscript from the media pack, and looking up at Dr Power, blinked myopically. "Interesting," he said softly. "The chapter emphasises the chess game at the heart of the book. Of course, chess is meant to be a game of war, between two sides. But this chapter makes you think about the conflict more, and it makes you wonder who was the wargame in *Looking Glass* between. The pieces imagine that they are running the game, but this chapter implies that the game is between two controlling sides, an altogether different level. Just, I suppose, as in a real game of chess. Who did Carroll mean was playing the game in *Looking Glass*? Whose hands were moving the pieces, I mean."

But before anybody could respond to this observation, a journalist had made his way across the meeting hall to the microphone just in front of the stage.

"Mike Roberts, BBC North, How much did the University pay for the manuscript?"

"I am not at liberty to say," said McFarlane. "There was a non-disclosure agreement with the family member who sold the manuscript." Lynch wrote this down.

"One last question," said Roberts "Where is the manuscript for us to see, and how much do you estimate it is now worth?"

"That's two questions, Mike," said McFarlane, with a smile. "Whilst we have been speaking in here, the porters have placed a secure display case in the foyer and the open manuscript can be viewed and photographed in its case after this presentation. As to the value now? Well, Allminster does not intend to sell the manuscript any time soon, but it has been valued at five million pounds." Lynch made a note, slowly shaking his head.

Another journalist took the microphone. "Sylvie Betts, Granada News. My question is to Dr White. How many copies of the new *Alice* book do you expect to sell?"

Dr White looked pleased to have finally been included in the event at last. "Our first print run – or first edition – of hardbacks will be fifty thousand. This afternoon we took an advance order from . . . er . . . a certain online bookstore . . . for two hundred thousand paperback copies and so we have been on to the printers. We expect they will be kept very busy."

Lynch made a rapid calculation of the likely profit.

A journalist from *The Sunday Times,* the *Telegraph's* rival, jostled Sylvie away from the microphone to ask his own needling question. "Simon Oliver, Sunday Times, you've had your own expert, the late Sir Robert Willett, appraise the manuscript and give it a clean bill of health, but he was *your* expert, an employee of this University. Have you had an *independent* academic evaluation?"

McFarlane stepped forward. "As I said before, Sir Robert made his analysis through an academically verified computer analysis, using independent, internationally recognised and thus unbiased software. It's the same software that any other academic would use, and they'd get the same results."

Simon Oliver pressed the point, "I hear what you're saying, but will the manuscript be available to other academics to analyse – say, to perform a chemical analysis of the inks and the paper used?"

"The paper has been verified as being from the nineteenth century. We consider that it is the intellectual content of the chapter which matters and which proves indisputably that the origin of the manuscript was the mind of Lewis Carroll." McFarlane beamed at the journalist, defying him to ask another question.

Before he could get another word out, the head of the University Press, Dr Cherie White, interrupted on cue. "Excuse me, Professor McFarlane. We must press on now to the display of the manuscript, which is ready for viewing out in the foyer. There will be some Oxford sherry – the very same kind that Charles Dodgson used to buy for the Christchurch Common Room – and a buffet of savoury steak pies and buttered mash." The mention of sherry, being an alcoholic beverage, was a brilliant stroke, forestalling any further potentially awkward questions, and supplying sufficient motivation to the assembled journalists to rush out of the meeting room for their glasses of sherry.

"Sherry saves the day, seven letters," said Lynch to himself, and put his notebook away. He turned to Power. "She dodged the real questions, but that manuscript is worth millions to the University in book sales alone, and so the questions will keep on coming." Lynch asked the Bishop, "Are you a fan of Lewis Carroll, your Grace?"

"I've written a book on the theological thinking contained in his work. Dodgson was brought up to be an Anglican cleric like his father, who was also called Charles. Lewis Carroll books are absolutely soused with theology."

Dr Power smiled wryly at the idea and was about to comment when Lynch interrupted him.

"And the chapter – is it genuine in your opinion?"

"If it's a fake, it's a very good one," he said.

"That's not a ringing endorsement, your Grace."

"When I read the chapter just now I felt the author was talking about war, that it was written by someone with the image of trench warfare in their mind, maybe someone who had seen footage of the First World War, or served in it – and the first world war, of course, was decades after Carroll died."

Lynch bowed his head in thought.

The journalists had decanted themselves from the hall and were either clustered around the manuscript in its reinforced glass display case, or quaffing golden sherry. A few academics were left scattered around the hall chatting across the tables. Power was suddenly aware of a figure advancing towards them across the hall – the imposing figure of Bridget McFarlane, in her black and white costume as the White Queen of Allminster. Power stood up for manner's sake, as did the Lynch and the Bishop.

"A very striking presentation, Bridget," said Power, swallowing down his feelings about the use of Sir Robert's verification. He gestured to the dress, "I wouldn't have recognised you."

"Thank you, Dr Power," she said. "The things we do for the University . . . I was dreading the questions."

The Bishop coughed. "I was very interested to see the missing chapter, Professor McFarlane. It will provide the academics with material to debate. I hope it doesn't prove too controversial."

"Why should it prove at all controversial?" Bridget said, haughtily. "It's the genuine article."

"So you say," said the Bishop, and looked down at the table slightly despondently. He gracefully resumed his seat and drained his cup of tea.

McFarlane turned her gaze upon Lynch. "Mr Andrew Lynch, I believe," she held out a black satin-gloved hand for him to shake. "The retired policeman."

"I've never been busier or more productive," said Lynch. "I feel as if I'm on active duty."

"The University commissioned a single piece of work from you, but that was a discrete piece of work. And yet you keep on digging, when the proper authorities are the more appropriate people to investigate."

Lynch paused and looked her directly in the eyes. "I have this unhappy habit of being a completer. I like justice. When I complete an investigation I feel I have been engaged in the Lord's work, and I always feel that He would prefer me to complete that work and to see justice done."

"Amen to that," muttered the Bishop softly as he gathered his papers together, preparing to leave.

"Nevertheless, the University would prefer it if you called off your quaint little quest, and asked your associate Mr Beresford to steer clear of the campus. He has been interrupting the University's employees in their work and asking questions of them. There have been complaints that he is distressing them by asking them to find facts for him. This is not an officially sanctioned exercise. Will you ask him to desist, please?"

"Mr Beresford is always the soul of discretion, I am sure," said Lynch. "He . . . we always seek to set things right. Surely only those with something to hide would oppose our very gentle enquiries."

"I don't know what you are implying, but *my* actions are beyond reproach. We don't like unofficial investigators prowling our corridors."

Lynch wondered if she was using the royal 'we'. "As it happens Detective Beresford has completed the first phase of his work and he has found something important."

"What? What has he found?" asked McFarlane.

Lynch smiled. "He will be making a full report to me tomorrow about various . . . anomalies."

"But I have a right to know," said McFarlane. "I'm in charge of the University now."

"You said that the investigation was not officially sanctioned, and separate from the University, and now you want to know the results of that discrete investigation? Just now you didn't want any part of it." There was an unaccustomed edge to Lynch's voice. "It's a bit like that saying, isn't it; 'you have to be part of the solution, or you're going to be part of the problem.'"

"I don't know what you could possibly mean," said McFarlane. She turned on her heel and stalked off to the foyer. There she mingled with the journalists and posed in front of the manuscript for their photographers.

The Bishop and Erin Marsh had departed and Lynch signalled to Power that he too would be on his way. He thanked Power for inviting him to the press event. The food at the event held no temptation for him; Mrs Lynch had promised him a fine supper at home. "This manuscript is worth millions in itself and also in sales revenue to the University. We need to know a lot more about its provenance. But all that can wait until tomorrow, I have an excellent Shepherd's Pie waiting for me. And Pamela worries if I am late."

Power watched his friend walking away through the foyer and was about to follow him, when a figure, who had been waiting for Lynch to leave, detached itself from the shadows at the side of the hall and stood in front of Power.

It was Caroline, McFarlane's lover.

"Hello," said Power, trying to steer his way round her. "I am just leaving. Excuse me please."

"So anxious to be off? Guilty conscience, maybe?"

"No, I just want to get home, thank you."

As he tried to move past her she blocked him, and stood in the middle of the doorway to do so. "She made a beeline for your table. Are you denying she did that?"

Power suppressed his exasperation and tried to appear calm. "Bridget only talked to Andrew Lynch. She didn't even look at me."

"You saw her just before though, in her office, and you told her, didn't you? *You* told her I wasn't having therapy."

"Which is only the truth, isn't it Caroline? Will you let me pass?"

"Why did you tell Bridget I wasn't seeing you? Couldn't you just have played along like a good boy? I could report you for breaching doctor-patient confidentiality . . ."

"Caroline, you can go ahead and report me if you so wish, but as you are not my patient, and never have been, your complaint simply would not stand. Now, please step aside."

Grudgingly, she moved to one side and allowed Power to pass through the doorway.

As he edged past she hissed, "You think you have all the answers, don't you?"

"Just leave me alone," said Power. "And treat Professor McFarlane better than you do." The anger she radiated made him anxious and his hands were beginning to shake. He walked away as quickly as he could, feeling that if he said any more there would be an unnecessary note of anxiety in his voice. His voice would betray him, and he felt it was important with her, not to show any weakness at all.

* * *

Dr Power parked his ancient Saab in the drive of the Old Rectory and stepped out into the crisp winter air. He pulled his coat tightly around himself. The air was largely clear but tinged with distant woodsmoke. He had parked next to the Vice Chancellor's six-litre black Bentley Continental GT which gleamed even in the pale light of that February morning.

Morning in the sleepy village of Davenham was blessedly quiet, apart from the occasional caw of a lone rook which sat atop the spire of the church opposite and viewed Power and his Saab with lofty disdain.

Power's feet crunched in the gravel of the drive as he walked to the glossy black front door and climbed the steps to pull at the old-fashioned bell. He could hear the bell echoing inside the hall beyond. As he waited, Power looked back at the cars standing side by side – the dusty, battered Saab and the pristine sapphire-blue Bentley. What did the contrasting vehicles say to the world about the two owners, Power wondered?

Mrs Armitage opened the door wide enough to see who was outside. She regarded him warily, "Hello, who is it?"

"My name is Professor Power. From Allminster. I am sorry to intrude, I was just wondering if the Vice Chancellor was at home and if I might have a word with him, please?"

"I don't know, he's been very unwell, don't you know."

Dr Power put on his friendliest expression and contrived to appear as benign as he could manage.

"I'm the doctor at the University who's been working with your husband on the medical school project," he said.

"He has mentioned your name, I do recall it now." Recognition had dawned on her face. "Yes, I remember the name, he has spoken of you on several occasions. Do you like chess? Are you the colleague he plays chess with?"

"Not me, I'm afraid; my son plays a better game of chess than I do, and he's only seven."

"Well, he has spoken of you favourably, let me say that. He may be pleased to see you, although he has been difficult to predict. Restless. Going for long walks at night, trudging slowly down the village lanes. I tell him it's dangerous in the dark, but he won't listen.

He gets up in the early hours. I tell him to wrap up warm and wear something white, and off he goes. This morning he is sitting out in the garden at the back of the house. In this weather!" She sighed. "You'll find him if you follow the path round the side of the house. Across the lawn . . . watch your step. The path's icy." She smiled, and closed the door gently, leaving Power to walk the Oxford stone path round the side of the house. At the rear of the Old Rectory he discovered an ancient, mossy lawn that stretched over to a clump of trees and in front of this, in the corner of the garden, was a hollow, wooden shelter.

The trees were leafless, their branches etched black against the dull grey canvas of the sky. Overnight fog had condensed on the branches and had frozen into glassy icicles, which hung glistening from the twigs. Hoarfrost coated the grass which poked up through the thick quilt of powdery snow. Power stepped up from the icy path onto the lawn. Crunching his way across the frozen white snow he made his way towards a still, slumped figure in a chair within the lee of the arched wooden shelter.

The Vice Chancellor was seated with his back to Power as the doctor trudged through the frozen white snow. The snow had built up into a deep drift against the bank at the back of the rectory garden. The Vice Chancellor's only shelter was nestled under the skeletal trees and comprised of an arched wooden windbreak, rather like the prow of a boat. In front of this he had set up a table and chairs, and there he had come to rest in the clear, fresh air.

"What possessed him to sit out here?' thought Power. "Is he trying to kill himself?"

Armitage had swaddled himself in two duvets and a tartan blanket. His feet were resting up on a stool and his head fallen back, lolling against a large red woollen cushion behind his back. He did not turn as Power came closer to him. Indeed, he did not move at all.

Power froze in front of the slumped body. He noted the pallor of the face, the absolute stillness of the moment. Although Power's breath steamed in the winter air, there was no visible issue of breath from Armitage's mouth or nostrils. The silence was so complete Power could hear the patter of water drops from melted icicles as they plopped into the snowbank. This fragmented moment of time seemed to stretch into eternity.

He looked back over his shoulder to the house, his gaze scanning the rear elevation to see if Mrs Armitage was watching at a window. Power wondered if she would be altogether surprised to learn that she had become a widow.

Dr Power thought that he should comply with the formalities of the situation. Reluctantly he approached the Vice Chancellor, intending to confirm his passing. He needed to peel back the Vice Chancellor's eyelid to check for a pupillary reflex and feel at his neck for the absence of a carotid pulse.

Power put a hand on the Vice Chancellor's collar.

Armitage opened one eye and glared at him.

Power jumped back. "Vice Chancellor!"

Armitage blinked sluggishly. "Professor Power, hello," Armitage lifted his head from the cushion and opened both eyes. "I was just having forty winks," he chuckled. "Did you think I was dead?"

"I'm so sorry. I mean, good morning," Power was flustered by the sudden revivification of the Vice Chancellor. "What are you doing out in the perishing cold?"

"I expected you a week or so before now," he paused, looking Power up and down. "How is Bridget McFarlane doing holding the fort?"

"Actually, I did want to talk about that," said Power.

Armitage chuckled, "I bet you do. Take a seat," he pointed to a wooden chair by the table, which was mercifully free of ice and snow. Armitage watched him sit down. "Actually, I am not cold."

"That could just be hypothermia," said Power. "People with hypothermia don't feel the cold."

"I have brought two duvets and a thick woollen blanket out with me." He twitched one of the duvets aside. "And my wife brought a stone hot water bottle out. I've got my feet on it. There should be a hat somewhere. It slipped off, I think." He pulled the duvet back into place and retrieved a brushed cotton nightcap from his lap and pulled it on. "I wanted some peace, some silence, some rest from all the turmoil after Willett died . . . and they would keep on phoning me – and drip their poison into my ear. So I leave all the phones inside for my wife to field and come out here. And I sit in the silence, muffled against the cold. I keep hot refreshment by my side. So you really shouldn't worry about me, although I thank you for your concern." He gestured to the table by his side. And indeed, there was a samovar on the table with a pair of cobalt-glazed, Lomonosov porcelain cups. Power could see that a spirit lamp was burning under the samovar. Armitage watched him admiring the silverware. "You can have a cup if you want? It's an original silver samovar made in Tula, by the Lyaliny brothers. Part of an Imperial set made for Czarina Alexandra."

"Then might the Czarina have poured tea from it herself?" ventured Power.

"I doubt it," said Armitage. "There were probably many samovars in a set made for the Imperial household . . . but if you like to be sentimental about these things, then why not?" He reached over and poured some tea out from the samovar and handed a steaming gilt-edged cup over to Power. "I'm pleased to see you," he said, Power could see a degree of colour coming back into the Vice Chancellor's complexion, and wondered how he could possibly have imagined that this animated face in front of him was dead.

"Watch out, it's piping hot," said Armitage, as he handed the steaming cup and saucer over. "It's a blend of tea from Kusmi, flavoured with orange blossom and bergamot. They call it Anastasia."

Power sipped the steaming brew speculatively. He was cold in the thin sunlight and began to covet the thick cocoon of duvets wound about the Vice Chancellor. "It has been so long since we met to talk about the medical school," said Power. "I'm afraid that the project is running out of steam. It's so important to have enthusiastic support like yours."

"And Bridget is at best lukewarm about Medicine, she sees it as a cuckoo in her nest; you are the interloper that will edge out her own children."

"I wouldn't want to worry you unduly, or to seek in any way to make you cut short your convalescence. But the deputy Vice Chancellor has assumed control of everything, and I wondered if you could signal the direction you wish things to go . . . it would help us, it would help me."

"Did she use that phrase?"

"Which?" Power was puzzled.

"Deputy Vice Chancellor? You said Deputy Vice Chancellor. Did she use those exact words?"

"Yes, last night, at the launch of the new Alice edition – when she presented the chapter to the press."

Armitage frowned. "There was a press event? For *The Wasp* chapter?" Power nodded, and experienced a sinking feeling in the pit of his stomach. He hadn't wished to appear to be telling tales. And yet it seemed clear he had borne bad news to Canon Armitage who seemed to have been blissfully unaware that whilst he had been recuperating, McFarlane had assumed control of his University, awarded herself a new title, and taken over a pet project of Canon Armitage's, presenting it to the media as her own.

The Vice Chancellor coughed and looked up at the sky. "I think maybe I have spent enough time here, indulging my feelings of guilt – the snow cannot wash that away – I am abnegating my responsibilities, punishing myself with the cold. I fear I must fall well again."

"Fall well?"

"As opposed to falling ill, of course, of course." He tried to pour himself another cup of tea, but the samovar was running dry. He leant over and blew out the spirit lamp. "Did the press welcome *The Wasp* chapter?"

"They did. I think it will be reproduced in the Sunday papers."

"I missed the news last night. You can be assured I will be back at work before Sunday. That will be a 'signal' to Bridget. Is there anything else I need to be 'signalling'?"

"Well," said Power. "My colleague, Andrew Lynch, has been continuing the investigation into Professor Shacklin's death. I know that the University cannot fund this work, but Andrew Lynch is a completer; he doesn't like leaving unanswered questions."

"I never imagined, for a moment, that you, or he, would leave it alone," said the Vice Chancellor. "I always thought you would keep on with that particular piece of work. Do you know, I'm feeling hungry again? I had lost my appetite altogether for while. If I remember correctly my wife promised me a gigot of lamb, with garlic and ginger. Would you care to join us for lunch?"

Nothing would ever induce Power to eat a gigot of lamb nowadays. Power wondered whether he had ever told the Vice Chancellor that he was a vegetarian, and if so, whether the Vice Chancellor was teasing him. However, he mumbled a simple apology, and moved back to the subject of the investigation. "We have had a detective working on leads; Beresford, he's an ex-police Inspector, and I gather he has been making progress. But Professor McFarlane, only last night, insisted that he stop work, and leave the University altogether."

"Did she indeed?" The Vice Chancellor sat more upright in his chair and put his feet back on the ground. "Doesn't that seem a bit suspicious to you? After all, why put obstacles in the way of a legitimate inquiry into the death of a colleague?"

"Possibly," said Power, cautiously. "She implied she didn't want employees harassed at work. But I'm sure we are on the brink of finding out something really important."

"I see," said Armitage. "And what would you like me to do? What signals would you expect me to make?"

"We'd like your leave to continue our work. And although we do not ask for further funds, we'd like access within the University and co-operation from staff. And your blessing for Lynch and I to return to Malta. No fees or expenses are involved. If you could just signal that I can take the time off to finish the work and Beresford can resume his investigations at Allminster – all with your blessing?"

"How could I reasonably refuse?" asked the Vice Chancellor. "You must go, of course, of course. You can have all the time you need." He paused, gathering himself for a decision. "I don't think it would be prudent for me to stay away from work any longer, and so, as I feel a lot better for seeing you, I think I will return to the University tomorrow. I will mend bridges and re-start the medical school project, while you complete the investigation. I can't see what motive Bridget could have for impeding the Foundation's work. As far as I am concerned, as I think it says in Corinthians, '*The race must be run, and the game must be won*'. And now, I think, my gigot of lamb will be done to a turn . . ."

Chapter Twenty-Three

Was there, after all, any green door in the wall at all?

H. G. Wells

D r Power reviewed his inpatients and left them in the capable
hands of his Specialist Registrar the day before boarding the early
morning plane to Malta. Lynch had flown out previously and was there
at Malta International Airport to greet him. Lynch had arranged for
them to meet Azzopardi later that morning and, after Power had
emerged from customs, he drove them north east to Valletta in a
scarlet, rented Fiat Barchetta.

There was sufficient time to park in Valletta and have a swift
breakfast of hot coffee and Imqaret date pastries at De Bono's café.

"I can taste the aniseed," Power said, as he munched the flaky
diamond-shaped pastry with relish. Power took a swig of black coffee
and looked closely at Lynch. "What's new then?"

"I need to bring you up to speed with the investigation before we
see Azzopardi," said Lynch. "I was emailed the SIS post mortem report
on Felfe last night. This was a report from a second post mortem, by
a more experienced pathologist who performed additional
investigations. At your suggestion."

"Go on, tell me."

"Well, you were right, Carl. When we saw Felfe on the stone of the
Cathedral floor you pointed out what had happened to his eyes. And

the slaver round his mouth. And your observations tally with what the pathologist found in his blood stream."

"Ah," said Power. "And what was that?"

"Snake venom," said Lynch. "The pathologist thought it had been taken orally. The venom probably came from a snake of the black mamba species, *Dendroaspis polylepsis*. Only two drops of venom would kill a man in minutes. The neurotoxins in the venom shut down the nervous system. Without anti-venom being given almost immediately the black mamba venom is one hundred per cent fatal."

"So he *was* murdered," said Power. "It wasn't a heart attack."

"As you can imagine the SIS is now trying to work out whether the death of their agent was at the hands of foreign security agencies. Felfe may have risen to the top of some historical hit list and been dispatched by a current service, or someone operating on behalf of a defunct service like HVA who wanted revenge for his historical betrayal."

"Poor Felfe," said Power. "Of course it might be someone else, an individual who killed him and not an intelligence service, but where would anyone get a mamba?"

"I was told that mambas come from sub-Saharan East Africa. They aren't exactly encouraged as pets in England, as you can imagine, although some aficionados will do anything, even break the law, to get a rare or banned species for their collection. Somehow, I doubt it was a live snake that caused Felfe's death. I can't imagine a black mamba was slithering about the pews of the cathedral. The pathologist thought that a stored venom was to blame – perhaps a dried venom powder that was reconstituted for use in something Felfe ate or drank. They keep dried venom powders in a tropical school of medicine to make anti-venom. But there are very few schools like that in England – there are only two – in London and Liverpool. And they aren't missing any samples, I've checked." He paused, a verse of scripture had come into his mind and it puzzled him. He muttered the line from Deuteronomy to himself, "'*Their wine is the venom of serpents, the deadly poison of cobras*'".

"The zoo?" said Power, still wondering where the venom might have originated. "Does Chester Zoo have a black mamba?"

"No," said Lynch. "They did have once upon a time, but they wouldn't now, not in recent years with Health and Safety." He looked at his watch. "Come on, we'd better go, Azzopardi will be waiting." Power stood and brushed pastry crumbs off his shirt as Lynch paid the waitress. As he handed over a tip, he could see that Dr Power was still deep in thought. Indeed, Power followed Lynch wordlessly along the sunny streets of Valletta, musing on his final conversation with Felfe.

They paused outside the peeling green door behind which the SIS maintained their residual presence on Malta.

Power touched the flaky, crumbling surface of the ancient door and its architrave. The tips of his fingers traced the recessed letters on the engraved brass plate of the ghost sign; 'Degiorgio and Azzopardi, Merchants and Agents'.

Lynch was just reaching up to the door knocker when his phone started ringing. He reached into his pocket. Power was deep in reverie in the morning sun. He was imagining what Felfe's last few moments on this earth must have been like. Despite the burgeoning heat of the day, he felt cold. Distantly he was aware of Lynch answering the call. "Lynch speaking . . . yes . . . of course, where? . . . yes . . . we'll find that, yes . . . see you soon, goodbye."

Lynch folded the phone up and said, "Change of plan." He noted Power's dissociated expression and asked, "Are you all right?"

"I was thinking about Felfe. Poor man. The neurotoxins in the venom would have paralysed his muscles. That's why his pupils were dilated. He would have been alert, able to see and hear what was going on around him but unable to move and unable to breathe or swallow either. He would have salivated but been unable to clear his throat, that's why he drooled . . . he was like a fish out of water, drowning on that cold stone floor. If his murderer was still around he would have been able to see him, in his last moments, but been unable to do anything."

"Horrid," said Lynch. "You've gone pale."

"I also remember a detail from a conversation with Professor McFarlane," said Power. "At least I think it was her. She was talking about the Bursar, Grieg. I'm sure she said that he had an unusual hobby; that he kept rare reptiles."

"Does he?" asked Lynch. "Are you sure?" He started composing a text to Beresford.

"About Grieg keeping reptiles, yes, yes. But who told me? I can't remember for sure. Was it McFarlane?"

"You're sure it was Grieg, though?" asked Lynch. Power nodded. "I'll text Beresford and he can make enquiries. But just supposing, even if Grieg had a black mamba snake, and used the venom to poison Felfe, wouldn't he get rid of it afterwards? Kill it and dispose of the snake's body?"

"I don't know," said Power. "He's a very odd, obsessional man. What we used to call an anankastic personality. A real collector. If he'd acquired a rare snake for his collection, however he did it, he wouldn't want to lose a prize item from his collection. It would kill him to do that."

"If he is so obsessional, would he have complied with the Dangerous Animals legislation and have a DWA Licence, sorry, a Wild Animals Licence?"

"It would depend what took precedence in Grieg's mind – would the desire to complete his collection be more important than complying with some external legislation? For instance, some extreme egg collectors will prioritise their own collection over the rights of a wild osprey and the law that protects it."

"Beresford will look into it, anyway," said Lynch. "Come on, we have a bit more of a walk to do."

"I thought we were meeting here," Power gestured to the splendidly dilapidated door.

"Azzopardi phoned, we are meeting at the Lascaris War Rooms instead."

"At the War Rooms?" asked Power, as he hurried to catch up with Lynch, who was already striding away down St Paul Street.

"Today they are closed to the public. He has access and wants to show us round."

"But what are they?" persisted Power, as they turned down Melita Street.

"A network of tunnels under Valletta's citadel," said Lynch. "Some very old, from Templar times, hewn from the bare rock and others mined from nineteen-forty onwards whilst Malta was besieged and being bombarded by the Luftwaffe who were flying in across the Mediterranean from Sicily, sixty miles to the north."

"It sounds like Valletta is always being besieged," said Power, a little out of breath as Lynch began. "It must be a most strategically important island."

"The Muslims besieged Valletta in fifteen sixty-five – and catapulted the severed heads of any captured Knights of St John over the battlements, and later the Axis forces in World War Two pounded the buildings of the city with bombs, flattening whole neighbourhoods," said Lynch, as he turned right onto Triq-Il-Batterija and they hurried down a long flight of steps. "The Maltese endured a solid one hundred and fifty days and nights of bombing in nineteen forty-two. And the fight back against this onslaught was controlled from the War Rooms – here." Lynch pointed to a curved arch where they had arrived, and down into a long, gated tunnel beyond, which evidently led deep into the rock. "We've arrived."

Power peered past the locked iron gates down into the darkness beyond and shivered. A sign was affixed onto the padlocked gates saying, 'Closed Today. Essential Maintenance Work.'

As he gazed into the tunnel, his eyes adjusted to the dimness and Power began to observe a shadow moving against a distant light. It was the silhouette of a man walking towards them. He called out, "Detective Lynch? Professor Power?"

"That's right!" Power called back. His voice echoed in the stone tunnel and the man, now discernible as Azzopardi himself, waved back.

Azzopardi, nearing the gates, fished in his pocket for a hefty bunch of keys and began trying to locate the precise key for the padlock and chain. He deftly unlocked it and slipped the chain off the iron railings. The links of the chain rattled loudly against the metal. He grinned as he swung the gate open. "Come in, come in. We have the War Rooms to ourselves, all the tourists are gone today. I just thought you might like to see the rooms when they are free of the crowds."

Azzopardi introduced himself to Power and shook his hand. "The name is Pawlu Azzopardi, Professor Power. Detective Lynch has told me all about you. We could do with a few psychiatrists in the Service, I think. Some of us are as mad as a box of frogs." He beckoned them inside and wrapped the chain back around the iron railings to secure the entrance against any stray tourists. "Welcome to the theatre of war. How it used to be sixty years ago. The curators are installing a new room to extend the tourist attraction. They are recreating the old number station from Cyprus and have managed to acquire the original machinery used at the time. Follow me."

They walked down the inclined tunnel and turned right into an old guard room, where once upon a time all the war time staff, such as signals operators and decoders, were identity checked on entering and leaving the intense secrecy of the headquarters. "The Lascaris War Rooms are named after Giovanni Lascaris, one time Grand Master of the Knights of Malta," said Azzopardi, over his shoulder. "Why not invoke the mighty Knights of Old, even if they are long dead? Dying is just a matter of finally running out of luck, hey? For all of us, I mean."

As he followed Azzopardi, Power noted that although he was not a tall man, Azzopardi walked swiftly and confidently, his back was straight and head held high, suggesting good self-esteem. He wore a crisp Rael Brook shirt and his light-grey suit was well-tailored and pristine. His skin was as pale as milk though, surprisingly pale for someone living on this sunny Island.

Inside the wartime complex Power saw the hinged frames of bunks folded up against the wall and wondered which officers would sleep here at night and which would go home to whatever house, billet or berth was left after the aerial bombardment. As they walked deeper into the tunnel network Power imagined the ghosts of air force and naval commanders striding down this corridor. The smell of cigarettes and whisky, used to numb anxiety and ease their duties, floated with them on the air. The shoulders of their khaki drill and white uniforms brushed past his own as they walked past switchboards, wireless and radar rooms to the command centre. He imagined the click of the soldiers' polished shoes on the concrete floor, their salutes to senior officers, their taut laughter borne of camaraderie, and also tinged with fear. Power would often teach his students about Spencer's observation that laughter was the release of nervous energy.

"There were three thousand, three hundred and forty-three air raids on poor little Malta," said Azzopardi, slowing his walking as they approached the RAF Sector Control Room. "They dropped fifteen thousand tonnes of bombs on the population. And it was a siege. Like a medieval siege. No plane or ship could get through the Axis Forces' blockade without being attacked or destroyed. Everything ran short: food, clothes, ammunition, planes, and ships. Even if you had the planes that hadn't been bombed to smithereens on the airfields of the Island, you were running out of fuel to fly them. And here is the RAF Control Room, where they directed the defence of the Island with what fighter planes and pilots they were able to get into the air."

Power noticed a vast plotting table, with a map of the ocean and the Island of Sicily painted upon it. On the wall was a map of Malta, with the smaller islands – little Comino and larger Gozo alongside. The ceiling was high and arched above their heads, allowing a mezzanine to run around three of the four walls. There were twelve seats up above the mezzanine like thrones in the Gods, a central chair seemed distinctly prominent, with an air of authority about it.

"This was the nerve centre of the defence of Malta during the War," said Azzopardi. "The Captain sat up there, in that chair." He pointed up to the central seat, high above them. "All the information fed into here. He could see the plotting table where the positions of all the incoming Italian and German plane squadrons from Sicily were moved around the board. And from here he could see details of all his own airfields, his own squadrons; who was in the air, whether they had sight of the enemy, whether they were engaged, and the resulting details of planes downed and lost, or returned."

Power imagined the women clustered round the plotting table, using rods to push models of squadrons, each marked with the squadron's aircraft numbers and altitude, and others – enemy Axis planes – detected by radar and zeroing in, mercilessly to wreak havoc on the besieged island.

"The room operated on a system called the Dowding system," said Azzopardi. "A system controlled from the ground, or, here, under the ground, designed to provide interception of the enemy fighters and bombers. Messages from the Dingli Radar station and the observer teams around the Island were all fed here to this nexus. There are other rooms clustered around the control room where staff decoded signals and radar data – in one room there were forty people frantically doing maths on objects detected from three angles and calculating height and speed and numbers. And sitting brooding above, up there in his chair, like some Olympic God, the Captain would watch the squadrons moving across the Map, like he was some kind of chess player." Power imagined the squadrons of planes skimming across the silvery surface of the ocean towards Malta and the Captain adjusting plans for the few fighter planes he had, the few pieces he had left to move, and making decisions that might expend their metal fuselages and pilots in countering the Axis wings of death. And, Power thought, this was no board game with fiat paper currency, because the currency in this arena could not be any more real and it was measured out in actual lives, in blood and souls, saved or lost.

"And the Captain here on Malta, did he have an opposite number, some equivalent Luftwaffe officer in Sicily. A counterpart? Someone to match his mind against?" asked Power.

"I believe so," said Azzopardi. "There was an opposing Luftwaffe headquarters on Sicily that the Nazis used slaves to build. They forced them to burrow deep into the very rock of Mount Erice with jackhammers and pneumatic drills. Many enslaved men died in the construction of those Luftwaffe headquarters. They ripped out the heart of the mountain under *Castle de Venere* and created something just like a Bond villain lair. And from deep inside the mountain they directed the Messerschmitts and Heinkel bombers on the airfields below at Trapani." Azzopardi continued in his urbane manner. "The relentless bombing of Malta was controlled from there. Day and night the bombs rained down. Imagine the noise, the dust, and the dead civilians lying in the rubble. The Maltese lived in ancient catacombs and tunnels under the citadel whenever they could. The aircraft we had were sometimes blown up on the airfields before they could ever get into the air.

"There was an operation in April 1942 – Operation Calendar – to get Submarine Spitfires onto the Island – to fight the bombers before they could reach Malta. USS *Wasp* managed to bring forty-eight Spitfires here through the blockade and onto the airfields, but spies had forewarned the Sicilian Command of their arrival and whilst they stood on the airfields, before they could be fuelled for flight, they were pulverised to shreds of metal under a carpet of Nazi bombs.

"Then came Operation Bowery in May 1942. The pilots and spare engines were sent ahead on a decoy ship HMS *Welshman*, which was disguised as a French vessel *Léopard*. USS *Wasp*, again, sailed from Scapa Flow with forty-seven Supermarine Mk Vc Spitfires with Merlin engines. Seventeen more Spitfires were sent in the accompanying HMS *Eagle*.

"This time things were different. Entirely different. *Wasp* and *Eagle* managed to get through and unloaded their planes." Power was somehow reminded of the characters fighting in Allminster's Carroll chapter. "This time the planes were instantaneously refuelled and manned by their pilots who took them into the air immediately. The fastest turnaround from unloading to being airborne was six minutes. Six minutes! This time the Spitfires were in the air and ready to meet the enemy as they closed in. Forty-seven Axis planes were destroyed that day. They call it the Battle of Malta, and it was that that stopped the daytime bombing of Malta." Azzopardi was flushed with pride on re-telling the story. "And so the darkest times must pass – they always do – although it often seems impossible at the time."

"'*And ye shall hear of wars and rumours of wars: see that ye be not troubled: for all these things must come to pass, but the end is not yet,'*" quoted Lynch. "*So all things must pass, with God's will.*"

Azzopardi continued, "After the Siege was broken General Eisenhower worked from these War Rooms on Operation Husky – the Allies' liberation of Sicily. And after the war, in the 1960s, the rooms became a NATO control centre. So, Malta would have been a Russian nuclear war target in 1963 during the Cuban Missile Crisis. In fact, this command station was still very much operational up until 1977.

"Of course, when they first constructed the command centre they also built tunnels that connect it elsewhere, almost like a labyrinth.

There is a shaft tunnelled up through the rock from here – stairs climb directly up to our SIS office," Azzopardi looked at Lynch. "There's a direct link into the basement of the building where we first met. That's how I got here today to meet you.

"So, here in this room where so many vital decisions have been made over the decades, shall we decide how to fight the problems you face?" said Azzopardi. "Can you brief me on where you are up to?"

Lynch looked over at the wartime map of Malta, Gozo and Comino. "Well, we think the solution to our problems may well lie here. Dr Shacklin, the Executive Pro Vice Chancellor of Allminster, was killed here. His body was never meant to be found. It was meant to have been devoured by pigs, but . . . identifiable remains were found, and the murder is, presumably, still being investigated by the Maltese police. Shacklin was due to meet somebody, a person with the alias, The Banker. Shacklin frequented casinos whenever he visited the island on University business, and had built up considerable gambling debts. He was also compromised by various liaisons, due to his remarkable libido. We do not know whether he was an active member of some criminal conspiracy, a knowing participant, or if he was attempting to make money to pay off his debts by breaking into the conspiracy or blackmailing the criminals." Lynch paused.

Power took over. "We know that another senior Allminster figure, Bridget McFarlane, was in the Mediterranean recently. She said she was visiting her family on Sicily." Power pointed to the map of Sicily on the plotting table. "And from your description of Operation Bowery we know that Sicily is relatively close to Malta by sea and air."

"Forgive me," said Azzopardi. "But McFarlane is certainly not an Italian surname. What family does she have on Sicily?"

Power tried to remember the detail of his conversation with McFarlane. "She said her grandmother's family name was Bacchi."

Azzopardi burst out laughing. "Bacchi? Really? The Bacchi's are well known. The family owns pharmacies here on Malta. They own pharmacies and at least one casino." Lynch was listening pensively.

Power continued, "McFarlane said that she kept her links to the family in Sicily separate from her life in England, because her catholic grandmother would not understand," said Power. "Bridget has a female partner and I assumed this was why she was cautious – because she was afraid of any prejudice."

"And, I think you said she has a qualification in finance and business, Carl," said Lynch. "So, could she be The Banker?"

Azzopardi walked over to the blackboard with the painted map of Malta on it. He wrote SHACKLIN at the top and by the name he added: Casino – Debt – Banker – Dingli meeting. And beneath this name he wrote MCFARLANE and by this: Sicily – Bacchi – Finance – Lover. He turned to Power, "Is McFarlane bisexual rather than homosexual? Could there have been a sexual relationship between Shacklin and McFarlane?"

"I really don't think so, although her partner seems jealous of any contact she has with any male or female." said Power. "McFarlane has always behaved as if she hated Shacklin. But sometimes love and hate are close allies, psychologically speaking. They both dwell in a part of the brain called the insula. On balance though, I don't think there was any . . . attraction."

"And our mutual acquaintance, our sleeping agent Felfe," said Azzopardi. "Do you know any more about him?" He wrote Felfe on the board expectantly, hoping to write an *aide memoire* for any pertinent detail.

"We now have a cause of death for Felfe," said Lynch. "He was poisoned by snake venom, and died minutes afterwards. The poison chosen made it look like a sudden heart attack. And the murder would indeed have been written off as a routine cardiac event except for Dr Power's forensic observations about the body shortly after death."

Power at once took notice that Azzopardi's face betrayed no surprise, and he wondered what else Azzopardi was already aware of.

"A poisoning," mused Azzopardi. "How very typical of a Soviet-style service assassination. Like the ricin administered to Georgi Markov by a passer by, using the tip of a sharp umbrella in the street. Do you remember the case in the papers? Markov was a Bulgarian defector who was quietly living out his life working for the BBC World Service. Felfe was an East German defector quietly living out his life working for a northern university. Was this just another case of delayed revenge?"

"Maybe," said Power. "Except we know Felfe had uncovered something – some operation in the Mediterranean, and that he was researching three words – *Wanderlust, The Banker* and *Sannik Law Co.*"

"And his investigation may have been discovered by who? The Banker?" asked Azzopardi.

Power nodded. "Somebody wanted his investigation to stop. Now is the bursar The Banker? We know he keeps reptiles . . . and we have someone looking into that right now."

"And, of course, I suppose a bursar would consider himself a money man. So, the bursar could be The Banker," said Azzopardi. "What's the bursar's name? For the board."

"Grieg," said Power.

Azzopardi chalked the names of FELFE and GRIEG on the blackboard. He wrote: Banker – Wanderlust – Sannik Law Co, by FELFE and: Bursar – Reptiles, by GRIEG's name. He turned to Lynch. "Are there any other names? Any other suspicious deaths?"

"There was a professor," said Power. "He was my friend, really, who killed himself, ostensibly speaking. One of the few positive people on campus. But he had relationship problems. Drank too much. He was being pressured to certify that a fake manuscript was real. If the manuscript was deemed genuine it would be an asset worth millions. As a fake, well, obviously, it would be worthless."

"So the professor's academic certification of this manuscript would be like an alchemist transmuting mere lead into gold?" pondered Azzopardi. "And this validation of dross was a feat of magic that was just one step too far. Too much for him to bear?"

"It would seem so," said Power.

"But we don't *know* for sure that the manuscript is fake do we?" said Lynch. "I took a look at it in the glass case. It looked real enough. They put it alongside a facsimile of the previous *Wonderland* manuscript, the real one he wrote for Alice Liddell when she was a girl. I'm not a graphologist, but the writing looked identical to me."

"Maybe I didn't explain it properly on the day," said Power. "There were too many people at the Press Event, too much going on, to say it all out loud. There are things in the manuscript – factual errors – which mean the manuscript couldn't have been written at the same time as the *Looking Glass* book."

"OK," said Azzopardi. "Let's include this man in our list, even if his death does look like suicide. After all 'being suicided' is an assassination method in secret services the world over. An apparent suicide by jumping from a flat window even has a name in the Service

– *defenestration*." Azzopardi went back to the board. His hand with the chalk hovered over the list of names. "Who was this unfortunate academic?"

"Sir Rob Willett," said Power.

Azzopardi wrote WILLETT and: Manuscript – Hanging, on the board.

"This . . . this whole case," Azzopardi pointed at the names on the board with his chalk. "This is all about the transmutation of things."

"It's all 'for the love of money'," said Lynch. "That's not hard to work out."

Azzopardi nodded, but seemed not to rise to Lynch's implied criticism that he was stating the obvious. "Let me explain. The Island is like an alchemist. The Island itself transmutes things into gold." He chose an empty blackboard and drew an outline of Sicily north of an outline of Malta and wrote 'Sicily/EU' upon it, and south of Malta he drew the coast of North Africa and labelled it 'Africa/Rest of the World'. Then he began drawing arrows and cashflows all over the map, for instance Azzopardi drew two arrows to and from Sicily and Malta and labelled these 'Euros'. He drew a little building on Malta which he labelled 'casino', and small boats and planes plying between Malta, Turkey and an area he labelled 'the Maghreb'. He drew arrows around the boats and planes describing the flow of cannabis, and prescription drugs.

Dr Power followed the complexities of the diagram for a while, but there came a point when his mind's eye blurred and he could not process any more of the detail. This felt similar to the feeling he got whenever accountants or financial advisers tried to explain mortgages or pension law to him. Power looked over at Lynch, who seemed to be following intently, and envied him his comprehension of Azzopardi's thesis.

Power thought it would help if he reviewed what he had learned so far to consolidate his own understanding.

Azzopardi had explained that Malta's entry into the European Union was crucial and it meant there could be a free flow of Euros between Malta and the rest of the EU. Euros earned in Malta could then flow virtually unhindered all around the EU and be used to buy any commodities and services Europe could offer – German luxury cars, French chateaux, or Spanish vineyards.

Malta could be used for money laundering – for changing illegal goods and products into legal Euros.

Casinos, especially online casinos, were key to this in Malta. The Maltese legislation governing gambling was particularly lax. Dirty money could be laundered here. An oligarch on a Russian yacht sailing around the Mediterranean could arrive in Valletta harbour with dollars, roubles or other currency, and visit the casino to LOSE money in order to have it laundered for them. The casino could then use the lost stakes to buy legitimate goods, which could include anything. But these funds could equally well include other items which could be sold at profit, so possibly more drugs. Any earnings on a deal could be then paid to back to the Russians as WINNINGS. The nature of the deal, the contract as it were, was hidden behind the apparent winning or losing. The whole system relied on trust between the two parties – those 'losing' the money having to trust the Casino to process it, and also to trust the banker to hold the money for them in Euros until such time as they wished to spend it.

The laundered profit from the trades processed by the casino and held by the bankers might involve cocaine or amphetamines manufactured in labs in Rabat, or cannabis and opiates from Kasserine and Sousse in Tunisia and synthetic drugs from Tripoli. The entire Maghreb was involved in drug production – and drug consumption – as they smuggled addictive prescription drugs in – bringing in Trazodone and the like for domestic consumption whilst they sent home-grown cannabis resin out. The goods flew in and out, and dollars or whatever currency flowed back and forth as necessary. The cargo from the Maghreb might be cannabis resin or cocaine, or it could even be people smuggled in rafts. Spain had only recently deployed a surveillance system in the western Mediterranean to spot and track the transport boats and larger planes. Traffickers would use fishing vessels, helicopters and light aircraft, and would switch routes as necessary to avoid detection from the western Mediterranean to the eastern Mediterranean . . . including routes from Tunisia to Malta. Money flowed in and out of Malta, goods flowed in and out of Malta and money to pay for them flowed in an out of Malta, and Malta was now the gateway to the EU, a cog in a machine to launder dirty, criminal money that couldn't be declared. And so the Island of Malta was like a home to an alchemist turning base lead into gold. In this case The Banker was the alchemist directing the very complex flows of monies between the various parties.

Lynch surveyed the very detailed diagram that Azzopardi had built up on the blackboard in front of them and gave an appreciative nod. "I don't dispute that this is the bigger picture," said Lynch. "I can see how very clever The Banker must be. But how do you think our names," Lynch pointed to the names on the other blackboard, "SHACKLIN – MCFARLANE – FELFE – GRIEG – WILLETT, fit into all this?"

Azzopardi looked at Professor Power. For a moment Power was anxious he would be tested on the economics of smuggling, Azzopardi said, "I have some ideas about how these people fit in, but as I don't usually encounter psychiatrists in my work, and I've heard a lot about your cases, do you have any observations on these characters?"

Power was relieved the question was a little more suited to his talents He looked at Azzopardi's list on the blackboard:

SHACKLIN:	Casino – Debt – Banker
MCFARLANE:	Sicily – Bacchi – Finance – Lover
FELFE:	Banker – Wanderlust – Sannik Law Co
GRIEG:	Bursar – Reptiles
WILLETT:	Manuscript – Hanging

"If you want to put it in military terms, and this seems a fitting place to do so, as we are in the war room, Shacklin was effectively the University's second in command. I surmise he had a distant father, perhaps someone altogether too busy or successful to spend much time with his son. Shacklin was always more uncertain than he chose to appear. He would be asked to do the jobs the Vice Chancellor hated. Firing people. Tiresome inquiries into bullying. Travelling to inspect overseas Universities with teaching contracts, setting up external contracts. His underlying self-esteem was low and he sought reassurance by seeking quick gains in gambling, and the solace of as many women as he could, to bolster his ego. He was probably impulsive and always calculating how to make the money to pay off his debts.

"McFarlane is different, her insecurities are more about her sexual identity and these lead her to acquire more and more responsibility and kudos. Unfortunately, as soon as she feeds her self-esteem with more acclaim or success, her partner becomes jealous of this and acts to undermine her with violence and negativity. McFarlane is governed by an envy of position and wealth. She undoubtedly has the mathematical intelligence to succeed at being The Banker; and she could certainly co-ordinate the finances behind a crime organisation."

"And certainly she has enough family connections if she is a Bacchi as you say," said Azzopardi softly.

"But McFarlane doesn't reveal any great emotional intelligence or insight," said Power. "And you need that acuity to evaluate your enemies and sense your effect on them. McFarlane tramples over people's sensitivities and I don't think she sees how much danger she is in.

"Felfe? If he was in the Secret Service you could probably find out more about him than I can discern. I bet he has a thick file that you could access." Azzopardi raised an eyebrow. "I thought so," said Power. "Felfe was too canny to reveal anything much of himself to me. For cover, he had been wearing the mantle of a mild-mannered academic so long, that the fabric of it had grown into his skin. If he had been a little more forthcoming, then maybe we could have helped him more." As he said this Power felt a pang of guilt. After all it was Power who had cut short the lunch at the Grosvenor where Felfe might well have asked for his help."

He turned his observations to the bursar next.

"Grieg? Grieg is an obsessional, dried husk of a man. Whatever he is defending inside in terms of a personality is guarded behind an impregnable psychological defence system of behavioural rules. He is an anankast. I hesitate to say he is on the autistic spectrum, as the term is so misused these days that it has lost its currency. He is a man beset by guilt. Would he have the strength to commit any misdemeanour, such as keeping banned snakes? He literally punishes himself with hair shirts. If he is late to a meeting he punishes himself." Power gestured to the map with the flows of dollars and euros and drugs on it. "Although he probably could master the financial aspects of such a scheme, could he kill to protect the scheme?"

Azzopardi smiled. "Let me play Devil's advocate. Maybe you have noticed his guilt, and think it only concerns his petty latenesses. And you, therefore, judge it inappropriate as his guilt sounds immense. What if it is an appropriately matched reaction to what he knows he is responsible for?" He pointed to the chalkboard and the mechanism upon it.

Lynch shrugged. "Well, our colleague Beresford will be checking as best he can to see if Grieg has, or ever had, a black mamba in his collection."

Power began to speak about the last name on the list. "Sir Rob Willett. A friend who seemed to unravel before my very eyes," said Power. "From being an energetic, bouncing bombast of a man to a spirit soaked, divorced, depressed wreck, sleeping in his office. He was riven with anxiety about having to disclose that the manuscript he was meant to verify was in fact a fake." Power sighed. "I should have done more."

"You feel his suicide reflected badly on your professional standing? Well, wearing a hair shirt yourself certainly won't help." said Azzopardi. He patted the doctor's shoulder. "You know, suicides leave us all with guilt. And in a way – I am speaking as a Catholic in this most catholic of cities – there are only two certainties in life. Death and a mountain of guilt."

"Much depends on whether you believe in God," said Lynch. "As He promises us an afterlife and forgiveness."

"Well," said Azzopardi. "Leaving matters of Faith aside, can I thank you both for your briefing? Let's see if we can pull the pieces together and fit them with what is happening in Malta or rather in the seas around Malta.

"We haven't mentioned Savina Daidalos have we?" Azzopardi added her surname DAIDALOS to the list of names on the blackboard. "She was killed near the old Radar Station wasn't she? Somehow she was manoeuvred to the edge of the cliff and over she went. Then her battered body found its way to the mortuary in Valletta, just like Shacklin's hand. The Service had been interested in her father, and suspects that her father and brother were assassinated in England in a plane crash. That ties everything together in a way. Despite hiding behind a mask of virtue as a respected member of the community Papa Daidalos made all his money from the drug trade. He was working as part of all this," he waved to the map and his model of how the Maltese smuggling trade worked. "We have no doubt that Daidalos was working with The Banker. He and The Banker were partners and both involved in the research going on at the Radar Station. Professor Xuereb's weapons research. Well, with the Daidalos family all conveniently gone, and with The Banker still left standing, maybe we can assume that Papa Daidalos fell out with The Banker. Had The Banker used Daidalos's money, or lost it? Or perhaps Daidalos wanted to cash in his investments early and switch allegiance to another crime organisation? Did he want to bank elsewhere? Whatever it was they fell out about, it was enough to get Daidalos and son killed. And then when his daughter rolled up and knocked on the door of the Research Station at Dingli, well, that got her killed, too. She should have stayed at home in Gozo."

"Did The Banker kill her, then? Or did The Banker persuade Professor Xuereb to use his weapons on her?" asked Power.

"Whatever it was, you need to find Paul Xuereb . . . and his weapons," said Azzopardi. "Satellite imaging shows that the Radar Station has been deserted since we last met. Where Xuereb went to, nobody knows."

"It's a small island," said Lynch. "Surely someone must know."

"We don't have enough people on the ground to make systematic enquiries, there is only one of me," said Azzopardi. "We three will need to work together as a team if we are to beat this. And we all need to get something out of this. You need something and I need something, too. Which brings me to the *Wanderlust* and its role."

"I tried to track it using a program on my phone," said Lynch. "But the *Wanderlust* is too small a vessel to have to carry a transponder."

"Convenient for the *Wanderlust*, isn't it?" said Azzopardi. "A boat small enough to escape notice, but large enough to be a big source of trouble to us."

"What kind of trouble?" asked Power.

"Until we catch her in the act and impound her the exact nature of the trouble can only be guessed. I suspect her function involves three criminal activities, but we will only ever know how she works when we catch her in the act. Occasionally *Wanderlust* carries drugs or currency – ferrying them from A to B, but that isn't her main function and generally speaking, if you were to drop in on her uninvited you might not find either drugs or currency on board. You might find some nets, some evidence of work as a fishing vessel perhaps, but all that is just window dressing. There is no fishing done on the *Wanderlust*. We know she docks in Malta for only a few days a month. A vessel of her sort will usually be based in a fishing town like Marsaxlokk and she'd spend her time either in port or fishing. Have you been to Marsaxlokk? Quaint place with a fleet of small blue and yellow fishing vessels. Each one of them with that Mediterranean eye painted on the prow to ward off evil. If *Wanderlust* was a fishing vessel, she'd be in the harbour most of the time. But the only time *Wanderlust* docks is in the north – in Valletta – in the harbour at Birgu. There she is, fleetingly, a shabby little scrap of a boat with peeling paint, and sun-bleached timbers nestled between these sleek, white superyachts. Those are the vessels you get in Birgu, the yachts of billionaires – and they look huge compared to her. Imagine what would happen if they drifted – say in a storm – the huge white yachts would clamp together like jaws and crunch her into matchwood.

"Perhaps the captain thinks he can achieve all he wants on shore and be off again before anyone notices. But some people have noticed. And they have told us. Our service wouldn't usually take any notice of the information, individual acts of smuggling are not our remit. But we took notice because of Felfe's intelligence. We respected his instinct. And our friends in the harbour have noticed a pattern to *Wanderlust's* appearances. *Wanderlust* appears around the time of the full moon, which seems rather romantic, don't you think? The captain ties the boat up and heads off, returning several hours later with some packages. He fires up the engines, casts off and is away. Where he goes next, we don't know. Our eyes aren't everywhere any more."

"And what is there at Birgu for him to visit so regularly?" asked Lynch.

Azzopardi unfolded a modern, large scale map of Malta and its Islands and spread it across the plotting table. He pointed to Valletta. "We're here, approximately speaking, way down under the Barakka Gardens. If we could look south east, across the expanse of the Grand Harbour we'd see a promontory, which is the Fort St Angelo. Behind that are the streets and buildings of Birgu, which some refer to as a city, distinct from Valletta, but it's a very small and ancient one, and it has its waterfront here, where the *Wanderlust* visits. The waterfront has cafes and bars, a chandlery, and a couple of casinos. And I believe that a casino is the reason for the Captain's visits." He pointed to his diagram on the wall with its arrows describing the conversion of currencies and smuggled drugs. "That brief touch of the vessel to the shore is our opportunity to better understand the cycle."

"Then why don't you get the Customs officers to arrest the Captain and impound the *Wanderlust* when it moors at Birgu?" asked Power.

"Because our interest is not aligned to same interest of the Customs officials. Of course, ultimately, I'd like to see the Captain prosecuted and his part in the drug trade finished, but . . ."

"Ah," said Power. "You're after the bigger fish. If you let them run their business they will lead you to the bigger fish."

"Not that either, really," said Azzopardi. "No, I'm far more interested in what *Wanderlust* does for the other twenty-nine days of the month. Any trafficking the *Wanderlust* does is its secondary function. And really, any drugs the *Wanderlust* ferries are not our main focus. The *Wanderlust* is something quite new and much more special. You will have heard of offshore banking, the preserve of the rich to hide their funds, legally, from the tax man? You will be aware how very lucrative it can be for all concerned? Offshore banking goes on in physical places like the Turks and Caicos and Panama. Hold on to that thought. Now, you may remember in the twentieth century that there were ships in international waters who ran radio stations without official broadcasting licences."

"Radio Caroline and Radio Atlanta, I recall," said Lynch. "They were called pirate radio stations," said Lynch.

"Well remembered," said Azzopardi. "Now I'll tell you what I suspect *Wanderlust* really is. It spends most of its time out in International Waters; *Terra nullius* or *Mare Librum*, if you like your Latin. As the United Nation says 'No state may validly purport to subject any part of the high seas to its sovereignty.' And so, as long as the *Wanderlust* doesn't spend more than a day or so in the national waters of a country it can go an acting as its does as a *floating*, offshore bank."

"A bank? You said it's practically a wreck," said Lynch. "Who'd use a bank like that?"

"It might look like a wreck, but that's just *Wanderlust's* disguise. It's structurally sound. You don't need a network of flashy offices and chief executives to function as a bank, not this kind of bank. If you have money that is not yet laundered you need somewhere to store it. The bank merely has to be connected and trusted, to loan money and charge interest. It doesn't have to look like a bank just hold those dark funds for people who can't use legitimate banks. *Wanderlust* is a kind of offshore bank, but instead of being in the Marshall Islands or Vanuatu, it moves in International waters, outside any jurisdictions, outside the EU. Out there in international waters it roams free and only tethered to this world via satellites and virtually plugged into the dark web. Instead of being a pirate radio station, this is a pirate bank. Although with minimal crew and much less 'Ahar, me hearties' about it.

"The *Wanderlust* has its old fishing gear as a decoy. But it also has an array of state-of-the-art satellite dishes, out of keeping with its shabby cover. We think its cabins are full of computer servers. Infra-red imagery taken of Birgu harbour suggests those cabins are very warm, despite the industrial standard air conditioning that has been added to the fishing boat.

"For a few weeks now, GCHQ have been attempting to trace and lock on to the boat's signals. We are keen to track the transactions and crack the cryptography, but they simply can't get a hold on what is going on. These are the best cryptographers in the world. They describe the technology as 'slippery'. So that's why my employers are vitally interested in *Wanderlust*. The lives The Banker has taken, the sums of dirty money involved and drug trafficking – all of these things are of secondary and minimal importance to them – compared to the prize of the cryptography involved in the *Wanderlust's* servers.

"Five years ago, a man called Stefan Konst published an idea for cryptographically securing chains of information. It's very technical, but you can pass information along chains without individuals in that chain being able to decrypt the information, even though they are passing all the information on. It is brilliant stuff and a key step towards implementing a whole new digital currency described by a man called Szabo a few years earlier. He called it 'bit gold'. It looks like The Banker has either invented this or has invested in the research that yielded the technology. And we want those servers."

"We are part of some larger game, then?" asked Lynch.

"I will help you achieve what you want, as far as I can," said Azzopardi. "But I can only do that in return for your help. Can I count on you?"

Power and Lynch looked at each other. Power nodded first and then Lynch spoke for both of them. "If it gives us the identity of The Banker and solves our case, then tell us what we have to do."

Azzopardi reached into a briefcase and withdrew a bottle of *Ledaig* single malt and three glasses. He grinned. "To seal the deal," he said. He poured a goodly glass of whisky for each of them and they toasted to their work together. "The Banker is no fool and The Banker's investments are shrewd – cutting edge technology – whether it be sound weapons or secure transaction cryptography. We need The Banker's encryption system – it is vital to our own operations and we don't want anyone else to have it. We will try to assist you with any details that will help prosecute The Banker, whoever they are, but it is the technology behind his transactions we want – we believe this is all on the servers, and they are on that shambolic boat. And I must warn you not to underestimate this operation. The boat may look a wreck, but that is a deception. Who knows what defence systems it has? We know that The Banker is not afraid to protect himself. So there is a real risk involved – you need to know that."

"Regrettably," said Power, 'there is always a risk to Life."

"Are we agreed to be allies, then?" asked Azzopardi. Emphasising the word 'allies' and gesturing around them to the Allies' war room.

"Agreed. Let's go to war, then," said Lynch. "What's our plan?"

Chapter Twenty-Four

Thou ominous and fearful owl of death.
Shakespeare, Henry VI, Part One

The old man with the long, grey hair sat on deck basking in the afternoon sun. He had brought a foldaway chair and, content to sit on this, he looked down over the deck railings at the water. The water of Birgu harbour was still, rather like a deep blue jelly. Every now and then the surface wobbled and glittered. He wondered what such a deep blue jelly might taste like if it was conceived as a dessert. His stomach rumbled. He had missed his lunch hurrying to the harbour at the urgent behest of Dr Power. Here he sat, alone, on board the *Wanderlust,* waiting for its captain to return.

His mind journeyed back through the years and settled on the memory of a child's party. There had been jelly there too; green, glistening and transparent. Mrs Xuereb had invited him. The party had been in the yellowed kitchen of her flat. He remembered the windows open to the blue sky, the serried lines of her washing draped and drying outside, facing the balconies of the apartments opposite. He had thought twice before attending; did he want to spend a frenetic hour surrounded by noisy children, running and jumping and shouting to birthday music? He was the boy's tutor after all. Was it seemly to attend a pupil's birthday party? But he had no wife, no children himself, and the boy was, perhaps, the nearest he would ever get to having a son of his own. When he arrived at the party, however, and was standing on the yellow and black squares of the kitchen lino he heard the immaculate quiet of the apartment and realised that he, the boy's tutor, was the only invited guest to Paul Xuereb's thirteenth birthday.

Memory visited, considered, mulled over and relinquished back into the vaults of his mind, Ramon Calleya, in the present, on board the *Wanderlust* awaiting the Captain, adjusted his broad-brimmed hat, and peered over the top of his sunglasses along the dockside, hoping to see the absent mariner. Occasionally Ramon reached into his pocket for a Maltese Water Biscuit and munched on it. He tried not to glance over to Dr Power who was sitting outdoors in the shade of a café awning, sipping a lemon pressé, and affecting to read the *Times of Malta*. Ramon kept Power on the periphery of his vision. He did not wish to break Power's cover. Power's pale skin and general demeanour marked him out as a probable tourist, either English or German. Ramon looked like an Islander, born and bred, which he was. And that was why Ramon was sitting where he was in the blazing sun, while Power was sipping a pressé in the shade. Ramon sighed, and accepted his lot with good grace. Without volunteering to do the job himself, Azzopardi had insisted that a Maltese should wait for the Captain. If Lynch or Power set foot aboard the *Wanderlust*, the Captain would immediately be suspicious. He would, in due course, be disgruntled that anyone should board his vessel in his absence, but Ramon could at least put forward a plausible cover story and offer it in that near – Tunisian Arabic that the true Maltese use as their native language.

Ramon had to keep Power at the edge of his vision for a signal as to what he should do. If Power got up and walked away, then Ramon knew he too had a cue to disembark and walk away, without encountering the Captain. But Power was still at the café, pretending interest in the gossip pages of the *Times* and so Ramon must stay, and if the Captain returned, attempt to charm him and delay his departure.

Ramon had already explored the boat as much as he could, without actually breaking and entering. The Captain had locked the cabin doors, and only the deck was accessible. He had explored the deck fore and aft, taking in the masts and furled sails, the stored nets and folded outrigger booms. The overall air of the ship was of casual neglect. The paint on the cabin doors was peeling, the marine varnish on the taffrail was wizened and crinkled with the sun. On peering through a porthole into the wheelhouse Ramon could make out two navigation charts. One was of Gozo and Comino, the two nearest islands, and the other was of the island of Pantellaria, and the nearby Tunisian coast. He noted that the wheelhouse had a range of state of the art communication equipment including two large, curved computer screens that belied the boat's down-at heel exterior. Ramon was a curious man, and if the cabin doors had been unlocked he might have risked a look inside the cabins, but these had whitewashed windows, precisely to prevent such snooping as Ramon was engaged in. Lynch had specifically warned him not to explore the boat, because of the potential danger. And so Ramon, feeling that he had probably pushed the boundaries further than Lynch had wanted, sat in the sun and waited for the arrival of the Captain or Power's signal from the shore.

Dr Power tried to make his citron pressè last by giving it only an occasional small sip. He evinced an air of calm detachment as best he could. He had been instructed by Azzopardi as to how a service operative might behave in the field, but Power was finding it difficult to exude nonchalance when he was eking out a single drink in a café without anything more than a newspaper to occupy him. Azzopardi had briefed them all, and supplied hardware that they could use, but he declined any personal involvement in the field. His superiors could conscience only so much intervention in their investigation, he said, and besides, this was a relatively simple matter he was sure they could manage without him. Dr Power was less confident. His assigned task was to wait onshore for the return of the Captain and only to intervene if there was a sign that a confrontation was developing between Ramon and the Captain on the boat. Power thought a confrontation inevitable as Ramon had made himself at home on the rear deck of the *Wanderlust* and was clearly trespassing. Power glanced at the dowdy vessel again. The contrast between the *Wanderlust* and the sparkling white yachts on either side was marked. The *Wanderlust* had salt encrusted windows, and split grey woodwork, naked unless covered by a few residual patches of marine varnish, crinkled with the *craquelure* of a decade's decline. There was an air of decay and abandonment. The cast nets, made of hemp and flax, with their cork and lead weights looked tangled and partially rotten. Power noted the traditional Mediterranean sea vessel's eye on the portside bow, a crude depiction of eye of Osiris. The large black pupil of the eye seemed to be looking accusingly at him, which rendered Power vaguely uneasy. He wondered about the other eye to starboard and what that was looking at.

The scuffed hull sat low in the water and Power imagined that there were heavy computer servers in the cabins, causing the water displacement. He suspected that despite the cosmetic and deliberate scruffiness of the deck, the *Wanderlust's* hull was nautically sound, watertight, and only recently overhauled. If Power could only remember his A level physics he might while some time away calculating, scribbling on a napkin, what the mass of the servers might be, the displacement of water, and the average density of the boat. The mathematics was too daunting however. On the port side he could not see the antenna and satellite dishes, but Azzopardi had assured them that the apparently decrepit *Wanderlust* was equipped with the very latest communications equipment.

Power stole a glance over at Ramon with his long gray hair and rumpled appearance. He seemed content and relaxed in the sun. Lynch and Azzopardi had been eager to use the old man as a decoy – he didn't look at all like a tourist, a policeman or a customs official. He was indisputably, an Islander. Power had been mildly surprised that Ramon had been at all enthusiastic to be included in the endeavour, but he was. The only reward he begged for, was to be allowed to see his errant pupil, Paul Xuereb, if he was ever located. Lynch and Power wanted to interview Xuereb in depth, as he might know something of Shacklin's fate. Ramon's motivation was perhaps to counsel and redeem his lifelong pupil and colleague.

The immediate aim of Ramon and Power's joint enterprise on the *Wanderlust* and the Birgu waterfront was to delay the Captain on his return in order to allow Lynch sufficient time to finish his own separate task. If he could complete his task before the Captain's return he would signal Power, and Power would walk away from the café, and at this juncture Ramon would also know he could disembark and slip away.

The level of citron pressé in his glass was getting rather low, and Power had spent almost forty minutes at the café under a broad yellow awning advertising CISK. He was acutely aware of how unusual he might appear, sitting alone at the white table, behind glossy black sunglasses. Questions assailed him. He wondered about ordering a sandwich and regretted not bringing the book he was reading by Eric Ambler, rather than a newspaper to read.

At the back of his mind he then pondered what he would do if the Captain became violent with Ramon. How would he intervene? He wondered whether to phone home and, determined on this course of action, reached into his pocket for his mobile and rang Laura. She answered, sounding bright.

"Carl! How are you doing? Working hard or lounging in the sun?"

"Doing a bit of both, really. I'm watching out for someone at the waterside here in Birgu, and I'm sitting in the sun."

"Can't be bad," she said. "Jo and I are just off to the cinema. He deserves a treat, I think."

"I'm sorry not to be there," said Power, genuinely remorseful. "I'll be back in a few days. I hope we are getting close to a solution. What are you going to see?"

"The *Spongebob* movie," said Laura.

"I wanted to see that," said Power, sounding mildly petulant.

"Well, we deserve a treat. If I know you, you're probably in a café somewhere . . ."

"How well you know me," said Power.

"Well, we might buy you a packet of Maltesers at the cinema and airmail it to you," said Laura. "Here's Jo."

Power grinned as his son came on the line. "Dad, Dad, we're going to the cinema to see *Spongebob*."

"I'm very jealous," said Power. "I hope it's good."

"I've got a joke for you, Dad. It's about a film. You know the film *Dracula*?"

"I do," said Power.

"What was the sequel called?"

"I don't know," said Power. "*The Bride of Dracula*?"

"No, no," Jo chuckled. "It was Nosfera2." Power groaned. "Bye, Dad." Jo handed the phone back to Laura.

"I like that joke," said Laura. "Well, we'd better be off, enjoy your café!"

Power ended the call. A waiter stood near his table, eyeing the depleted drink meaningfully. "Can I get you anything else, sir?"

"Erm, another pressé please and . . . and a pizza al funghi."

"Of course, sir," he said, and whisked away.

Power looked up just in time to see the Captain of the *Wanderlust* returning, he had nearly missed him whilst he ordered pizza! He was carrying a vast purple rucksack on his back, something that he had not been wearing when he left the boat. He had come from the direction of the casino, just as Azzopardi had predicted and he was nearly upon them, just fifty or so yards away. Ramon had glimpsed the Captain too, and Power saw him getting to his feet in readiness, and brushing biscuit crumbs from his jacket.

The Captain strode determinedly up the gangplank and stood on deck glaring at Ramon. He stood in such a way as to deliberately block any exit down the gangplank for the old man and demanded, "Who are you? What are you doing on board my boat?"

Ramon smiled sheepishly, and tried to look deferential. To him, the man in front of him looked too thin to be a Captain. He wore a blue linen cap, was unshaven and dressed in a white T shirt and baggy blue trousers. His pale green eyes looked watery, like an old man's, but he was scarcely thirty years of age. Overall, his forlorn appearance radiated such a persistent melancholy that his anger and alarm at seeing a stranger on his vessel were reverting to his default depression.

Ramon noticed that the Captain's right hand was unconsciously searching his belt and trouser pockets for the weapon he presumably usually carried.

"You shouldn't be on here, this isn't a pleasure vessel taking people round the harbour. Those tour boats are at the opposite end of the waterfront. Can you get off now?"

"Do I look like a tourist?" asked Ramon. "I'm sorry to alarm you though, I didn't mean to intrude . . ."

"But you have, nevertheless." The Captain eyed the old man's appearance and could see Ramon was right – he was no tourist. And he didn't look like a police officer either, even an undercover one. He wasn't dressed smartly enough, and what was he doing with that long hair?

"I'm Ramon Calleya, from the University."

"A professor?" The Captain could imagine this old one as an academic.

"Yes, yes. A professor of physics and keen astronomer. I also host a television programme about the night sky and the stars. I'm the presenter. Have you seen it? On TVM2."

"I don't watch the television. I catch fish. No reception on here." The Captain was curt, but at least his hand had stopped searching for a weapon to use.

Ramon noted that he spoke Maltese, but his accent was unfamiliar. Maltese was not his native tongue. Ramon smiled as innocently as he could, deciding the Captain needed a deal of reassurance. Ramon knew that if he pointed out that this flaky old fishing tub had the latest satellite receivers, this would not reassure him.

The tidbit of information about the fact his unwanted guest had a TV programme had sunk in, for the Captain now appeared to mellow his response. "Mr Calleya, let me stow this and we can talk about how I can help you." He shrugged off the heavy rucksack and stowed it in the cabin, locking the door carefully behind him. He returned to the deck and gave Ramon the thinnest of smiles.

"I am Captain Christoforou," he offered a moist and bony hand to shake. "Tell me please, before you leave, what interest can a Professor of Physics have in the *Wanderlust?*" There was a hint of a threat behind the words.

Ramon assumed a beatific demeanour to reassure the Captain. The surname he had given – Christoforou – if correct, was Cypriot, and this explained the singular accent he spoke in. "I am always looking for items of local interest for my programme. I saw this Maltese fishing boat here, sandwiched between the foreign millionaire's yachts."

"Billionaires," the Captain corrected him. "There are at least two Russian billionaires moored at Birgu today, and an American who owns most of the Internet."

"Well, you see the contrast," Ramon waved a hand towards the glossy white superyachts and then pointed at the worn wooden deck. "Local working vessels and the playthings of foreign billionaires, just lying idle in case their masters choose to pay them a visit. I know where the real beauty lies. In tradition, yes? In hard work, yes?" The Captain nodded thoughtfully and Ramon pressed on, "Tell me Captain, how old is the *Wanderlust?* What is her story?"

"Her past is a matter of public record. Your researchers can check the shipping registers. She was built in 1922 in Bergen to carry salt fish along the Norwegian coast. Then she was sold and sold again. She was once a floating brothel off Casablanca, and ran contraband on the North West coast of Africa. She smuggled guns to the Angolan rebels in the Civil War. She used to be called the *Flora* and took cargo and fish from Valletta to Gibraltar. She's led a varied life."

"She's almost a hundred years old," said Ramon.

"Not quite," said the Captain.

"But she's lasting well? Although she has a new hull."

The Captain frowned. This man was too observant for his taste. "She has had new planking. She has a double skinned hull. The waters of the Mediterranean are warm and the worms attacked the old oak timbers. Her owner extended her life by giving her a new hull."

"Expensive work," said Ramon. "Who *is* her owner?"

"You ask me all these questions, but I ask you, what is your interest? What do you want of me? We have a tide to catch, as they say."

Ramon could sense the Captain's rising irritation. "We want to celebrate stories about Malta, first and foremost. I wondered if we might make a feature of the *Wanderlust* on the programme – perhaps broadcast live from out on the waters. Away from the light pollution of Valletta you will have a very clear view of the Milky Way."

"If it was up to me, maybe," said Captain Christoforou. "But the owners would never agree. I work to their timetable. A strict timetable, you understand. And now, I must ask you, again, if you would leave. We are sailing now."

"Of course," said Ramon. The Captain was resolute. Whatever Ramon might say otherwise could only lead to a scene. Lynch had expressly said that there must be an avoidance of any conflict. "Thank you for listening to me so kindly." He fished in his pocket for a card, brushed off the biscuit crumbs that clung to it, and smiled. "My card. Please phone me if the owners ever change their minds." And with that Ramon climbed down the gangplank and stood smiling on the concrete waterfront watching the Captain preparing the vessel to leave. The Captain glared at him and Ramon retreated politely away from the edge to the pavement near the shops. He knew Power was on his left hand side, but he did not look at him, merely sauntered off and merged into the crowd.

A moment later, Power's phone rang and he put down a slice of pizza to answer it. "Dr Power? It's Ramon. I had to leave – I didn't come over to you, because I didn't want the Captain to see us together."

"Thank you for your help, Ramon," said Power. "Did you learn anything?"

"The Captain is called Christoforou, he's from Cyprus, I think. He usually carries a gun in his waistband or pockets. When he first saw me he reached for it. He didn't have it because he'd been onshore, in public. But I'm sure he usually carries one. You'd better bear that in mind, Carl. And also, although I only saw the Captain . . . I'm not sure he is alone on there. I felt that there was at least one other person on board. That's just a feeling – that I was being watched. Maybe being watched remotely on CCTV? But watched by someone all the same.

"In the wheelhouse, there's a range of computer equipment that a simple fishing boat would never have. And on the table there were large-scale maps of Gozo and Comino. Do you think that's where Paul Xuereb might be?"

"I don't know," said Power. "But we need to find him."

"If you trace Paul tell me, please, I beg you. I need to talk to Paul. Counsel him. He shouldn't be mixed up in this."

Power thanked Ramon for being on deck to stall the Captain's departure and put his phone down. The *Wanderlust* was pulling away from the stonework of the pier as the white-hot afternoon sun dimmed and became the apricot glow of the evening sky. Power watched the boat chug its way into the broad, open harbour and then, gaining speed, head off towards open waters.

Lynch appeared quite suddenly, as if by some enchantment. He pulled out a chair opposite Power and sat down grinning, pleased to have completed his allotted task in the afternoon's mission. Lynch reached over and took one of Power's remaining slices of pizza. "To save you from yourself!" he said, and munched away contentedly for a few minutes.

"Would you like a drink, as well as my pizza?" asked Power. Lynch nodded and Power ordered him a Cisk lager.

"Were you successful?" asked Power

"Yes, thank you," said Lynch. Droplets of harbour water dripped from Lynch's hair onto the linen table cloth. His shirt and shorts were patchily damp. Lynch had only just flung on some clothes after climbing up onto the dockside from the water. "An invigorating swim. I don't think I was detected. Ramon did a good job of diverting the Captain."

"Where did you manage to put the transponder?"

"On the starboard side. I was worried that someone or some instrument on the yachts moored alongside would spot me. I don't think they did."

Lynch had climbed down into the clear waters of the Birgu waterfront at Power's signal from the cafe that Ramon was in position. Whilst the Captain was engaged on his errand to visit the casino in town, Lynch swam around the great white hulls of the yachts and approached the starboard side of the *Wanderlust*. He trod water whilst unwrapping the small transponder that Azzopardi had issued to them. The task was not easy, and twice he had nearly dropped the device into the waters of the Mediterranean. The small, black transponder would signal the *Wanderlust's* position wherever it sailed – as long as it remained undetected. Lynch peeled the backing off the device to expose the adhesive and reached up out of the water and gently pressed the glued side of the device to the round black pupil in the centre of the painted eye on the *Wanderlust's* bow. Lynch regarded his work with satisfaction. The transponder was firmly attached and, being black, was almost invisible unless the eye was scrutinised at close quarters.

As he was admiring the transponder on the hull, Lynch heard the Captain returning and his initial altercation with Ramon. Lynch slipped back down into the water to the sounds of Ramon's voice expertly reassuring and calming the Captain. Mindful not to fall foul of the yachts and their natural movement in the water Lynch swam warily round their hulls, anxious lest anybody start up the engines and set the propellers in churning motion near him.

"Well done," said Power, watching Lynch swigging beer. "What do we do now?"

"We join Azzopardi in the citadel, and track where the Captain is taking the *Wanderlust*."

"From what Ramon saw on the table in the wheelhouse, we need maps of Gozo and Comino," said Power.

* * *

Azzopardi and his Head of Section had been talking intermittently all morning. Azzopardi required permissions for his actions, as the Valletta station was now 'merely observational' according to the Ministers responsible. For the station to actually act required permissions from a bewildering array of folk in the Service and the Foreign Office. So many people had seemingly been consulted for this particular operation which had evolved from information supplied by Power and Lynch that Azzopardi felt he might as well climb to the rooftop of Valletta station and shout out his intentions via loudhailer to a crowd of startled locals and tourists on the streets below. Nevertheless, despite the accretion of administrative bureaucracy slowing their joint endeavour like barnacles encrusting on a ship's hull, Lynch had made genuine progress; the transponder beacon was attached to the *Wanderlust* and working. So now the next stage of the operation could begin. Azzopardi had imagined it would be a simple operation to cut out the *Wanderlust*, but he was very anxious that everything should be smooth sailing. The problem with being 'observational' and thus holding the dirty work at arms length was that he had become somewhat apprehensive of physical operations in the field. Nevertheless two undercover vessels had been requisitioned for that night, with appropriate naval staffing, and the associated costs had been minutely explained to him as being allotted alongside his name, and any loss or disaster would come with blame pre-attached. Furthermore the service bean counters were demanding that there be some 'profit' in the transaction. Azzopardi had promised them working servers, with the potential prize of access to, and learning from, a whole new encryption system. But 'why was he so sure the boats were required tonight?' his managers had asked. 'Might there not be a spectacular waste of public resources if the Captain merely took off into International Waters where he could not be followed?'

Azzopardi had answered that the Captain had that day taken on board a valuable cargo. He said he was sure the rucksack contained items of great value from the Casino, (although this was purely a guess on his part). The Captain could not endure the presence of such valuable and incriminating evidence on board his vessel for a moment longer than necessary. There would be a meeting somewhere and a handover within hours, of that Azzopardi said he was most sure. The Captain had not lingered a second more than was necessary at the docks in Birgu and would want to be free of the rucksack, whatever it contained, as soon as possible. He would not want to stay in EU territorial waters with contraband. To avoid being stopped and searched, the Captain needed to keep the boat outside in International waters. There he could safely resume offshore banking – the *Wanderlust*'s primary function.

Having given assurances to the Head of Section and GCHQ that the *Wanderlust* would imminently transfer its cargo and be vulnerable to a cutting out operation, Azzopardi watched the screens monitoring shipping round the Island with rapt attention. If the *Wanderlust* – now a flashing cursor on the face of the Mediterranean started heading westward to disappear in Atlantic waters, Azzopardi would have lost his bet with his employers, and would be watching the prospect of any future promotion sailing westward too. If, however, Azzopardi's gambit paid off, and the GCHQ got its hands on the *Wanderlust*'s servers, then his promotion was a copper-bottomed guarantee.

Power and Lynch travelled from Birgu into the citadel of Valletta to join Azzopardi there at his office. They drank Darjeeling tea and watched the icons representing shipping flowing around the Maltese archipelago. Lynch watched the flashing dot that was the *Wanderlust* in the midst of the shipping with a justifiable feeling of pride. His actions that afternoon, swimming in Birgu harbour to attach the transponder to the painted eye had rendered the invisible boat visible.

There was a frantic clutter of vessels in the Grand Harbour of Valletta, but the shipping traffic thinned out in the open waters northwest of the capital. *Wanderlust* stood in splendid isolation and seemingly static, in the sea north of St Paul's Bay.

"He hasn't found the transponder and ditched it?" asked Lynch, looking at the static icon. "It's not moving. Maybe he stuck it to a buoy or something for a joke."

"*Wanderlust* was moving until just before you arrived," said Azzopardi. "I think he's waiting until dark before he makes landfall again. Don't worry, everything is going according to plan."

Power looked more closely at Azzopardi. It was quite remarkable how pale he was for a man who claimed to be a native of Malta. Power discerned that Azzopardi usually wore a wedding ring on his left hand, but that this was not present. "Mr Azzopardi?" Power noticed the tiny delay before Azzopardi responded to his name. "You mention a plan," said Power. "Whose plan is that? The Captain's cunning plan or ours?"

"He has his scheme," said Azzopardi. "And we have ours." Power looked at him expectantly and he continued. "Which is to follow him on screen, until we have a good idea where he is making landfall. I expect he will want to transfer that rucksack of cargo he picked up today as quickly as possible. It's like a game of pass the parcel . . . but instead he wants to pass the parcel on *before* the music stops. Because if the music stops and he is caught with the parcel by EU customs, then he faces five to fifteen years in jail . . . and if he is caught by a North African regime like Libya or Egypt he faces capital punishment. And the *Wanderlust* is primarily intended as a bank, not a smuggling operation."

"Ramon said that there were maps of the islands of Gozo and Comino on the table in the wheel house," said Power. "Could the Captain be heading there?"

"Both islands are quite a bit smaller than the main island of Malta. Gozo has thirty thousand residents and about a dozen small police stations. Comino is tinier still and has only four residents and no police station! Realistically there's no-one to witness or prevent any handover of the cargo on Comino. But of course, Gozo is the island where the girl, Savina Daidalos, and her family came from."

"Do you have maps of those islands?" asked Lynch.

"Of course," said Azzopardi, and spread a pair of maps over a table top. "Here's Gozo and here's little Comino, just one and a half square miles in area."

Power pored over the map of Gozo. "Where did the Daidaloses live?"

Azzopardi consulted a database on the computer. "They had an estate overlooking the bay – near Mgarr ix-Xini. We can get you a current satellite image."

"Please," said Power. "The name you mentioned?"

"Mgarr ix-Xini?"

"Is that name Maltese? I find the language difficult to understand. It's not like Italian."

"It's a semitic language," said Azzopardi. "It has an ancestor in medieval Sicilian Arabic." Power noted the academic style of Azzopardi's answer – which was not the answer of a man about his first language – Power wondered again about this man's identity and nationality. In the meantime, Azzopardi printed the satellite image off for Power. He pointed to its position in the Southeast of the Island of Gozo. "The bay is quiet. People swim and go diving there. Once upon a time the Order of St John used it as a safe harbour for their galleys."

"So, a boat like *Wanderlust* could easily anchor there?" Power observed. "And on the Daidalos's estate nearby is there a landing strip where Daidalos could take off and land his plane?"

"There is no formal airstrip, but there is enough flat ground around the estate to land a Cessna," said Azzopardi.

Power scrutinised the satellite image of the Daidalos's estate. "How recent is this image?"

"The latest satellite pass. At most a few days old," said Azzopardi.

There was a central house with four wings, a vineyard and surrounding this, acres and acres of woods. Two large swimming pools near the house stared up at him like a pair of big, blue eyes. The lush green of the lands about the house, contrasted with the sundrenched brown land that lay beyond the periphery of the estate. "How much would an estate like this cost?"

"Well, probably tens of millions of Euros. It's quite spectacular isn't it? And as a result of supply and demand the prices are soaring. It's the kind of real estate that is being snapped up by rich Germans."

"And with the Daidaloses gone, who owns it? Who lives there now?" asked Power.

Azzopardi accessed the Maltese Land Registration Agency database. "The land registry entry has not changed in the last ten years. The Estate is still registered to Daidalos's company. But it must be empty now, abandoned?"

"If Xuereb was part of Savina's disappearance, then he may have known of the estate," said Power. "He fled from the Research Station at Dingli. Could he be at the estate on Gozo?"

Lynch nodded. 'That's more than possible. Do you think the *Wanderlust* is heading there?"

"The transponder on board will tell us. I have a team ready for tonight that I had to beg the Mediterranean Desk and head of E Squadron for. If we have the heading for *Wanderlust* we can be there almost as soon as she makes landfall. Wherever the Captain goes, we can, and will follow."

"Can we go too?" asked Lynch.

"I appreciate your help so far, Andrew, we all do, but this is too dangerous for civilians," said Azzopardi. "Placing a transponder is one thing, but boarding a vessel and taking command of it is a task for specialised operatives."

"We'd really like to help if at all possible," said Lynch. "This is *our* case after all. We've flown here precisely to finish things. Surely, we could observe the action as stakeholders, please?"

"We think that the *Wanderlust* will be a very special prize for SIS and GCHQ. And because *Wanderlust* is vital – as a floating bank – to legions of criminals to process their money they will protect the *Wanderlust* in any way they can. It's worth millions and millions to them. There *will* be a fight."

"When Ramon was on the deck meeting Captain Christoforou he thought that the Captain was well used to handling guns. And, before, when he was waiting for the Captain's return, well, Ramon didn't think that he was alone. He thought he was being watched," said Power, who didn't quite share Lynch's enthusiasm for being involved.

"I think we have more than demonstrated our usefulness," said Lynch, still grumbling.

"The Service appreciates everything you have done. After tonight the Service will withdraw and so the conclusion of the investigation will be entirely your operation, I promise you," said Azzopardi. "Our involvement ends with the seizure of the *Wanderlust*. It has been impressed upon me that we have no role in the solution of the crimes you are investigating. We have no interest in policing the illegal money and drugs trade or solving these murders. That may sound odd at first, but agencies should only operate within their limits."

Power was poring over the map of tiny Comino, tracing the coastline with his finger. He had first noticed a defence Tower set up by the Knights of St John, and an isolation hospital built by the British. Then he had fixed upon an outline of a set of buildings in the north. "What are these?" he asked.

Azzopardi moved away from Lynch and studied the map over Power's shoulder. "It's a hotel. Only open in the summer; closed at this time of year."

"It must be very quiet even in summer," said Power. "Not much nightlife to be had on this rock." Besides these few buildings he had found, the Island of Comino was barren. And then, he noticed something else on the map. Power paused in thought for a moment. He had known Lynch for years now and he could tell just how much Lynch wanted to be involved in the actual operation. "Mr. Azzopardi, if I can tell you exactly where the *Wanderlust* will land, will you promise to let us be involved tonight?"

"You can't know," said Azzopardi. "Nobody can be sure."

"Felfe has already told us where it will be," said Power. "So, is it a deal? If I tell you where – can we come along?"

Azzopardi sighed, "If you can convince me you know where the *Wanderlust* is going, *and* if you promise me that you will stay out of the crossfire, then you can come along. But we can't afford any civilian casualties, understand?"

"What have you seen on the map, Carl?" asked Lynch.

"Well, Felfe gave us three pieces of information," said Power. "The Banker, Wanderlust and what we thought was a firm of solicitors, Sannik Law Co. We found out what The Banker and Wanderlust represent, but we couldn't find any law firm of that name." He pointed to a bay on the coast of Comino. "Look here at the name of this bay."

Azzopardi read it out, "San Niklaw Bay."

"Yes," said Power. "And the Co at the end of Sannik Law Co. stands for Comino. Felfe was indicating the importance of this particular bay. Sannik Law Co should read San Niklaw, Co."

Lynch and Azzopardi stared at the map of Comino and the little blue bay with the words San Niklaw Bay in italics. "I believe you are right Dr Power," said Azzopardi. "Comino is often abbreviated to Co. I am not sure how I overlooked that, but I did. That is most helpful. I think it gives us a reasonable target for tonight's mission. And I can see why the Captain of the *Wanderlust* chose this particular island for transferring any cargo. There's a safe harbour to anchor, the land is basically unpopulated. In the winter the hotel on the coast of the bay is deserted. There is no one there to witness any landing. And that works for us too. There will be no-one to see our operatives boarding the *Wanderlust*. And they will board when the Captain leaves to make the transfer of the rucksack, which I think will be managed as a dead drop. If the transfer was just between two ships that could be done at sea, but this kind of transfer is usually made on land. If Dr Power is right about the *Wanderlust*'s destination, then the Captain will leave the *Wanderlust* in San Niklaw Bay and the transfer will be made somewhere on Comino."

"And what is a *dead drop*?" asked Power.

"It's a way of passing things along a chain, but without members of that chain getting to know each other. If they want security, say, or deniability. If they don't meet, then they can't know anything if they are interrogated, they can't for instance testify that they handed x to y if they don't know who y was. It does require trust, however. The Captain will have to leave the illegal package somewhere on Comino and walk away. That's the *dead drop*. It might be a physical transaction – he leaves something, and picks something else up. Like a trade of money or drugs. Or it maybe he leaves goods for some payment that's already been done on-line. Anyway, whatever it is, he leaves the illegal package somewhere on Comino. Then, shortly after, maybe minutes or an hour or so, the person who is the other link in the chain comes to pick up the package. They never meet. That's the system we think will be in play."

"It does require a lot of trust," said Power. "To leave a valuable cargo unattended and walk away. What if someone else picks up the package?"

"Then woe betide them. That would be very unwise," said Azzopardi. "But seriously, what are the chances that the package will be interfered with – in the dead of night – on an island with only three inhabitants?"

"I see," said Power, thoughtfully. He was still thinking of Ramon's warning that there might be other armed men on board the *Wanderlust* besides the Captain.

"So, knowing that there may be some danger, and despite my warnings, are you still intent on joining us tonight?" asked Azzopardi.

"Of course," said Lynch.

Azzopardi looked at Power who had remained silent. Power nodded, trying to mask any wariness he felt inside.

"Well, then," said Azzopardi. "Let me brief you on the operation and how I think you can help tonight."

* * *

That night at 11 p.m. Lynch and Power were picked up from the Grand Harbour in Valletta by the Archer class patrol vessel, HMS *Pursuer*. Azzopardi accompanied them on board to a point a few hundred yards off the Southern coast of the Island of Comino. The sky was an inky blue, pierced by the light of a steely grey moon that was only obscured occasionally by the scudding shadows of low-level altostratus clouds.

"Could be rain in the early morning," said Azzopardi. He handed them each a bundle of night operation clothing, and equipment for the mission.

Engines now disengaged; the *Pursuer* waited still in the waters off Comino. Here, the Southern coast was made up of corraline limestone cliffs intermittently pitted by deep caves. The *Pursuer* anchored and watched the GPS navigation screens for signs of the *Wanderlust*'s movements. For Azzopardi time stood anxiously still; the moment of his career hung on the actions of Captain Christoforou. At last Azzopardi found he could let out a justified sigh of great relief as the *Wanderlust* began to venture south towards the Northern Coast of Comino. The first part of his gambit had paid off. Power had successfully predicted the course that *Wanderlust* would take.

The SBS officer in charge of the commandos on the *Pursuer* had taken a dim view of 'civilians' being involved even as observers on the mission, and he would only accede to Lynch and Power playing a minor role after Azzopardi had employed all his persuasive skills. Accordingly, after a wintry ten minutes' briefing by the Commander, whilst they were surrounded by a group of silent commandos in night camouflage cradling HK33 assault rifles in their arms, Lynch and Power were put into a Zodiac inflatable launch and directed towards a semicircular notch in the coast called the Crystal Lagoon or, the unpronounceable L-Ghar ta Bla Saqaf, in Maltese. The *Pursuer* said its silent goodbye to the inflatable, weighed anchor and sailed guardedly round the periphery of the tiny island towards San Niklaw Bay, all the while seeking to remain out of sight of, and undetected by, the *Wanderlust*.

The island would now be bathed in the darkness of Mediterranean night, but for the moon and the stars shining bright in the heavens above, so that the rocky coast was blessed with a pale blue sheen of light. The waters were still and almost silent, and the noise of their outboard motor sounded perilously loud. As they entered the steeply rock-walled waters of the Crystal Lagoon, the throbbing noise of the engine bounced and echoed off the stone enclosure of the inlet. Lynch cut the motor and proceeded to row quietly towards the shore. The water gently lapped and splashed about in the lonely Lagoon. On board the *Pursuer* Lynch had felt their presence was keenly resented. He had felt obliged to point out to the SBS commander, that he, Lynch, was a senior police detective of many years' standing. Nevertheless, they had been sidelined, marooned here in a bay that might see them insulated from any action. And Lynch yearned to be at the centre of things, in the thick of the action, and riding the excitement of the present. Power on the other hand had felt increasingly wary through the evening and noticed he was holding his breath anxiously, and uncomfortably so. The boundary of the Lagoon here was, for the most part, a craggy wall of rock, which neither of them could begin to climb, but in one place the rock dipped down and there was a horizontal slab that offered somewhere both to moor and to clamber onto, allowing them a brief purchase on the Island's edge.

There was a rusty iron ring set into the rock and Lynch, being the most practically gifted of the pair, used two ropes, from the bow and stern respectively, to tether the launch to the land.

"Have we decided who is going and who is staying with the boat?" Lynch asked in barely more than a whisper.

Power looked around the dauntingly high walls of rock that bounded the obsidian-black waters of the Lagoon. The night-time rendered the cliffs ominously forbidding. He didn't relish the idea of waiting here. At some point, if Azzopardi was right about the Captain making a dead-drop of his cargo, the men who were picking up that cargo would have to arrive on the Island. Although the SBS Commander had suspected they would use a more open bay like Santa Marija, no one was quite sure. Any boat entering the lonely Crystal Lagoon where they were now would undoubtedly take exception to Power and Lynch being there. The only alternative task on offer to Dr Power was to wait inland by the isolation hospital, and maintaining his distance, keep an eye out for the arrival of the Captain. When the Captain was sighted by Power in the middle of the Island, the Patrol Boat could begin the cutting out operation and extract the *Wanderlust*, whilst the Captain was occupied onshore. This precaution would reduce the risk of a firefight and associated casualties.

Lynch could see his friend's discomfort over making a decision, and chose for him. "I'm all right staying here," he said. "I will guard the boat for us both. I'm perfectly capable of defending our means of retreat." He took a Naval issue Glock 19 from his waistband. "They gave me this," he said. "But if you would rather carry it, you're welcome?" Power shook his head vigorously. "Then, I'll be waiting right here when you get back. Have you got the PNG – the night vision goggles – and the radio?'

"Yes, mother," said Power.

And so it was that Dr Power clambered out of the inflatable and onto the flat rock, which was still warm from the day. The waters of the lagoon were calm and he was pleased he had not fallen clumsily into the sea on transferring himself from the launch to shore. He waved a silent goodbye to Lynch, and began to scramble his way upwards, following the craggy path from the bay to the headland.

Power walked north and within several metres of the cliffs, his view of lagoon and the boat had disappeared. Power looked around to try and discern a marker in the environment to pinpoint this spot for his return, but beyond the tufts of dragon-tongued aloe eking out an existence in the dusty grit of the Island, there was no landmark here.

Power reasoned that on such a small island he could always navigate a way back to the lagoon by the stars, or just by following the coastline. The constellation of Orion was overhead and he fixed it in his mind's eye against the landscape. The three stars of Orion's belt, Alnitak, Alnilam and Mintaka, were set just over the Lagoon. Power walked south-east, treading softly on a meagre carpet of vegetation that closely covered the ground. As the soles of his feet fell on the plants the scent of cumin floated up on the air. The island of Comino is named after the cumin plant and clouds of its balmy, warm aroma wafted around him in the night as he stole towards the low, flat buildings that were the ruins of the deserted isolation hospital. Power felt totally alone. Somewhere ahead in the night, beyond the ruin of the hospital, was San Niklaw Bay, and *Wanderlust,* if it was not already there, would soon be entering in the waters of the Bay. As he crept along Power rehearsed in his mind what he might say if he was challenged by anyone he encountered on the island. Azzopardi had advised that Power and Lynch share the same cover story. Power, now on the Island, was to say he was a birdwatcher. The Island was a well-known bird sanctuary, with dozens of species like shearwaters and skylarks. Power rehearsed his lines. He was a birdwatcher who was lost, possibly he had been marooned on the Island, and was searching for the boat and the local fisherman who had arranged to take him back to the mainland. He even knew what nocturnal bird he had been seeking to find, an owl, called the Scops owl. In his turn, Lynch, now guardian of the inflatable, was to say, if he was challenged by smugglers, that he was waiting for a fool of a birdwatcher who had failed to turn up at the appointed place and time.

Power felt the nature of the ground change beneath his feet and become more solid. He had found an old road, its surface largely submerged beneath waves of sand, blown there on the breeze. Its surface was infinitely easier to traverse than the scrub, and once he was on the road he walked more swiftly towards the ruins. Variously the building had served as army barracks, as a fever and plague hospital, as prisoner of war camp, and still later as a school. Now the sandstone walls stood empty and peopled only by the drifting ghosts of the long departed. The various elevations of the hospital were punctuated by rows of rounded arches, which opened on to the corridors and quadrangles within. The arches stared at Power like sunken orbits, in a pale, skull-coloured wall.

There were very few buildings on Comino that Captain Christoforou might visit to make any dead drop. Two had been assigned to Power to watch – the hospital and the tower. If the Captain of the *Wanderlust* dead-dropped his cargo anywhere, the hospital, or the solid, square-built tower a few hundred yards away, might be candidates. The forty-foot tower, with its twenty-foot thick walls had been built by the Knights of Malta as one of a series of towers across Malta and the Islands – a chain of towers, permanently manned, that would set signal fires if a fleet of the Moors' ships should ever re-materialise on the open turquoise seas. The lit beacons would transmit a call to arms to the Grand Master in Valletta, and he would send forth a countering fleet of ships and Knights to trounce the Moors. In those times Comino had been a place to exile errant Knights. Earlier still, in the thirteenth century it had been a place of exile for the prophet Abulaifa. He endured years of solitude on the Island and wrote his Kabbalistic texts in confinement. Power found a group of bushes nestling under an Aleppo pine tree. After ascertaining that he could see both hospital and tower from this vantage point, he crouched down amongst the foliage. From here he could see any man approaching these two buildings from the northwest; the direction of San Niklaw Bay.

And so Power hunkered down, seemingly at the crossroads to everything; the answers to the riddle of the *Wanderlust*, the answers to the deaths at Allminster, and the answers to the murders on Malta.

He wondered what forces contrived to bring him here – to a place and a time where he could very well lose his life. How had he arrived at this particular moment, when he could be sitting at his own hearth – at home with a partner who was bearing his child and a son who adored him? He wondered, 'Why do we do what we do? Why do we do that which we know is neither safe nor wise? Why do we, at some point in our lives, begin to defy the good advice of our parents? Was it perhaps to chance all? To feel the thrill of cheating death and thereafter live on borrowed time? How would this all end?' Power shuddered in uncertainty. A line of Shakespeare came back to mind from his schooldays, and crouched there, he let it play in his mind; '*Be not afear'd: the isle is full of noises, sounds and sweet airs, that fire delight and hurt not.*'

Power could smell the Aleppo pine – and focused on the tree's sweet and citrus aromas – deliberately preferring the reality of his senses, rather than his inner fears.

A shadow suddenly whirred against the night sky and settled in the tree nearby. Power looked into the branches above and saw huge eyes, set in a disproportionately small body, glinting down at him in the moonlight. The owl hooted and its fluting voice sounded as if it was saying 'oh doctor, oh doctor'.

The first Power knew of the Captain's approach was the distant sound of his running feet scuffling through the dirt. The sound travelled easily in the empty night air. Power put on his night vision goggles and saw the sturdy figure of the Captain coming over the rise, perhaps some two hundred metres away and jogging determinedly towards him. On his back Christoforou was carrying the heavy rucksack Power had seen after the Captain's return from the casino in Birgu.

Power fumbled in his pocket to feel for the radio. He had to alert Azzopardi on the patrol boat and so he silently pressed the signal button three times, as pre-arranged. This three note message would tell Azzopardi that the Captain was now inland and well away from the *Wanderlust*.

Power sank down, edging deeper into the scanty foliage by the tree, lowering his head behind some desiccated bushes and a prickly pear, hoping to avoid detection. The Scops owl had mercifully stopped hooting, and was staring out into the night at the Captain, who was nearing the ruins. Power hoped the owl would maintain her silent watch and not draw attention to their shared position.

When the Captain was perhaps only twenty metres from the Aleppo pine he veered left towards the old isolation hospital, slowing his stride to a careful walk up to one of the square entrances to the colonnades. He paused by the entrance to reassure himself he was truly alone and then disappeared within. He was gone from view for about five minutes, and then reappeared, minus his rucksack. The Scops owl in the branches above shifted and hooted tentatively, as if alerting Power to the reappearance of the Captain. The owl and Power observed thoughtfully as the Captain retraced his steps away from the abandoned hospital, to work his way northwards again to San Niklaw Bay.

All at once the relative silence of the night was broken by the staccato sound of gunfire in the distance. Power couldn't discern the exact direction the sound came from. The Scops owl on the branch above Power's head took fright and fluttered off into the darkness. Ahead, Power saw the Captain pause, apparently dithering in ambitendence. His dilemma was whether to retrieve the rucksack or to hurry to San Niklaw Bay to defend his ship and the precious servers on board. The Captain's dilemma did not last long though and he started sprinting up the rise, back towards his vessel.

Power stood up cautiously and scanned the landscape around him. He could not know how long it would be before anybody came to pick up the dead-dropped cargo. Curiosity stirred within him, and although he had been told to make his escape as soon as the Captain was sighted, he began to wonder if he had time to look at whatever the Captain had been carrying in the rucksack. The curiosity suddenly overwhelmed his natural caution. There seemed to be no-one about, and no sound nearby. There had been distant and sporadic sounds of gunfire, which Power had attributed to events in San Niklaw Bay. Perhaps, as Ramon had warned, there had indeed been other people on board the *Wanderlust* besides Captain Christoforou.

Power's inquisitiveness finally overcame any reservations. He rationalised that the hospital ruins were practically on his journey back to the Crystal Lagoon and set off towards the shadow-filled opening in the walls where the Captain had entered the old plague hospital.

Moonlight outlined his shadow on the red Mediterranean soil as he hurried to the L shaped ruin. The Scops owl had settled back on the tree just as soon as Power left the undergrowth. The owl kept its glossy black eyes on the doctor's receding shape.

Power paused at the threshold to the deserted hospital. Inside he could see a long, covered colonnade, with a stone wall on one side, bearing deeply inset doors on the right. On the left side of the colonnade were columns supporting the upper floor. Through the columns he caught a glimpse of a courtyard, with the rusted skeleton of a car and the marooned hull of a boat abandoned therein. The hull had long since tumbled from its supports and smashed like an eggshell upon the ground.

Power stepped inside, and in utter silence, used the night goggles to investigate. The Captain had not taken any steps to conceal the rucksack. It stood, propped against a pillar, straight ahead. Presumably he was assured that the tiny Island was truly dead at night and that no-one had ever disturbed any cargo he had brought here. Uncomfortably, Power began to suspect that the Captain had known the cargo would be picked up almost immediately by those it was intended for.

Power hurried over to the rucksack and tugged the top flap open to see what lay within. Despite the night vision goggles he still could not quite make out the contents in the light conditions. Power swore softly under his breath and dragged the heavy rucksack out into the starlight. In a panic, he ripped the top of the rucksack open further and picked the entire sack up by its base and emptied the contents onto the dry dust.

The bulk of the contents strewn on the ground were numerous thick wads of paper money. Power saw high denomination notes – slabs of 100 US dollars, 50 Tunisian dinar and 500 Euro notes. In addition, there were dozens of blister packs of synthetic pills. He peered at the silver backing and struggled to make out the printed name of the drug – 'Buprenorphine' – an opioid taken under the tongue. Each tablet had 8 mg stamped upon its surface, a high dose.

Power started, suddenly, at the repeated noise of gunfire. But this time the shots seemed nearer. He had to go. Impulsively he reached into his pocket and pulled out a packet of matches he had once picked up in a hotel and which had lain unused in his jacket. Now they would be put to use and fulfil their destiny. If he had given it more thought he might have reconsidered his action, but he gathered the scattered money, plastic packs of drugs and the synthetic rucksack into a semblance of a pile and, striking a match, began to light the paper money here and there. The rucksack, half buried now in the mound of paper and opioids, leapt into bright flame and burned with sudden fury. The acrid smell of burning plastic and paper stung his nostrils. It was at this point of no return that Power began to worry whether he had acted sensibly. If the intended recipients of the cargo appeared now they would surely shoot him without further question. Any protest that he was a birdwatcher lost on the island would be immediately discounted. No cover story or pretence of bird watching would explain the wilful destruction of a cargo worth hundreds of thousands of pounds. Power began to run away from the fire; back the way he had come towards the Crystal Lagoon, now desperately seeking the safety of the inflatable and his friend, Lynch.

From her perch the Scops owl gazed after Power as he ran, then turned her head to watch the bonfire, the flames glinted in her ebony black eyes. The bright orange flames danced and crackled as the paper money became an inferno that lit the stone walls of the ruins a vivid, leaping yellow.

Power kept his head down and hurried over the dry terrain following the coast, taking care not to get too close to the cliff edge. He imagined Lynch would chide him for his impulsive act of arson. A destruction of evidence, certainly, a waste of money that could have been diverted to better causes? Why had he done it? He had wanted to do something, anything, to interrupt the well-oiled gears of the criminal machine, to jam the mechanism of death, and, perhaps only for a moment or two, cause the machine to hiccup. He had seen the human wreckage of drug addiction all through his career in medicine; the people used up, chewed up and spat out by the drug pedlars. It was this relentless, regressive decay; of crime begetting more crime that Power had sought to interrupt, however briefly. Just for a moment he looked back towards the hospital. He could still see a roseate radiance cast upon the walls of the ruin.

Power ran down the abandoned road, and once more over the sweet-smelling carpet of cumin, his eyes now on the sky ahead, trying to match the starscape to the earth. He identified the stars of Orion's

Belt, Alnitak, Alnilam and Mintaka, over the edge of the world and judged that he was now back at the point where he had left the Crystal Lagoon. He bent low and crept to the edge of the cliff to look down into the circular walls of the lagoon. He knew intuitively that something was very wrong, the silence of the place around him was eerie, and the hairs of the back of his neck tingled with apprehension.

Down in the bay the sea was calm, and the waters reflected the moon above. Power's heart sank. The Zodiac launch they had arrived in should have had been the only vessel in the Lagoon. Their launch had been joined by another boat. This was a small wooden fisherman's boat; now seemingly adrift, in the bay. Power saw two figures on the boat, and both were sprawled on the wooden deck. They lay so unnaturally and so still that Power immediately understood that they were dead.

Power's attention darted back to their Zodiac inflatable. This was tied up just as before, although the boat was clearly empty. He scanned the surface of the water in the enclosed circle of the Lagoon and then the rocks and cliffs nearby.

Then Power saw it. There was another body lying on its side on the great slab of rock that he had clambered on when first they landed. The body was curled into a semi-foetal position. Immobile. He could see a dark and spreading stain on the rock and deduced that the stone around the body was slick with blood. The body was that of Lynch, his friend.

Chapter Twenty-Five

What we know is a drop,
What we don't know is an ocean.

Sir Isaac Newton

Reeling; rendered unsteady by the shock of seeing Lynch's body, Power half-stumbled, half-fell, on the slope of scree and rocks down to Lynch's body. He skirted the dark pool of Lynch's blood which glistened in the starlight. He knelt by Lynch's side. The fresh blood had that distinctive metallic smell which was both familiar and unwelcome to Power. He felt for Lynch's carotid pulse. At first he thought his friend was gone, but there was a pulse, albeit rapid and weakened by blood loss.

Dr Power passed his hands over Lynch's cooling body, inspecting him, hurrying to locate the source of his haemorrhage. There was a deep puncture hole in the inner aspect of Lynch's right thigh. The bone of the femur seemed intact however, and Power assumed that a bullet had passed through the flesh and muscle taking out the distal part of the femoral artery.

Lynch was still alive, but deeply unconscious and the blood loss so swift and severe that, unless Power acted as swiftly as he could, the wound would prove fatal.

Power thought back to his house job with Mr Charlesworth, the vascular surgeon, always lecturing him, even at the side of the operating table with a patient opened up on it, deeply sliced from groin to calf. The memory he was focused on was of his chief surgeon deftly sewing a femoral wound together and as he sutured describing the risks of femoral haemorrhage: 'Dr Power, the flow in the distal femoral artery is 100 ml/minute. That's rapid. The human body can only lose up to two litres of blood. That's death in less than twenty minutes unless you can arrest the haemorrhage.'

Power undid the leather belt of Lynch's trousers, pulled the belt out from its loops around his waist and passed it around Lynch's mid thigh, adjusting it above the gunshot wound. Using the barrel of his torch as a windlass Power tightened the belt – as hard as he could – to control the haemorrhage. Lynch moaned, and rather than being alarmed at his friend's complaint about the pressure of the makeshift tourniquet, Power was delighted to hear the noise. Lynch was still alive and his ability to groan meant he had not yet fallen into a hypoxic coma.

Power fished in his pocket for the radio he had used to signal the patrol boat about the Captain. He fiddled with the buttons on it, switching the volume on and adjusting the transmission from signal to voice. There was a crackle of static as the radio came alive. He spoke into it, "Hello? Power here. Is anybody there?"

There was an ominous dead silence from the radio. Power repeated himself, "Power here. Please respond! Is anybody there?"

"We're not having a séance, Dr Power. Azzopardi here. I hear you, over."

Power did not appreciate the momentary levity. "Azzopardi. Where are you? Lynch has been shot. He needs air evacuation now, over."

"Are you sure, over?"

"Of course I'm sure, I'm a doctor." said Power. Fear rendered his voice uncharacteristically aggressive. "He needs a surgeon in the next thirty minutes."

"The Captain of the *Pursuer* is with me, Dr Power. He has heard your emergency. He is radioing for an air ambulance as we speak. He's asking if you are both at the Crystal Lagoon, over?"

"We're by the Lagoon, yes. On the cliff edge. Lynch had company. There's a boat adrift near ours. Shots were fired. Two bodies that I can see, over."

"If Lynch has his gun nearby can you secure it? Just in case there is a third man unaccounted for? *Wanderlust's* Captain is still stranded somewhere on the Island. We saw him standing on the shore of San Niklaw Bay as we left. We're on our way round the coast to you now, with one prisoner and the *Wanderlust* under tow. We came under fire when we boarded the *Wanderlust*. Our prisoner is the on-board computer engineer, although he's not speaking at the moment. Look, Dr Power, we'll be there as soon as we can. Then you'll be safe until air evacuation. And we have an emergency medical kit with IV fluids – you can put a drip up. I'm sorry about Lynch, but technically speaking the operation has been a success, over."

"I'm glad you think so," said Power, his friend's body silent and still beside him. "Out."

* * *

Doctors would have us believe that time and surgery heal, but chance dictates whether that the tattered raiment of our bodies can be sewn back into life or sewn into a shroud. Our bodies, restored to anatomical wholeness are nothing without the vital spark some call the soul. It was, of course, Lynch who was the man of God and Power could only cling on to the hope that science afforded him. And yet, with his friend's life balanced on a needle point, Power could not resist the primal urge to pray. And time saw his prayer answered.

Ramon Calleya found Power sitting by Lynch, under a sun umbrella by the hotel pool. Despite the warmth of the morning sun, Lynch was wrapped in a blanket and looked deathly pale. He had left the University Hospital that morning, only the day after his emergency operation.

Ramon pulled out a chair, and sat down, "Good morning, Carl." He reached over to shake his hand and then turned his attention to Lynch. "Good morning, Andrew. I'm pleased to see you. Shouldn't you be resting? In bed?"

"I've had quite enough of being ill," growled Lynch.

"Lynch is a very bad patient," said Power definitively. "Not only was he shot, lost a deal of blood, and had a major artery repaired, but he has discharged himself – against all medical advice, including mine."

"I've had a transfusion of four units," said Lynch. "I'm feeling fine.

If we don't secure Professor Xuereb today he will have fled overseas. We are losing time, and Azzopardi can only help us so much. He got what he wanted with the servers from the *Wanderlust*. His battles are not our battles. Xuereb is the key to everything. He will know who The Banker is. But we are running out of time."

"You're in no fit state . . ." Power began, and then stopped when he saw Lynch's expression of irritation.

"*We are God's handiwork, created . . . to do good works, which God prepared in advance for us to do,*" quoted Lynch.

"And yet when God created the world, doesn't it say in Genesis that He Himself rested?" Ramon said softly.

Lynch nodded slowly.

"Having been shot and nearly died, you must take care of the life restored to you," said Ramon. "You must rest. If you need anything doing, *we* will do it. We will take care of anything. Just tell us what needs to be done, yes?"

Lynch assented, with a reluctant nod of the head.

Ramon asked. "What did happen to you?"

"I'm not keen on even thinking about it, let alone talking," said Lynch, looking out over the harbour.

"It might help," suggested Power.

"I can't see how," said Lynch. There was an edge to his voice.

"It would help you process the experience," said Power. "But if you'd rather not . . ."

Power turned to Ramon. "Would you like a coffee or a tea? Have you had breakfast?"

"I will take morning tea, if you please," said Ramon. There was already a silver pot of tea on the table, steaming gently, and a honey-scented pile of pastries lay neatly on a blue-rimmed dish. Ramon observed that a place had been laid for him. Following Power's gesture of invitation Ramon politely selected a sticky pastry and rested it on his plate.

Lynch decided he must have appeared uncivil to his friends. He sighed deeply, and made an effort to overcome his pain and respond to Ramon's question. "I was alone in this Crystal Lagoon place, a bay, in an inflatable, sitting there 'on guard'. It was all quiet, lonely even. I was waiting for Carl to return. The water wasn't choppy, more like a millpond, but I'm no sailor. There was this slow heaving of the water, up and down, and I began to feel a bit queasy. I made sure the boat was tied up at two points and I climbed out onto the rocks . . . so I could feel solid ground beneath my feet again. Then I heard the sound of a motorboat out on the ocean, coming closer. And I stood up to see. They suddenly appeared in the lagoon – moving quickly. As soon as they saw me, they shot. There was no warning – nothing. They didn't check who I was or why I was there. They just shot me in the thigh and I fell – half through the impact and half, I suppose, by instinct. Throwing myself on the ground. I remember the sound of the shot – it echoed and bounced off the rock walls round the Lagoon. I couldn't feel the pain then. That came after. I pulled out my gun. I was so glad I hadn't left it in the boat. And I remember I was absolutely incandescent with anger. Like it wasn't me. There was, as they say, an 'exchange of fire'. I shot them both through the head, without a moment's hesitation. And I am puzzled that I don't feel guilty. I don't feel anything. I feel nothing. And then I remember feeling dizzy. And very tired. An ache in my thigh. And then it faded away to nothing. Nothing." He paused, that was the most frightening memory for him, but he didn't want to elaborate upon his fear. "But here we are," Lynch forced a smile onto his face for Ramon's sake. "In the sun, taking tea, and eating honey pastries. Who could ask for more?"

"Who were they?" asked Ramon. "The men in the boat?"

Power spoke, "We assume they came to Comino to pick up the rucksack left by the Captain of the *Wanderlust* – it held a whole heap of cash and synthetic opioids. Where the men came from, though, and where they were going to, I don't know. Libya? Sicily?"

"What happened to the two bodies?" asked Ramon.

"I didn't get a good look," said Power. "I think the marines on the *Pursuer* took them on board. I was busy trying to find a vein in Andrew's arm for the drip. It's not easy finding a vein in the dark, especially when someone is hypovolaemic."

"Hypovolaemic?" asked Ramon.

"In shock through blood loss," said Power. "I'm sorry if I left a few bruises in trying to find a vein, Andrew."

"Nothing compared to the bruise on my leg from the surgeon," said Lynch. "It is the precise shape and size of Africa."

Ramon sipped his tea and radiated sympathy. "Maybe you should fly home and rest?" He suggested.

400

"We are on the brink of a solution," said Lynch. "We can't lose the case now."

"All right, then you can rest here and make all the plans. But leave it to Dr Power and me to confront Paul Xuereb in person."

Lynch was rousing himself to protest, but the insistent aching pain in his leg made him think better of this, and resignedly he grunted his assent. "Azzopardi has been interrogating the Captain. It sounds a very aggressive word, interrogation, but I gather the Special Service is very gentle these days. At any rate, the Captain will have fewer bruises than me by the end of the day. Nevertheless, despite the threat of a few years in an EU prison, the Captain is adamant he never met The Banker and doesn't even know who The Banker is. Azzopardi believes he is telling the truth. The Banker has been very careful to keep his employees at a distance. They can be contacted by The Banker and so be made aware of The Banker's will, they can be paid by The Banker in electronic monies once they have done The Banker's bidding, but they can never *know* The Banker."

"We can't go back to the Vice Chancellor without knowing who this person is," said Power.

"Beresford phoned me this morning," said Lynch. "He has confirmed two things. One, that there was an audit of the stocks of specimens in the Life Sciences Department. They audit the science departments every so often. To make sure the plutonium, or whatever, hasn't been lost down the back of the sofa presumably."

Ramon frowned at this flippancy. "It is a necessary thing in every University, Andrew. Some items in the collections of Departments are very costly; equipment costing millions, or artefacts that are thousands of years old."

"Or dangerous," said Lynch. "Forgive me – I didn't mean to be facetious. I was told that some reptile specimens are missing from the biology department at Allminster."

"That information sounds familiar," said Power. "I wonder why . . . was it venom that was missing?"

"Indeed it was," said Lynch. "A small collection of freeze-dried venoms dated from before the Millennium, has disappeared."

"Old venoms would be inactive," said Power. "The proteins would denature, wouldn't they?"

"Beresford checked that with the School of Tropical Medicine," said Lynch. "If the venoms were kept dry and weren't subjected to extremes of temperature in storage, then even old venoms would be fully active once they were rehydrated."

"And how good is the security in the labs?" asked Power. "Who had access?"

"Anyone who could lay their hands on an electronic University staff pass could get in there," said Lynch. "That is to say, there are two thousand staff at Allminster and a pass is easily begged, borrowed or stolen – in other words the security was less than ideal . . ."

"You said Beresford found out two things – what was the second?" asked Power.

"Beresford audited the annual leave of the senior staff at the University. When Shacklin was in Malta losing money in the casino, seeing the University folk and falling foul of a herd of pigs, Bridget McFarlane is confirmed as taking the same number of days off, and she said she was on Sicily – a ferry journey of an hour and a half or so from Valletta."

"It could be coincidence," said Power. "Did Beresford audit everyone? The Vice Chancellor included?"

"According to Beresford, the Vice Chancellor was visiting North Wales."

Power nodded. "If we could just find Professor Xuereb."

"I've known him since he was a boy," said Ramon. "If he could surrender to anyone it would be me, I hope."

"As to where Xuereb might be, it seems Azzopardi has helped us, one last time. He sent us this," Lynch unfolded a piece of paper from his pocket and laid it on the table for Power and Ramon Calleya to inspect. "It's an enhanced satellite image of the Daidalos's family estate on Gozo, latterly occupied by Savina Daidalos."

Power scanned the image of the estate with its buildings and grounds. "It's a vast place," he said. "Who inherited it after Savina died?" He peered more closely at the paper. The aerial view showed the land just outside the boundaries of the estate as parched, brown earth, dotted with scrub-like plants. The estate itself was green and lush. There were two oval swimming pools. The satellite image had captured the water in the instant it was glistening under the Mediterranean sun. The detail on the image was so good that Power could even see a couple of red and white, candy-striped sun umbrellas by the pool. There was a cluster of seven linked flat-roofed buildings surrounded by an arboretum. A thick white wall encompassed the estate, punctuated at one point by a set of gates. To the south of the enclosed land was a car park with a single vehicle parked in it.

"The vehicle in the car park is familiar," said Lynch. He proffered a second sheet with an enhanced aerial image of the car. "I last saw it parked in the compound at the research station in Dingli. It is registered to Professor Xuereb."

"He's squatting at the Daidalos's estate on Gozo then?" said Ramon.

"I believe so," said Lynch. "After Savina's murder, he, or The Banker, would know it was empty. And it would have been a perfect place to hide himself for good, had he not parked his car right where the spy satellite could see it. There are no neighbours to speak of to observe him. He's on the high ground there at Mgarr ix-Xini surrounded by scrub. No-one to rat on him. The Daidalos family was extinguished. He could have sat up there for months if need be, but we have spotted him. And I'm going to have to ask you both to pay him a visit."

* * *

The sun poured down from a cloudless sky as their ferry sailed out of Ċirkewwa. Power revelled in the sight of dolphins jumping in the wake of the ship, the black commas of their bodies clashing with the white surf of the wake and the deepest blue ocean. The salt scent of the sea spray tingled in his nostrils as a rainbow mist danced in front of Power's eyes. By his side, Ramon leant on the taffrail and hummed to himself.

"Strange that Xuereb should be so sensitive to sound, and yet make sound his life's work," Power reflected thoughtfully, listening to the thrashing sound of the churning water, cleaved by the sharp edge of the bow.

"I once showed Paul an experiment – this was when I was tutoring him at home. He would have been about twelve. I was demonstrating waves . . . we had a large, shallow bowl of water on the kitchen table. We closed the blinds of the kitchen until it was dark in there. I turned a light to shine on the water to reflect off its surface and up onto the whitewashed ceiling. I started a motor on a flat paddle that dipped up and down every few seconds onto the surface. You could look up and see the light and shade – the waves on the surface of the water, rippled on the ceiling. We discussed the physics of sound waves. He was entranced, staring at the ceiling for hours. Captivated. You could see him thinking, calculating the frequencies. I think his interest in waves, in sound waves started that day. He was transfixed. I demonstrated various things using the waves – coherence, diffraction . . . he was rapt with it all. His mother was delighted because he was so enthusiastic about something."

Thirty minutes later, when the ferry reached Mgarr, Gozo's port, Dr Power drove a hire car, a blue Renault hatchback, off the ferry. The brooding Ta' Cenc Cliffs loomed watchfully over the harbour. Ramon navigated as Power drove out of the harbour and up into the hills and towards interior of Gozo.

"You've not said much about Paul's father," said Power, "What happened to him?"

"His mother told me very little indeed," said Ramon. "You know, I think we turn left here, that sign is pointing towards Mgarr ix-Xini." Power swung the Renault round the next curve and took the dusty road off to the left. "She said that his father deserted them when Paul was a toddler. He couldn't take to Paul. He didn't recognise himself in the boy. He couldn't understand the intensity of the relationship between boy and mother and he felt . . . excluded."

"Did you feel Paul was difficult to understand, too?"

"Not at all, because we could always communicate through mathematics, and the realm of physics. That was sufficient for both of us. Once or twice I wondered . . ."

"What did you wonder?"

"Whether his mother had been altogether truthful about his father leaving. She had rather sought me out and . . . fostered . . . my relationship with the family. Just briefly, I speculated whether time had changed her so much that I hadn't recognised her from earlier in my life – had I perhaps known her before? When we were both younger and children of the hedonistic sixties? Was Paul *my* son?"

"You mean . . . ?"

He exchanged an eye-to-eye glance with Power. "I suppose it is a wishful fantasy without a grain of truth in it. Paul is not my son. I never dated his mother. I would have liked a son, once, but . . . I never got round to all that . . . sometimes I really don't know where my life has gone."

"Time just gets away from us," said Dr Power.

They were in the countryside of Gozo now, speeding through roads flanked by an expanse of sun-drenched bleak, barren earth. They were just a few miles from the Daedalos's estate.

"Your friend Lynch, his faith is so simple, refreshing, but his God is a Newtonian God set in linear time and space. We are children of the Quantum Age and we must adapt our gods."

Power frowned. "Lynch would say that God is a changeless being and our creator."

"We make reality," said Ramon. "Reality only exists, because life perceives it."

"So you and Paul bonded over physics and Paul Xuereb's métier is sound waves, sound particles. But how can sound be used as a weapon?" asked Power, hoping to first guess what awaited them at their destination. "I know there are laser weapons that focus light waves, but using sound as a weapon?"

"Waves transmit energy. Sound is a wave form. Energy can affect . . . can disrupt matter. Why should you think that sound waves are different? It's just a matter of how you package them. Take the brain, your specialty, doctor, how would you describe the brain's consistency?"

"Well," said Power, thinking queasily back to anatomy sessions in the dissection room. "I always tell medical students that the human brain has the consistency of a jelly, or a blancmange."

"Indeed," said Ramon. "Like pink and white blancmange . . . thank goodness evolution gave us a thick skull and a layer of spinal fluid between brain and bone to protect the jelly. But you must remember what happens if you shake a jelly?"

"Yes," said Power, uncomfortably. "It wobbles."

"It responds to the vibration – it carries the wave. And if you vibrate it faster, more violently – have you ever done that? What happens?"

Power slipped into a madeleine moment. "When I was six there was a family party. There was this brilliant red jelly my grandma made. Turned out from the mould and glistening on a white porcelain dish. I was asked to put it on the tea table. As I was walking from the kitchen to the dining room I thought I'd give it a wobble. Well I did, and it shimmered, so I wobbled it some more, and then more."

"And . . . ?"

"It tore apart," said Power. "Half of it flopped out of the dish onto the carpet. I looked at it, and I knew I'd never be able to scrape it up and put it back in the bowl. I wasn't popular with my grandma that day."

"Exactly so," said Ramon. "And a sound weapon can deliver exactly the right sound waves – pulse, amplitude, frequency to disrupt matter. Maybe start with 19,000 Hertz, pulsed at 81 decibels to cause discomfort, a quiet hurt, then trigger headaches. Dizziness develops next, then pain, and you know how delicate the brain is, ramp it up and you get unconsciousness; vibrate enough and you induce small haemorrhages, torn microvessels, in other words strokes."

"Do you think Xuereb used sound weapons to kill Savina Daidalos and David Shacklin?" asked Power.

"Sound weapons could be used to disorientate, certainly to stun and to kill." Ramon paused. "The Lord knows what he has developed, I'd never have imagined Paul to be a killer."

"But if he were frightened enough? If he felt completely isolated, terrified and that the whole world was against him?"

"In those circumstances? Wouldn't any of us use a weapon to defend ourselves? And I ask you, have you brought one? A weapon?"

"Lynch insisted I do." said Power. "A Glock, I believe it's called." Lynch had been mindful of how his attackers had shot him without any prior warning.

"And are you trained to use it . . . would you use it?"

"I have been trained," said Power. "I don't like guns. And these sound weapons – they work at a distance don't they, Paul could fire it remotely, from indoors – and what could a gun do against an unseen adversary? You have to see your target with a gun and be in range. So to tell you the truth I was planning to leave the Glock in the car. And I hoped Paul would listen to you. I thought negotiation might work."

Ramon chose not to point out that negotiation requires even more proximity, a closer range, than a gun. "I brought something as a defence," said Ramon. "Not a weapon."

"What?" asked Power. "What can you use against sound weapons? Earplugs?" As an alternative he imagined being cocooned in a thick blanket of foam to keep the sound out. But as far as he was aware Ramon had brought nothing like that. He had though, bizarrely, brought a large A1 flip chart pad. Was he going to lecture Xuereb into submission? With notes?

"I was going to ask you not to use any weapon on Paul," said Ramon. "But I don't really feel I have the right to deny you any defence. I wanted you to give him a chance but take a gun if you wish." Power shook his head. "OK, so be it."

They had arrived at the Estate where, once upon a time, the whole Daidalos family and their servants had slept and eaten and lived. Now the family was no more, the servants dispersed and the Estate had only a lone squatter hiding himself there. There was a single entrance set into the long white wall that crawled, seemingly forever, around the house and its gardens. Power drove the hire car through the gap in the wall to find Xuereb's Toyota Landcruiser in the car park, sitting heavily on a pair of concrete ramps, all set in limestone gravel. The gravel crunched as Power braked and parked the Renault alongside Xuereb's vehicle.

The warmth of the day enveloped them as they climbed out of the car. For a moment Power luxuriated in the brilliant sunlight. "Do you think he can see us from here?" he asked Ramon.

"We're out of direct view of the house, but I saw a CCTV camera on the car park wall as we drove in, it'll pick us up for sure as we walk round the Landcruiser," said Ramon. The old man was busy in the back of the hatchback. He had laid out the flipchart pad on the car's parcel shelf and was detaching pieces of white paper that gleamed in the sun to the extent that Power had to shield his eyes from the glare.

"What are you doing?" he asked.

Ramon was using a thick marker pen to write in large black letters on one of the sheets. The smell of the pen's alcohol wafted over to Dr Power.

Ramon rolled up one piece of paper, (the one he had written on), into a tube and tucked it into his jacket. The other, the blank piece, he rolled up and gave to Power.

"Keep hold of that," said Ramon. "This is our defence. But hold it behind your back as we walk so he doesn't see. I don't want to forewarn him. I will tell you when to use it."

Power frowned, perplexed as to what two pieces of paper could offer as a defence. Admittedly they were very large pieces of paper, but to Power's eyes there was no reason to explain Ramon's use of a flipchart.

"Can you explain what this paper is for, Ramon?" he asked.

"Only if we need it," said Ramon. "Otherwise you will think me insane and refuse to go ahead. If I am right, then I am right, and then you will thank me."

Power shook his head but did not wish to argue about carrying a large tube of paper. "Shall we go?"

"Yes," said Ramon. "Let's head towards the house. I think we've given Paul just enough time to see us on CCTV and prepare for our visit."

Sight of the car park's hideous, brutalistic design was spared from the main house by its being hidden behind a high, white stone wall. Power and Ramon emerged on to a rolling green lawn which sprawled and undulated gently up to the mansion and its complex of linked buildings. For a moment Power looked at the view enjoyed by residents of the villa. From its windows any inhabitants would glory in an unhindered and splendid view of the ocean and its deep Mediterranean blue. Ahead of them clusters of automatic sprinklers began to play glittering fountains of water over the lush green lawn.

Ramon pointed to a white brick path that bisected the lawn and led all the way up to the villa's porticoed entrance. "This way I think, but we must be quiet, now. He will be listening to what we say, as well as watching us."

"There's no-one near," said Power. "I know you said he was sensitive to sound, but his hearing can't be that acute!"

"He has all the technology he needs, you can be sure," said Ramon, as they walked up the bright white stone path towards the Daedalos's mansion. There was a warm and soft zephyr like breeze that carried a hint of spice; of rosemary, thyme and honeysuckle. In such a gentle, perfumed air, Power was lulled into a sense that all was well – and again the small island of Gozo reminded him of the sorcerer's enchanted island in *The Tempest*.

"Are we journeying to see Prospero in his cell?" Power wondered aloud.

"My worry is that on this Island we will not be met by a hospitable, urbane and mature Prospero, but by monstrous Caliban," whispered Ramon. By now they were almost half of the way to the shade of the portico. The noon-day sun made Power perspire.

All at once a harsh voice sounded right in their ears, as if a mouth were pressed up close against their skulls. "Stop! This is your only warning. Turn round. Go back to your car. Never come back." There was a residual soft buzz inside Dr Power's ear, like the angry sound of a colony of wasps. He automatically looked about to see who had been standing next to him, but there was only Ramon, who seemed much less alarmed.

For an instant Power wondered whether he had succumbed to the persecution of hallucinations and traded places with his patients at last. His medical training taught him that a hallucination is a 'perception without a corresponding stimulus from without', and here was a commanding voice, real and urgent near at hand, and without any human presence to explain its proximity.

"It is Paul," explained Ramon. "He is using sound projection. It's a function of the sound cannon I described. Even using low energy levels he could project his voice for several miles." "Miles?" Power was incredulous.

The disembodied voice spoke again, "Professor Calleya is quite correct. I can speak to you and hear you from a distance."

Ramon looked at Power and put his finger to his lips to counsel him to keep quiet.

"We are no threat to you," said Ramon. "We just wanted to talk to you, to see if we can help."

"A bit late," said Paul Xuereb. "Years late in fact. All my colleagues turned their backs on me. And even you betrayed me, Ramon. Now, you can turn your back on me again and go, before I make you pay."

Xuereb's voice seemed more intense, just as if it was now inside Power's ear, next to his ear drum. Power shook his head, but the voice did not diminish. The buzzing noise had become intense and angry. Power felt he needed to say something, "Professor Xuereb, can we talk to you, please? You sound annoyed, perhaps . . ."

"Who *are* you?"

"He's a friend," said Ramon. He signalled urgently to Power to be quiet. He knew how volatile Xuereb could be. "I'm still your friend too, Paul. I wanted to help you, to get you out of whatever trouble you're in."

"I'm in trouble? I haven't murdered anyone. I haven't stolen anything. There's nothing to warrant an intrusion by an ex-colleague who betrayed me. A mentor who became my tormentor. Go! I could kill you both right now."

The voice was deafening and the buzzing had become distinctly uncomfortable. Power's scalp felt heavy with a throbbing aching in forehead and neck. He fell to his knees.

"I have only ever had your best interests at heart," said Ramon, with some difficulty. His voice was more of a gasp than anything. "I've known you since you were a child. I've nothing but love for you, please stop, let's talk."

Xuereb's response was to ramp up the buzzing, to become a frantic clicking then a sharp piercing whine jabbing into Power's ears. He shook his head and crouched, like an animal trying to shake off an attacker, but the pain deep in his head was now unremitting. He felt dizzy, as if he might fall over and never get up. He thought, 'Here is where I could die'. He kept shaking his head. He moaned in pain but nothing helped.

Somehow, he registered that Ramon was shouting, although his voice was drowned out by the sound cannon. Ramon was making signals to him to unroll the thin piece of flipchart paper he had brought with him. It seemed surreal to him, to watch Ramon unrolling his piece of paper and hold it up in front of his face by the corners.

Power brought his own loosely rolled piece of paper out from behind his back and let it unroll and held it up, hanging in front of his face. The noise abated at once, miraculously. Power sighed with relief, and found he could hear Ramon again.

"It's a highly focused directional beam of sound waves," said Ramon, holding the paper high. "The paper resonates with it and absorbs the sound waves. We should press on through, before he tries something else." They half ran, half loped across the lawns towards the house. Power could imagine they looked ridiculous, but Ramon's simple defence of paper *had* stopped the sound and the corresponding pain completely.

"What did you write on the other side of the paper? Is it a message to Paul?" asked Power.

"Two words, written large." said Ramon, somewhat breathlessly. "I wrote 'YOUR MOTHER.' I hope her memory stops him for a few seconds and makes him think."

They had reached the portico of the villa and by moving out of the direct beam of the sound projector, escaped the sound weapon that Xuereb was operating from an upstairs window.

The absence of noise was blissful to Power. He slumped against a column, sank down onto the warm stone of the portico and closed his eyes in relief for a few seconds.

"Don't relax now," warned Ramon. "Who knows what else he has prepared?"

Power struggled to his feet clutching the paper that had defeated the sonic attack.

The double front doors of the villa's portico swung open slowly, remotely and automatically triggered. The grand hallway beyond was revealed. Power and Ramon held the defensive paper sheet up in front of them, at the ready.

From out of the darkness of the hallway stepped a single, painfully slender figure. It was Paul Xuereb, with pale, pinched face and straggly curled hair. His distant brown eyes were watery and surrounded by dark rings as if sleep had eluded him for weeks.

Xuereb held his hands up in submission, his gaze directed down at the floor. "I shouldn't have fired on you," he said. He risked a swift glance at Ramon and Power. "I knew someone would come to find me and make me pay. You can borrow energy from the Universe, but it always has to be repaid. Newton's Second Law, hey?" He paused. "And it was you two that came. You look like priests on a house call. Have you come to take confession?"

Ramon perceived Xuereb's starved appearance and the desperation in his voice. "Paul, I've come to rescue you from this . . . from this solitary life you've been leading. Bring you back from the brink. I owe that to you, and to your mother." Paul looked up briefly, but could not tolerate the eye contact, his gaze reverted to the crevices between the Travertine floor tiles. "And if you feel a need to confess as you say, Paul, well, I'll hear you. This is my friend Professor Power. He's a doctor. He can help you in his own way."

"I didn't kill anybody," said Xuereb, quickly. "I'm not confessing that!"

"I heard you when you said that before," said Dr Power.

Xuereb chanced another appraising glance, this time at the doctor. He thought that Power had the quiet, kind face of someone you could tell anything to. He nodded to Power. "Shall we find somewhere to talk in the garden? Before we go?

"You want to leave here?" asked Ramon.

Xuereb nodded. "And never come back," he said. "I want to go home to Gzira and see Valletta again."

"Let's find somewhere out in the open, under some shade," said

Power. "A bench somewhere under the trees. I want to ask you all about The Banker."

* * *

The concierge at the Phoenicia, all smart uniform, slick efficiency and smiles, announced to Dr Power that Mr Lynch had gone for a walk to the Gardens. Power found him standing on the parapet of the Upper Barakka Gardens, looking out over the glittering blue waters of the harbour with a pair of binoculars. Lynch was training their heavy lenses on the Birgu promontory opposite.

Power had been excited to tell Lynch of Xuereb's confession; his role in the investments and schemes of the Daidalos family, The Banker and the true purpose of the *Wanderlust*. Power had learned how Xuereb had been seduced by Daidalos's promises of unlimited finance for his research, luring him ever deeper into a clandestine sound weapon development scheme. After Daidalos's untimely death, Xuereb had compacted with The Banker, and an offer of further support for the project.

More importantly, Power had discovered the identity of The Banker from Xuereb, and he was keen to tell Lynch. But one look at his friend Lynch, who was still unaware of his presence, persuaded Power to tread carefully. Lynch's attention was firmly fixed on the other side of the harbour.

The sun was setting, and the golden light danced on the deep blue waters. Power's keen eyes discerned a slight, irregular tremor to his friend's hands as they gripped the binoculars. To mitigate this Lynch was leaning on the parapet, his elbows forming a stable base for the binoculars. Lynch's breathing was fast and shallow, denoting an inner tension. Suddenly, in the distance to the South East, there was the unmistakable sound of gunfire. Power saw his friend flinch, his breath catch and the tremor became more pronounced. Power decided to approach Lynch with care, and pace his conversation to Lynch, rather than weigh in at once about his experiences on Gozo.

"I thought," said Power, walking up behind the detective, making his approach sound as loud as he could to warn Lynch of his presence, so as not to alarm him by creeping up on him, "that you were confined to the hotel. You are meant to be resting by the pool, or in the lounge, with your leg elevated."

Despite the noise of Power's arrival, Lynch still jumped, but sought to cover his alarm. "I fancied a walk," said Lynch, briskly. "The hotel lent me a walking stick."

Power had already seen all the signs of his friend's anxiety while he was concentrated on distant events. "You shouldn't be putting any stress on the wound or the vessel repair, you know," said Power, admonishing him as gently as he could. "A bleed from a rupture in the repair could be deadly."

"Your bedside manner could do with polishing," said Lynch irritably. "I'm trying to relax."

"No, you're not relaxing, and you know it," said Power. "You're up to something."

"Maybe," said Lynch. He handed the binoculars over to Power and picked up the walking stick that he'd rested on the parapet, to point over the water. "Take a look over there, towards Birgu. Look at the quayside."

Power adjusted the binoculars to his eyes and peered through them across the Harbour to Birgu. The road on the quay was dotted with armoured vehicles about which were clustered troops in camouflage gear, shielding themselves from gunfire. At this distance the gunshots sounded like firecrackers on bonfire night.

"Azzopardi told me that the EU customs agency was raiding the casino. Lent me these binoculars to watch but forbade me to get any closer than this. Not that I think I could," he added. "Whatever part of the crime syndicate runs the casino is putting up a deal of resistance. They are not going easily." He sighed. Part of him wanted to be there, on the Birgu quayside, not a passive spectator at a remove, watching passively through binoculars. "We now think the role of the casino was to supply cash and synthetic opioids to the Captain of the *Wanderlust*, who, in turn, transferred the same to Comino ready for collection by a gang from Tunisia to pay for raw cannabis, grown in the Maghreb, and later supplied to mainland Europe. The complexity of the transaction is entirely deliberate. The more complex and obfuscated the transfers are the less traceable they are. The *Wanderlust* was acting just like a trusted bank, albeit a bank for criminals. A kind of smugglers' escrow. I'm afraid it was you that disrupted the machinery and broke the chain of trust between the criminals when you destroyed the rucksack." There was the sound of yet more gunfire, the reports staccato and urgent amidst drifting smoke and tear gas that intermittently obscured the quay and floated on the waters of the Harbour.

"They clearly don't want to go quietly," said Lynch. "They must be trying to buy time to destroy evidence, there's no other explanation. They are outnumbered and the only outcome is arrest or death." He paused and spoke, quietly, as if to himself. "It's hard to justify killing someone. And now I must live with it, again." Power assumed Lynch was referring to any guilt he felt over the deaths of the two traffickers who had shot at him. "*I take no pleasure in the death of wicked people. I only want them to turn from their wicked ways so they can live.*"

"I didn't think anything was going to happen to these other criminals, Azzopardi said he was not interested," said Power. "That's why I burned the cash. I thought they should be made to feel some pain. I thought Azzopardi was only concerned with the server technology?" asked Power.

"It would be outside the remit of SIS, yes, but he probably didn't mind passing on information to Europol," said Lynch. "Giving such information is part of the *quid pro quo*. He'll expect their co-operation in return one day." Lynch looked Power up and down. "Looks like you survived your trip to find Professor Xuereb. I gathered you found him from the text you sent me. Where did you leave him?"

"Ramon is with him. He took him home."

"Home?" queried Lynch. "Is that safe? Is it wise?"

"I think so," said Power. "Ramon felt it was for the best. He has known Xuereb for decades. Ramon is a father figure, I suppose." Power thought back to the afternoon spent with Xuereb at the villa on Gozo. Paul had shown them the interior of the house which had been well ordered. There had been no grime, no dirty plates, all was scrupulously cleaned, although everything was dark and quiet as a sepulchre. Xuereb had closed all the shutters and fitted heavy layers of fabric over the windows 'to keep out the screeching birds and the whistling wind' he said. In this obdurate silence he had endured weeks of concealment; eking out his meagre supply of tinned and frozen food until perhaps at last the solitude had proved too much even for Xuereb. The accumulated burden of loneliness, guilt and privation had broken his resolve once he glimpsed his old tutor Ramon, carrying a reminder of his link to their shared past, his mother. "Xuereb tried to resist at first," said Power. "He fired a sound cannon at us. But he was the one who broke. I think he just crumpled and folded when he was reminded of better times. He wanted to confess to Ramon . . . it all came pouring out. He has invented fearsome and deadly new weapons, but I don't think he could bring himself to kill us. And actually, I don't think he killed anyone. That was someone else."

"Very well," said Lynch. "You can tell me more when we get back to the hotel. The show at the casino in Birgu is over." There hadn't been an exchange of gunfire for some time. "I sense our time here in Malta is coming to a close and we can report back to the Vice Chancellor and Bridget McFarlane."

"Agreed," said Power. He offered an arm to Lynch to help him walk the distance back to the Phoenicia hotel. Lynch waved him away slightly irritably, for the pain was playing upon his patience.

"I'll manage with the sticks," he said. "I'll need some more of the damned pills when we get in."

"Pain?" asked Power.

"They only work for a bit," complained Lynch.

"Well, they're not designed for people who aggravate their wounds by walking across a city a day or so after a vascular operation," said Power.

Lynch held his tongue. They walked very slowly across the squares and streets of Valletta toward the City Gate.

"The drugs also make you feel spaced out," reflected Lynch. "A bit elated, a bit drunk. A bit neglectful of reality and what is sensible. Maybe it wasn't wise of me to leave the hotel." He sighed and they paused. Lynch feigned an interest in the architecture around them. Power could sense that he was resting and gathering strength for the final few hundred yards. "I think you will need to drive us back to the airport when we leave," Lynch said wistfully. Then he mustered his remaining stamina and returned to the theme of Power's mission to Gozo. "So Xuereb fired on you, did he?"

"It was like nothing I've experienced before. It was as if he was *inside* my head. Jabbing inside my ears and brain. It was quite . . . unearthly and very frightening to . . . lose control."

"I dare say Azzopardi would be interested in *that* technology, too," said Lynch, resuming their plodding journey back to the hotel. "He would probably jump at the chance to debrief Xuereb."

"Xuereb looked as if he needed three square meals all in one go and a week's sleep afterwards," said Power.

"Speaking of food, you'll be wanting an evening meal, won't you? But I'm not very hungry. No appetite."

"The dihydrocodeine has affected it I dare say," said Power.

"I'll sit with you while you eat, if you like," offered Lynch.

They had limped past the Triton Fountain and reached the grand entrance of the Hotel.

"I am rather hungry, now you mention it," said Power.

"You always are," Lynch said, with a wan smile.

They strolled straight into the restaurant, where Power ordered a main course, a side salad and a carafe of Maltese Sangiovese wine. Lynch ordered himself a clear soup and a mineral water.

"Did Xuereb confess the name of The Banker, then?" asked Lynch.

"Yes," said Power, as he buttered some exceedingly thin and crisp Melba Toast. "Yes, he has met The Banker and he told me . . ."

Suddenly Lynch's phone began to ring; urgently, and insistently. Lynch looked around the elegant restaurant, embarrassed at the strident interruption. The other diners didn't seem to mind too much, however. Nevertheless, Lynch wanted to take the offending phone out of the restaurant to answer it but couldn't bear the pain of standing up. Lynch handed the still agitating phone over to Power. "Please can you take it outside and answer it. I can't get up and I can see it's Phillip Beresford calling. It's important."

Power was reluctant to leave his food, which had just arrived, but he hurried dutifully out to the hotel lobby with Lynch's phone. He cursed this appurtenance of modern life for its unpredictable inconvenience. He hesitated, trying to fathom how to answer Lynch's phone, and then he was listening to the crisp, authoritative tones of detective Beresford.

"Hello, it's Carl." said Power. "Andrew asked me to take your call. It's difficult for him to get around after his op." Power found a vacant sofa and sank into its plush upholstery.

"Hi, Carl. I hope you've finished your work out there, because you will both need to get back here as soon as possible. Tell Andrew that there's been an arrest."

"An arrest?"

"The police arrested Caroline Diarmid late this afternoon."

"Caroline? What for?"

"On suspicion of murder, Carl. Bridget McFarlane's body was found in her office at the University this morning. As you know there was a history of domestic violence."

"Yes," said Power, automatically. The blood in his veins suddenly ran chill and thin. It was difficult to assimilate this new information. "Bridget McFarlane?"

"Yes, that's right," said Beresford. "They found her body in her office this morning. Her head was caved in like a smashed boiled egg."

Power thought of the earlier conversation he had had with Ramon about the blancmange-like texture of the human brain, and felt the remainder of whatever appetite he once had evaporate.

"Caroline used a heavy ornament from the table. She held it up in two hands and brought it down on McFarlane's head. A crime of passion, so the detective in charge of the case believes. Jealous rage."

Power remembered his conversation with McFarlane in her newly decorated office. He had admired the heavy purple stone on her meeting table; how it glistened and sparkled, reflecting the light.

"Was it that heavy amethyst quartz ornament?"

"Yes," said Beresford. "They found it wedged in the wreckage of her skull – I mean it's very heavy, but she must have hurled it down on her head. And the provisional forensic sweep of the evidence shows the quartz had Caroline's fingerprints all over it."

Chapter Twenty-Six

God moves the player and he, the piece.
What author, behind God, describes the plot
Of dust and time and dreams and agonies?
Jorge Luis Borges, Chess

D r Power sank into the ruby-coloured armchair opposite the Vice
Chancellor and smiled at him. The Ormolu clock ticked steadily
in the background. There was the mellow aroma of woodsmoke from
the fireplace. Blazing logs of ash, split from trees felled from the
University's own woods, crackled away in the grate and their eager
combustion generated a welcome heat that held the chill of the winter
at bay.

The bronze statue of Carroll regarded Power with a curl of a smile.
The statue overlooked the chess table. All the pieces except the two
Kings had been put away in a rosewood box. The Red King appeared
to be held at bay in a corner of the board.

Here, in the plush comfort of his grand office the Vice Chancellor
appeared relaxed in his smart suit. His face was ruddy, and his eyes
shone with vigour, quite at variance with the pale shadow of a man
that Power had encountered in the snowy garden. Canon Armitage sat
across the way from Power, smiling benignly at his employee.

Power spoke first. "I wanted to inform you as soon as I could, Vice
Chancellor. We have concluded the investigation and a solution has
presented itself."

"Have you finished, then?" asked the Vice Chancellor. "That is a
relief. Am I the first to know your solution?"

"Of course you are," said Power. "You commissioned me to find
out what happened to Professor Shacklin and thus his murder, and so
it seemed only right that I should let you know as soon as I could."

"How kind," said the Vice Chancellor. "And I assume you are

certain of your 'solution'; that this is 'checkmate' and not merely 'check'."

"If you wish to use that analogy, then yes."

The Vice Chancellor rose to go over to a Butler's tray below the elegant sash window. He poured two cups of coffee from the silver jug and placed one on the table in front of Power. "Freshly brewed," he said. "I asked the chef to make it when I heard you were coming." He resumed his armchair. "It's a decaffeinated coffee from the Blue Mountains. I seem to remember decaffeinated is what you take. Chef brewed it to go with an almond syrup, which I've added, of course . . ." Power noted a bottle of Monin's Almond syrup on the tray.

"Thank you," said Power. "I had a drink just before. Maybe I will have some in a moment."

"Are you sure?"

"Quite sure," said Power.

Power reached over and pulled his cup and saucer a little nearer, to seem polite. He watched the Vice Chancellor's expression carefully. "Maybe later."

"Never mind," said Armitage, lifting his own large cup from its saucer. "Well, don't keep me in suspense, the tension is becoming unbearable; who is responsible for the murders?"

"A person called The Banker," said Power. "And that would be you, of course."

"I see," said Armitage. His smile did not waver. Instead he took a sip of his coffee. "That syrup is remarkable," he said, and took a long draw of the coffee and swallowed it in one long gulp. "Will you tell me all? Demonstrate your acuity? Go through the crimes and prove your astuteness. Or would it be quicker if I confessed?"

"You don't deny it, then?" asked Power, frowning. He had expected at least a token resistance.

"Why should I deny the truth? It would be so time consuming. It is far better manners to resign – I concede your checkmate." He rose again to refill his cup from the Butler's tray and returned to his seat with a tape recorder and microphone, which he set on the table in front of them both. Armitage switched it on. "I think you might find it useful to have a recording, especially to rely on later. Shall I confess to you like that psychiatrist/priest of Eliot's?"

Power felt uneasy; puzzled by the Vice Chancellor's behaviour. It felt as if Armitage was playing with him, and perhaps now continuing a game he had been playing all along.

"You *can* drink your coffee," said the Vice Chancellor. "I wouldn't poison you, you know." He paused, and looked at the ceiling for inspiration. "Where to begin?" he asked. There was a long pause.

"If you really are going to confess, why not start with Savina Daedalos," said Power. "I was going to begin with her myself."

"Of course, of course. What would you like to know?"

"How did she cross your path?"

"She sought me out," said the Vice Chancellor. "Her family had died . . . in an accident. She was an orphan, trying to understand her late father, coming to terms with the fact that he was less a benign god and more a career criminal and drug lord. Poor girl, she had no idea about him. She found an email from The Banker on her father's computer and wanting to meet to discuss his business affairs she emailed The Banker back. The email to The Banker, of course, came straight to me."

"And what happened?"

"She tried to blackmail me! Quite ineptly, I might add. She knew too little about her father's methods and yet knew a little too much about The Banker. She had gathered a few ideas about his smuggling operations, and the Weapons research, which he was a co-investor in. She was a *naif* though. Her dear father was a crook and she couldn't quite accept that, and certainly couldn't match her father's guile or innate self-preservation. My main work with her father was the establishment of the weapons laboratory around Paul Xuereb. Daidalos wanted the weapons to guard his drug operation and I wanted the profits. Do you know how much revenue the arms industry generates? The UK is the second largest exporter of arms. Exports of arms to South Africa alone are worth a billion a year to the UK. And there – all of a sudden – was Savina – stumbling about in confusion and guilt – threatening me that she would go to the Maltese press – knowing full well what havoc she would cause if she did. She turned herself from an orphan into a risk that had to be managed. She had just enough information about the weapon station, to be a significant problem to me, but did not enjoy enough sense to shut up.

"You know, the main problem with turning an illegal profit is how to process the money – you have to launder the money in different ways. The University – being semi-autonomous – proved ideal for this. I moved money sideways, downwards, upwards, in fact, in every which way. Bidding for art in my own name using cash from the *Wanderlust* then being refunded by the University, was just one way." Armitage waved airily towards the portrait of Tudor Queen Margaret, who looked down from the wall upon them. Power thought she wore a disapproving frown, but who for? For him or for the Vice Chancellor? "Paintings and old manuscripts allowed me to move money between pools, cleansing it of sin at every stage, until ultimately it became my own clean money."

"And poor Savina threatened all that, did she?" asked Power. "So what did you do?"

"The internet is a marvellous thing. Most of the time I could manage everything remotely from home, or here. The operation can be run like that. Keeping everything in the virtual world – in a looking glass world, if you like. But when Savina started to mither at me I had to switch over and act in the physical world. I flew out to Malta after I'd arranged to meet her. Most inconvenient to be dragged all the way out there. She wanted to see the Research Station and gauge what her father's 'investment' had bought. When she turned up early at the Station before our arranged meeting Xuereb phoned me and I instructed him to give her a sedative in a drink. He took some persuading as he is a good man at heart. I arrived later that evening and whilst she was still unconscious – when it was dark enough – we put her outside on the scrubland, beyond the wall, and waited. It was an opportunity to try the sound cannon out, and I used that to nudge her, again and again, to the edge of the cliff, until over she went." He smiled. "Xuereb was not involved in that. He couldn't even bear to watch. Too timid by far. But it was reassuring to me to find out that the weapons I'd invested in actually worked."

"Did you feel any remorse for what you had done?" asked Power.

"She was a pretty girl, and it was a shame perhaps, of course, of course," said Armitage coldly. "But you can't allow sentimentality to cloud your judgment when there are risks to your very existence. I suppose she was a bit like her father, a risk. And he had to be managed too." He paused to see if Power would ask him a further question, but he did not and Armitage pressed on. "You did well to link her death in. That was superior play. I always knew you would be a worthy opponent. I saw you once on TV news being interviewed about a case and I knew then that you would offer a stimulating challenge. So I invited you in to the University, brought you on board, so to speak."

"Do you imagine this was all a game?" asked Power. "Did you fantasise that you were playing me?"

"You speak as if you had no conception. That you were playing without even knowing you were in a game. Perhaps you were playing unconsciously? Or perhaps you started playing along instinctively?"

"When, exactly, did *you* decide that we were playing our game?" asked Power.

"I had heard of you. National newspaper reports of your deductive successes –matching your wits against various notorious minds. So I thought I'd like to play you and I invited you in to the University, with flattery to your ego and the bait of a new medical school to dazzle you. And then, later, I remember seeing you on the television news – pacing about a crime scene at Lindow – deep in thought. And I knew then that you were going to be a really worthy opponent to play."

"I see," said Dr Power, weighing what words to say next. He wanted to encourage further confession, but he found the Vice Chancellor's blatant lack of remorse and conceit of playing with people's lives uniquely chilling. There was also his dented pride, an irritation that he had failed to see through Armitage's flattery from the beginning. "You are being quite . . . candid, Vice Chancellor. I expected some reluctance to admit anything on your part, especially on tape."

"You will understand why I see no reason to withhold any information at all. There's nothing to be gained by being cagey with you. There is no physical escape for me. I know, for instance, that your colleague, Detective Lynch, is outside. My exits from here are effectively blocked."

"Very well," said Power, bemused by the apparent ease with which the confession was unfolding. "We might as well talk about Professor Felfe now. Felfe was a quiet gentleman. After a lifetime working in intelligence, helping the West survive the Cold War, and himself surviving the Eastern Bloc secret service, he died in the Cathedral."

"Professor Felfe . . . yes," said Armitage softly. "The Berliner." Power suspected a Berliner was a kind of jam doughnut, but saw no reason to correct the Vice Chancellor.

"I feel guilty," said Power, knowing that he was probably the only person in the room with such an emotion. "Because I underestimated Professor Felfe and regarded him as no more than an old gossip, but in fact he deserved my help, desperately. I believe you poisoned Felfe and intended his death to be confused with a simple heart attack. I noticed some anomalies with his pupils, and the drooling, but I was persuaded by others, who I thought knew better than me, that his death was from natural causes, when it was anything but."

"You know, I thought that his death, and the death of Savina, were almost perfect crimes," said Armitage. "Nobody should have remarked on their passing as unusual." He sounded almost gratified by his accomplishment. "I wonder how many 'natural' deaths are anything but natural?" The Vice Chancellor's eyes twinkled at the thought. "How many murders are missed because people, even pathologists, make a lazy assumption that what they are encountering is just another normal death?"

"Very few," said Power, cautiously.

"By all means comfort yourself with that thought," said the Vice Chancellor. "But only fifty miles from here, your medical colleague, Dr Shipman, killed dozens of old people over the years, didn't he? And no-one did anything for decades? Other doctors just signed the cremation forms in good faith. They all saw only what they expected to see, another old person dying alone at home. Old people are meant to die. That is the mindset of our society. People tend to believe what comforts them, and it is unsettling to contemplate otherwise. People don't like to be troubled by the unexpected. It puts them out. So people elect to think along well-travelled lines. It's easier to believe the authorities; it's easier to believe the Government rather than question anything.

"Savina's death was assumed to be suicide – understandable in a bereaved girl – or misadventure. And they assumed Felfe had a heart attack. An old man. A sudden death. No-one would begin to suspect a death by snake poison. I believe *envenomation* is the correct term."

"And you acquired the venom from the Biology Labs, then?"

"Of course, of course. My electronic pass, as Vice Chancellor, has the highest security clearance in the whole University. I can move anywhere; invisibly too. The system is purposely programmed not to track me; so it doesn't capture my moves. At night, if I wanted, I could prowl round the entire campus. It was easy to walk into Biology and remove the dried venoms. They were extracted from the reptiles at the zoo years ago and I have had them by me for ages. Just in case. For Felfe it was just a matter of sprinkling the powder in the communion wine before he took a sip. It works very quickly, as you observed. A matter of minutes."

"You administered the dose in his communion wine?" Power kept his voice as level as he could, so it signalled no surprise or disdain.

"I knew Felfe was meeting you in the Cathedral that day, your electronic diary is synced across the University servers, and perfectly visible to me – so I knew your moves ahead of time . . . and he wanted to see you, presumably to relay everything he knew about the *Wanderlust.* Whatever he suspected about its financial operations in the Mediterranean and Atlantic. He would have told you his suspicions about The Banker. And so rigid were his habits I knew he would take Communion before your meeting. He was a regular at that particular weekly service. He liked the intimacy of St Anselm's Chapel.

"You knew I was a canon in the Cathedral and if you'd checked you'd have found I was officiating in St Anselm's Chapel that day, handing out the communion bread and the wine. I wonder whether Felfe wanted one last look at me before he sold me to you, like a sort of Judas? Any way you look at it, it was a beautiful opportunity. It's so gratifying when a plan comes together."

"I never saw you that day though," said Power. "Even though you were in the Cathedral."

"That chapel only has a few worshippers who celebrate morning communion. The public use a stairway at the rear of the chapel, but there is also a private way out for clergy. So if you were waiting in the nave down below, you would not have seen me enter or leave."

"To clarify, because Felfe knew too much, you silenced him?"

"Traditionally he made a virtue of quietness, of merging into the background. Never voicing his opinion, so you'd hardly notice he was there at committees. He just wanted to blend in. He'd had enough jeopardy when he spied in Berlin. You can burn out when you're living under a constant threat, I would imagine. He taught students occasionally, but he never published. He never attended academic conferences. He was so . . . inhibited, and he made me uneasy. Was he sitting there quietly analysing everything for some dossier, or was he just disinterested? He probably felt forever on guard, hiding away from ex-Communist assets who might turn up unannounced one day. Haunted by old spies who were still loyal to the past regime and craved revenge. Wrinkled spies who hadn't quite moved on to the afterlife and who still harboured a grudge against double agent Felfe. The academic post here was really just a front Allminster provided as a courtesy to him, at our Government's entreaty. I should have made Felfe retire long ago. The thing is, the quiet ones, they don't say anything – they just persist – and they notice everything. And I knew he had found something. I suppose it was his *modus operandi* to spy, but rather than show his hand and DO anything himself, he wanted to give *you* the ammunition, so you could use it. And I couldn't allow that."

"And so you pride yourself that his death was a perfect murder?"

"Nobody to miss him. No family. Of such an age that a sudden, silent heart attack would be predictable." Armitage paused. "He was a relic, a burden imposed on the University and arranged through my predecessor. I blame myself for not having the courage to rout him out and pension him off years ago. He was an unwanted pawn, best discarded."

"You thought him unimportant," said Power. "But he *did* pass on his information. He told us there was a Banker, and that there was the *Wanderlust,* even mentioned San Niklaw Bay. Sometimes the actions of a pawn can win or lose you the game. Maybe you overlooked his potential."

"Yes, some games really are like war," conceded Armitage. "Where the actions of every piece count."

Power felt irritated by Armitage in a way he had never been before. The fragility of his ego and the way he decried Felfe's tendency to keep his own counsel rankled the doctor. Power stifled the temptation to vent his frustration on Armitage, or to point out the errors in his thinking or his *weltanschauung.* This was not therapy, where he might work with Armitage's defence mechanisms. Power was intent on making it as easy as possible for Armitage to let information flow unimpeded. He suppressed any growing annoyance, and merely gave a bland smile to encourage the man opposite to disclose every detail.

"Savina and Felfe, they were both part of the 'game', then?" asked Power.

"Savina was not part of *this* particular game, our game. I did not intend her to be a piece on your 'side'. She didn't know you. You didn't know her. She was separate to the main game. It is a mark of your worth that you linked her death into this at all. But Felfe was one of your supporters. He was on your 'side', as it were."

"I never asked to play any 'game' with you, did I?" Power observed, unable to bury this particular aspect of his irritation any longer. "I never wanted to play. Anything. I never consented to play. Surely you can see that?"

"The game of life plays us, Dr Power. We don't get an option about *whether* we play. God doesn't ask for our consent, does He? That's why life often feels unfair to us because some thing, or someone else, is in control. Sometimes life makes you play the game from the beginning, and sometimes you have to start halfway through, and you have to do the best you can with the board you're allotted."

Power could think of a dozen things to say in response to Armitage, but he decided he must shift the focus of the interview ever forward. He looked down to check that the recorder was still working, capturing their conversation for later analysis. "And Professor Shacklin . . . whose remains I saw in the morgue in Valletta . . . was he on my 'side' too? Theoretically speaking . . ."

"Of course he was. He began playing for you when I delegated the chair of the medical school committee to him."

"I see," said Power. "And do you consider his end, his murder, less than perfect? I ask as you did not mention his death in the same breath as those of Savina and Felfe."

"It was shoddy work," said Armitage, self-critically. "Far from perfect, and certainly not elegant." He chuckled. "I wasn't as feeble as I led you to believe. It was a bit of a struggle managing the dead weight of his body out of the Landcruiser and into the pig shed. A body is a cumbersome thing to manoeuvre. But I managed it. When I upended him into the pig pen, I obviously hadn't ensured he was wholly dead. Very remiss of me. The pigs were intended to dispose of his body, not eat him alive, as they eventually did, in a sort of feeding frenzy. By then I'd left, of course. If he'd been properly dead, and not just brain damaged, I doubt that a morsel of him would have survived. Instead he was scrabbling about to try and escape, and the pigs didn't eat him whole. And leaving the ring on. That was a mistake. Maybe, as a psychiatrist, you might interpret that oversight as a *parapraxis*?"

Power decided not to engage with this comment, which he regarded as some kind of taunt. "So you were in Malta when Shacklin was killed? And that was you? Not Xuereb?"

"Xuereb is a physicist. He's content to design weapons and not to use them. He doesn't have the will, the vibrancy and life force inside him, to act, and to impose his design on the world, to affect reality. There are two kinds of people in the world. Submissives and Dominants. I don't mean in sexual terms. You are either one or the other. There are shepherds and sheep, hunters and prey. Most people are just submissive victims, meek passengers on this spinning earth; unable to form even one truly original idea and bring it into effect.

"I sent Shacklin over to Malta. Shacklin is a case in point. He liked to think he was an original man. He liked to think he could be a leader, become Vice Chancellor. But he was just a follower, governed by greed and his impulses – he couldn't impose his rational will on anything, even his own life! He thought he'd enjoy a holiday at the University's expense. He could be expected to gamble away the shirt off his back and sleep with anything that had a pulse. I sent him there partly because he queried the existence of the Research Station. He'd learned of the existence of the Maltese Research Station through a cross reference in an application to Allminster's University ethics committee. The paperwork had briefly crossed Shacklin's desk, and as ill fate would have it he noticed it and he particularly wanted to learn details of the Research project's sponsor, which would have been The Banker, of course. The details were obscure, so well hidden in the application I felt sure that he'd never notice them, but as ill fate decreed it, Shacklin noticed. He scented a potential line of credit. The Banker's identity was not specified in the documentation, but Shacklin saw a source of relief from his debts. He emailed The Banker without knowing precisely who The Banker was. And his email wended its way to me. When he went to Malta he had high hopes for a meeting with The Banker. What his pitch would be, I never found out; I didn't want to take the risk of actually meeting him. I don't really believe he had the capacity to begin to understand what I had designed. He was a very limited man, but a man in considerable debt, and therefore desperate. His debt was so severe that he could have been seriously injured or killed by his creditors at any stage. I'm sure he would have wanted to tap The Banker for money, to make good his losses at all the gaming tables. I sent him to Malta, and he willingly travelled to his own death. That was the most elegant point in the plan."

"So what happened at the meeting Shacklin arranged?"

"When Shacklin went out to Malta I took a long weekend leave on the pretext I was going to holiday in North Wales. Shacklin had emailed to arrange a meeting with The Banker at the Research Station. And, with everyone thinking I was in North Wales, I took my own flight to Malta.

"When he arrived at the Research Station, I was hiding inside watching him on CCTV. I had decided to use the sound cannon again, like I had with Savina. But this time I thought I would test out its full capacity to destroy. So I focused the beam on Shacklin almost as soon as he got out of the car. I cranked the dial up to eleven, as they say. And he dropped like a stone! Xuereb was by my side and he was so frightened when he saw Shacklin drop, that he wet himself," Armitage chuckled. "Feeble man. Too late for him to wonder if you should create something, after the fact."

"Xuereb wet himself?"

"And wept like a baby, too," said Armitage frowning. "I gather some of the physicists who worked on the Manhattan project in nineteen forty-five and designed the atom bomb wept when they watched it explode. They only understood what destruction they had wrought at the very moment of detonation. Idiots. And Xuereb is an idiot too. To work on some new device as if it only exists in a virtual world, barely acknowledge at some intellectual level that it is a weapon, and then be horrified when they see it fired in the real world. Pathetic. Like someone who eats a processed chicken nugget in a fast food restaurant, but couldn't bring themselves to wring a real chicken's neck in a farmyard."

"And how did *you* feel when you saw Shacklin 'drop like a stone'?" asked Dr Power.

"I sense you keep wanting me to express some kind of remorse, of course you do. Of course, you do. But to be honest, and why shouldn't I be honest this late in the game? I felt nothing but relief . . . and excitement. I felt *alive*." Armitage looked closely at Power. "I heard the irritation in your voice just now – I am sorry to annoy you by being honest. When time is limited why waste any maintaining a social façade. I've done with all that, or rather time has done with me. People always self-censor what they say. They feel an obligation to censor their thoughts, their words and their acts for the benefit of someone else's feelings. They might hate someone but they won't ever say so – to preserve what? To shore up a mutual pretence of civilization? We have murderous thoughts – all of us – but we can't admit them to others – sometimes not even to ourselves. It's just that I have ventured further on my journey than other people ever can. I've acknowledged my murderous thoughts, nursed them, and acted upon them. Why be irritated by that, Carl Power?"

Armitage picked up his coffee cup and peered at the remaining third or so, then looked over at Power's untouched coffee. "You haven't touched a drop. You could at least try it before it goes altogether cold. Have one last drink with me?"

Power was musing on issues of psychiatric diagnosis. Whether Shacklin or Armitage had diagnoses that he had missed. For Shacklin he remembered research on early Parkinson's Disease and manifestations of frontal lobe pathology – uncharacteristic sexual excess, overspending and gambling, and for Armitage he speculated on violence and narcissistic personality disorder. But he pushed these meandering academic thoughts to one side and placed his attention firmly back into the here and now. This seemingly benign man opposite was a self-confessed murderer. To lose one's concentration might prove fatal. The Vice Chancellor seemed desperate for him to drink from the coffee cup.

"No thank you," said Power, and he abruptly pushed the cup to one side. "I rather think not."

"I assure you I did not poison your cup," Armitage said softly. He drained the last dregs of his own coffee. "I hope I am holding your attention," he said. "I wouldn't want to waste your time by prattling on. If I can be candid, my motives for killing Sabina, Felfe and Shacklin were largely self-interested ones – to preserve myself and my lifestyle. But at the end of last year I learned that my life could not be preserved anyway, and this changed my . . . motivation. I learned of a diagnosis – a rare tumour around the pancreatic ducts, something that could not be cured. You will probably know the name – 'Oddi's tumour'. I pretended cardiac symptoms to get my own way at Allminster, from time to time. In recent weeks I have wondered if the universe was paying me back for pretending. Like the karma of an able man who uses disabled parking spaces being rendered wheelchair bound. Well, you may or may not believe me now regarding the terminal diagnosis I received, if so I understand, but I assure you it altered the rules of the game for me. I reminded you before that we don't always choose the rules. Thereafter, I struck out more at a world I no longer really understand. I was . . . enjoying myself until you caught up with me."

"How was I to catch up with you?" asked Power. "Playing a game that existed only in your mind, according to *your* rules."

"Oh, I still conformed to the rules of chess so you could follow along," said the Vice Chancellor, peevishly. "You know your tone has shifted from irritation to bitterness, Dr Power. You played along well enough. You must have done, or else I would not have conceded the game. You came here to win it, by accusing me. You are what we call an intuitive player, responding unconsciously to my moves. You certainly always made a move in response to every move of mine, even if you are feigning ignorance of having done so consciously. If you reflect on it, you will see I am right. You worked it just like Newton's third law – *'For every action there is an equal and opposite reaction.'*"

"I could argue the point," said Power. "But what would be the use?"

"You're the opposite of a bad loser," said the Vice Chancellor. "You're a bad winner, Professor Power. Accept the compliment from me; you won." He paused. "Have we finished with Shacklin? What more is there to say? I watched him park his rental car and I just hit him with the sound cannon, full blast. He dropped like a stone and I assumed he was dead. He looked dead to me. And then I needed to move him. Xuereb just couldn't bring himself to help. You know when I was young, my aunt told me to always have a little story prepared. My heart problems, as I said, were a little story that allowed me a great degree of latitude. So I was never really the cardiac cripple I pretended. But it still took all my strength to bundle him into Xuereb's Landcruiser on my own.

"I drove him to the pig farm and dragged him into the pig shed. He seemed lifeless, his limb's all limp. I took off his jacket and his shoes, because I didn't think the pigs would eat those, and I didn't want anything left over after they'd finished. I genuinely thought he was dead when I heaved him over the gate into the pig enclosure. They didn't mind his underclothes and shirt . . . they tore at them. The pigs seemed very . . . enthusiastic about him. I forgot to take his ring off his hand though. The heat of the moment. That assisted you no doubt?"

"You see your behaviour as perfectly reasonable, don't you?"

"Don't you think I was fully justified? Think about it. Not only was Shacklin going to be in a position to blackmail me, but there was also the University to think of. We're a premier University. We can't have people like him, sleazy, persistently lascivious beasts, ogling teenage students, putting his hand up the skirts of research fellows. Gambling, using cocaine . . . no, I put up with him, as much as I could. I'm not a monster, I tried to guide him; I cut him some slack and hoped he would mend his ways. And every time I guided him in such a way he always repaid me with further indiscretions. He was a threat to me, and ultimately a threat to the probity of the University. And what about the women he used and abused? Odious man. I prefer to think I was acting like an editor really; deleting him. My actions were justified, for the greater good." He paused and reflected again on what he had earlier termed his *parapraxis*, "Failing to ensure he was properly dead and failing to remove that vulgar ring he always wore. They were mistakes in play that helped you far too much."

Power shifted uncomfortably in his seat, "Perhaps we should move on? Who to? Bridget McFarlane? For a while I wondered if Bridget McFarlane was the one that met Shacklin in Malta and that she was The Banker."

"I'll talk about Bridget last," said Armitage. "I'm following a chronological order here. I'll talk about Sir Robert, the Knight next."

"Very well," said Power, checking the recorder was still working. "When I told you that Rob Willett was depressed I believe you then contrived to murder him, and depicted it as a suicide. But why kill him? Surely a broken man was no threat to you . . ."

"It was a mixture of factors that made his execution imperative. He was going to be tiresome about the manuscript. Critical of me, ultimately. Not entering into the spirit of things at all. A 'Knight mare' of an employee. I thought *The Wasp* manuscript was an exciting asset for the University's collection and a celebration of our founder Lewis Carroll. Not only that, but it was a perfect purchase to launder more cash from the *Wanderlust*. So there was that – his bleating protests would just draw attention to the financial aspects of the purchase. And also, what a drab, spent man, drunk and unfaithful, dossing in his office; a fallen Knight. I was just drawing an untidy life to a tidy end." He looked across at Power and assessed his reaction to the words. "You seem to have an affinity for him, but you also have a blind spot, I think. There are, put simply, some lives unworthy of life. Life's 'useless eaters'."

"A cruel philosophy, unworthy of humanity," said Power.

Armitage shrugged, "Why should I care?"

"Wouldn't simply firing him have been easier?"

"Oh, these days you can't fire anyone without a long, drawn-out process of appeals and Employment tribunals. And what would he say in court about the manuscript? Believe me, (I'm not being facetious), when I say it's easier these days to murder someone than fire them."

Power sighed. "How was it done then? Rob had locked himself in his office to hang himself – seemingly. I remember you arrived at his office *after* we cut him down."

"You thought that?" Armitage was gladdened that Power had not worked everything out. "Willett had asked to meet. I suggested first thing in the morning before any of the secretaries had arrived. He'd been sleeping on the couch in his office. He was unshaved, dithering with nerves and reeking of stale alcohol. He didn't really require any more, but I encouraged him to have a morning sherry into which I slipped a fast acting sedative. It all happened quite smoothly after that; as if fate had ordained it." Armitage nodded contentedly. "If anyone had come in when he was groggy – well I could say that he was merely drunk, but once he was unconscious I locked the door and pocketed the key. I had brought a rope with me in a briefcase, which I wrapped around his neck, tighter and tighter. Once he was dead, I hooked the other end of the rope round the neck of the grotesque to act as a pulley. That reduced the weight of him, so I just tugged on the rope and hoisted him out of the window. He was somewhat cumbersome to manage, but as I said, I was never as frail as I pretended to be. Then I hid in the alcove, behind the long velvet curtain and I waited patiently, because I knew someone below was bound to see him. I was there inside the room when you were hammering on the locked door. And later, when everybody was focused on the body I chose to emerge.

"It was a risk to hide there, but it was exciting and fate was with me. When people chance across something like a hanging man they focus on that – they simply don't take anything else in. So nobody noticed me stepping out from behind the curtain. All I had to do then was appear shocked and breathless. I must say you were very kind to me at the time. You seemed genuinely concerned about me."

"I was concerned about you then. Although I did wonder, when I took your pulse, why it was strong, and regular. Not the pulse of a man with a weak heart, nor the pulse of anyone frightened by what he had just seen or done. It retrospect it was the pulse of a man who was quite composed. Just as composed as you are now."

Armitage smiled as if Power had just paid him a compliment. "I think the University is a tidier place without Willett."

"Which brings us to Bridget McFarlane," said Dr Power. "Are you willing to talk about her?"

"Of course, of course, if we have the time," said Armitage. "Do you remember when you came to see me in the garden, in the snow? You sat there in the cold and requested my permission to return to Malta. I knew then we were starting the Endgame."

Power thought back to the conversation with Canon Armitage in the snow-blanketed garden of the rectory. "When Andrew and I flew out to Malta I expected to find proof that Bridget was The Banker. She'd boasted about her financial qualifications. We knew her grandmother came from a crime family in Sicily. We calculated that she could have travelled to Malta from Sicily to meet Shacklin. And she hated him as much as you did. She could easily have managed Xuereb remotely, just as you did, and also run the *Wanderlust*. She could so easily have been The Banker. But you chose to remove her from the equation? Someone you could easily have shifted blame on to."

"Shifting the blame in that way would have been the faintest of hopes. Maybe I could lead you to suspect McFarlane was The Banker for a while, but a circumstantial explanation without proof is no defence. You were bound to work out the truth. You know – you say she was financially qualified, but you never asked me what my primary background is. European Banking Systems are my *forte*. My library in this room has every text published on the system in the last ten years. I've published research papers on European Banking Institutions and Regulation. It was time to stop maundering at home, feeling sorry for myself, and return to work and whilst you were abroad, finish her off."

His eyes were suddenly ablaze with determination. "Never has one woman wanted the hollow crown more than she. You can imagine her delight when she thought I was ill. She'd have trampled on my throat and danced on my coffin lid with pleasure. So I don't regret her death for one moment.

"You thought she was your opposition, stopping *your* medical school, but she was only pointing out realities to you about your ambition. If you'd only known it she was really on your team, you know. There never was any real money to do the things you wanted or build any kind of medical school. She was being cruel to be kind. Building and staffing a medical school – that kind of endeavour would require tens of millions that she knew the University never had. I just sold you a dream, because I wanted to you to play a game with me.

"She was so ambitious that she burned with envy for my position. I knew the game was already over for me, but I just couldn't bear the idea of her profiting by my defeat. Spiteful of me to kill her I concede. And her lover was there to take the blame, (in the unlikely event you failed to solve the case)."

"How was it done?" asked Power. He spoke to prompt the confession for the tape recorder, but at the same time he was deep in thought and considering diagnoses, trying to make medical sense of the Vice Chancellor's behaviour. Power wondered if the Vice Chancellor's line about a terminal illness contained a shred of truth. Maybe something lurked in the older man's head, growing inside his frontal lobe. The frontal lobes house what Lynch would call a conscience, and Armitage seemed to lack this. Maybe some tumour cells had spread from the Vice Chancellor's pancreas and lodged within his brain, squeezing out any sensibilities and judgement he might have had, disinhibiting him, and making him enact things he might once never have considered. Or was this just self-centeredness, a feature of Armitage's underlying personality?

"How was it done?" Armitage mulled over Power's question. "This was hardly well-planned. Perhaps because I knew I was about to resign the game anyway? I no longer really cared if I was discovered. Killing her was sufficient. The prognosis for my cancer was disagreeably final. There was also the sense you were closing in on me, inevitably. McFarlane had practically crowned herself the next Vice Chancellor, while I was at home. She flaunted herself as a Queen at the manuscript's launch. The deepest hatred for her grew inside me, like the cancer. I think you found her odious, so I am not alone. I only returned to work to end her brief reign.

"I confronted her in her office. I remember I was shaking with anger. I told her the plain truth – that she would never be Vice Chancellor – that she was universally loathed. I'd put on white cotton gloves to avoid leaving any prints in her room. Perhaps I was still trying to prevent discovery. Self-preservation is a habit and some habits die hard. Anyway the ornament presented itself, right there at my fingertips. The purple quartz was remarkably heavy, I remember that, and I was so toweringly angry I threw it down onto her head with all my might, and, you know, when her skull caved in it made the most satisfying noise. A sort of cracking sound then a squelch."

The Vice Chancellor observed Power wincing and smiled at his discomfort. "Her murder was an indulgence, and I knew I was running out of time."

His mention of the word *indulgence* led Power to recall his very first meeting with Armitage. They had met at the Indulgence Café in Manchester. Armitage had ordered a tableful of cakes and tea for them both, but had contrived to eat most of the spread himself. At this first meeting Armitage had invited Power to become a professor and baited the offer by dangling the prospect of a new medical school. Power wondered how long the Vice Chancellor had been planning the moves in his game. He found himself again exploring other diagnoses, like narcissistic personality disorder, that might explain what had happened, and remembering a paper he had read by Nestor about narcissistic personalities and the risk of violence if they were slighted.

Power looked more closely at the Vice Chancellor. His face was pallid and there was a slight sheen of perspiration on his forehead.

"Bridget McFarlane could have helped you," said Armitage. His voice was thick and he seemed to be having some difficulty in forming his words as crisply as he would have liked. "I think you failed to see how Bridget could have helped you if you got her on your side. Such a rare and powerful piece can move in any direction."

"Back to your notion that you were playing a game," said Power. "Do you perhaps see people round you as dispensable, like dolls or automata – just there for your amusement?" asked Power.

Armitage scoffed. "Not *just* a game."

Power regarded the Vice Chancellor's eyes which were filled with a dangerous sincerity. He recalled the very last line of Ibsen's play *'People don't do such things!'* And yet the confession of the man in front of him merely underscored the fact that people did behave like this. As a forensic psychiatrist Power had seen the actions of men with psychosis, but by and large, he deemed the apparently sane much more deadly, as the organised mind could function with devious cunning. Outside, Lynch and Beresford would be waiting to make their version of an arrest. Looking at Armitage's face now, however, Power thought the prospect of any arrest had become remote.

"At one level, why shouldn't I do whatever I damn well liked?" asked the Vice Chancellor, his voice beginning to slur. "And at another conscious level, why can't I pretend it was a game. To make my time here just a bit more exciting. Have some fun?" Armitage paused for a moment. He licked his lips. "And now I've confessed all. Am I shriven?"

"I'm no priest," said Dr Power, "and you're no man of God." He frowned at the self-obsession and cruel finality of the man. And then he saw Armitage's lower jaw sag a little way, and a dribble of saliva crawled its way down the side of his mouth. And, observing these physical changes, Power realised that the Vice Chancellor had been truthful when he said that he had not poisoned Power's coffee. He had, however, added powdered venom to his own drink.

"I think this is it," said Armitage. "Goodbye." He seemed to stare unremittingly at Power, and slowly his pupils began to dilate. He made no further move.

Murder and Malice
Commentary

The commentary contains spoilers so please don't read it before you finish the book.

Prologue

Each of the Dr Power books is a stand alone story, but I like to add in extra details and sometimes continue with themes, characters or events that have featured in early stories. Sometimes major characters are deliberately introduced as minor characters in earlier books.

The prologue in Murder and Malice contains elements from the beginning of Son of Darkness. Mr Daidalos and his son both die in a plane crash that initiates the story in Son of Darkness, which is set in 2003/4, but the events behind the crash are not explored. At the beginning of Murder and Malice, Mr Daidalos's bereaved daughter, Savina, investigates her father's last business deal with the mysterious Banker.

Daidalos has invested money in a weapons project on Malta. The Malta of 2004/5 (when the book is set) is at the start of its joining the EU, a multicountry project which allowed the dissolution of barriers to the free movement of people, and money. Without boundaries, money could wash around the various constituent countries, and without boundaries, organised crime could move people and funds for money laundering purposes from north to south and east to west, without question. With police being localised to countries and essentially divided from each other, the advantages of this project to internationally minded criminals, would be obvious to any but the most naive.

In the book's world of 2004/5 the weapons possibility of focused sound was being explored.

Nowadays billionaire's yachts can come equipped with LRAD devices to fire at pirates. Such yachts also offer laser devices to fire at the digital cameras of paparazzi to avoid unwanted media surveillance. (The automated lasers fire when sensors detect the CCD of a digital camera. CCD stands for 'charge coupled device' – a mechanism which channels the battery's charge. The lasers fire a burst of light at the camera rendering it impossible to take an image of the yacht).

Woody Norris, who founded the LRAD Corporation, discussed the military application of ultrasound and hypersonic sound in 2004, revealing the device had already been used by the US military in Iraq; deceiving the enemy by beaming the sound of troops at them to make them think they were being attacked. He also discussed using the device to alter the temperature of enemies.

> We make a version with this which puts out 155 decibels. Pain is 120. So it allows you to go nearly a mile away and communicate with people, and there can be a public beach just off to the side, and they don't even know it's turned on. We sell those to the military presently for about 70,000 dollars, and they're buying them as fast as we can make them. (Norris, 2004)

In the prologue such a beam of focused sound is fired at Savina, (at least on one occasion, and possibly two) causing her to become profoundly frightened, disorientated, heated and nauseated, before systematically shifting her as she flees towards and over the cliff.

Chapter One

We receive a formal introduction to the Vice Chancellor of Allminster University and learn that the University was founded by Charles Dodgson, an academic and mathematician of Oxford University. Dodgson was, of course, better known as author Lewis Carroll. As Dodgson, he wrote 11 books on mathematics and, as Carroll, he authored 12 books of fiction. The works of fiction sold incredibly well; millions of copies were bought across the world. *Alice's Adventures in Wonderland* has sold over 100 million copies alone. He became very wealthy indeed, but he was reluctant to alter his donnish bachelor's lifestyle. Indeed, he viewed his success and fame as an encumbrance. In 1891 he wrote, *'All that sort of publicity leads to strangers hearing of my real name in connection with the books, and to my being pointed out to, and stared at, by strangers . . . I hate all that so intensely that sometimes I almost wish I had never written any books at all.'*

It would have been feasible for Dodgson to fund a new educational establishment in his home county of Cheshire. For the purposes of the fictional University of Allminster I chose Dodgson to be its founder.

Chapter Two

Dr Power's well-intentioned strategy to develop a new medical school is accurate in its involvement of the General Medical Council and other key players. The dire need for more doctors to support the health service in the UK has been apparent to all concerned for many years and represents a tragic failure of leadership. Power is developing his strategy in a somewhat unfamiliar and semi-hostile environment amidst people who may be tempted to misjudge him, given his unfamiliarity to them and his deliberately unassuming nature. The Vice Chancellor, aware of how febrile an academic environment can be, warns Shacklin, 'don't underestimate him, however blithely inoffensive he might appear.'

Chapter Three

Dr Power is introduced to the University hierarchy and meets the characters that inhabit its highest echelon. He attends meetings with them all in good faith, the better to follow his mission to found a new medical school. He is surprised by the backlash against his proposals, and soon learns that he is viewed more as a threat to the status quo than a saviour.

Chapter Four

Power begins to learn that beneath an external academic veneer Allminster has a disquieting interior life based upon motivating forces such as greed, envy and lust. Felfe discloses he has worked in Berlin and also hints that he likes to stay apart from academic politics and the machinations within committees so he can get on with his real work. At the time Power does not pick this up, but this clue will be picked up in a later chapter. Felfe has a mild Germanic accent and still uses various idioms from another life; a life before Allminster. Idioms are interesting as they display similar ways of thinking across different languages and cultures. Felfe alludes to various idioms in this chapter such as *'um den heißen Brei herumreden'*, which means 'to talk around the hot porridge', 'beating around the bush', or *'da kannst di Gift drauf nehmen'*, which literally translates as 'you can take poison on that', or 'you can bet your life on it'. He describes one academic as 'being prone to make an ape of himself'; *'zum Affen machen'*.

Power's sense of fair play is somewhat affronted by Felfe's forthright description of his University colleagues' negative characteristics, but Felfe feels he really needs to know what's going on, unfortunately Power leaves before Felfe can explain one or two other hidden matters. Psychologically speaking, Power is protecting his dream of a medical school and leaves before Felfe can move it out of reach by a series of disclosures. Power isn't ready to accept his dream project may be nothing more than that, a dream.

Chapter Five

Power takes his son to visit the birthplace of Charles Lutwidge Dodgson (the real name of Lewis Carroll) in Daresbury, Cheshire (All Saints' Vicarage). Dodgson's father was the vicar at All Saints Church in the 1830s. Charles Dodgson became a mathematician at Oxford from 1850 onwards where he met Alice Liddell, the daughter of the Dean at Christ Church, Oxford, and subsequently wrote the two Alice books: *Alice's Adventures in Wonderland (1865)* and *Through the Looking Glass (1871)*, based on the tales that he told Alice Liddell.

Power's son, Jo, is less impressed by a trip round the Church with his father than he is by a meal of scampi and chips afterwards. Jo was brought up by his mother for the first seven years of his life, before her early death.

During the meal Jo reveals that his maternal grandfather taught him chess. He must have taught the boy well as he very quickly solves the initial chess problem set by Dodgson (Carroll) in *Through the Looking Glass (1871)*. The chess game is a device that frames the story in *Through the Looking Glass (1871)* as Alice interacts with chess pieces such as the Red Queen as she works her way across the board in her journey from pawn to Queen herself.

The theme of Alice is referred to again in later chapters of this novel.

Dodgson's books went through dozens of reprints in his own life and were an overwhelming commercial success, earning him fantastic sums for the day, but he continued with his seemingly disliked academic post at Christ Church.

He might very well have founded a small University of his own such as Allminster in Cheshire, but he did not do this, and indeed Cheshire had to wait until 2005 (after this book is set) before it got a University. It is not entirely clear how Dodgson spent the vast sums that must have accrued from his works, and so the history of Allminster is entirely fictional.

Chapter Six

Professor Power is horrified to hear that Hamish Grieg, the self-denying and miserly bursar wears a hair short to continually punish himself. The wearing of a hair shirt for religious penance is an ancient custom, known in medieval times. Lutheran adherents sometimes wore it at Lent, for instance to mortify the flesh. The prickly hair shirt, or *cilice*, is made from a coarse, uncomfortable fabric woven with coarse hair, like goat hair, or other materials like sackcloth or hessian burlap. In Grieg's case this seems to be a lifelong habit, but Power feels unable to analyse the fetish too closely, because Grieg is not his patient.

Chapter Seven

Power is surprised to find, when he talks to the Vice Chancellor about the intolerable behaviour of the deans, that he not only predicts how the deans reacted, but is sympathetic to how Power feels. The Vice Chancellor explains, as best he can, that he gives the deans a degree of free will, but that ultimately he is in charge. This does reflect the kind of power that most Vice Chancellors used to have over the fiefdoms that Universities represent.

Over time some controls have been introduced to temper their whims with Senates, and Councils, but at Allminster these teams are neutralised, partially through the Vice Chancellor allowing them to be divided and dysfunctional, but also because he has to initiate and endorse almost every significant financial transaction.

This god-like power is reflected in his conversation with Power; allowing his employees free will, but retaining ultimate control to step in. When McFarlane attempts to wrest control of the medical school project from Power, he neutralises her attempts and over-rules her. Armitage references Macchiavelli's *The Prince* (1513), when he talks about tolerating small evils in pursuit of a greater purpose. He has an overview of the necessity of the University's continued function, and the misdeeds of the deans, pale into insignificance for the Vice Chancellor if the University continues to teach and process students through exams.

When Power suggests limiting the actions of the deans or taking them in hand because they are 'dangerous', Armitage shows great interest and even excitement that Power himself is encouraging this.

Lynch is concerned about a different kind of danger at the end of the chapter and calms himself to sleep by using banana porridge and prayer. Banana porridge is something Power would probably recommend; the oats would provide slow release of carbohydrates, and bananas would provide a boost of potassium and magnesium which are natural muscle relaxants, and also boost L-tryptophan which can produce 5-HTP which in turn is converted to serotonin, beneficial to mood and sleep. The prayer, he says, is also meant to be said before sleep and would help Lynch, with his faith, with a degree of reassurance.

Chapter Eight

The paragraph about Chester Cathedral standing through all the centuries and passing through famine, plague and war (at least three of the four horsemen of the apocalypse) is technically accurate. Parts of the cathedral date from Norman times. After these times, there was at least one famine in Cheshire in 1433, several wars (Wars of the Roses, Civil War and two World Wars) and plague (sixteenth century).

Envenomation is the term for the effects of cobra venom on a human after a bite. The visible effects of the venom in Felfe's case, seen by Lynch were due to respiratory arrest, which occurs in a matter of minutes after ingestion of the venom, following profuse salivation, nausea and vomiting. Felfe's wild look is likely to have been due to pupillary dilatation.

Chapter Nine

Willett says several things, which are potential clues. Firstly he gives Power the news about Felfe and seems to believe the idea that Felfe simply died of a heart attack in the cathedral, but later on he quotes from T. S. Eliot's *Murder in the Cathedral*, and Power wonders whether this selection of quote was an unconscious error, a Freudian parapraxis, and if so, he wonders how much Willett does know about Felfe's death?

Earlier on in the conversation with Power, Willett uses a phrase:

"I've had plenty of practice." Willett said very gravely. "Plenty of practice."

This phrase is adapted from *Through the Looking Glass* and is intended by the author to be a clue as to which chess piece Willett symbolises.

The Wasp

Male wasps can't sting, so the wasp's comment that he chooses not to sting, rather than admit he cannot sting Alice, is something of an attempt to cover his lack of potency.

Paul Gent commented on the illustration of Alice and the Wasp as follows: 'The slightly dodgy feel of the wasp picture was intentional as I felt it somehow fitted with other images I have seen of Alice by Tenniel – you may have noticed a nod to Goya's *El Caballo Raptor* from *Los Disparates*. The image is supposed to represent the shock of the wasp lifting Alice into the air.'

Chapter Ten

For those that are keen to know the answers to the questions Power asks, in sequence are: Dura Mater, William Harvey, Günther Blobel, Acetabulum, Sir James Black, Finnegan's Wake, Hangsaman, William Faulkner, Julius Caesar, Samuel Johnson, Just over one Year, *Yersinia pestis*, 1918, 1985, and Czechoslovakia.

Chapter Eleven

Sir Rob Willett recalls lines from Larkin as he crosses the University Memorial Gardens. His mind replays lines from *Aubade* by Phillip Larkin, possibly the grimmest, most disquieting, and brutally honest poem ever.

Hamish Grieg shares some character traits with Sir Thomas More – his habit of wearing a hair shirt for instance. Grieg's speech also includes paraphrases of some of More's quotations including *'You wouldn't abandon a ship just because you couldn't control the winds'* and *'An absolutely new idea is one of the rarest things known to man'*. Hamish's strategy for avoiding the calamitous eventuality of Sir Robert's denouncement of the *The Wasp* chapter as a fake, is to suggest Sir Robert issue a carefully worded interim report. Thus the bursar seeks to defer rather than avoid the publication of any finding that the manuscript is fake. This echoes More's quoted phrase *'What is deferred is not avoided'*.

The bursar's final comment about old manuscripts inevitably dirtying hands is perhaps a sly reference to the ideas of Machiavelli.

Power and Lynch discuss the Crown Prosecution Service (CPS) on the train down to London. For some years the police had dubbed the CPS the Criminal Protection Society. In 2004 the recently appointed Director of Public Prosecutions (*ex officio* head of the CPS) was criticised in the press as having been a defence lawyer for terrorists who had never acted for the prosecution. He reportedly founded the same human rights chambers in which the Prime Minister's wife practised. It was a controversial appointment as he also had a past conviction for supplying cannabis. (The Guardian, February 2004). Later in 2009, the same lawyer was highly critical of Tony Blair saying *'intoxicated by power, Blair tricked us into war'*.

A symbolic phrase occurs when Power offers to be his 'glass' or mirror and help him reflect on his work. The phrase chimes with themes of the book drawn from *'Alice through the Looking Glass'*. In reply Lynch quotes the phrase *'through a glass darkly'*. To see 'through a glass' — a mirror — 'darkly' is to have an obscure or imperfect vision of reality. The expression comes from the writings of the Apostle Paul; by which Paul means that we do not now see clearly, but at the end of time, we will do so.

In his dealings with the world Lynch feels he and Power are often required to act whilst surrounded by wolves and quotes Matthew 10:16 – *'Behold, I send you forth as sheep in the midst of wolves: be ye therefore wise as serpents, and harmless as doves.'*

Chapter Twelve

Sir Bernard Lovell was the larger than life figure who founded the Jodrell Bank Observatory in Cheshire in 1945. For many years Jodrell Bank was at the forefront of radio astronomy internationally – tracking Sputnik and playing an important role in researching pulsars, quasars, masers and the like – Lovell claimed that he was subject of a cold war assassination attempt during a 1963 visit to the Soviet Deep-Space Communication Centre using a potentially lethal radiation dose.

Chapter Thirteen

Various characters that Power meets at the University have personalities which match the seven deadly sins. The tragic couple Bridget McFarlane and Caroline Diarmid are pride and envy (jealousy) personified. Bridget is envious of Dr Power, amongst others, and Caroline is so jealous she could be said to have morbid jealousy and, without any real evidence, accuses Dr Power of having an affair with her partner.

The seven deadly sins are variously categorised and which ones are included are a source of debate. They have been characterised as lust, gluttony, greed, sloth, wrath, envy and pride. (In Latin; luxuria, gula, avaritia, acedia, ira, Invidia, and superbia). Readers can try and decode which of Power's various academic opponents correspond to these, but the author would concede that the correspondence is not always perfect. The seven deadly sins were formulated as a model to contrast with the seven virtues, which are antidotes to the sins. These are, in an order which tallies with the sins above; chastity, temperance, charity, diligence, patience, gratitude and humility.

In this chapter the Vice Chancellor and Power discuss, in vague and elliptical terms, the violence that Caroline inflicts on Bridget.

Most people associate domestic violence with an overbearing and violent male and a passive female victim, in the context of a heterosexual couple. Where morbid jealousy is involved in this kind of relationship it is sometimes termed 'Othello Syndrome', and often associated with alcohol dependence, paranoia and male impotence. Interpersonal violence is not confined to a stereotyped male on female heterosexual couple. Rolle et al (2018) quoted that over 50% of gay men and almost 75% of lesbian women have reported being victims of psychological abuse. Severe violence affected 29% of lesbian women and 16% of homosexual men compared to 23% of heterosexual women and 13% heterosexual men.

Chapter Fourteen

If readers are interested in the factual basis for the fictional money laundering operations in *Murder and Malice* this is derived from various sources. Information about the stages of money laundering was derived from the United Nations report on *'The World Drug Problem'* (1998). The information about the explosion of the Maltese economy after its EU accession comes from reports like the 2017 report in *L'Espresso* – 'Malta Nostra: how Italian Mafia is using the island to launder money' by Malagutti et al. This features crime reports from 2005 and details the kind of activities that the fictional Azzopardi describes as going on. Subsequent investigations did find that 10% of the Maltese GDP was dependent on online gambling, and that around 2.5% of its GDP (£200 million plus) was lost to the legal economy through tax evasion. So eager were Maltese politicians to attract outside investment that external corporations paid 5% tax, whereas local businesses paid 35%, leading to internal stresses and disharmony between the people and their representatives, culminating in mass demonstrations, and political resignations, including the Prime Minster of Malta in 2020 after revelations in the leaked Panama papers.

Chapter Fifteen

In terms of organised crime the 'Ndrangheta do not yet feature in popular culture as often as the mafia. They hail from 18th century Calabria and have become one of the most powerful crime syndicates worldwide. It specialises in drug trafficking, but also deals in arms, money laundering, prostitution, loan sharking and extortion. By 2013 they had achieved an annual turnover of €53 billion. In 2015 the 'Ngrangehta was investigated for running 21 gaming outlets in Malta. It is likely that Shacklin's losses to any 'Ngrangehta gambling establishments in Malta would have put his life at risk.

The World Health Organisation (WHO) introduced the diagnosis of Gambling Disorder (6C50) in the ICD 11 (International Classification of Diseases) which post dates the year when *Murder and Malice* is set. In this disorder the individual loses control of the gambling, and prioritises it above all over interests in terms of their job, relationships, education and social life. Despite all deterioration and negative consequences in their personal life affected individuals continue to focus on gambling.

Chapter Sixteen

'If you want to find the secrets of the universe, think in terms of energy, frequency and vibration,' said Nikola Tesla. Many readers will be aware of the paradoxes inherent in quantum physics. For example, light can be characterised in terms of both light waves and light particles, photons. It is perhaps less well known that sound can be characterised as sound waves, and also as particles, which are called phonons. The concept of the phonon hails back to 1932 and work by Soviet physicist, Igor Tamm. In 2019 scientists managed to isolate individual phonons. Besides sound, phonons have roles in thermal and electrical conductivity including superconductors.

Chapter Seventeen

Azzopardi makes passing conversational reference to the deliberate poisoning of Viktor Yushchenko, the President of Ukraine, in September 2004. Yushchenko was rushed to the Rudolfinerhaus Hospital in Vienna, with severe pain and vomiting, and suffered facial disfigurement through 'chloracne' as a result to the assassination attempt with TCDD, a potent form of dioxin. There was rumour his soup had been poisoned by a Russian agent to skew the result of the Ukrainian elections towards a candidate favoured by Russia. By December 2004, when this chapter is set, Yushchenko was reported as largely recovered.

Chapter Eighteen

Having imparted the news of Shacklin's gory death to the Vice Chancellor, Power is puzzled that he and Lynch are summoned home. Armitage explains his commission was only to locate Shacklin, and now that mission is complete, he could not conscion any interference with the local police investigation. This superficial explanation is a strictly correct interpretation of Power and Lynch's mission, but suggests the Vice Chancellor has a deeper anxiety that Power might be getting too near the truth.

Chapter Nineteen

The Vice Chancellor is considering purchasing another art work as part of his financial machinations. This time it is a picture by Heyden, after Breughel, called *La fete des fous.* This phrase translates as the Festival of Fools, and the picture depicts a raucous, joyful Medieval gathering. The Festival of Fools was first described in Paris in the twelfth century and was an annual event on New Year's Day which instead of being presided over by a Bishop or Pope was reversed and lorded over by a page or junior clergyman. Despite the Church's disapproval of such levity the custom spread through Europe. In England, the president of the Feast was the 'Lord of Misrule', in Scotland the 'Abbot of Unreason' and in France the 'Prince des Sots'. By the middle of the Fifteenth Century the Church began issuing decrees forbidding the Feast and the tradition of misrule gradually died out. The Vice Chancellor, as Canon, would be a relatively junior clergyman. It could be that the topsy turvy tradition of the Feast of Fools appeals to the perversity of Armitage's psychology.

Chapter Twenty

The haunting Welsh folk tale in this chapter, *The Lady of Llyn y Fan Fach*, hails from Myddfai, in Carmarthenshire, on the edge of the Brecon Beacons. Power relates this story to Lynch because it encompasses the destructive nature of jealousy in a fashion that transcends dry fact and narrow research. This is the paradox of folk tales; that they are not literally true, but nevertheless reveal a truth about humanity and its emotions.

There is something of a sequel to *The Lady of Llyn y Fan Fach,* known as the *Physicians of Myddfai.* This relates that in the aftermath of the Lady's leaving, the distraught husband was looked after by his three sons. Sometimes the boys would stand at the edge of the lake to call for their mother, hoping to see her once more. One day she appeared to the trio out of the lake and taught them the arts of medicine. She predicted that they would be great healers who would go on to teach the arts of the physician and the herbalist to others. They became renowned as the *Physicians of Myddfai.*

Carl Power's namesake Carl Jung always emphasised the psychological importance of myths and folk tales – *'Myths and fairy tales give expression to unconscious processes, and their retelling causes the process to come alive again and be recollected, thereby re-establishing the connection between conscious and unconscious'.*

Chapter Twenty-One

In the refectory scene, where Power talks with the reticent Caroline Diarmid, in front of a 'reflectory' mirror, he quotes lines from a play, seemingly at random. The misremembered quote that Power makes to Caroline Diarmid is from T. S. Eliot's *The Cocktail Party.* In the play Dr Harcourt-Reilly, a psychiatrist, speaks the lines. The use of a quotation here is a deliberate technique on Power's part, and not so random as it might first appear to the reader. The reflection of an image dredged up from Power's unconscious is deliberately used to see if it accords with something in Diarmid's unconscious. (Sometimes this technique works and sometimes it doesn't). It is described in a classic book, *'Mutative Metaphors in Psychotherapy'*, by Cox and Theilgaard.

Chapter Twenty-Two

With the Vice Chancellor sick at heart and punishing himself at home by maundering in the snow, the ever ambitious Dean McFarlane capitalises on the publicity surrounding *The Wasp* to try and cement her position for a bid to be Vice Chancellor. She takes advantage of his absence to promote his manuscript and herself at a florid press launch. Professor Willett's death is forgotten, his absence merely another stepping stone for her ascent.

Power's visit to the Vice Chancellor's home in Davenham is partly motivated by care and sympathy and partly because he also seeks to galvanise the Vice Chancellor, if indeed he can be rallied, to champion the Medical School project.

The Vice Chancellor's house in Davenham is based on a real rectory near the church. At the time of writing it was on sale for £2.5 million.

Chapter Twenty-Three

I made a visit to the Liverpool School of Tropical Medicine (LSTM) to research the black mamba species, *Dendroaspis polylepis*. The species itself is fairly rare, and knowledge about the early clinical effects of a bite (beyond being ultimately fatal, and rapidly so) is not certain. Power's observations of the effects on Professor Felfe are probably correct. I am greatly indebted to Dr Abouyannis of LSTM for his advice about the scientific literature regarding mamba bite deaths in 2020. I take responsibility for any errors in the description of Felfe's death from black mamba venom.

Chapter Twenty-Four

Will Nicoll of *Forbes* magazine, writing in 2021, noted that in 2004, *'the Mediterranean island nation of Malta began its transformation from sleepy tourist spot to international gambling mecca'*. The fervid alacrity with which Malta embraced online gambling has been replaced by a degree of regret. Some seventeen years later Nicoll reported that the Malta Gaming Regulator's former anti-corruption tsar had been charged with corruption and there were accusations that the Malta Gaming Authority-licensed site RaiseBet24.com laundered $74.2 million for the Cosa Nostra. The Malta Gaming Authority oversaw licenses that delivered tax receipts of more than $1.4 billion in 2019 approximately 12% of the nation's entire GDP. Lax supervision of gambling reportedly led to suspicious financial operations, money laundering and other criminal practices so that allegedly the EU's smallest country had become the destination of choice for the Cosa Nostra intent on money laundering billions of dollars over the years.

Chapter Twenty-Five

Mr David Charlesworth was a vascular surgeon at Withington Hospital in Manchester so it is conceivable that Dr Power trained with him. Power learned his lessons from Mr Charlesworth about the dangers of femoral artery injuries well enough. Undoubtedly, Power's quick thinking and action in using a tourniquet saved Lynch's life as blood loss from the femoral artery can swiftly prove fatal. Power's later disapproval of his friend mobilising so extensively after surgery is well founded although Lynch does listen to a degree, sending Power and Ramon on a journey to Gozo to seek Xuereb out at at Mgarr ix-Xini, rather than journeying himself.

The physics behind Xuereb's sound weapon is, forgive the pun, sound enough. The human body is more sensitive to vibration than we allow for. The reader might share Power's scepticism that a simple sheet of paper would provide any protection, but this is feasible in some circumstances. More intuitive protection methods – like padding or synthetic foam – do not work nearly as well.

There are various pointers in the novel to the possibility that Xuereb is partially autistic. He harbours a lifelong sense that people do not understand him and resents their failure to perceive his unique intelligence. It is unlikely that he would have been so keen to research weapon technology had some people not rejected his ideas and others exploited his brilliance.

Although he uses his technology on others, I like to think that he would baulk at killing others. It is likely that it was the Vice Chancellor who controlled the technology when severe damage was done to others, and Xuereb feels remorse about his involvement, which is why he is ultimately susceptible to Ramon's intervention when he reminds him of his mother, and Ramon's long association with the family.

How likely is it, do you think, that Ramon is Xuereb's father?

Chapter Twenty-Six

This final chapter seeks to unravel the mystery behind the deaths explaining the various questions the reader might have regarding the who, what, when, where, and why of every single murder. This was a complex undertaking, and to ensure everything was satisfactorily covered in Power's final conversation with the Vice Chancellor, I had to resort to the use of a spreadsheet.

A writer must abide by the time-honoured rules of the game when composing a murder mystery. This means that all the clues necessary to allow the reader to reach the correct solution to the mystery must be present. These explicit clues should lead the reader of this book to accept that the murderer, The Banker, was the Vice Chancellor. Although the important clues are buried within the text, they are there.

In addition to the basic clues, for amusement and on a whim, there are some additional allusions to the identity of The Banker, which are included as an indulgence. If you notice them all well and good, but if you don't' – all the basic clues are already present.

There is a song from my childhood by Paul McCartney, a personal favourite, called Penny Lane. The song features various characters such as a barber, a fireman and a banker. As a child I would be taken past the actual bank and shown the real banker's car, and past the barbers where the banker waited for a trim. The banker, is described in Paul's song as being 'very strange' for not wearing a mac in the pouring rain and has little children laughing behind his back. And so, the Vice Chancellor in this book has students laughing behind his back, he goes for a trim and he meets Power in a suit all wet from the rain because he didn't wear a mac. I didn't expect anyone to notice these things reading through the chapters, but maybe someone, familiar with the Beatles' song, did subliminally.

Do you think the Vice Chancellor intended Power to be his final victim?

Explore the world of Dr Power

Visit www.hughgreene.com

THE DARKENING SKY
Hugh Greene

Brilliant. Very much enjoyed – a new detective series based in England

A brilliantly written plot with lots of twists and turns, this book had me gripped from the first page. I loved the mysticism and the dark undertones

Well written, with great development of characters. I look forward to further volumes in this highly entertaining and somewhat edgy series.

Brilliant story line and a welcome change from recent crime/thrillers I have read.

The Darkening Sky is a tense psychological thriller and the first in the Power and Lynch series of murder mysteries.

Dr Power is recruited by Superintendent Lynch of the Cheshire Police to help him solve a murder in leafy Alderley Edge. Power and Lynch are challenged by a series of mystifying events and realise that they are caught up in a desperate race against time.

THE FIRE OF LOVE
Hugh Greene

This is a gripping story, I was hooked from the first page.

Another great and gripping read from Hugh Greene.

After the first chapter I could not put it down.

Good plot, good read, loved it.

Dr Power is drawn into the urgent investigation of a fire at Heaton Hall, Cheshire and the murder of its owner, a Government Minister. Power is asked to write a court report on a suspected arsonist who is accused of his murder. He believes she is innocent and so begins a fight, with the help of Superintendent Lynch, to prove her innocence and find the real killer .

This is the second novel in the Power and Lynch series of mysteries.

THE GOOD SHEPHERD
Hugh Greene

In Hugh Greene's books you can just escape to places that seem more real than the chair you are sitting on.

A very enjoyable and intriguing read.

The pace of the plot is gripping and makes me want to know what is next.

There was drama and suspense and a nice twist at the end. It was quite compulsive.

Dr Power, consultant psychiatrist, is asked to report to the Coroner on the life and death of Dr McAdams, whose body is found drifting in the sea.

Power comes under pressure to label the death as suicide, but suspects that the dead scientist was trying to protect a most important secret. As Power tries to uncover the secret he realises his own life and the lives of many people across the world are in the greatest danger.

DR POWER'S CASEBOOK
Hugh Greene

'The Dark' has to be one of the best short stories I have ever read.

If you have not come across this series yet, I highly recommend it.

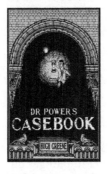

Read this as well as the rest of the series – don't make it our first excursion to the Alderley edge of Dr Power. I loved it.

This is worthy companion to his other works.

A collection of fourteen short stories concerning Dr Power's life as a psychiatrist, and his patients, each story having a particular diagnosis in mind.

The stories are woven around the events of the first three thrillers in the Dr Power murder mysteries series. In two of the stories there are mysteries to be solved, but this is a different kind of Dr Power book.

SCHRÖDINGER'S GOD
Hugh Greene

An incredible piece of writing. And the more I think about it all the more impressive it gets.

The St James Way makes a really special setting for an ingenious thriller.

I found it hard to put down and was eager to carry on.

The story is well told and the twist at the end was exceptional. I enjoyed this book very

A peaceful holiday walking the St James's Way to Santiago del Compostela takes a tragic turn leaving Power and Lynch trying to solve two shocking murders, while unravelling a conspiracy that spans the Continent. Something is very wrong.

Who can be trusted when smiling friendly faces are masking guilty secrets.

SON OF DARKNESS
Hugh Greene

I have no hesitation in recommending this author to anyone who enjoys a well-crafted well-written psychological thriller.

There are plots and sub-plots with gripping, tense moments and unexpected twists

It's all here – Greene's meticulous plotting, and convincing professional details combined with archetypal horror from the past.

The prologue is brilliant, it got me hooked, and then I couldn't put it down.

The farm by the dark lake at Lindow had been thought deserted for years, but after a light aircraft plunges out of the sky into the farmhouse, police make a shocking discovery that leads them to call in Professor Power and Detective Lynch as consultants.

Can Power find the answer of missing persons from the present to the distant past by unearthing secrets buried deep for generations, before ghosts from his own past catch up with him, which are threatening to either end his life – or change it forever.

DR POWER'S MEDITATION
AND COLOURING BOOK
Hugh Greene & Judith Eddles

Hugh Greene takes you through the steps of two simple but effective meditation techniques, and answers many questions you may have on meditation, such as, its benefits, any side-effects it may have, the science behind it, and much more.

Give yourself some relaxing and calming moments and enjoy colouring the 40 exquisite designs by Judith Eddles. Mandalas, floral and geometric patterns, varied and imaginative, some intricate, some simple – something for everyone. Printed on one side of the page only.

DR POWER'S BOOK OF PUZZLES
Hugh Greene & Judith Eddles

Hugh Greene takes us through the history of some of our favourite puzzles, what puzzles were popular with people in the 18th and 19th century, who invented them. And considers whether puzzles can be of real benefit to the brain.

Enjoy a collection of challenging and absorbing puzzles by Judith Eddles. A wide variety including cryptic and quick crosswords, wordsearches, codes, word ladders, knights tours, word ladders and much more.

OVER 150 PUZZLES

Printed in Great Britain
by Amazon